# THE COYOTE WARS

*To the people of Bridgewater .*

*Michael DelaPeña*

MICHAEL C DE LA PEÑA

ISBN: 1492992682
ISBN 13: 9781492992684

This novel is dedicated to my sister Dagny, who inspired me to turn an idea years in the making into action.

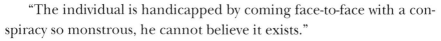

"The individual is handicapped by coming face-to-face with a conspiracy so monstrous, he cannot believe it exists."

J. Edgar Hoover, FBI director 1924–1972

# PROLOGUE

## Boston, June 1998

Anita Migliore watched him intently from behind her desk, her brown eyeglasses perched precariously at the end of her nose. She read some of Carlos Sullivan's file then glanced up to observe him as he waited for her to usher him into the boss's office. It was a ritual at the Boston office of the FBI, where Anita had worked for forty years. Every newly arrived agent received the same scrutiny from her. She was the secretary for the special agent in charge. Anita played the role of gatekeeper, a job she enjoyed immensely. She judged every one of them based on their attire, demeanor, and interaction with her. Once her judgment was formed, nothing could alter it. Being "blessed" by Anita could cement an agent's reputation for good or ill in the Boston office. With this in mind, most agents approached the ritual with a certain sense of trepidation. As she periodically glanced from the report to Sullivan, she sensed that he was quite unconcerned, which only presented her with more of a challenge. She had to admit that his appearance was clean and professional. He wore a black suit with a white shirt, punctuated with a purple tie. She liked his look. From a review of his file, Anita could see that Sullivan also had an impeccable record in his previous two offices. She nonetheless had to challenge him.

"This report indicates you had quite a good track record on the drug squad in San Juan." She looked up at Sullivan, who sat patiently, a slight smile on his face. "Do you think that means you're some sort of expert in the field?"

Sullivan's smile widened. "Not at all, ma'am." He had noticed some family photos behind his questioner. He reacted in his natural manner. "Is that a picture of your daughter?" He pointed at one of them. "She has your eyes."

Anita turned, smiled, and seemed to melt before him. "Oh, my dear!" She became flustered. "That is my granddaughter. You are a darling."

"You have a lovely family, it seems," he answered.

Anita looked him up and down, reevaluating him. She decided he was sincere. "I would like you to meet my daughter, Emily; she is a bank manager in the North End. She can set you up if you need to open a new account."

"Actually, a referral at a bank is just what I need. I'm going to need a car loan," Sullivan replied.

"Excellent. I will take you over there on our lunch break."

"Thank you," he said as he leaned forward in his chair. He consciously used his body language to telegraph his thoughts, a tactic he always found useful. Anita received the subtle message clearly.

"I'm sorry, Carlos, the boss is ready for you. Go right on in." She waved him in.

"Thank you, Anita, I will see you when I come out." With that, Sullivan had received his stamp of approval.

———

The North End Credit Union was a small banking institution tucked in a corner of Boston's fabled Italian section. It was sandwiched between two Italian restaurants for which the neighborhood was known. Anita leaned on the counter as she waited to introduce Sullivan to her daughter, Emily Scola, the bank manager. When the customer Emily was attending to left, she made the introduction.

"This is the young man I mentioned on the phone." Anita beamed.

As Sullivan reached for Emily's hand, two men with guns stormed into the bank through the front door. One yelled, "Everybody get your hands in the air!"

Their loud voices rumbled through the quiet bank, startling everyone, much like roaring motorcycles passing down a serene rural street.

"Oh my god!" screamed Emily. One of the men trained his gun on her and Sullivan. The other jumped the counter. The employees lay on the floor, trembling, as the robber started opening their teller drawers, furiously pulling out fistfuls of money.

With the first gunman pointing his weapon at them, Sullivan took Emily and Anita by the hand and ushered them to the floor. As they looked out the glass door that led to the street, Sullivan saw a Boston Police patrolman approach the entrance and put his left hand on the door. He glanced inside warily, a pistol dangling from his right hand. One of the gunmen noticed the officer.

"Shit!" he yelled to his partner. "We're trapped."

The bond between Sullivan and the Migliore family was about to be forged forever.

——

Patrolman Jonathan Fallon had worked the streets of Boston for almost ten years. In that time, he had seen enough criminal activity to discern when it was best to seize the moment and intervene and when it was more prudent to wait and call reinforcements. The situation he had stumbled on fell in the latter category. Fallon watched the door as his fellow officers responded to his call for assistance. Within minutes, the area was swarming with police officers. The FBI was alerted and was en route to establish a command post staffed with hostage negotiators. The responding units were as yet unaware that the FBI had two employees trapped inside the bank—one of them determined to shape the course of events.

——

After nine hours, the two gunmen who had taken over the bank were becoming increasingly agitated. Anita trembled in fear, and Sullivan gripped her hand tightly. The men paced back and forth. Their leader, a gaunt white man in his mid-thirties, held a pistol in his right hand but cradled it against his chest with his left hand, almost like a child. FBI negotiators had been speaking with "Tim" on and off for hours, with no progress. The gunmen had threatened to kill their hostages if the police moved in. The robbers had closed the curtains, so law enforcement had no way to see into the bank.

While everyone else appeared frantic, Sullivan seemed serene. He was one of six hostages; aside from Ms. Migliore and himself, the rest were bank employees. There were no other customers. He watched the scene unfold; all the while he coldly calculated the situation. He observed the distance between the gunmen and himself, the distance between the robbers themselves, the nature of the weapons, and the obstructions between all the parties. He had not been searched, so he had his weapon available, but he would not take chances with the safety of the hostages. Sullivan waited for the right moment to strike. Inside, Sullivan was tense and coiled. To anyone watching him, he appeared detached, unobservant. Sullivan knew they were desperate amateurs. He heard them call each other "Jim" and "Bill." However, at one point Sullivan noticed that Jim had slipped up and called his partner by the name Mike. They had no plan.

Mike was in charge of attending to the hostages. As they needed to use the restroom, Mike would escort them and wait outside. He made them keep the door ajar. Sullivan had asked to use the bathroom at one point for the sole purpose of assessing the gunman. He observed that he was packing a black Sig Sauer 9 mm pistol with an extended magazine. The pistol contained at least fifteen rounds.

As the tenth hour of their captivity drew near, the bank manager, Emily Scola, asked to use the bathroom.

"Didn't you use the bathroom before, you dumb broad?" Mike barked at her.

"I'm sorry. I have to go," she answered, trembling.

x

"You stupid bitch!" he screamed at her. "Get up...Come on, you whore!" Spittle came out of his mouth.

It took all of Sullivan's restraint to stay silent. He knew the partner was watching, a threat to them if he attacked Mike. He watched quietly as Mike escorted her to the bathroom, which was in a back room, out of their sight.

After ten minutes, Sullivan became concerned.

"Carlos, why is my daughter not back yet?" Anita asked in a whisper. She started shaking uncontrollably as she became increasingly nervous.

Seconds later, they heard Emily crying, not loudly, but perceptibly. Sullivan noticed Jim grinning broadly, looking toward the back room, and he knew.

His training had taught him that action is always quicker than reaction. He would not wait any longer.

Sullivan whispered to Anita, "Close your eyes. It's all about to end." He released her hand and rose from the floor.

Jim was caught by surprise at the sudden sight of Sullivan approaching. He froze. Without warning, Sullivan pulled out his pistol and fired two rounds into his chest. Blood splattered across the desk next to him. Sullivan quickly ran to the back room, his gun drawn, as Mike emerged with his gun out.

"FBI! Put it down, or I will blow you away!" Sullivan warned him.

The gunman paused, deciding what to do. When he noticed Sullivan's resolve, he dropped the gun.

"Keep your hands up and follow me," Sullivan ordered, as he walked behind Mike toward the back room.

Inside, he saw Emily, semiclothed, crying on the floor. She was disheveled, trying to put her clothes on. Sullivan winced in revulsion at what had occurred.

"Mrs. Scola, please go and wait with your mother." She got dressed and ran frantically out of the room, closing the door behind her.

Mike looked at him and smiled. "I never figured you for a G-man," he said.

Sullivan looked down at him with unbridled anger.

"That whore asked for it. She asked for it!" Mike cried out.

"Get on your knees," Sullivan ordered.

Seeing the hatred in his eyes, Mike started pleading, sweat forming on his brow. "Please, please, you can't shoot me...You're a cop! I'm unarmed!"

As Sullivan looked through the trigger sights of his weapon at his pathetic prisoner, he was convulsed with rage. He pointed his weapon at the man's temple and slowly, deliberately, put pressure on the trigger.

# PART I

# ONE

## Inception

The letter rested at the end of the bed, exactly where Kyle Grant had left it after reading it for the tenth time. He eyed it as he got dressed in front of his mirror. The sunlight was peeking in from a window, reflecting light off the envelope. It was the proudest moment of his life. His one lingering regret was he had nobody to share it with.

Very few people are accepted into the ranks of the FBI special agent corps. The Bureau likes to say that only one person is hired for every thousand applicants.

First, Grant had to meet the minimum qualifications to even take the entrance exam. He was a US citizen between the age of twenty-four and thirty-seven. He graduated with honors from the University of Arkansas with a business economics degree. He was physically fit. The FBI entrance exam is known as the Phase I test, much like an SAT exam; it takes about four hours to complete. Approximately 50 percent fail the exam. Unlike the bar exam, which can be taken repeatedly, an applicant is only allowed to take the test two times.

After passing the Phase I exam, Grant was invited to participate in a panel interview, known unimaginatively as Phase II. The panel consisted of three experienced FBI agents. Grant recalled rehearsing answers to questions he imagined they would ask him. Over and over again, he wondered how his interrogators would question him. In addition, he was told there was an essay requirement. He wasn't as concerned about that obstacle. Writing was one of his strengths.

The Bureau flew him to Dallas, Texas, and directed him to go to the Gaylord Hotel and Convention Center, a sprawling complex just outside of Dallas. It was August, and the sun was scorching. The car he rented was so hot, he had to roll the windows down before getting in. His undershirt was starting to get soaked. He worried how he would look to the interviewers if his shirt was wet with sweat. He was impressed at the expense the FBI laid out in the search for the best candidates. It appeared that there were at least a hundred other applicants, and they were broken down into two groups. One group was directed to begin the essay portion of the exam; the other group would begin their interviews. In the afternoon, the groups were flipped. He was lucky to start the essay portion first, since it allowed time for him to cool off. The industrial air conditioners were blasting cold air through the testing room.

He replayed in his mind the questions the panel of three agents peppered him with. The agents did their best to appear intense and humorless.

"Give us a concrete example of how you overcame an obstacle in a professional setting."

"What special skills do you possess that will prove an asset to the FBI?"

"Please tell us of your greatest weakness."

He batted each question back adeptly and without pause. A small black device was placed on their desk, a red light indicating that his session was being recorded. No doubt this was meant to put additional pressure on the applicant. His answers impressed the panelists, and his essay must have been acceptable. His day in Dallas was over. He was moved to the next phase.

The fitness portion of the vetting process was perfect for Grant. He knew the physical fitness requirements were on a point system. At least one point was required for each exercise, such as completing fifty sit-ups; in reality it was necessary to score substantially more in each category to be competitive. He was fully prepared for each fitness category, including pull-ups. He could also run two miles in well under the sixteen-minute requirement. In fact, Grant was an experienced runner. He felt it cleared his head. As he ran along the back roads of his Little Rock home, he smiled, amazed at how far he had come in the process he had dreamed of since he was a child.

His father, a Little Rock police officer, was killed in the line of duty when Grant was ten. He remembered sitting on his father's lap as a child, staring in wonderment at his dad's badge. He knew his father would be proud. As he neared the end of his run, he was saddened by the thought that his father would not be there if he made it all the way. He stopped, fearing that his final step in the application process would be the most daunting.

He went into his bedroom and read the letter again. It was his ticket to success. A job offer as a special agent of the FBI. He only had one last step to take, one final condition of employment. He wished desperately to share his experiences with the one person—other than his deceased father—who could appreciate his success. Yet his pride stopped him from calling her.

———

The Little Rock field office of the FBI is a large two-story structure, with a circular glass foyer beckoning visitors. It is surrounded by a black iron gate. Cameras monitor all areas of the exterior. It is a twenty-first-century castle. It has parking for visitors in the front, but Grant already knew this. He had been there before during various visits with Mary Walters, the staffing assistant who had been processing his application. Her job was to help Grant negotiate all the obstacles the FBI hiring process presented.

It was in this building that he had taken a drug test and submitted his fingerprints. He was surprised to learn that the FBI no longer took fingerprints with black ink, as you see in the movies. Instead, your fingertips and palms were placed on a modern scanning device. The prints are automatically downloaded and sent for comparison to the massive FBI data center in West Virginia. Grant knew he had little to worry about. He had a spotless record—only one speeding ticket in his entire life.

Taking a polygraph examination was another matter. He had heard horror stories from other people he knew who had been subjected to a polygraph examination.

The FBI routinely requires every applicant to submit to a polygraph examination. It is the final step in a long vetting process. Sure, background investigators would check with an applicant's neighbors, friends, and supervisors. But the FBI was still concerned that a dedicated liar, or worse, a dedicated enemy, might be able to infiltrate someone into the ranks of the FBI. This was no idle concern.

The FBI was aware that foreign enemies, terrorists, and hostile countries, including the Russians and the Chinese, were always attempting to penetrate the FBI by placing "moles" within the Bureau. They had come close on many occasions, but were ultimately thwarted by the polygraph examination, which proved to be a shield they could not yet penetrate.

Mary Walters greeted him at the reception area. She had orchestrated every phase of Grant's application process. She was wearing a white blouse and a conservative blue skirt. Although always helpful and encouraging to Grant, he seemed to detect a sadness in her eyes. She told Grant to have a seat. The polygraph examiner would be out to get him shortly.

As Grant waited in the reception area, he kept thinking he had no reason for concern. Still, the idea of being subjected to such an intrusive examination was making him sweat. He'd brought a *Newsweek* magazine. Even this detail he had debated. *What type of magazine do I want them to see me reading*, he asked himself silently. He finally settled on a news magazine—a politically middle-of-the-road weekly. As he

4

looked at the editorial he was reading, it finally dawned on him that he wasn't even reading it. He was just looking at the words, not processing them. He kept glancing up from the page.

Except for the security guard behind the desk, he was the only one in the room. Finally, a large door opened, and a man appeared. He identified himself as Special Agent Pat Hanford, the polygraph examiner. He was in his forties, tanned and neatly groomed, wearing a gray suit with a red tie. Grant, as he had rehearsed a thousand times, gave him a firm handshake and looked him right in the eyes. As he was escorted into the polygraph room, he couldn't help but notice that Agent Hanford was scrutinizing him from head to toe. The mental battle had begun.

After Grant signed a consent form, Agent Hanford started reviewing the application with him. It was obvious he had already reviewed it in advance.

"Why did you leave your job as a supervisor at Wells Fargo after only five months?" Hanford asked accusingly.

"Well, I was told I would be supervising a loan unit, but I was given a lesser assignment. I gave them several opportunities to try to work something out, but it wasn't a good fit for me. I'm sure you will find that the company has nothing but good things to say about me. In the end, I always had my eyes set on the FBI as my final goal." Grant had rehearsed that answer several times. It went on like this for a couple of hours, and Grant had the upper hand throughout.

Among the topics reviewed was Grant's use of illegal drugs, which was zero, to his use of alcohol, which was minimal. Also reviewed were any undetected crimes that Grant may have committed. Hanford had a list of "serious" crimes, from arson and assault to sex crimes and Internet crimes. Grant had no concern in that area and showed no emotion as the list of crimes was enumerated.

Hanford then spent considerable time on national security matters. This consisted of reviewing what he termed espionage and terrorism.

"What do you think of when I say the word 'espionage'?" asked Hanford.

"Espionage is the unauthorized passing of classified material to a foreign power, or the agent of a foreign power. I have no connection to any foreign power, and I don't even have access to classified information. So I have never committed espionage." Grant responded. Here again, he had read the statutes concerning espionage as part of his homework.

"Very good. Let's move on, then," Hanford responded dryly. "I'm going to ask you on this test if you have ever provided support to any terrorist group, Mr. Grant. I'm referring to any terrorist group, whether it is a foreign or domestic terrorist group. What comes to mind when you think of terrorism?"

"Terrorism is the use of violence to achieve a political, economic, or social goal. I have no links to any terrorist groups," Grant replied.

Agent Hanford scrutinized the young applicant before him. He had started evaluating him even before he had opened the door to the reception area. He had gone to the security camera and observed him as he sat in the waiting area. Hanford wanted to see whether the applicant was dressed appropriately and what he did as he waited. He remembered one applicant who sat in the reception area, his leg bouncing up and down uncontrollably. That was not a good sign. Like so many others, Grant had brought a prop, as Hanford called it. He saw that it was a news magazine. Hanford considered it a boring choice. But then again, the applicant didn't particularly impress him. His answers seemed rehearsed.

"Tell me, Mr. Grant, how could a person help a terrorist group if he wanted to?" asked Hanford.

The question seemed to take Grant by surprise. He paused. "I guess you could give them money," he finally answered.

"You guess? What else could you do to help a terrorist group, if you so wanted?" Hanford finally spotted hesitation in his subject.

"I could give them material support, such as weapons, as well as money. I could give terrorists shelter. I could help them commit criminal acts. I could attend their meetings. But I have never done any of that," responded Grant. He had regained his footing.

"Very well, Mr. Grant. Now let's begin your examination."

Hanford moved Grant from the interview chair to the large polygraph chair. It was black with wide arms. There was a motion sensor on the seat pad. It looked like an electric chair.

The interview had taken almost two hours. The actual examination took only about twenty minutes. When it was over, he drove home in a daze. The examiner had tried to mess with him, but he kept his composure. He recalled how Agent Hanford extended his hand after the polygraph and said, "Congratulations, Mr. Grant. I see no problems with your exam. Good luck at Quantico."

As Grant turned to leave, Agent Hanford stopped him "Oh, one other thing, Mr. Grant. I noticed you have PVCs."

"PVCs?" Grant asked. "What is that?"

"Premature ventricular contractions. They manifested themselves on your cardiograph tracings. They were quite pronounced every ten seconds. I don't see that often. At least not in healthy people," Hanford explained.

"Yes," replied Grant, "I do have a heart flutter, a lifelong murmur, as my doctor has called it. But it is asymptomatic, and I was given a clean bill of health by the Bureau physical."

"No matter," concluded Hanford. "I just thought it was interesting. As I said, I don't see that often at all." Hanford held the door for him.

With that, Grant stepped outside into the clear Arkansas air. He had passed the final obstacle. He was headed east. Or so he believed.

# TWO

## The FBI Process

The FBI hiring process is not centralized but instead is spread out throughout its fifty-six field offices across the United States. Budgetary considerations are a deciding factor in how many special agent applicants are hired each year. During lean times, the Bureau has instituted hiring freezes. One such freeze occurred after 2012, following severe fiscal constraints—the fallout of the great recession of 2008–12. Once the hiring freeze finally ended, the Bureau authorized the hiring of one thousand special agents.

All initial applications are submitted online. Each office processes applicants, who then compete against each other for slots at the FBI Academy at Quantico, Virginia. Large field offices, like New York, Washington, and Los Angeles, send the bulk of applicants to Quantico. Smaller offices like Little Rock process only a handful of applicants who meet all the criteria. Grant was only one of seven people whom Little Rock sent to Quantico that year. He was the only one from Little Rock in his class, commencing in June.

The FBI is broken into two camps. The special agent corps, and the support staff. Special agents are authorized to carry firearms, carry badges, and make arrests. The support staff, as they are known, are a critical component of the FBI and handle a wide variety of duties. They represent many roles, including intelligence analysts, clerical staff, paralegals, mechanics, nurses, and staffing assistants.

Mary Walters had started in the mail room of the Little Rock office ten years ago. She had moved up slowly, not having a college education, which is not required for many entry-level support positions. Her father, a mailman, died of a heart attack when she was fifteen. Mary was emotionally devastated and didn't come out of her room for a year. Her mother, Judy Walters, worked as a secretary in city hall and was close to collecting a pension. Mary eventually rose to be only one of two staffing assistants in the office. She liked the work. Dealing with different applicants was never boring.

Mary had trouble catching the attention of what she considered "good" men, and this bothered her. She was a plain girl, of medium build and height. She was very habitual. Every Friday, she could be found at her local watering hole. She sat at the same stool and ordered the same drink, week after week. Mary always left tipsy, but despite the flirtations of some of the men who approached her, she never took them home. They never measured up.

It was in this manner that she first met Tim.

Tim Wallace was an enigma to Mary. When she first saw him two years ago at the bar, he seemed oddly out of place. In some ways, he projected an image she had in her mind of her own father. He was tall and muscular for a man in his fifties. He wore glasses with thick frames. His hair was black, with flecks of gray. When he first spoke to her, she seemed to relax. Unlike the other men she met, he wasn't the least bit interested in taking her home. He talked about matters she had never considered, like philosophy, art, and history. He had traveled the world, he told her, as a freelance reporter covering some of the most compelling stories. As he learned what Mary did for a living, it occurred to him that he wanted to do a piece on the FBI, with the focus on how a person becomes an FBI agent, from the first step to the last. He wanted to profile one of the FBI's finest candidates.

From their long discussions, Tim learned that five years ago Mary had had a car accident, which left her in considerable back pain. The alcohol she consumed was as much medicinal in nature as it was a vice. However, the painkillers she had become addicted to were indeed a vice that she went to great lengths to conceal. Tim had a contact that allowed him to supply Mary with painkillers, which he gave her every Friday afternoon. In exchange, he asked her for what she believed to be innocuous information about the FBI.

Tim asked her to let him know whenever one of her special agent applicants looked promising. He had a particular type of person he wanted to profile. He was looking for a white male, approximately twenty-eight years old. Over the course of about eighteen months, she told Tim about several prospects for his profile story, but it seemed that he kept finding a flaw in each one. One time, Tim rejected the person because he had blond hair.

"You don't want to profile Jones because he's blond? Last month you rejected someone because he lived with his girlfriend," she once objected, frustrated. "What possible difference does his appearance make? What gives?"

"I know it may seem strange, but I just have a particular look in mind," he answered.

It went on like this for months, until she described Kyle Grant. As she described his background and appearance, Tim became more animated.

"I think you may have finally found my subject," Tim declared with assurance. "I will need his contact information and a copy of his file," he added. "Remember not to tell him about me, I want it to be a surprise." She had never seen him this excited. Mary objected to sharing Grant's file, but Tim insisted, all the while assuring her that he could be trusted. Mary had come to depend on him.

As she finally nodded in assent, he added one more request. "I need to know when he plans on leaving for Quantico."

"Tell me I'm doing the right thing," Mary said softly.

Tim leaned over to her, placing a hand on her hair, gently. "You can trust me, Mary."

Two days later, they met in the parking lot of the bar they frequented. She handed him a copy of Grant's file. In exchange, Tim slipped her a small container that held a dozen pills: her Oxycontin fix. They would never meet again.

—

Grant had finally made all his arrangements for his move to the FBI Academy at Quantico, Virginia. He had gone to the post office to have his mail forwarded. He shut off the water and gas. His bags were packed. He had even written a letter to Tina and mailed it that morning. Also, as Ms. Walters had requested of him, he had called to tell her about his departure first thing in the morning. It was almost ten o'clock, and Grant was packing his last suitcase when he heard a loud knock on the door. Upon opening the door, he was greeted by a middle-aged woman. She had long dark hair and black-rimmed glasses. She wore a white blouse with blue jeans.

"Can you help me?" she inquired.

Grant looked onto the dark street and noticed a brown Honda Civic parked in front of his house. The hood was up. Grant quickly deduced that she had car trouble.

"Sure," Grant answered helpfully. "What happened?"

"I'm not sure. I think I have a battery or electrical problem. Maybe you could jump it for me?" As they walked toward the car, she directed him to the trunk, which she opened with the remote.

"I have cables," she added as he approached the trunk.

In that one instant, as he turned up from the trunk to look at her face, he sensed danger. He knew it was too late. With one quick movement, the woman had placed a stun gun to his neck, jolting him. Two million volts of energy surged through his body. As he convulsed, he flopped to the ground, smacking the side of his head on the pavement as he landed.

From Grant's backyard, a slender man appeared quietly from the darkness. He quickly helped the woman bind Grant's feet and arms, dumping him, helpless, into the trunk. They moved together with a highly trained efficiency. Although the street was deserted, if there had been a witness, he would not have even given them a second look. As she drove off in the Honda, the mysterious stalker used Grant's key to enter the residence. He needed to finish packing.

When Mary Walters did not show up for work the next day, Michael McGinty became concerned. He was the administrative supervisor, her direct manager. It was not unusual for Mary to be late, and he suspected she had a substance abuse problem. Despite her frequent tardiness, Mary had never failed to show up for work without calling. He was thinking about her when his phone rang. It was her mother, Judy Walters. They had met once. A couple of years before, he had a tax matter pending at city hall. When Mary found out he was going to be there, she told him he should stop and meet her mother, which he did.

He recalled that Judy Walters was very outgoing and gregarious, not at all like her daughter. Their meeting was short but memorable.

Now, on the phone, she sounded concerned. "Mr. McGinty, this is Judy Walters, Mary's mom. Do you remember me?"

"Yes, I do," he replied.

"I'm sorry to bother you, but have you heard from Mary?" Her voice was quivering. "I have an awful feeling. I've been calling her for several hours, and I get no answer. It's not like her. I'm going to her place, but I just wanted to check and see if she was working on something important, maybe"—she stumbled—"I was hoping she was traveling for the Bureau or something."

"No, Mrs. Walters, she's not." He quickly agreed to meet her at Mary's house.

McGinty arrived first, followed by a police officer. He had called the police. The last thing he wanted was for a neighbor to call in a report of suspicious activity. He convinced Judy to wait outside. When the police arrived, McGinty introduced himself to the responding officer. "I'm Mike McGinty, Little Rock FBI. We need to check on one of our people."

Using Judy's key, he and the officer opened the door and entered the residence. Once inside, they noticed the lights were on. They entered her bedroom, and McGinty gasped slightly when he saw Mary's lifeless body on the bed. Her face was as white as the freshly painted wall. Her lips were blue, her eyes closed. Next to the bed, on the nightstand, lay the bottle of pills.

"Officer, we need to keep this quiet. We don't need any bad press," McGinty stated dryly.

The officer nodded. "I understand."

The FBI did not need the embarrassing revelation on the nightly news that one of its employees was addicted to drugs. The official cause of death was listed as an accidental overdose. The media was only informed that Mary died of natural causes after an illness. Judy knew about her daughter's addiction and agreed to the cover-up, to protect her—and their—reputation.

# THREE

## The Fortress, the Family, and the Wolf

**D**eep in the Ozark Mountains of northern Arkansas, abutting the 1.2-million-acre Ozark National Forest, lay the Fortress. The dirt road leading to the Fortress was the only way to access the compound, and it was over two miles long. The entrance from the main road had no sign, only a rusted metal gate with a solitary No Trespassing sign hanging in the center. The gate was closed and padlocked.

The Fortress consisted of several wooden structures, among them a sleeping area, a kitchen/eating area, and the school. Tim and Susan Wallace also had a house on the property. Susan's brother, Bill, had a cabin within the compound. Although loyal to the family, Bill was not an intellectual. He had no formal education but was an extraordinary handyman. He had large hands that acted like a vise when he wanted. His strength was legendary in the family.

The Fortress itself was conceived as a training academy for special children. The idea of this school was not that of one single person but of a committee comprising the leftist revolutionaries from the sixties and seventies. They had the goal of destroying the capitalist under-pinnings of the United States and establishing a new order. Yet their attempt at transforming the United States through violent action had failed. Their bombings and kidnappings had not brought the change they envisioned. One by one, all of the groups in the leftist revolutionary vanguard were identified and neutralized by law enforcement, particularly the FBI. From members of the Weather Underground to the Symbionese Liberation Army (SLA), who famously kidnapped Patty Hearst, the revolutionaries were arrested or killed by the FBI. Sometimes they were captured individually and quietly, but occasionally they were captured in spectacular fashion. On May 16, 1974, the FBI and Los Angeles police surrounded a house sheltering several SLA members. The two-hour firefight resulted in more than nine thousand rounds of ammunition expended between the SLA and law enforcement. The SLA fired hundreds of rounds but never hit one officer. Instead, five SLA members were killed. The remaining members, including Patty Hearst, scattered and were eventually caught. They and their revolutionary movement had been vanquished. By the time Ronald Reagan assumed the presidency in 1980, their cause was only a memory. Thirty years later, most of the revolutionaries were either dead, in prison, or living ordinary lives among the population—those were the ones who had "sold out" and rejoined mainstream society.

The children of those few who escaped scrutiny formed the Committee. The Committee realized that to succeed in their goals, they needed to change tactics. Each member of the Committee decided to volunteer one of his or her own children to the cause. This was an act of altruistic self-sacrifice, which was at the root of what they believed. The cause was more important than any one member, or any one family. The goal was the establishment of a new world order, starting with the destruction of the United States and its financial system of oppression and corruption. In order to build a new structure, they believed, it was necessary to destroy the old foundation. To that end, their children were sent to the Fortress for a lifelong instructional program. The entire Committee did not even know where the Fortress was. They did not know what mission their children would be eventually assigned. They knew this was important in the event the authorities ever questioned them. The Committee also knew they would never see their children again. They knew this was part of the plan.

Each member handed his or her newborn child over to Tim and Susan Wallace. The Wallaces were themselves among the founding members of the Committee. Once they took possession of the fifth child, they broke all contact with the Committee. Each child would know Tim only as Father, and Susan as Mother. The adoptions were all processed legally and through the proper channels. Nothing illegal had occurred.

Living arrangements at the Fortress were spartan. The meals, however, were cooked by Mother and were high in protein and satisfying. Firearms proficiency training began at the age of twelve. Wallace did not believe it was prudent to handle firearms at too young an age. In addition to shooting at the Fortress's range, they also learned to hunt and track in the woods surrounding their compound. They often brought back deer for Mother to cook. One of their primary lessons was self-sufficiency.

Susan Wallace was medically trained. She ensured the children received proper medical care. She had even set the arm of the oldest, Michael, when he fell from a tree during one of their drills with Father. She also vaccinated the children, for she knew that one day they would be leaving the compound and would need that protection.

Their daily instruction began precisely at five o'clock in the morning. Father awakened the children for their morning exercises. For two hours they engaged in a series of increasingly aggressive exercises, ending in uphill sprints. Tim would always gather his children around him after each session. "Remember," he warned them. "The most dangerous weapon is always your mind. Now let's go study." Susan would be waiting in the schoolhouse with her lesson plan ready. In the afternoon, Tim would relieve her. The students were all too eager to learn. In reality, they had little choice and no unmonitored outside influences to alter their indoctrination.

Their instruction was diverse, incorporating all the essential areas of learning: mathematics, chemistry, physics, English, geography, economics, philosophy, and history. History was explained through the prism of the oppressed people on the planet. Most of the world's problems were laid at the doorstep of the United States. As the children grew, their instruction became more complex. Philosophy courses analyzed Emmanuel Kant. Political study focused on Marx, Castro, Chavez, and Mao. The capitalist works were also studied, but Adam

Smith's economic theories were dissected for their flaws. Father explained that they needed to know their enemy well, in order to defeat them. Learning occurred at a round table, where the discourse was free-flowing. They all listened in awe as Father explained how they were the vanguard of the New Movement, as he called it. They would change the world by their own hand, in their own lifetime.

Alexandra was the youngest. Her family called her Alexa. She had sharp blue eyes, shoulder-length, dirty-blond hair, and she sported a small dimple on her chin. She was always quick to ask questions and just as quick to soak up learning like a sponge. Alexa was considered the artistic one. She enjoyed drawing and was the least athletic of the group. She was also a skilled marksman and archer.

Ryan was the tallest, standing at six foot three. Strong and athletic, he had sharp features and piercing dark eyes. Although intelligent, he often required a little extra effort to keep up with the others intellectually. He knew he wasn't the smartest, and he knew enough to ask his siblings for extra help when he didn't understand something.

Samantha was the most driven. She was tall and slender, with long jet-black hair and deep-blue eyes. Samantha's goal was to always be number one, and she enjoyed beating her brothers in competition, whether in her studies, on the range, or at running. On most occasions, she did beat them. The more the brothers got upset at being defeated by a girl, the more she gloated.

Peter was generally considered by the family to be the prodigy of the group. He had dark hair and brown eyes, stood six feet tall, and was the most athletic. He was the smartest, with the ability to instantly recall verbatim anything he read. Peter was also the most social and charming. He could talk about any subject. He made connections between events instantly, like a chess grand master thinking thirty moves ahead. Peter was also the most physically aggressive. When engaging in the combat and fighting techniques that Father had taught them, he was relentless. Father would pair them up for instruction in close-quarter combat, as it is called by the military. Peter always disarmed his opponents by placing them in a chokehold until they tapped out. This bothered Samantha to no end.

The eldest, Michael, had assumed a mentoring role with his younger siblings. He was of average build and strength, but he possessed a quiet wisdom. Michael would never answer a question without pausing, reflecting, then giving a well-thought-out answer. Michael also seemed more intellectual, perhaps because he was the only one to wear glasses. When he was fourteen, Susan took him out of the compound and into the city to fit him for a pair of glasses. He absorbed the experience intimately. And he longed to repeat it.

It was inevitable that Michael would share his experience with the others later that night in the family room, which they shared next to their living quarters. The others listened raptly as Michael described the outside world in detail. They had already been exposed to the world through books, television, and the Internet, but it was not the same as experiencing it directly. Because their father knew they would one day have to assimilate into society seamlessly, he had allowed them to watch two hours of television every evening. He selected some of the more popular shows, so they would not seem culturally ignorant when dealing with people on the outside. Bill had set up the satellite system for them. They were also instructed on the options available in the cyber world, and how to access information. The children had enjoyed their TV and Internet time, but the idea of leaving the compound to experience the world had now infected them like a virus. Tim knew he needed to address this before the virus became deadly.

In order to address their increasing desire to learn about the world outside the Fortress, as well as to further assimilate them into society, the family started taking vacations. They were essentially working vacations, with each trip incorporating at least one mission for every child. Tim selected the missions. Peter was fifteen, the same as his brother Ryan—they were often called "the twins"—when they first traveled to New York City. Peter recalled how they had visited the Statue of Liberty, taking the ferry from Battery Park. It was 2003, and the attacks of 9/11 were still on the minds of most Americans. They visited Ground Zero. Peter remembered how Father had gathered them around as he so often did.

"What was the problem with the 9/11 attacks?" Tim asked them. He looked around the group for an answer.

After a few moments, Peter answered, "There was no follow-up."

Tim looked at the others. "What does he mean by that?"

They all looked at each other, seeking reassurance. Finally, Michael thought for a second as he always did and added, "You taught us that if your opponent can absorb your initial blow, he will most likely win. That's why you need to continue your attack until the enemy is down. No quarter is given." He looked at Father for approval.

"Exactly." Tim beamed. "Exactly."

Once that lesson was absorbed, Tim decided another mission was in order. He pulled Ryan aside in private.

"Ryan, this is your mission for this trip. We are going to leave you here. You need to find a way to get back to the hotel by yourself." With that, Tim turned and approached the others. "Let's go." He didn't even allow Ryan the chance for any questions.

Susan took two of the children in one taxi; Tim took the remaining two in another. As he looked out the window, he wondered. Had Ryan paid attention to where they were staying? Could he navigate the complicated subway system? Would he even know to use the subway system as the easiest course of action? If he had paid attention to his training, Tim knew, Ryan would make it easily. Yet he knew Ryan was possibly the slowest of the group. Perhaps he had selected wrong; he should have chosen another.

After traveling uptown through traffic to their hotel on Sixtieth Street, they paid their fares and got out of their cabs. When they entered the lobby, the group was stunned. There, sitting on a couch with his hands laced behind his head, was Ryan.

"Amazing. Truly amazing, son," Tim stated quietly. With that, they embraced.

As the group made its way to their respective rooms, Tim thought about the trip and its implications. Everything that transpired convinced him that their instruction was bearing fruit. He shared his thoughts with Susan, and she agreed.

—

Later that evening, the family assembled together at a park on the banks of the Hudson River. Under the glow of a full moon, Tim gathered his flock around him. He sat on a large stone; Susan crouched down at his side. Bill waited by the car, watching for any suspicious movements. The children looked up at him eagerly, waiting for what they had come to expect: a good story.

"Gather around, my little coyotes," Tim said to them, as he had grown accustomed to addressing them.

"There was once a large wolf," Tim began, "that was menacing the forest. None of the other animals could live in peace. One day, a family of coyotes came upon the forest. The other frightened animals urged the coyotes to leave the area, as their resources were scarce enough. The wolf took more than its fair share of food. It often killed the forest animals just for fun, they explained to the coyotes. Rather than heed those warnings, the coyote clan decided to fight the wolf. Attacking as a group, they started harassing the wolf, nipping at its heels, taking a bite here and there. They worked as a team, circling their enemy, so the wolf could never grab one of them and kill them." Tim paused. He could see they were interested; they listened raptly.

"Day after day they attacked the wolf, always at a different hour. The wolf was too strong for them to defeat, but that was not their plan. After a few weeks of these attacks, the wolf grew weaker. It was not able to hunt as it used to. It was too fatigued from the constant battles with the coyotes. One day, the wolf simply left the forest, defeated. The forest came alive with celebration. The animals rejoiced at their new freedom. Through their courage, the coyotes had saved the forest." Tim looked at his children with pride. "This is why we train, my children, for one day we will confront the wolf."

Even the youngest, Alexa, nodded in understanding that she was a coyote.

—

When Grant awoke, he realized he was in the trunk of a car that wasn't his. The most disturbing thing for him was that he had soiled himself when he was shocked. He imagined that it was a natural reaction to being hit with a direct electrical discharge. The stench was suffocating him. Several hours elapsed, and then he heard a change in the road conditions. It became clear that they were driving on a dirt road. After the vehicle stopped, he could hear the driver get out and slam the door shut. He heard the sound of two voices, but he couldn't make out what they were saying. One of the voices was female, perhaps the woman who had stunned him, he thought. Finally, the trunk opened, and he could smell fresh air. His eyes were covered, but his senses of smell and hearing were intact, and what he sensed reminded him of the times he had gone hiking. He instinctually realized he was in a forest.

Just as quickly as the trunk opened, he felt large hands reach down and grab him firmly. Whoever it was must have been very strong, as he was lifted easily and carried inside a structure. He was tossed on the ground like a rag. The man placed a knee on his back as he untied the bindings around his feet, then his arms. The man said brusquely, "Don't resist, or you will be hurt."

Grant thought it best to comply. The last thing he wanted was to get shocked again. Once Grant was freed, his jailer stepped out and locked the door. He was in a prison cell. From the outside, the man opened a small aperture that had been carved into the door at eye level. He stared at Grant, who could now tell that it was dark outside. He calculated it must be early morning.

The man spoke in a robotic manner. "Mr. Grant, you will find a change of clothes on that small table in the corner. There is a chair for your convenience. There is a bucket for your needs. You will be fed twice a day. How you are treated will depend on how you comply with our orders. No questions will be answered." The small door was closed, and Grant could hear his jailer's footsteps as he walked away.

Grant was more stunned than when he was shocked with the stun gun. He sat in the chair and cried.

# FOUR

## Quantico

The FBI Academy looks like a leafy college campus. It was the brainchild of the FBI's founding director, J. Edgar Hoover, who envisioned a world-class law enforcement training center, which is what he achieved. Ironically, Hoover died after forty-eight years in office, in May 1972, just days before the academy officially opened its doors. Located on 385 acres of Marine Corps property at Quantico, Virginia, it is about thirty-five miles south of the nation's capital. In addition to dormitories, classrooms, a gymnasium, firing ranges, and a dining hall, the academy also is home of the famous "Hogan's Alley." The alley is a recreated town, with a motel, cinema, apartments, a pharmacy, and a bank that is billed as the most robbed bank in the world. The Bureau hires actors to participate in role-playing scenarios with the new FBI agent candidates, known as new agent trainees, or more derisively by some agents as "NATs."

After the attacks of 9/11, the special agent training program was expanded from an eighteen-week to a twenty-one-week program. Training related to terrorism investigations was added to the curriculum. In the three additional weeks, there was a two-week program sponsored by instructors attached to the Combating Terrorism Center at West Point. All of this instruction was focused on the global problem presented by international terrorism. The course centered on Al Qaeda, Hezbollah, and other foreign terrorist groups that all have one thing in common—hatred of the United States. No attention was given to any domestic terrorist threat.

Prior to the 9/11 attacks, security at the academy was negligible. There was not even an outer security perimeter. Anyone could drive in and walk around. Certainly, there was a security checkpoint when someone entered the main foyer, located at the Jefferson building. Security was the responsibility of the FBI Police force, a highly professional corps of police officers whose duties are limited to protecting several sensitive FBI properties, including the academy. They operate much like the police departments that patrol college campuses. Subsequent to 9/11, the FBI Police force was beefed up, and an outer security checkpoint was installed on the road leading into the facility. During the immediate aftermath of the attacks, the marines had set up an additional checkpoint several miles before the academy entrance. That marine checkpoint is still the first line of defense for the academy.

As Peter Wallace approached the entrance to the academy, he recalled his last meeting with Father. During the course of several years, all of his siblings had left the Fortress, one at a time. Each had already set off on their missions. Even Alexa, the youngest, had left the Fortress for her assignment. He was the last. He remembered how his father looked concerned as he gave Peter his final briefing.

"Did you read the file?" he asked in a serious tone.

"Yes, Father, completely," Peter replied. In fact, Peter had read Grant's file twice in its entirety. The entire application submitted by Grant. The interviews of his employers and neighbors were also in the file. Everything the FBI spent a year researching about Grant was documented within its pages.

Peter spoke again. "You chose perfectly. His parents are deceased. He has no siblings. His neighbors said he never engaged with them. Even his last employer at the bank said he had his lunches at his desk and rarely socialized. He had a girlfriend, but they broke up. He even looks like me."

Tim looked at Peter sternly. "Nevertheless, Peter, don't take anything for granted. Do what is asked of you, but try not to stand out too much. Keep a low profile. You know your mission." With that, Tim handed Peter a driver's license.

"Good luck, son," Tim said as he hugged his son good-bye. He knew he might never see his son again. Peter recalled the exchange fondly.

As he approached the marine checkpoint, Peter slowed down to a crawl as he approached the military police (MP) officer. He handed his license to the guard, indicating that he was heading to the academy as a trainee. From behind mirrored glasses, the Marine wrote down his information on his clipboard. He then took down the license plate. As he did so, a line of cars was starting to form behind Peter's car. After a minute, the MP waved him on, and he was on his way. He started the drive to the FBI Academy's east entrance.

As he came closer to the FBI Police guard shack, he could feel his heart pounding more strongly against his chest. He knew this was a critical moment, and he could not be certain of the outcome. He tried to allay his concerns by recalling how Father told him what to expect from academy security. He didn't know where his father got his information, but it was always perfectly accurate. He comforted himself one more time by repeating a quote his father used to tell them all the time, from the poet Virgil, "Fortune favors the bold." He repeated the saying out loud three times as he pulled up to the gate.

The FBI Police officer looked directly in his eyes. "How can we help you?" inquired the officer. His uniform was neatly pressed. His sidearm was displayed at his side. He could see another officer inside the guard shack.

"Yes, Kyle Grant, reporting for training," he replied and handed over the license his father had furnished him. He was certain the officer could hear his pounding heart.

The officer looked it over and then waved him on with a warning. "As you approach the Jefferson building, you are not allowed to park in the first row, nearest the building. Anywhere else is OK."

He passed through the gate. Peter parked his car as instructed. Without hesitation, he grabbed one of his suitcases and walked into the main academy foyer. It was a Sunday, which was when new agent trainees were instructed to arrive. Training would commence the following day. He walked to the security counter and was greeted by an FBI employee at the reception desk. An FBI Police officer was seated behind the counter but said nothing. He was reading something on his computer.

The receptionist was a woman in her forties. She was dressed professionally and had glasses hanging around her neck, held there by an old-fashioned eyeglass holder.

"You are reporting for training?" she asked rhetorically. "Your name?"

"Kyle Grant," he replied. He handed his license over before she even asked for it. She never even looked at the license.

She looked through her arranged packets on the counter and found the one for Grant.

"You are in class 356," she said, almost to herself. She then waved to a group of other trainees who were sitting nearby on some couches in the lobby. They were from the previous class, assigned, by tradition, to escort the newly arriving NATs into their dorms and give them a tour of the facility.

One of the escorts, a young woman with black curly hair, approached Peter. "Hi," she said in an animated manner. "My name is Becky. I'm from class 355. I will show you to your room."

"Thanks," Peter replied in a friendly way. "I'm glad to be here."

He could not believe it had been so simple, just as Father had told him. Peter Wallace was now Kyle Grant.

———

The next morning, new agent class 356 was ushered together for their official photographs. They were all instructed to wear suits. Peter smiled broadly when it was his turn for a picture. Later that day, they were handed temporary credentials listing them as FBI special agent trainees. Peter placed it in his suit pocket, and he touched it more than once to make sure he really had his creds, as he learned they are called in the Bureau. Before the first day ended, they were all summoned to the auditorium where they recited their oath of office. It was a proud moment for all of them—even Peter, who had different motivation behind his pride.

As the weeks played out, Peter was careful to never stand out too much. Whenever 356 was on a class run, he made sure to stay in the middle of the pack. Peter laughed to himself at how out of shape some of the trainees were, by his standards. He could easily have beaten the pack every time, but he held back. He did the same at firearms training. Back at the Fortress, he rarely ever missed a shot on the range. At the Academy, the FBI requires a minimum qualification score of eighty out of one hundred. Each qualification consists of fifty rounds, two points per round. Peter made sure he always missed at least two or three shots, giving him a respectable score of ninety-four or ninety-six. Some of the trainees had never fired a gun before arriving at Quantico. Peter made an effort to help some of the other trainees, to establish bonds and trust. He knew that such relationships could bear fruit in the future.

This was how he came to mentor Jeffrey Wilson. As a trainee, Wilson was struggling. He had previously worked as an accountant at a financial firm in Chicago. He was of medium build, with small shoulders and a serious face. Cerebral and not athletic by nature, Wilson had the appearance of the proverbial nerd. He had scored only the minimum points on his physical fitness test. He was not a good shot on the range. But he was the valedictorian of his college class at Wharton, an accounting genius. It was for these traits that the Bureau had recruited him.

Peter helped Wilson with some stretching techniques he used before a run. He showed Wilson the best running posture, and it helped him. One of the things the instructors liked to do to the NATs was to make them do knuckle push-ups, on the macadam. It left many of them with sore and bloody knuckles. It wasn't unusual to see the trainees walk around with their hands bandaged, especially in the first few weeks. It was a type of hazing, and Peter helped Wilson get through this test.

"Wilson, just don't move once you get your knuckles touching the pavement," Peter admonished him. "Stay as still as possible. It will reduce the friction and pain."

Wilson followed Peter's lead, and it helped him get through that challenge. On the range, Wilson could never hit the target firing with his left hand, as is required during "weak-handed" shooting.

"I just can't get it," Wilson complained to Peter one day.

"I can solve your problem," Peter said confidently. "Let me watch you shoot."

After observing Wilson on the firing line for a bit, he noticed what he might be doing wrong. "Wilson, keep both eyes open and point at that tree over there with your finger. Stop when your finger is right at the center."

"OK. Got it."

"Good, now close your left eye."

Wilson did as instructed. "Yes, it's still centered."

"Now close your right eye."

"Aha! It's off-center now."

"You are right-eye dominant," he told Wilson. "Try using your left eye on the sights when shooting left-handed."

"You think?" Wilson asked. "OK."

He followed the advice. On the next qualification course, Peter scored an eighty-six. It was his first passing score. The relief Wilson felt was noticeable to the rest of the class. Wilson was considered to be a nice guy, and they had been rooting for him.

"I owe you," Wilson later commented to Peter at the dining hall.

"Sure," Peter replied. "Maybe you can do my taxes next year!"

As Peter walked away, Wilson observed that everything seemed to come easily to Grant. He could easily be the class leader. "What's holding him back?" he asked himself.

---

On the seventh week of training, the Bureau announces to each trainee to what office they will be assigned. The FBI has fifty-six field offices throughout the United States, including an office in San Juan, Puerto Rico. Each trainee is asked to select their preference by region and then to rank each city within each region. The Bureau does not guarantee a trainee will get his or her preferred city, let alone a preferred region. It is unusual, but not unheard of, for a trainee to quit on the seventh week because he might be assigned to Albuquerque when he has never left his hometown of Chicago. The Bureau has a policy, with limited exceptions, of not sending new agents back to the office where their applications were processed.

The announcement of assigned offices is such an important event for the trainees that the Bureau has a tradition of videotaping the process. The trainees are gathered in their classroom at the end of the seventh week. One of the instructors holds a bundle of envelopes in the front of the class, each with a trainee's name. As each NAT opens his envelope, he announces to the class where he has been assigned. The cameras capture his reaction and the reaction of his classmates.

Peter was not emotional about the process. He really didn't care where he went, as long as it was on the East Coast. Father had only instructed Peter to attempt to obtain an assignment along the East Coast. Beyond that, he was not given any guidance. After looking over a map of the United States, Peter selected Boston as his first preference in the eastern region, followed by New York City.

So Peter displayed little emotion as he unsealed his envelope.

"Boston," he told the class nonchalantly. The group applauded.

After a while, it was Wilson's turn. Peter watched him to see if he would get an office close to his beloved city of Chicago. Wilson had listed Cleveland as his first preference.

When he unsealed his envelope in front of the class, he seemed dumbstruck. "Little Rock," he said. The disappointment was written on his face. Unbeknownst to Wilson, Peter was equally upset. He approached Peter later that night.

"Hey, you are from Little Rock. I'm going to need you to hook me up," Wilson told him.

"Sure," Peter replied. "No problem." He realized he would now have to do some research in order to help Wilson. He knew nothing about Little Rock. This was a turn of events he had not anticipated. In the meantime, he would have to get word to Father about his posting to Boston. He would be pleased.

———

Tim Wallace understood all too well the technical capabilities of the US government and its intelligence agencies such as the FBI. One of the most utilized techniques for eavesdropping on terrorists or other "enemies of the state," was electronic surveillance, known by the acronym ELSUR. In the twenty-first century, this meant not just surveillance of telephone calls, but also e-mails.

Thus, although electronic communication is the easiest mode of contact, it is quite vulnerable to penetration. The use of the postal service, while more time-consuming, offers more privacy and protection. Although the government could ask for the postal service inspectors to implement what is known as a mail cover, this has limited value. In a mail cover, the postal service only takes a photocopy of the outside of the envelope. The mail itself is never opened, except with a warrant showing probable cause and then only in exceptional circumstances.

Tim was reasonably certain that he and his children were not on the government's radar screen at this point, yet he believed in taking all prudent measures. With this in mind, Tim had devised a simple method of communication with his children, which required no subterfuge or complicated technique. He believed correctly that the more complicated a plan, the more opportunity there was for it to fall apart. Further, the more complications embedded in a plan, the more likely a person could be seen as acting suspiciously. His communication plan was simple. When communication was necessary, each child simply sent a letter addressed to his or her own name at a predetermined address. As a countermeasure to any possible mail cover, they would not add a return address to their letters. The only clue to the letter's origin would be the postmark. In the case of Peter, he would simply write a letter to Kyle Grant, directed to a PO box he had opened in anticipation of such a need. Tim had access to these PO boxes. Peter couldn't send the mail to the house in Little Rock, which would have been simpler, because Peter needed to have Grant's mail forwarded to Quantico. In this way, he received Grant's bank statements and credit card reports on a regular basis, all of which Peter now had access to. One of the first things Peter did administratively after he checked into Quantico was to have his paycheck direct deposited into Grant's account. He had Grant's credit cards and personal checks. Still, there was one problem.

———

Tim and Susan had argued forcefully about the fate of Kyle Grant. Tim wanted to dispatch him immediately. Keeping a prisoner alive allowed an opportunity for him to attempt escape. Further, feeding and cleaning up after him was also a burden, a duty that would fall on Bill, who listened quietly as the two argued. Although he had a personal stake in the matter, Bill never revealed his preference.

Susan felt that it was impossible to predict what value keeping Grant alive might have as the weeks progressed. There were factors that might require some information from him, something that had not been anticipated, especially during the embryonic stages of their plan. She expressed deep reservations about Peter's mission in general, feeling that there were too many variables to account for. Susan argued that the odds of Peter's deception being successful were less than 50 percent, and the entire operation could be compromised. In the end, she relented to Tim's persuasiveness. She did, however, finally convince Tim that they should keep Grant alive, at least for a few weeks, in case something developed they hadn't planned for. Her concerns now seemed prescient.

As Tim approached the cell, he had to admit to himself that Susan was right after all. On the ninth week of his training, running low on money, Peter had attempted to access cash from Grant's ATM card. When he failed to submit the correct PIN number, the screen asked him to call the bank. Peter's second mistake, not having much knowledge of personal banking, was to call the bank and attempt to get the correct PIN number. He started well, offering his personal information exactly and without hesitation.

Then the representative asked Peter, "Now, Mr. Grant, as a security measure, you were asked to furnish a password. What is it?"

Peter was flustered. His face turned bright red. He was not used to not having an answer. "Well, I don't understand. A password?"

"Yes," she insisted, "the password you gave us when you opened the account."

He hesitated. He could hear the suspicion rising on the other end of the line.

"I guess I can't remember," he replied. "That was quite a while ago."

"Well," the representative replied, "I'm allowed to give you a hint. That was one of the features, in case you forgot. You can ask me for a hint that you provided us. Would you like a hint?" She asked half helpfully, half sarcastically.

"Yes," he asked in frustration. "What's the hint?"

"What is the name of your childhood dog?"

He searched his brain for a clue. He knew Grant didn't have a dog. But a childhood dog? He could not recall any photos of Grant with a dog in the house. Nothing in his background file mentioned a dog. He could not answer.

"Ma'am, I'm sorry, I don't feel well," he finally said in desperation. "I haven't felt well all day. I have a migraine. Let me call you back."

The customer service representative placed a note of a suspicious call in the file. The account was now flagged.

———

Grant sat bare chested in his jailhouse chair. He was gaunt and pale, his face ashen. He had lost almost twenty pounds since his arrival at the Fortress. Grant's hair was disheveled and matted together all at the same time. The food he received, although sufficiently nutritious to keep him alive, was practically tasteless. He was forced to eat with his fingers. Since his imprisonment, he had not spoken with his jailers.

His only recreation was his memory—the mental playback of the good and bad events of his life. His final talk with Tina was on his mind as he sat helplessly in his cell. Her words felt like a hammer on his heart. "I'm sorry, Kyle, but I want more excitement in my life. You are nice... but boring." He was now pleased that he had mailed that letter. No doubt, she would be impressed with his entry into the FBI. Except he now wondered if he would ever see Quantico.

Grant's attempts to engage Bill had been met with complete silence. As Tim observed Grant in his pathetic condition, he almost felt remorse. Then he remembered the greater good of their mission.

Grant felt he was being watched and turned to the door, which had been opened.

"Good morning, Mr. Grant," Tim stated dryly as he looked down at his prisoner.

Grant was escorted to a bench which was placed about twenty yards from his cell. It was next to a small stand of trees and was carved out of a giant log. This was the most exercise Grant had experienced in weeks. Grant noticed that his jailer had a gun holstered on his right side. The other jailer, who provided him his daily needs, was also armed and stood behind the man who had greeted him. He further noticed that that man also had a shearing tool in one hand. Grant wondered what purpose that tool was designed for, and it concerned him. He had a million questions about his situation, many of which he spent the long lonely hours pondering in his cell. Despite this, he felt it was prudent to listen rather than speak. He quietly took his seat on the bench as instructed.

"Mr. Grant, I'm sure you have many questions," Tim said thoughtfully. "Unfortunately, I'm not in a position to answer them at this time."

Grant was comforted by Tim's tone and demeanor, despite the lack of information he was getting. He thought about his dilemma as he looked up at his two foes. They seemed to be simply staring at him, waiting for him to speak.

Finally, he addressed them. "What do you want from me? Is this about money, because I will pay"—he stammered—"People will be looking for me...so it's best to just let me go."

"This is not about money, Mr. Grant." Tim cut him off in a monotone. "And nobody is looking for you, I'm sorry to say. It's best for you to simply cooperate in the questions I'm about to ask of you."

"Yes, what is it?" Grant asked.

"What was the name of your childhood dog?" Tim asked flatly.

Grant was stunned. His face became red. He clenched his fists. "What the fuck is this about?" he yelled as spittle came out of his mouth. "You've kept me here for all these weeks or months—who knows how long—and that's what you want to know? Well, fuck you, how about that!" He stared at his captors in a rage.

His tormentors displayed no emotion. They looked down at him as if waiting. As the seconds turned into a complete minute of silence, Grant's anger started to turn into anxiety. These were not normal people. He looked up at Tim and could see the heat had formed a bead of sweat on his forehead. He could almost hear the drops fall to the ground in the silence. As he assessed the situation, he realized he was at their mercy.

He also finally realized why they wanted to know about his childhood dog. He finally broke the silence. "I understand now. You are trying to access my bank account."

"Mr. Grant," Tim spoke in an eerily calm manner. "Why we need your cooperation is not important. What is important is that you must cooperate fully."

Tim pointed to Bill. He spoke again. "Do you see the instrument that my associate is holding?"

As Bill held the tool, the sun was glinting off its silver finish. Grant was quiet as Tim continued.

"If you do not tell me what I need to know, my associate will begin to cut off your fingers, one by one, until you cooperate. Do you understand? The issue is not whether you furnish the information I need, but how many fingers you will have once we are done." He spoke in an icy, efficient tone. His piercing, unblinking black eyes locked on to him.

---

Grant lay on the ground in his cell. It was dark now, and he could hear the sounds of wildlife outside. Through the cracks in the wood, he could see the stars in the clear sky. He was ashamed of how easily he had broken. He still had all his fingers. He closed his eyes and wept silently.

———

Wilson approached Peter as he was accessing some cash from the academy's ATM machine. Peter was counting his money as he heard Wilson come up on him.

"Are you psyched yet?"

They only had three weeks left in their training, and they had already fulfilled all their requirements for graduation. The last three weeks were going to be relaxing, despite the fact that they were itching to get on with their assignments. Most of them wanted to return to their families for final packing and celebration, but Peter was prepared for his assignment to Boston.

Peter turned to see Wilson smiling.

"Yes, absolutely," he replied, smiling back. Wilson's eyes squinted as he asked, "Kyle, are you absolutely sure you are OK with me renting your place?"

Wilson had convinced Peter to let him rent his house in Little Rock. Peter was initially reluctant, but after some thought couldn't think of any reason to deny his new friend this favor. Plus, he could collect rental income. Peter had sent word to his father to scrub the residence in anticipation of Wilson's arrival.

"Not a problem," Peter replied. "Just don't be late on your rent!"

They walked to class together to complete the final three weeks of their instruction, which centered on the terrorist threat faced by the United States. Peter found it simplistic and lacking, given its complete disregard for the real threat, which he knew all too well. He was elated that the training was almost over and was looking forward to the graduation.

———

Little Rock Police Detective Robert Johnson was a young patrolman when his mentor was killed in the line of duty. His mentor, Ross Grant, was already a senior detective on the force when he was killed during a high-speed pursuit of a bank robbery suspect. His patrol car had flipped over, and he'd died on the scene. Johnson was on duty that day and helped pull his lifeless body from the wreckage. He promised himself that he would look in on Ross's ten-year-old son, Kyle. For several years, until Kyle turned twenty-one, Johnson came to see him on his birthday. Kyle's mom, Rebecca, seemed appreciative of the gesture. She died of cancer while Kyle was attending college. Johnson was at the funeral and mass to comfort Kyle, who was now alone in the world.

When Johnson heard from Kyle that he was interested in the FBI, he wasn't surprised. He served as a reference for him and gave the FBI investigator conducting Kyle's background check a glowing recommendation.

Tim and Susan had read the recommendation when they reviewed his file, as did Peter while preparing for his mission. As before, they argued over how to handle this loose end. They concluded that the likelihood of Johnson encountering Kyle Grant at Quantico was remote. Besides, killing a policeman was a delicate matter, certain to attract all the resources of law enforcement. This was attention they did not need. So they did nothing.

———

With only one week to go at the academy, Peter was finally comfortable with his surroundings and confident in his assumed persona. It seemed as if he was in cruise control with the finish line in sight. As he liked to do, Peter sat reading a book in the Hoover Reading Room at the academy's library, under the shadow of a large framed photo of J. Edgar Hoover. Behind where he sat was a glass wall, which overlooked an outdoor memorial to the 9/11 attacks. On the other walls were photos of Hoover, some with past presidents. Books on Hoover and the FBI were laid out throughout the room. The room was essentially a shrine to the Bureau's most famous director. Peter enjoyed knowing that it was from within the inner sanctum of the FBI that he plotted the destruction of that very organization. As he mulled over the irony of this thought, he heard a set of footsteps approaching.

Quantico instructor Jedd Miller stood before him. Miller was one of the legal instructors, himself an FBI agent for almost twenty years.

"Wilson told me where to find you," he declared.

Peter looked puzzled. "What's up?"

"There's someone here to see you. A Detective Johnson, from Little Rock. He said he knew your dad. He's at reception waiting for you. If he wants to come in, you will need to escort him."

Peter's mind was racing. He knew who Johnson was instantly. He had worried countless nights about this very scenario in his sleep.

"OK," he replied after a second. "I will take care of it. Thanks."

As Miller walked away, Peter grabbed his phone and called Wilson.

Detective Johnson was sitting on a gray couch in the academy's reception area when he was met by Wilson.

"Are you Detective Johnson?" Wilson asked.

"Yes, that's me," Johnson answered.

"My name is Wilson. I'm a friend of Kyle's. When he heard you were here, he got real upset. He said it's bringing up some really sad memories. He was crying. I think it's best if you talk to him another time. He said he would call you after he graduates."

Johnson was a little taken aback. "It's just that I was in Washington for a police conference, so I thought I would surprise him. I'm kind of surprised he would be that upset. I know him well enough. It's never been an issue."

"Well, I guess it is now," Wilson replied, "I don't know what to tell you."

As Johnson drove off the academy campus that afternoon, he wondered what had just happened. He also pondered how Kyle had never returned his multiple phone calls to his cell phone. He could not think of anything he had done to offend Kyle. He had this on his mind for the next several days.

On the day of their graduation, most of the graduates had family members in attendance in the FBI auditorium. Peter was alone. One by one, they were called to the stage, where an unmemorable assistant director handed them their new official FBI credentials and badge. A photograph was taken as they accepted their identification. The ceremony was concluded with a new oath of office, which was recited by the graduates in unison. A reception followed the graduation at the academy's atrium.

Peter and a couple of other agents with whom he had become friendly walked to the FBI gun vault, where they were each issued their service weapon, a .40-caliber Glock pistol. He said his good-byes to Wilson and the others, holstered his weapon, grabbed his bags, and walked out of the academy as a special agent of the FBI.

# FIVE

## Boston

The Migliore incident, as it had come to be called in the Boston FBI office, had given Special Agent Carlos Sullivan considerable attention among his peers, all of it unwanted. For the first several months, he could not help but notice the extra stare and the whispers from his colleagues. They did not disapprove of his actions—to the contrary. However, they were too intimidated to ask him about what had actually occurred that fateful day. He spent more than a decade working quietly and intensely, doing everything to prove he was a great agent, not because of his tactical skills, but because of his sharp intellect and dedication. Despite his efforts to downplay his persona, there was always an unmistakable swagger about him.

Sullivan was like a cruise ship that leaves a large wake wherever it goes. Despite being of average build and height, the moment he entered a room, all eyes seem to be drawn to him. He was genuinely affectionate with those he engaged, charming without seeming like a politician. Sullivan was quick with funny quips, and he was often holding court with his peers, telling story after story, but he could turn in anger on a dime. His temper was famous within the Bureau, yet it always seemed in retrospect that the recipients of his lashings deserved what they got.

He was an avid reader and loved to recite famous quotes, often in Latin. He was also a dedicated athlete, running or cycling to keep his muscular frame in shape. He had been an agent for twenty-two years but was still two years away from retirement eligibility. Regardless, he had no intention of retiring. He liked his job too much.

Sullivan was the senior polygraph examiner in the Boston office. He was a tireless interrogator, often talking with criminal suspects for hours. In one memorable case, he interrogated a suspect for twelve hours until the man confessed his crime. On that occasion, as in many of his exams, he was being observed through a one-way mirror placed in the room. The case agents loved to watch the interrogation phase, which occurred once the suspect failed the exam. Sullivan seemed to feed off the idea that he was being observed; it mentally energized him to continue even when he was physically exhausted. The next morning, the supervisor of the respective squad approached Sullivan with two of his agents who had watched the interrogation.

As always, Sullivan was dressed impeccably. He wore a dark suit with a red tie.

"Sullivan," the supervisor said, "I have a question."

Sullivan assumed the supervisor was there to congratulate him on getting the suspect's confession, although he noticed that the agents accompanying the supervisor kept their heads down sheepishly. "Yes," he said. "How can I help you?"

"I noticed in your report how long your interrogation lasted. Did you give the suspect any breaks?" He added in a concerned manner, "If so, can you document that in a log?"

Sullivan tilted his head slightly to the right, as he often did when he was going to decimate someone. "Really," he said, his face red, his voice rising. "What about my break? What breaks did I get? Aren't you worried about that? Well, don't you worry. He got the same break I got!"

Sullivan stared at him. The supervisor stammered, not knowing how to respond. He was new in the Boston office and hadn't yet heard about Sullivan. He had just learned his lesson. When the supervisor abruptly left, one of his agents stayed behind.

"Sorry, Sully, we tried to stop him," the young agent said.

"Don't worry about it," he replied. "That's new Bureau management for you." Then he looked at the agent sternly and said, "Just don't become like that!" He pointed at the retreating supervisor for emphasis.

The young agent smiled and left.

As the story was retold throughout the office, Sully later received supportive e-mails and phone calls from other agents. The younger agents in particular looked to Sullivan for guidance. He took it upon himself to train the probationary agents on deception, interview and interrogation, and statement analysis, among other topics in that field. Sullivan's training had become mandatory in the Boston office for the "probies," as they were called.

He had a deep well from which to draw. His polygraph training was sponsored by the army, at a training facility located at Fort Jackson in South Carolina. All federal law enforcement polygraph examiners receive their basic training at this three-month intensive course. After graduation from the polygraph academy, he underwent an apprenticeship within the FBI polygraph program. During that time, he took other courses on interview and interrogation techniques. Indeed, FBI examiners are required to undergo forty hours of training on a yearly basis to maintain their skills.

Over the course of the next eight years, Sullivan had conducted almost two thousand polygraph examinations, in every conceivable setting and in far-flung corners of the earth. He had one temporary duty assignment (TDY) in Afghanistan and one in Iraq, submitting insurgents to the polygraph technique. He was always looking for a new challenge. In the Middle East, he used interpreters, but in South America and the Caribbean, he spoke in fluent Spanish.

Sullivan did not take a normal route to the FBI.

Sullivan's father, Thomas, was a second-generation Irish American who grew up in the Hyde Park section of Boston. He was vacationing in Miami in 1961 when he came upon a stunning beauty on Miami Beach. Her name was Katarina Robles. She was a Cuban refugee, only twenty-four years old at the time. She had long chestnut-brown hair and a beautifully tan complexion. Their connection was immediate, even with her broken English. They married a year later, and settled in Medford, Massachusetts, a mere five miles from Boston. A few months later, Katarina's parents moved into the first floor of their home, a three-story white Victorian house. A few months after that, Carlos Sullivan was born.

Growing up in the Boston area was not easy for Sullivan. His grandparents on his mother's side spoke no English, and the Irish kids in the neighborhood soon started calling Sullivan the spic in and outside of school. With the exception of one Chinese student, Sullivan was the only person at school who wasn't all Irish or Italian. He never knew why they insisted on being Irish or Italian, since they were all Americans in his view. His classmates did not agree.

The constant taunting was soon followed by physical assaults after school. To his credit, Sullivan always fought back, but he was invariably outnumbered, usually by four or more boys. He had no chance against a mob. One day, a pack of Irish kids had set upon him like rabid dogs, dragging him and throwing him into a construction ditch. There was a hole in one corner of the site, and they were intent on burying the twelve-year-old. Every time he tried pulling himself out of the hole, they would push him back in, as the others poured dirt onto him with shovels. Sullivan was crying, desperately convinced he was experiencing his last moments on earth. The sand was getting into every pore of his body. He begged them to stop, but his pleas only fed their frenzy. Then suddenly, a shadow appeared over them. The shadow's name was Jimmy Conrad.

It was impossible to discuss Carlos Sullivan without mentioning Jimmy Conrad. One year older than Sullivan, he had only recently moved to Medford. Conrad was a man of few words and had few friends, even in his old neighborhood. He had a profound sense of justice, and he felt compelled to jump into the fray. At that moment, their fates would be forever intertwined.

Conrad was big, even as a child. He had large hands and a powerful chest. His strength seemed superhuman. Despite his large frame, he moved with amazing speed. He had a sharp jaw and deeply set, dark-brown eyes. Conrad and Sullivan were both only children. They developed a bond closer than most brothers. Conrad saw in Sullivan a deep intellect that he had never before observed in a kid his age. He came to enjoy being in Sullivan's orbit. After that day in the construction ditch, nobody ever bothered Sullivan again.

As they grew up together, they decided they were going to become FBI Agents. Neither could recall who had the idea first, but they were both motivated by a strong sense of doing the right thing. They applied to the Bureau simultaneously, and both were accepted within a few weeks of each other. They were only one class apart at the academy, but they still managed to hang out together on their free time. They were posted to different offices after graduation, but after several years they were able to transfer to the Boston office.

They started out in Boston on the same squad, targeting drug traffickers. Because Sullivan was one of the few Spanish-speaking agents in the office, he underwent specialized undercover training at the FBI Academy. This led to many undercover roles, but Sullivan always insisted that his meetings be monitored by Conrad. Sullivan liked to say that his interest in deception began while he was in the murky world of undercover narcotics work.

During one particular undercover operation, Sullivan was portraying a drug supplier, as he often did. This was known as a "reverse" undercover operation, the goal being to confiscate the drug dealer's money as well as make an arrest. In a traditional undercover operation, the undercover officer poses as a purchaser. The meeting was held in a hotel room for logistical reasons. This allowed the FBI technical agents to wire the room for sight and sound. As always, Conrad was in an adjoining room listening to the meeting. Next to Conrad was a young Spanish-speaking agent, who served as the translator. Not that Conrad needed an interpreter. He had learned considerable Spanish just from being around Sullivan. Beyond that, he knew Sullivan's body language. He could tell instantly if there was a problem, just by watching his partner's movements.

On that day, something seemed off from the start. Conrad could see that Sullivan was extremely tense throughout the meeting. This was unusual. Sullivan had the natural ability to relax even in the most intense situations, and this in turn made the targets relax as well. The Dominican male who was the target of this operation suddenly started pacing the room nervously. The subject was getting increasingly agitated. Conrad could see Sullivan watching his target's movements, and then he noticed Sullivan looking at the door. He was looking for a way out.

Sullivan must have seen something they could not detect from their monitor. Then, within moments, Conrad could see the problem. The Dominican's jacket opened slightly, and tucked in his waist was a dark object—something Conrad could tell instinctually was a pistol. He pointed to the shape on the screen. Another agent disagreed, saying it could be a cell phone holder. The black-and-white image made it difficult to discern. Then the supervisor came to the screen and also said they needed to wait. Yet Conrad knew.

"I'm going in," Conrad whispered tensely.

Everyone in the room knew there was to be no debate. Conrad was too protective of his partner. It was his call. Just as Conrad pushed the adjoining door open, the suspect had pulled the weapon on Sullivan, demanding the cocaine Sullivan had been talking about.

Sullivan grabbed the pistol with a lightning-quick movement of his left hand. With his right hand, Sullivan was holding him by the throat. The suspect was yelling, spitting. They grappled savagely. The gunman had pulled the trigger, but Sullivan had locked the pistol's slide with his hand, preventing it from discharging. In the next second, Conrad barged in and planted a swift punch to the side of the man's face. He was knocked out instantly.

As the man lay crumpled on the ground, Sullivan looked at Conrad.

"You son of a bitch," he said, taking deep breaths.

"What?" Conrad asked his partner.

"What the hell took you so long?"

———

Almost a week later, they were having lunch together when Conrad spoke. "Sully, you need a change. I don't think you should keep doing this stuff." He looked at Sullivan intently.

"Go on," Sullivan replied, considering Conrad's words.

"Well, we're getting too old for this shit. Plus, honestly, I don't think I could live with myself if something happened to you on one of these gigs. I heard the polygraph examiner is retiring. I think you should put in for that. I think you would be good at that."

His new path was set in motion.

———

The probationary period for FBI agents lasts two years. During those two years, a probationary agent can be dismissed for practically any infraction. It is a time during which most probationary agents are cautioned to carefully toe the line.

In the FBI, the placement of probationary agents within a field office falls under the discretion of the special agent in charge of the office, known by the acronym SAC. Below SACs in rank are assistant special agents in charge (ASACs), whose numbers vary depending on the size of the field office. Each ASAC in turn manages a certain number of supervisors, who themselves are responsible for the agents on their respective squads.

Each of the fifty-six field offices within the FBI are known as divisions. In some divisions, probationary agents are placed directly into an investigative squad. Squads are given alphanumeric designations. In Boston, probationary agents are initially placed on the administrative squad, known as C-8. The C-8 squad is also home to the recruiter, the firearms instructors, and the polygraph examiners. All processing of FBI applicants in Boston is the responsibility of C-8.

As such, probationary agents' duties on that squad consist primarily of conducting background investigations of applicants or of people nominated for government jobs requiring security clearances. Cabinet members, for instance, are required to undergo background investigations. These investigations consist of interviews with former employers, teachers, neighbors, and others who might know the candidate.

The Boston SAC, Milt Wainwright, felt this was a good way for new agents to acclimate themselves to the city and get to know their way around. The probationary agents were seated in a bull pen area known affectionately as "the nursery." Peter was in the nursery for the first time, standing over his assigned desk. He was unpacking some of his belongings from the box he had mailed himself from Quantico. The other new agents he had met minutes before already had several weeks under their belts, and they talked quietly among themselves. One of them sat typing reports at his desk. Another, a female agent who had introduced herself as Jodi, was reviewing a map of the city. She seemed to be the most outgoing of the group. Peter watched them with one eye as he placed things about his desk.

As he did so, another female agent walked into the nursery. Her name was Kathy Fuller, and she was there to give him a tour of the office. Fuller had been in the FBI for almost thirteen years. She was thirty-seven years old, stood at almost five ten, and had black curly hair. She had started her work in Boston on C-2, the drug squad, alongside Sully and Conrad, who mentored her from her first day on the squad. She had previously been a state trooper in Pennsylvania for several years, and unlike most of the probationary agents, she was placed directly on C-2 upon graduation from Quantico.

Two years after Sully became the Boston polygraph examiner, he approached her about joining him. He had convinced his supervisor and ASAC that there was a need for a second full-time polygraph examiner. Conrad wasn't interested in changing assignments. She was his next choice. He offered to recommend her for the training, and she agreed.

Fuller was generally considered to be a by-the-book type of agent. Yet she possessed a quality that convinced Sully she was trustworthy: loyalty. One day, after conducting a long surveillance of a drug subject, he took his girlfriend to Logan Airport in his FBI car, known as a Bucar, short for Bureau car. He knew this was a violation of FBI policy that could result in a thirty-day suspension. He was tired, and it was a short trip, so he took the risk. As he sat waiting for a red light to change, he noticed Fuller standing on the corner, looking directly at them. His heart sank.

Fuller was only one of two agents—the other being Conrad—who knew his girlfriend. Sully was very private about his personal life and took pains to keep his personal and professional lives distinct and separate.

The next day, Sully sat at his desk, alternately staring at his phone and the door to his office. He waited all morning, expecting either a phone call from management to report to the front office, or for Fuller to confront him. Then, shortly before noon, Fuller entered his office. She stood over him, knowingly. He looked up from his chair, waiting.

After a brief pause, she spoke. "Lunch?"

They had their lunch at a deli behind the office. Fuller never mentioned the incident.

———

As Fuller finished her tour with Peter, she inquired of him, "You haven't met Agent Sullivan yet, correct?" She looked straight at him.

Peter knew she already knew the answer to her question. He had already heard a story about the legendary Agent Sullivan from an instructor at Quantico, on hearing he was being assigned to Boston.

"No, not yet," he replied with a sly smile.

"Well," she said. "You will have to do so before you leave C-8." With that, she spun around and walked out of the room. He could tell she was trying to freak him out.

Peter was unconcerned. He knew he could not be bested. He was, after all, the prodigy.

# SIX

## The Secret Service

Tim once told his little coyotes that for every lock, there is a key. For every puzzle, there is a solution. Likewise, for every security measure, there is a countermeasure. Samantha had paid close attention to her father that day.

———

John Livingstone was sitting in his office one day when the phone rang at his desk. He was fifty-one years old and had been pondering his possible retirement from the US Secret Service after twenty years of service. He also had prior military experience—six years in the army.

The female voice on the other end of the phone was pleasant and polite. She had an accent he couldn't quite place. He listened intently.

"Mr. Livingstone, my name is Samantha Wallace, and I'm a senior at George Washington University. I'm writing a term paper on the polygraph technique, specifically as it is used by federal law enforcement. I got your name from the community liaison person at your office, Mrs. White. She told me you are a polygraph examiner, and she suggested perhaps you could help me." Her voice was soft, almost sensual.

Livingstone wasn't necessarily bored with his job; he was bored with life. His marriage of eighteen years had been over for three years, and he had not dated anyone in that time. He knew he had no particular charm and was plain-looking, but he didn't understand why his luck was so bad.

"Sure," he said after a moment. "Let's meet."

———

It only took two meetings before Livingstone was certain he was in love. Samantha always had an uncanny knack for persuasion. She possessed a certain magnetism that made people want to be around her, especially men. There was no doubt that most men found her irresistibly sexy and approachable. Her eyes had a hypnotic effect on them.

———

After the family's trip to New York—or mission as their father called it—none of the other siblings were able to learn how Ryan managed to beat them back to the hotel. They pleaded with him to no avail. He repeatedly told them he would not reveal his secret. Their father would not ask Ryan, as he felt that part of the lesson was to maintain operational secrecy. After a few days, however, Samantha approached him when he was alone.

She smiled at him in her radiant manner, placing a hand on his shoulder.

"Ryan, won't you tell me how you got to the hotel?" she asked.

He was helpless before her. "OK," he said. "I just went over to a police officer who was standing on the corner. I told him I got separated from my family. Next thing I knew, they put me in a cruiser, and I was in the lobby in no time. They confirmed at the desk that I was staying there and left me to wait for you."

"That is amazingly simple. I don't think I would have thought of that. Thanks," she replied gratefully and walked away.

It was the same charm she used a few years later during her admission interview at George Washington University. Despite her lack of demonstrated extracurricular activities, the admissions officer placed her application on the top of their list. The school had a certain number of students admitted every year who were home-schooled. Samantha would prove to be one of the school's best students.

Several months after Samantha had beguiled Livingstone, she informed him that after being with him, she decided that upon her impending graduation from college, she too wanted a career in the US Secret Service. He encouraged her and offered to help her in the application process. Livingstone did not yet fully understand how much Samantha was expecting of him.

———

The US Secret Service was created in 1865 as a branch of the Department of the Treasury. Initially the Secret Service's mission was to tackle the problem of counterfeiting, which was taking a large toll on the country. The chaos created by the Civil War had allowed counterfeiters to run rampant. After the assassination of President McKinley in 1901, the Secret Service was given the added duty of protecting the president and vice president. Today the Secret Service maintains two branches, the uniformed division and its special agents.

As their name implies, the former are a uniformed corps, responsible for the physical protection of the White House, the vice-presidential residence at the Naval Observatory in Washington, and foreign embassies in the capital. The latter are the special agents who conduct investigations related to counterfeit currency, credit card fraud, and other financial crimes. In addition, they form protective details responsible for the security of current and former presidents and vice presidents. Following the attacks of 9/11, the Secret Service was transferred from the Treasury to the newly formed Department of Homeland Security (DHS).

Secret Service special agents are required to be US citizens between the ages of twenty-three and thirty-seven, possess a four-year college degree, pass an entrance exam, and be physically fit. In addition, they have to pass a polygraph examination.

Among the ethical obligations required of polygraph examiners, one of the most important is to avoid conflicts of interest. For this reason, a polygraph examiner is never to test somebody with whom he has a relationship. Even having a casual relationship with someone he is testing can be perceived as a conflict of interest. A personal bias can affect the way a test is administered and how the results are evaluated. Unlike DNA testing, polygraphy is a subjective science. Livingstone had explained these protocols to Samantha at their first meeting.

At the age of twenty-three, Samantha graduated summa cum laude from George Washington University. As promised, she initiated her application with the Secret Service. This was no surprise to Livingstone, who had encouraged her application. However, now Samantha was asking more of him, and he had to remind her of his ethical obligations.

"But, sweetie," she implored him. "I want you to test me."

"I told you I can't do that," he insisted. "Besides, what difference does it make?"

She looked at him in that way she did when she wanted something. "*You* told me that there are cases of false positives, where innocent people can fail the test." She looked at him and repeated, "*You* told me that. You did."

"I said there are rare cases. Nothing is perfect. It's not likely." He shook his head.

"Not likely. You want me to place my future on 'not likely'? That's not very comforting. Don't you trust me?" she asked him, holding his hand.

After ten more minutes of pleading, Samantha convinced him that it was viable. As she had insisted, he never told any coworkers her identity. He did tell his coworkers that he had a new young girlfriend—he couldn't help himself, but he never told them she was applying to work with them. Livingstone assumed that she didn't want it to appear as though she was getting into the Secret Service on anything but her own merit. And he respected her for that.

Before even applying for the job, Samantha went out of her way to never meet any of his coworkers. She never went to his office. She never let him take pictures of her or of them together. He assumed that she was a private person, or she didn't want to be judged about their age difference. She usually insisted on meeting at night, at his apartment. She never invited him to her place. She told him her landlord didn't allow visitors. He was in love, blind to her unusual behavior and requests. He accepted her word without question.

On the day of her scheduled polygraph examination, Livingstone came out to the reception area and called her name coldly. He was nervous. He trusted Samantha, but he knew what he was doing was a serious violation of policy that could result in his forced retirement. He did not want to leave service on bad terms, as it could affect his prospects for employment in the private sector. Yet he didn't want to lose Samantha. She made him feel so alive.

She was dressed in a white blouse with fringes, a black skirt, and black heels. The receptionist, Serena Washington, thought that the skirt seemed to be a little too short for the occasion. She recalled Livingstone's previous description of such attire as a "DI dress." He had explained to her that in polygraph, DI stood for "deception indicated." In polygraph circles, a woman wearing such a skirt, dress, or low-cut top was deemed to be wearing clothing designed to bias the examiner in her favor, away from her deception. Thus, the term DI dress was coined.

As she sat in the chair he pointed to, Samantha said nothing. She crossed her legs seductively.

"OK," Livingstone said. "Let's keep this is as professional as possible."

In most circumstances, the polygraph is preceded by a lengthy pretest interview. During this interview phase, the polygraph examiner reviews the application and background with the candidate. The process involves an in-depth dissection of the applicant, a probing for weaknesses, and an assessment of his motives for applying for the position. In this case, Livingstone decided he would dispense with this phase of the test. He simply reviewed the questions to be presented. As with the FBI polygraph, questions are asked regarding espionage, terrorism, criminal activity, illegal drug use, and the truthfulness of the person's application, among other things.

Livingstone placed Samantha in the polygraph chair and quickly placed the components on her. First, two rubber tubes, known as pneumograph tubes, were placed across her chest and stomach. Then a blood pressure cuff was placed on her forearm. Finally, two finger plates were strapped onto the tips of two of her fingers. Livingstone explained to her that each series of questions would be asked three times, which is the normal protocol. He also explained that he would be sitting behind her as he asked the questions. Samantha said nothing but listened intently.

After the first round of the questions, Livingstone reviewed the data before him and became concerned. As a polygraph examiner, he was trained to detect and evaluate deviations from the norm, essentially looking for strong physiological reactions in comparison to the planted control questions. In most cases, the control question is a known truth, such as "are you sitting down?"

As he reviewed the chart, he noticed that Samantha's reaction to the terrorism question was twice as strong as her reaction to any other question. While he was concerned, he was not panicking. He knew from experience that some people react to a question the first time out, and then the reactions diminish. So he initiated the second round of questioning.

He was apprehensive as he approached the question he'd flagged the first time, hoping that her first response to that question was only an anomaly.

He asked again, "Have you ever provided support to any terrorist organization?"

This time, her reaction was three times that of any other question. Livingstone's heart began beating more strongly. He did not like the situation he was in, and now Samantha was having a problem with the examination. He also knew from experience that when a reaction increases during a second or third asking of a question, this is a sign of a deceptive person. He was almost in a state of panic as he began the third session.

As he began the third session, he knew the terrorism question would be the fifth one in the question string. As it approached, he started feeling a pit in his stomach.

Livingstone asked question four. "Have you ever used any illegal drugs?"

"No," she replied in monotone.

No reaction.

Then, "Have you ever provided support to any terrorist organization?"

"No."

Livingstone was stunned. Samantha's reaction to the question was now stronger than ever. He knew in every previous case he had seen that this was a sign of deception, or DI as it was called. But this was Samantha, the woman he loved. It had to be a mistake. He took a moment to compose himself. He grabbed his chair and wheeled it in front of Samantha.

"Sam." He looked at her seriously. "You are having trouble with this test. What's on your mind?"

"Which question?" she asked incredulously. Her eyes widened.

"The question regarding terrorism. How is that possible?"

"Well, that's crazy," she stammered.

"What were you thinking about related to terrorism, Sam?" he said intently.

"Well, maybe it's because I was thinking about the 9/11 attacks. I did a major research paper on the attack, and it kept flashing in my mind. That has to be it, Johnny."

She knew he had a soft spot every time she called him Johnny. For the next fifteen minutes, Livingstone went back and forth with Samantha over the results, and whether her explanation was plausible. He knew Samantha. She could not be connected to anything related to terrorism. Her future was in his hands. He also knew that if he failed her, she could turn around and disclose their relationship, ruining him. She sat crying softly as he pondered what to do. Finally, he decided.

"OK, Sam, we are going to run through the test one more time."

She silently nodded.

Livingstone went to his computer and deleted her file. He opened a new one. He began an entirely new series with the same questions. This time, however, each time he was supposed to ask her about terrorism, he mouthed the question silently. She never heard him ask the question. Thus, she could not produce a reaction. He did this three times.

Livingstone had just committed the first corrupt act of his long career.

———

Training for Secret Service special agents begins with a course at the Criminal Investigator Training Program at the Federal Law Enforcement Training Center, known as FLETC (pronounced Fletcy). The FLETC trains candidates from dozens of different federal law enforcement agencies, including agencies like the ATF, Immigration and Customs Enforcement (ICE), the US Capitol Police, and the US Park Police. After finishing their instruction at the FLETC program, Secret Service agents complete another eighteen-week training course at a Secret Service facility in Virginia. The FLETC is located in Glynco, Georgia, which is between Savannah, Georgia, and Jacksonville, Florida.

Samantha was a model student. Her coursework was exceptional. Her firearms proficiency was flawless; she never missed a shot. During the fitness drills, she was always ahead of the pack. Unlike Peter, who was involved in a deeper deception, Samantha felt no need to keep a low profile. Just as at the Fortress, she was determined to be the best student. All of her instructors were impressed with her skill and poise.

One day, Samantha walked past a wall which contained the class pictures of all of the previous graduating classes. She stopped to peruse them, glancing quietly at each photo for the last several years. Then, as she reviewed a photo of a graduating class from three years before, she stopped. There were about fifty students lined up in the photo. She looked at the picture again, pointing at one particular student with her index finger. She found who she was looking for. The image was small, but she was sure. It was her brother Ryan.

Ryan had been an officer in the US Capitol Police force for the last three years.

# SEVEN

## Arkansas

**W**ilson had begun to accept his transfer to Little Rock with more optimism. He realized he was far from the Chicago of his upbringing and all that the big city offered. On the positive side of the ledger, he had a low cost of living in Arkansas. He was settling into Peter's home and found that it was quite warm. The rent was cheap, and his commute to the office was less than twenty minutes. He could never get to work that easily in Chicago. While he had furnished the home completely, he had yet to explore the old house in its entirety.

—

Mount Judea, Arkansas, was an unlikely place to find a Secret Service agent. Just north of the Ozark National Forest, the only things visible to a passerby, except for small shanty homes, were a small church and the Mount Judea General Store in the center of town. Agent Michael Crowley had just spent two hours driving up and down rural roads looking for the residence of Samantha Wallace, whose background investigation he was responsible for. He had left Little Rock early in the morning, hoping to conduct a routine neighborhood investigation. Normally, this procedure was quite straightforward. Simply find some neighbors of the applicant and interview them about the candidate seeking employment. In this case, he could not find the residence; thus, he found no neighbors. He stopped at the general store for guidance.

Two elderly men were inside the store, arguing about something they were reading in the newspaper. The manager identified himself only as Kenny.

Agent Crowley identified himself and inquired about the Wallace residence.

Kenny responded, "I know that family…well, at least the husband and wife. I've never seen them kids."

"You don't know their daughter Samantha?" he asked.

"No. Never saw the kids. Years ago, I figured they had kids, cuz they came here buying diapers or milk and such. The head of the family, I think his name is Tim. He got his mail delivered here for a time. Then he stopped that, too. I haven't seen them in years."

Crowley continued, "Can you tell me where their house is located? I'm trying to find their neighbors."

Kenny looked at him with a smile. "They ain't got no neighbors." He added, "Nobody's ever seen their house. It's in the woods."

"I see," Crowley replied in frustration.

He had no desire to spend another two hours looking for a residence nobody could find in the woods. He headed back to Little Rock. His official report would indicate that the Wallace residence was located in a deeply rural area, and the local grocer had indicated the family had no neighbors.

———

Tim sat in his favorite leather chair inside the Fortress, with two separate messages in his hand. His feet were propped up on a matching futon. A table lamp next to him illuminated the letters. His brow furrowed. He read them each twice, absorbing the sobering news they contained. The first was from Samantha, and she was concerned about her situation. Livingstone had been calling her at FLETC, and with each call he sounded increasingly unhinged. He was having pangs of conscience, he told Samantha, and was thinking about turning himself in. She had managed to contain him temporarily—he agreed to await her return from training, which was only two weeks away. Samantha suggested no course of action. She knew her job was to recount the facts in as detailed a manner as possible. It was her parents' duty to decide on a solution. For this reason, she signed her letter simply, "For your consideration, Samantha." Tim chuckled when he read her signature.

The second message was from Peter. He had described the incident at Quantico. Peter was not as circumspect as Samantha. He finished his letter with the statement, "This threat must be neutralized." This elicited no smirk from Tim.

He called for Susan's counsel. Together they strategized, as Bill sat in the corner, listening. They agreed that too many pieces had been played on their strategic board to let the plan fail now because of some loose ends. They had to take action. They decided to handle Peter's situation first. After all, they had all the information about Detective Johnson at their immediate disposal. The FBI interview of Johnson was in the file in their possession. It contained Johnson's address and telephone numbers. A quick Internet search revealed a photo of Johnson. In March 2009, Johnson had received an award for valor, after rescuing two teenagers from a burning car. The photo, which ran in the local newspaper, showed the mayor handing a beaming Johnson the award.

Finally, they had the most important resource of all: Grant. With each subsequent interview, Grant had become more compliant. He was a broken man. He had lost more weight, and his pale skin seemed to sag. His arms and neck were covered in mosquito bites. Some of them were scabbed from his constant picking at them. He was emotionless as they asked him about his knowledge of Johnson. Tim sat in a wooden chair asking the questions, Susan sat by his side taking notes. Bill observed. By the time they had finished, they had an impressive dossier on Detective Robert Johnson. They could not imagine that Grant would omit one detail from his debriefing.

Before concluding their interview of Grant, Tim asked him one last question.

"How many other people did you tell, or have knowledge of the fact, that you were going to the FBI Academy?"

As Grant feebly elaborated, Susan wrote down two other names into her notes, with their descriptions and addresses. He was so defeated; he did not hesitate to furnish the name of his unrequited love.

———

Once the decision was made to kill Detective Johnson, they assessed the problem in the most logical manner. The killing of Johnson while on duty was a nonstarter. He would be armed. He would have radio contact or be in the presence of other officers. In addition, it would be impossible to predict his movements or patterns. As a detective, he had freedom of movement. He did not have a patrol route. Further, the ensuing response and media coverage would pose enormous risks. The attack had to appear random, or at least not related to his police duties. Although his death would certainly result in a massive police response regardless, it would be far greater if it was perceived he was killed because he was an officer. Then it would be an attack on the system. And they believed—indeed they knew from history—that the system always won. Unless, they hoped, the system could be decapitated with one massive blow.

———

As was his habit, Johnson had decided to take a jog from his house after his shift ended. Because of the Arkansas heat, he preferred to wait until dusk to exercise outside. Typically, he drove home, secured his weapon, changed clothes, and went on a three-mile run just as the sun was starting to set.

The Wallaces had already driven the route Johnson took several times, based on the information Grant had furnished. On at least two occasions, Grant had gone for a run with Johnson. They took notes about the course, selecting the most remote location on his route.

Johnson jogged along a long field of uncut wild grass, almost three feet tall. There were no homes on either side of the roadway. Crouched and waiting in the grass, obscured from view, were Tim and Bill. Susan stood by their car, which had its hood up. On cue, she appeared distraught.

Tim had always believed that if a plan had proved effective in the past, it was best to use it again, rather than reinvent the wheel. Of course, he also had a backup plan.

As Johnson approached Susan, he stopped jogging and walked over to her. Tim was taken aback at how much bigger Johnson appeared in person compared to his photo. He estimated that Johnson was approximately six two and easily weighed 225 pounds. He seemed muscular and fit.

"Do you need help, ma'am?" Johnson asked.

"Yes, actually," Susan replied. She motioned him over to the exposed engine. Her confederates were coiled, ready to spring from the field.

"It won't run. I'm not sure what the problem is." She waited for the right moment. Johnson started to lean into the engine. As he did so, Susan retrieved the stun gun she had tucked into her waistband.

Johnson started to check the radiator, when he sensed a movement. The setting sun had cast a shadow against the engine block. He spun around as Susan was inches from stunning him in the neck. The device was in her right hand. With one arm, he quickly slapped the stun gun out of her hand. With his other hand, he slapped her strongly in the face. Each move was so fast it seemed like a single motion. As she fell back, he heard footsteps.

Before he could turn, Tim was behind him, and in an instant a wire was around his neck, choking the life out of him. From his training, Johnson knew he had no more than a minute before he would be dead. He had to break free. As he gasped for air, he tried to hit his assailant's face with the back of his head. But the wire was tight, and he could barely move his neck. He couldn't even cry for help. As he struggled, Bill had come up next to him, trying to force him to the ground and further limit his mobility.

For an instant, Johnson could see that Bill's leg was in a vulnerable standing position. Before Bill could react, Johnson crushed his calf with one strong thrust of his foot. He used all the energy he had left, and Bill's leg snapped. Tim kept on top of Johnson for a few more seconds, like a cowboy riding a bull flailing wildly. Eventually, Johnson slumped to the ground. They dragged his lifeless body into the field. They hoped it would be several days before his body would even be found.

Susan was bleeding from a cut to her face, but she was otherwise unharmed. Tim helped her set Bill's leg once they returned to the Fortress. Despite his obvious pain, Tim was impressed with Bill's silence during their escape. He knew Bill was actually more embarrassed than hurt.

Whenever the family engaged in a mission, they always conducted an after-action review. They now needed to assess how their plan had been so poorly executed.

—

It didn't take long for the family to realize why their plan was nearly thwarted. Before dumping Johnson's body, they had taken his wallet; in the hope the authorities would believe that robbery was the motive for his death. Among his many IDs, Tim found papers identifying Johnson as a former member of the US Army, a retired Special Forces officer. Tim had suspected as much. Johnson's moves displayed training beyond what is received at a police academy.

The next morning, he visited Grant in his cell. The disappointment on Grant's face was evident. It was clear he had hoped never to see his jailer again.

Grant flinched slightly when he saw his tormentor carrying the shearing device he had previously seen. Behind Tim was Susan, a scratch and bruise visible on the left side of her face. Grant saw only the same cold visage Tim displayed every time they met. There was no emotion behind his eyes. Grant waited to be addressed.

"Surprised to see me, Mr. Grant?" Tim asked sarcastically.

Grant stayed silent. Tim continued, "It seems, Mr. Grant, that you have been less than candid."

Grant looked from Tim to Susan, looking for any opening. He found none.

"For that, Mr. Grant, there must be punishment." He stared at Grant.

Grant spent the next minute pleading with his jailer, trying to convince him that he was unaware of Johnson's military training. As he did so, he knew there was no point. His words finally trailed off.

After they left, Grant looked at what remained of his left hand. His index finger had been sliced off. The bloody digit was still in the dirt at his feet. They left him no bandages. He was in agony. In his mind, he replayed the moment when he was sliced and pictured how the female was grinning, enjoying the moment. Beyond the pain, he could not get the image out of his head.

———

The next morning, Grant awoke to the sound of a squealing pig. He found a small crack in the wooden door, from which he could see his jailer pulling a large pig on a leash into a shed. Grant had previously seen the shed about thirty yards from his cell but had thought nothing of it. After shutting the pig in the shed, the man circled around to the other side of the structure, out of his sight. After a minute, the man returned, looking at a stopwatch. The other jailer approached him and Grant could see they were talking, but he couldn't hear them. After several minutes, they opened the shed. The pig lay dead inside. It had not made a sound as it died. Grant felt sick to his stomach; he could not fathom the horror he had become a witness to.

———

It took the search party two days to find Johnson's body in the field where he was discarded. By then, it had been mangled. Some animals had started to pick at his flesh. Crime scene investigators quickly established the manner of death. Yet there were no immediate leads, witnesses, or apparent motive. A task force was established to investigate his murder, which was front-page news. They initiated the time-consuming process of reviewing all of Johnson's current and former cases in the hope of finding a connection to his murder. Their review would yield no clues to his assassination.

# EIGHT

## Washington DC

Following his divorce, Livingstone had moved to a small apartment in Reston, Virginia, just outside the nation's capital. It was a five-story brick building with six units on each floor. It had ample parking and was surrounded by a ring of large trees, which gave the complex considerable privacy. Entry to the building was either with a key or an intercom with buzzer access.

Livingstone sat in a cheap plastic chair by his kitchen table. He had just finished eating a plate of microwaved ravioli. It was almost midnight, but he was restless and hungry. He knew that if his employer discovered his misdeed, they would force him to retire in disgrace, at the least. He also worried that his act might also incur some criminal penalties. Yet he could not live with himself. He had not slept for more than two hours at a time since that fateful day. He had decided to turn himself in, and he had told Samantha as much. Out of love for her, he would give her the chance to also turn herself in at the same time. He was prepared to tell her this after she graduated. She had convinced him to wait. But his resolve was solid.

As he considered his predicament, his buzzer sounded. He ignored it at first, not expecting any visitors. Then it sounded again, loudly. He finally answered through the intercom. "Yes, can I help you?"

"Yes, Mr. Livingtsone." The voice was serious but friendly at the same time. "This is Michael Wallace, Samantha's brother. She has a message for you."

Livingstone was momentarily taken aback. He did not remember Samantha mentioning a brother. Yet who else would know where he lived? It seemed reasonable to him. He had to hear the message he brought.

"OK," he said. "Come up." He buzzed Michael into the building. Michael walked up the three flights to Livingstone's apartment. Nobody saw him enter.

Livingstone cautiously cracked the door slightly to observe his visitor. He had started having doubts in the short time it had taken Michael to walk up to his unit.

"How do I know you are her brother?" He quizzed Michael.

"Who else would I be?" he responded flatly.

Livingstone hesitated. He looked Michael up and down and noticed he was wearing a small backpack, which appeared empty. Michael became concerned that Livingstone might be concealing a weapon behind the door.

"OK," Michael finally said, "here's my ID." He handed Livingstone his military ID card. "I'm a captain in the US Army."

With that, Livingstone opened the door and handed Michael his ID back. Michael entered the apartment and immediately swept the area visually for weapons. He saw none.

Michael stood before Livingstone and said, "Sam is concerned about her privacy. How many people did you tell about your relationship?" Michael knew that by phrasing the question in that manner, he was more likely to get an honest response. As a polygraph examiner and skilled interrogator, however, Livingstone also recognized what his visitor was doing.

"How many?" answered Livingstone. "None."

Livingstone did not notice that Michael had quietly placed his right hand inside his pocket as he was speaking.

"I hope that's true," Michael said, "because otherwise Samantha will be very unhappy."

As he heard what Michael was saying, he could not process what he was now witnessing. As Michael spoke, he retrieved a sharp knife from his pocket and lunged at Livingstone. Before he could react, the knife was deep into his chest. From his training at the Fortress and in the army, Michael knew exactly how to effect a swift kill—with a knife thrust directly to the heart. Livingstone was in shock; he fell to his knees and clutched his chest. He looked up at his killer in dismay.

As Michael looked down at his dying victim, he leaned down and, without mercy, whispered, "Sam says good-bye."

Once Livingstone lay dead on the floor, Michael quickly put on a pair of gloves. He knew if he had worn them earlier, Livingstone would not have granted him access to the apartment. He took the knife to the kitchen sink and wiped it down. He folded the blade and placed it in a plastic baggie, then back in his pocket.

Michael spent the next several minutes methodically searching the apartment for any evidence linking Livingstone to his sister. He found a laptop and placed it in his backpack. He searched a desk and found some papers, all unrelated to his search. In the bedroom, he found a digital camera on a nightstand, which he also took. In the drawer he discovered Livingstone's service weapon, which he left untouched. It was under Livingstone's mattress that Michael's search ended. There, he found a small black journal. Michael flipped through the pages, especially the last entries, and discovered that Livingstone had been keeping a diary. He placed it in his sack and walked out of the apartment.

He took the rear stairs and walked out of the building into the muggy Virginia air. He went quickly to a waiting vehicle that was idling in the parking lot. Behind the wheel, was his sister Alexandra. She served as both driver and lookout.

⸺

Later that night, Michael placed two bricks into the backpack with the items he had retrieved and dropped the backpack into the murky Potomac River. The knife he dropped into a different section of the river. The journal he kept, in order to burn it. His message to Father was simple and direct. "Mission accomplished."

———

Fifteen hundred miles away, Cynthia King was reading a magazine in her living room. Her radio was tuned to a local Little Rock country music station. She lived only three doors down from the Grant residence. Cynthia had long been friends with Martha Grant, who had died of ovarian cancer only a few years before. She was fifty years old, almost the same age as her friend Martha. Cynthia recalled how the cancer had ravaged Martha's body aggressively; she died within six months of her diagnosis. The loss had devastated her. Cynthia's own husband had died of lung cancer ten years earlier.

Cynthia took it upon herself to look in on Kyle after his mother's death. Occasionally, she would stop over with some home-cooked food. Kyle was appreciative, offering to help her with chores in return. She had been excited to learn about his acceptance to Quantico and had been surprised that she had not heard from him since he left. Her calls to his cell phone had gone unanswered. Two days previously, she had left a note in Grant's mailbox. She had hoped the young new tenant had some news about Kyle.

Cynthia was startled when she heard a rap on her front door. Through her peep hole, she could see a blond woman. Sensing no threat, she opened the door.

Susan stood before her and asked, "Are you Cynthia King?"

"Why, yes, I am," she responded clearly.

Without saying a word, Susan pulled a gun from her waistband and fired a round directly to her forehead. The hollow-point round practically exploded her head. Her blood splattered across the hall as she fell back into her foyer, lifeless. The silver pistol had a silencer attached to the end of the barrel and made very little noise upon discharge. With a gloved hand, Susan closed the door and walked away. She silently slipped into the passenger side of a car driven by her husband. She had insisted on handling this mission herself.

The family had decided to remove all of its loose ends.

———

The killing of a federal agent falls under the investigative jurisdiction of the FBI. When Livingstone's body was discovered the next day, the FBI's Washington field office (WFO) initiated an immediate investigation. The WFO's area of responsibility covers the entire Washington metropolitan area. The investigation was spearheaded out of its satellite office, the Northern Virginia Resident Agency (NVRA). Out of professional courtesy and respect, the Secret Service was allowed to participate in the investigation. The murder of a federal agent is a rare occurrence, and the first priority is always to determine if the motive for the killing was in any way connected to his law enforcement duties.

Secret Service Supervisory Special Agent (SSA) John O'Neil waited patiently in a conference room to meet the agents who would be managing the investigation of his colleague's murder. O'Neil was tall and slender and always dressed professionally, in the finest suits. O'Neil had known Livingstone for almost ten years. He knew his associate to be a good man and a good agent. O'Neil wanted his killer brought to justice. His office had carefully selected him to run point with the FBI on the case. He had twenty years of service and had worked with the Bureau before, in a handful of financial fraud cases. Although he preferred that his own agency take the lead in the case, he knew there was an advantage to being emotionally detached from the victim. A dispassionate mind was an asset in this situation.

O'Neil had waited less than five minutes when the door opened, and two agents barreled into the room. They were in a hurry.

"Mr. O'Neil," said one of the agents, "My name is James Roberts, and this is my partner Stan Hernandez." Roberts looked at O'Neil with empathy. "I know how this must be affecting you and your people. A few years ago I also lost a colleague." Roberts seemed sincere as he spoke. "I can tell you that we won't rest on this case until it's solved. You have my word on that."

O'Neil was relieved at their attitude. They seemed genuinely committed to the case.

"I appreciate that Mr. Roberts," he answered. "Now, where do we begin?"

"First, we will be canvassing all of his neighbors. Second, we will want to interview people close to him, including coworkers. Hopefully they can give insight into any enemies he may have had. I have an analyst who has already begun dumping all his toll records, both from his home phone and his cell phone." Roberts smiled slightly as he finished.

He saw that O'Neil had looked at him oddly when he caught his smile.

"It's just that I'm a big believer in telephone analysis," Roberts said. "I want to know who he was talking to."

———

The US Capitol Police force was established in 1828. Its mission is to protect the US Congress, including its 435 congressional members, one hundred senators, and their families, anywhere in the United States. Practically speaking, most of the seventeen hundred members of this police force are deployed to the Capitol, protecting congressional buildings and the legislators while they are in session. However, if a specific threat is assessed against a particular legislator, he or she is assigned a protective detail, which travels with the congressman. This is rare. Few Americans can even name their congressmen or senators, and most legislators work in relative obscurity. Nevertheless, there have been attacks at the Congress and against its members. In 1998, a deranged gunman, Russell Eugene Weston Jr., stormed the Capitol, killing two Capitol Police officers before he himself was killed. In 2011, Congresswoman Gabrielle Giffords did not have a protective detail when she was shot in the head by a crazed gunman in Tucson, Arizona.

Neither of these attacks was a planned attack on the political system. They were random acts of violence by unstable men. The US

Capitol Police are an effective force, yet all their training and preparation is focused on threats from outside their ranks.

Ryan Wallace had established himself as an outstanding Capitol Police officer in his three years on the force. He had followed his parents' advice from the outset, which was to gain the confidence of his superiors, move up in rank as quickly as possible, and establish alliances within the department. At every performance review, Ryan received the highest marks.

His hiring process had been uneventful. A background and criminal check was conducted, which of course revealed no prior record. His high-school equivalency was sufficient education for the police, and unlike the Secret Service and FBI, the US Capitol Police do not require a polygraph examination for admission. This was one hurdle he did not need to overcome.

As a Capitol Police officer, Ryan had full access to the Capitol building and its surrounding grounds.

# NINE

## Assessment

Last winter had been brutal in the city of Boston. Nature unloaded more than seven feet of snow on the city, which took each storm like a body blow. Residents had trouble finding space to dump the unwelcome snow. The mayor, for only the second time in the city's history, authorized the dumping of snow into the harbor.

For this reason, Bostonians revel in the sun when it first makes a significant appearance. Restaurants and pubs open their windows, and whenever possible tables are placed outside. On an unusually warm and sunny June afternoon, Sullivan, Conrad, and Fuller sat outside enjoying a beer at a restaurant in Boston's Quincy Market. Bostonians seemed to be walking about in a more relaxed way now that the Boston Marathon bombings were receding from their collective memory.

The selection of meeting place was Sullivan's, as he was always the most paranoid of the trio. There were some restaurants closer to the office, but Sullivan preferred to keep a safer distance from any FBI managers who might be checking on them. Some managers felt obliged to take note of agents they observed drinking in public. Furthermore, they were waiting for Sullivan's girlfriend, Lena, who was meeting them to have dinner. Sullivan had never introduced Lena to any coworkers, with the exception of Conrad and Fuller.

As they waited, Fuller opened the conversation. "So Sully, have you met Kyle Grant yet?"

"No, not yet," he replied. "What's his story?"

"He's been in the nursery for six months now, and all the other probies hate him."

Sullivan listened intently. He looked at Fuller, then to Conrad. "Why?"

Fuller replied, "The word is that he's a know-it-all. He keeps trying to give them pointers about how to do things better. It's not going over well."

Conrad nodded. "That might have played well at Quantico, but now that he's in the field for a few months, not so much." He adjusted his sunglasses, watching the people walking past them. Most of the people out that day appeared to be tourists.

Sullivan looked at them and frowned. "Well, I have a lead to cover tomorrow. I think I'll ask him to join me. Maybe he's getting a bad rap."

Fuller looked at him incredulously. "Whoa, wait a minute. Where is my partner, and what have you done with him?" she asked, lifting her palms upward.

Sullivan answered, "I just want to make sure he gets a fair shake."

Conrad interjected, "Sully, just so you know, the word is that he is a major ass-kisser. I personally saw him coming out of the ASAC's office twice in the last week. What's up with that?" He added in disgust, for emphasis, "The ASAC, Sully...the ASAC."

Sullivan asked seriously, "Which ASAC?"

Conrad looked back with a frown. "Gibbons, that's who...not that it should matter."

Sullivan pondered Conrad's comments, as he scanned the passersby for Lena. "Well," he finally offered, "Gibbons is a major asshole. Maybe the probies are right after all."

They sat quietly for the next several minutes, people watching. They all silently recalled the many run-ins Sully had with Gibbons over the years.

———

Although no longer required to manage and operate cooperating informants, also known as sources, Sullivan still kept one of his old drug informants on the books. Her code name was Isabel, and she was a longtime FBI asset. She was from the city of Ponce, Puerto Rico, and could easily blend in the underworld Latino community that was prevalent in Lawrence, Massachusetts. Located twenty-five miles north of Boston, Lawrence was rife with corruption and had a thriving drug trade. Isabel provided Sullivan with consistently reliable information of value to the Bureau. Usually, they communicated by phone, but the Bureau required periodic face-to-face meetings. On this latest occasion, Sullivan was going to pay Isabel, which by policy required another agent to be present to witness the payment. Sullivan asked Special Agent Kyle Grant to accompany him to the meeting.

As they drove north, Sullivan counseled his passenger. "In the Bureau, you probably know by now, we have hundreds of rules. Some of those you can break, but others you most certainly cannot. Among the latter, you never meet a female source alone, and you always have another agent witness a payment."

Peter listened intently.

Sullivan continued, "If you ever get caught breaking a rule—any rule—just admit what you did. The Bureau will forgive almost anything, as long as you don't get caught lying."

"OK," replied Peter.

"As for today," Sullivan said, "you don't need to engage the source in conversation. Just observe."

They arrived at their meeting point, a shaded area beneath a large oak tree in a cemetery on the western side of Lawrence. Sullivan turned the car off, and they waited. There were no other people within eyeshot. After a few minutes, Isabel pulled in behind them and jumped in the backseat. She was petite and tanned. She wore a tank top and low-cut jeans, which Peter felt was inappropriate for a woman of forty years. Sullivan noticed Peter arch an eyebrow as she settled into the backseat.

Isabel and Sullivan spoke in Spanish for about twenty minutes. Peter had a basic understanding of Spanish, but he made it appear as if he understood nothing of what was said. When the discussion ended, Sullivan pulled out an envelope and handed it to her. In their presence, she counted the $500 it contained. She signed a receipt. They then signed as witnesses.

As they drove back to Boston, Sullivan began to question Peter. "So, Kyle, tell me about yourself."

———

Upon returning to work, Sullivan called Conrad and Fuller into his office. As they entered, he asked them to close the door.

"Uh-oh," said Fuller, "this can't be good."

"I just had a little conversation with Kyle Grant," he explained.

"OK," answered Conrad. "So what happened?"

"What happened is that he is lying," Sullivan said plainly.

"About what?" asked Fuller.

"About his background."

His unexpected answer took them by surprise. Conrad and Fuller looked at each other, puzzled.

———

It didn't take Agent Roberts's analyst long to determine that Livingstone had been placing late-night telephone calls to the FLETC complex. In fact, it seemed that he called very few people. The calls to FLETC were among the last ones he ever made. With the cooperation of the staff there, the calls were traced to Samantha Wallace's room. Despite Samantha's entreaties to him, Livingstone had continued to call her frantically.

Interviews of his neighbors and coworkers had yielded no leads, although some reported that Livingstone spoke about a new love interest. Livingstone lived a quiet, simple life. He had no apparent enemies. Although they had confirmed that Samantha was at FLETC at the time of the murder, these phone calls were their most promising lead.

With only one week until her graduation, Samantha was summoned for an interview. One of the instructors escorted her into a conference room.

Inside the room was a long rectangular conference table. At the head of the table sat Roberts, with Hernandez and O'Neil at either side, facing each other. Samantha was dressed in the khaki pants and polo shirt which are required attire at the training center. She took mental note of their serious demeanor as she took a seat at the table.

After identifying themselves, Roberts spoke first. "Do you know why we are here, Ms. Wallace?" He waited to assess her reaction.

Samantha had already prepared for this moment, which she considered inevitable. "I assume this is related to the murder of Agent Livingstone."

O'Neil stepped in. "What do you know of it?"

"Well, people have been talking about it here. It's also been in the news. It's a horrible tragedy," she offered in a sincere tone.

O'Neil replied quickly, "So why would we need to talk to you?"

"Well, it must be because of his phone calls to me here. I assume you are following a natural lead." She looked straight at him.

Roberts asked, "So what was the nature of your relationship with Mr. Livingstone?"

"There was no relationship," she answered flatly.

Hernandez finally spoke. "Then why the phone calls?"

The question hung in the air for several moments. Samantha started to fidget uncomfortably. They waited for her reply.

"Look," she said. "I don't like to speak ill of the dead. But you give me no choice."

O'Neil appeared angry. "What does that mean?"

"He was stalking me. He conducted my polygraph, and then he started calling me. He was obsessed with me. He kept asking me out. I asked him to stop calling me, but he wouldn't listen. If you check carefully, all the calls were incoming. I never called him."

As she continued, it appeared she was on the verge of tears. "I didn't know what to do. I didn't want to get him in trouble. I know this sounds horrible, but in a way I'm glad he won't be calling me anymore. Of course, I wish he had just stopped on his own."

The three agents looked at each other.

Samantha sensed that she had caught them off guard. She went in for the kill. "I want to say another thing. As of right now, I've decided not to pursue any kind of sexual harassment claim against the Secret Service, as long as this all just goes away. I don't want my future coworkers knowing about this. It would be scandalous." Samantha had composed herself and now seemed more serious as she sat before the agents.

O'Neil was surprised but not finished. "Do you have a boyfriend, someone who might have been protective of you or jealous of Livingstone?"

"No." She paused briefly. "I'm too focused on my training and my goals. I don't have time for a boyfriend."

The agents left disappointed. Their most promising lead had just fizzled.

———

Sullivan's problem with FBI management was not philosophical, but practical. It was not the idea of authority that bothered him. It was more the manner in which that authority was exercised, especially by some leaders whom he deemed to be unfit. He had maintained good relations with most of the old school managers who had served in their respective fields for several years before seeking promotion. Their numbers were diminishing with each passing year as they started retiring. The newer FBI managers had considerably less experience. Many of them served the minimum requirement of three years of field experience, then sought a promotion to FBI headquarters. After four or five years at FBIHQ, they would transfer to the field to take command of a squad of agents. Many of the agents they would supervise had many more years of experience. The smarter among these supervisors would seek the counsel of the senior agents before making decisions. Others, lacking common sense and eager to exert their newfound authority, sought to micromanage the cases and agents on their squad. Those supervisors were often the ones who sought even higher promotions, becoming ASACs with little or no field experience.

Gibbons was such an ASAC. Tall and brooding, with a perpetual scowl etched on his gaunt face, Gibbons made few close friends in the Bureau. He transferred to Boston after a stint at FBIHQ five years previously, and he quickly tangled with Sullivan. He felt that Sullivan did not confer upon him the proper respect an FBI manager was entitled to. Sullivan felt that respect was earned, not conferred like a title. Now that Gibbons was an ASAC, he always was watching for an opening to teach Sullivan a lesson.

Sullivan seemed to know how to go right up to the line and then not cross it. Gibbons never had enough ammunition to go after him. His performance was unquestioningly superior. His confession rate was higher than most polygraph examiners nationally. In addition, he also managed an informant who supplied valuable information. Gibbons had also been unable to secure an alliance with any respected agent in the office.

The latest confrontation between Gibbons and Sullivan was typical. During a briefing in preparation for a polygraph exam, Ronald Colson, the squad supervisor responsible for the case, asked a question that Sullivan deftly ignored. Several agents in the briefing noticed Sullivan had done so, but they said nothing.

After the meeting, the supervisor approached Sullivan in private. "Sullivan," he asked, "why did you ignore my question?"

"It was a stupid question," he answered calmly.

Colson shook his head and walked away. Several minutes later, Sullivan was summoned into Gibbons's office.

"Sullivan," Gibbons began, "why did you tell SSA Colson that he asked a stupid question?" He waited for an answer.

"Because it was," Sullivan responded.

Gibbons face reddened. "You can't say that…there is no such thing as a stupid question!"

"Mr. Gibbons," Sullivan answered, "that's what we tell children in first grade, so they won't be scared of their teachers. This is the big leagues." Sullivan stood still, his hands behind his back, waiting.

Finally, Gibbons waved his hand dismissively. "Just get out of here."

Sullivan knew that because his comment was made to Colson in private, he was immune to a charge of insubordination.

# TEN

## Doubts

Conrad and Fuller were used to Sullivan's often bizarre theories and schemes, but they were also aware that he was usually right in the end. Yet now, despite the fact he was talking about an area within his field of expertise, they had grave doubts.

"Seriously, Sully?" Fuller looked exasperated.

"Yes, seriously." Sullivan was unwavering.

Conrad looked at Fuller, then to Sullivan. "I don't know, Sully. What you're saying is a little far-fetched."

"I know I'm right."

"You want me to believe that Grant isn't who he says he is because of 'microhesitations.'" Fuller was in full debate mode, using her fingers to air quote the last word.

Conrad stepped in. "Yeah, what the hell is a microhesitation anyway? I took your course, and you only mentioned simple hesitation as one of the cues to deception."

"It's a pioneering new field in the study of deception. As you know, we're all familiar with microexpressions— brief, involuntary facial expressions that reveal a person's emotions. Well, this is similar, only from an auditory perspective. I'm working on a study to analyze the minihesitations surrounding an answer. It's an indicator of deception. Plus, he gave off other clues."

"I don't know," Fuller said. "It sounds a little thin."

"I'm telling you, his story didn't sound true. It sounded scripted...even about simple things." Sullivan was determined to win them over.

"Like what?" Conrad was throwing him a lifeline, as Fuller rolled her eyes.

"I asked him about where he went to school in Arkansas. He was very vague...deceptively vague, as if he wanted me to change the subject. I don't believe he studied at that University of Arkansas." Sullivan stood his ground.

"But Sully, the Bureau has vetted him!" Fuller had her hands together, as if she were pleading with him.

"Maybe they missed something."

Conrad started leaning in Sullivan's direction. "It couldn't hurt to look into it."

"Conrad, you're buying this?" Fuller said.

"He's been right before, Kathy. That's all I know."

Fuller thought for a second. Then she said, "So even if you are right, we can't send this up the chain without more meat. What do you propose?"

Sullivan looked pensive for a moment. "Let's just make some discreet inquiries for now. We should start by getting a copy of his background file."

"I once dated a girl who works at HQ in the records section. I can probably get a copy of it on the QT," Conrad offered.

"May I remind you, gentlemen," Fuller remarked, "that initiating an unauthorized investigation is a violation of the offense code. Would you like me to get the disciplinary offense manual?"

"Not an investigation, Kathy, an inquiry...a simple inquiry."

"Very clever, Sully, but not much of a difference," Fuller responded.

"I'm in. I don't like the kid anyway." Conrad looked at Fuller.

Sullivan wanted her to be on board. He looked at her with a slight smile. "Are you in?"

She closed her eyes and nodded silently. Then, before leaving, she pointed at Sullivan. "Reluctantly, Sully, reluctantly." She had her doubts, but she was part of the team.

———

Their decision to proceed cautiously was wise. Peter had quickly established a friendship with ASAC Gibbons. The friendship appeared to be one-sided to those who observed it, because Peter had essentially become Gibbons's lackey and informant. However, Peter knew that at some point the relationship would be to his advantage. He realized quickly that he was unable to establish any meaningful alliances with his coworkers. He decided to seek Gibbons's mentorship and protection, in exchange for keeping Gibbons informed about the goings-on in the office. It was a symbiotic relationship, as far as Peter was concerned.

One day, Gibbons summoned Peter into his office. The secretary, Millie Spencer, had become used to Agent Grant's visits to the sixth-floor office. Spencer had been an FBI secretary for twenty years. Typically, when an agent was called into the ASAC's office, it was to receive bad news. She noted that this was not the case with Grant. She had made a mental note of each visit.

As he usually did, Peter sat in one of the leather couches in the spacious office without asking permission. From behind his desk, Gibbons looked up from some papers he had been reading.

"Grant," he started, "what do you know of Agent Sullivan?"

"Not much," he answered, "but he seems to be well respected."

"By some, perhaps," Gibbons replied derisively. "I'm not so impressed." He gave Peter a serious look. "If you hear anything about him, let me know." Gibbons turned back to the papers he was perusing.

Peter stood after a moment and looked directly at Gibbons. "Absolutely, sir, I will let you know immediately."

He turned and walked out without Gibbons even lifting his eyes up again. Peter considered how this could present a future opportunity.

———

Little Rock Police Detective Jim Pruit stood over the lifeless body of Tina Jones and was perplexed. Not with the manner of death—this was quickly observed to be from strangulation. Instead, he was concerned that Little Rock had just suffered its third murder of a seemingly law-abiding citizen in as many days. Three murders in a drug-infested housing project might not attract much media attention. But now, Jones' murder occurred only two days after the death of Cynthia King, who was murdered in her home. Of course, all of their minds were also on the murder of Detective Robert Johnson, whose murder three days before was still unsolved. There were still no leads in that murder, and the case was frustratingly cold. With this latest killing, the media might start speculating about a possible serial murderer in their midst.

Tina Jones's murder in her apartment bore no semblance to the other homicides, which involved a gun in one case and a garrote in the other. Aside from the fact that King and Jones were killed in their homes, there were no other similarities or apparent links between the victims.

Given the facts available, Pruit could not be expected to make a connection, at least not without a thorough review of Jones' life; she had dated Kyle Grant until she ended their relationship about a year ago. Despite his extensive search of Jones' apartment, he had no reason to open the sealed envelope from Grant which was in a stack of mail in her kitchen. Tina had never even opened the letter. She would never know the true impact her breakup had on Kyle. More important, Tina would never know how that connection would lead to her demise.

---

On a beautiful Saturday in July, the Charles River was teeming with activity. Sailboats were out in force, as were some crew teams. The sun shone in Sullivan's eyes as he stood on the Boston side of the river, watching a team of rowers aggressively pull their boat down the river. In a four-man sweep boat, two oarsmen row to the port side, while the other two row starboard, in an alternating order. He watched as the four women sat in a single row, pulling their oars feverishly. They rowed without a coxswain, but they really didn't need one. They were former members of the Boston University crew team and had plenty of experience rowing together. They made it a tradition to row together at least once a year.

Sullivan noticed that Lena was sitting closest to the stern as they approached the River City boathouse, their final destination. Suddenly, he heard a loud snapping sound. He couldn't immediately see what had happened, but he noticed that they had stopped rowing. Then he saw that the stress on one of the fiberglass oars had caused it to snap in half.

As they reached the shore, Sullivan was waiting.

"I didn't know those things could break like that," he said, partly in the form of a question.

"They can if they have a structural defect," Lena answered as she got out of the boat, drenched in sweat. Even after so many years in the United States, Lena still had a detectable accent from her native Russia. Sullivan found it adorable. At his request, she had started teaching him the Russian language and Russian customs.

He waited as they placed the craft in the boathouse. He noticed they placed the two pieces of the broken oar inside the boathouse, next to the undamaged ones. She came out smiling.

"Hey!" she said, grinning. "How about a big hug?"

"Ha-ha, very funny," he replied. "Maybe after you shower!"

"What?" she joked. "Don't you love me?"

"Yes," he answered, "I love you clean."

They continued to joke with each other as they walked toward her Beacon Hill apartment.

———

Other than Bunker Hill in Charlestown, the Beacon Hill neighborhood is the highest point in the city of Boston. It is a quiet residential area, and brownstone apartments house some of the wealthiest citizens of the city. The one-way streets are all narrow, and parking is strictly restricted to residents only. Some of the picturesque alleyways are still cobblestoned. At the top of Beacon Hill sits the gold-domed

Massachusetts State House. At 21 Beacon Street, next to the State House, is the eleven-story Belvedere residential building. The building has a roof deck, with a stunning view of the State House, as well as much of the financial district. It was a coveted spot during the Fourth of July fireworks celebrations.

After graduating from Suffolk Law with her JD, Lena Hall had started her own legal practice. Her focus was real estate law, and she also handled wills and estates. She obtained a real estate license, but she only handled a handful of properties at a time. That was a side gig. Over time, she developed an impressive clientele, and one of them recommended the Belvedere to her. When she saw an opportunity, she bought a one-bedroom condo there on the eighth floor. It was her pride and joy, living in the heart of Boston. She lived there with her small beagle, Toby, until she met Sullivan.

At first, he only stayed one night a week. By the second month of their relationship, he was staying two nights a week. At their current relationship stage, he was spending most weeknights with her, and he had a spare set of keys. His mother, Katarina Robles, checked in on his upstairs apartment in Medford from time to time, but she usually only saw him on weekends. The Belvedere had one additional benefit that was very important to Sullivan—it was two blocks from the FBI office.

The Belvedere had a doorman, and as they approached the door, they could see that Joe was at his post. Lena swiped her key pass to open the door, and they casually walked up to Joe.

"Hello, Lena and Sully!" Joe said in a welcoming manner. "It is a beautiful day, isn't it?" He sat behind a wooden desk. A copy of the latest *Boston Globe* lay next to his computer.

They chatted with Joe for a minute or so before going upstairs. They both felt it was important to maintain good relations with the building staff.

Although Sullivan was physically attracted to Lena, his link with her was more intense emotionally. She had left Russia as an adolescent, becoming a naturalized US citizen. He felt this was something she had in common with his own mother. He felt that he had finally met his match with her. She was the one person in his personal life whom he could not out duel mentally. She was also one of the few people who could make him genuinely laugh. Her wit was legendary in her circle, so much so that within a month of meeting her, he had introduced her to Conrad and Fuller. They were the only two people he allowed into his zone of privacy.

Sullivan very rarely spoke about his business with Lena. On this day, however, he sat down with her and talked about his doubts. He wanted her opinion.

———

"All right, so you think this Kyle is impersonating somebody because he 'microhesitated'?" Lena had listened to his story in its entirety, without interruption, at times playing with her long black hair. They sat in her small living room. The TV was playing a Red Sox game, but the sound was muted. Toby rested quietly on Sullivan's lap, his eyes closed.

"Why is everyone so hung up on microhesitation? I just gave you five other reasons why he's lying." Sullivan was frustrated. Still, he loved her Russian accent when she said "microhesitation." It was endearing.

"It's just that I've never heard of that before." Lena shifted on the couch.

"It's the auditory version of microexpressions, which are used to evaluate a person's feelings or moods. The theory is that when a person answers a question, the response time will lag by small fractions of seconds when there is deception."

He seemed to be entering a lecture mode as he continued. "Obviously, many factors have to be considered, for instance, the nature of the question, its complexity, the intelligence of the person, and so on. So a baseline must be obtained for each person under evaluation. There's a technique to it. And I did that. He was deceptive, Lena, I'm certain of it." Sullivan was adamant.

"So let me guess," Lena answered. "This pioneering technique you've described, are you the pioneer?" She smiled as she finished the sentence.

When he didn't answer, Lena smiled again.

"I see," she said. "Well, then, it must be true...he is an imposter!"

"This is serious, Lena." He touched her shoulder. She could tell it was bothering him. He rarely talked about his work with her.

"OK, I see that. Well, Carlos," Lena said, "I guess it's plausible. It begs a question, though, right?" Other than his mother, Lena was the only one to call him Carlos.

Sullivan looked at her inquisitively. She could tell he wanted her to continue. "I mean, if he is an imposter, there has to be a reason, right? I mean, what would be the point?"

"Right," Sullivan said, pondering her point.

Before he could say more, she asked another question. "Carlos, doesn't every FBI employee have to take a polygraph exam? If you're right, then he would have had to pass that test, correct?"

The question troubled him. He thought for a few moments and reached down to pet Toby's head. "Yeah, I guess so...I guess so." His voice trailed off quietly. Sullivan made a mental note to follow up on that angle.

Lena stood up to get a drink from her minikitchen. As she was fishing through the refrigerator, she voiced one more thought. "You should follow your own advice."

He gave her a puzzled look. "Oh, yeah...what's that?"

"You know that line from *The Godfather* you're always quoting?"

Sullivan chuckled. "You mean I should make him an offer he can't refuse?"

"No silly," she countered, "the other one." She paused for effect and then said with her best faux-Italian accent, "You keep your friends close, but your enemies closer."

Sullivan pondered her comment as he got up from the sofa. He chuckled to himself—a Russian girl faking an Italian accent. He stood over her work desk, taking note of the way in which she laid out her things. He noticed four three-by-five cards, each one with a different Beacon Hill address. Lying on each card was a set of keys. It was Lena's way of keeping track of the properties she was handling; she had a tendency to misplace her keys.

Sullivan asked, "Lena, you're down to just four properties?"

"Yeah, honey, I sold one last week, finally."

They sat back down and made plans for lunch.

———

John O'Neil couldn't sleep. He lay awake at night, staring at the ceiling. His wife awoke one night and noticed him brooding.

"Honey, you can't sleep? It's this case, isn't it?" She laid a hand on his chest.

"Carol, it's just bothering me. I need to resolve this case."

"What are you going to do?"

"I'm going to see Agent Roberts tomorrow. I have to shake things up." O'Neil looked over to her. "Go back to sleep, Carol." He patted her hand gently. He stared at the ceiling for another three hours.

———

Agent Roberts listened to O'Neil patiently. At one point, he caught himself wanting to look at his watch but refrained. He knew how emotional this was to the Secret Service. When O'Neil finally finished, Roberts spoke.

"I get that you have doubts about Samantha Wallace...I understand that our telephone analysis indicated she was his last contact, but as you know, she has an airtight alibi."

"I know that, but we have nothing else, right? Have you come up with anything else?" O'Neil was exasperated.

"I'm afraid not," Roberts conceded.

O'Neil covered his face with his hands. He was surprised that he was displaying emotion in front of another agent.

"I'm sorry, John," Roberts said sincerely. "We will continue to interview people who knew him. It's our only avenue right now. The forensic analysis gave us nothing."

O'Neil stood up to leave. "I understand."

He shook Robert's hand and walked out of the office. Outside, he resolved to do what he could independently.

# ELEVEN

## Michael

To those around him, Michael Wallace was the quintessential American hero. At the age of eighteen, he enrolled in the Army ROTC program at George Mason University in Fairfax, Virginia. The ROTC program is designed to produce students, known as cadets, with the necessary skills to become US Army officers. During his four years in the program, Michael was among the best cadets ever to walk through the doors of the institution. He was a natural leader and soon gained a reputation among the other cadets as someone to emulate. As part of the program, he and the other cadets planned and executed numerous training exercises. Michael had already been familiar with such exercises, which were routine at the Fortress. He had internalized the army ROTC warrior ethos, which was placed on a wall near the ROTC office.

*I will always place the mission first.*
*I will never accept defeat.*
*I will never quit.*
*I will never leave a fallen comrade.*

Upon graduating with a degree in public policy, Michael was commissioned as a second lieutenant in the US Army. He served one tour of duty in Iraq and one in Afghanistan. By his seventh year in the army, he had reached the rank of captain.

It was in Iraq, his first deployment to a theatre of operation, that he met Colonel Gus Armstrong. The colonel was legendary in the army, not so much for having studied at Harvard, but for his tough demeanor and salty language. He always wore his helmet without a chin strap and was usually chomping on a cigar.

His first encounter with the colonel would be a turning point in his career.

"You are a real quiet son of a bitch, aren't you?" The colonel said to him after Michael returned to the base one day with his men. They had been providing security for a convoy dispatching food for troops in a forward operating base. Three days previously, Michael lost three men in his unit to an improvised explosive device (IED). He was not in a festive mood.

The colonel had been watching Michael over the previous weeks, taking mental notes. Michael had developed a reputation among his peers as a deliberative thinker, never saying anything impulsively. He said nothing in response to the colonel's remark. Several other officers sat around the room, observing the exchange.

Armstrong continued, "Well, if you aren't saying anything, I guess you're thinking. What the fuck are you thinking about, Wallace?"

Michael looked at the colonel in a serious manner and responded dryly, "I'm thinking we might still lose this fucking war…sir."

Never before had the troops witnessed the colonel laugh so loudly. He practically spat out his cigar. From that moment on, Colonel Armstrong decided to take a personal interest in Michael's career.

---

In the army's culture, an officer who stayed single for too long would draw suspicious looks. Certainly, an officer approaching the age of thirty would be expected to marry. Given that he was the oldest child, his mission would naturally be the longest. Therefore, he had asked his parents for permission to wed.

The Wallaces had been wary of the concept of their children having partners. They felt it could diminish their enthusiasm for their respective missions and possibly compromise their very carefully laid plans. However, given Michael's situation, and the fact that he was very deliberative and committed to their common goal, they felt that a marriage might actually allow him to better inoculate himself against any suspicion. Their concerns were also allayed when he assured them he was not in love with Kathy. He merely wanted to solidify his cover.

He had met Kathy Simmons at George Mason University, and they married shortly after he was commissioned in the army. She had studied economics, and after obtaining a master's degree, obtained a job at the lobbying firm of Madison & Booth.

The wedding was a small affair, and the Wallaces flew out from Arkansas for the ceremony. His youngest sister, Alexandra, was in attendance, as were several of his former cadet friends from the ROTC program. Kathy's long white gown was a family heirloom, passed down to her by her grandmother.

As both clans posed for their obligatory photographs, the bride's family could never have suspected they had just wed their daughter to a family of terrorists.

---

By floor area, the Pentagon is the largest office building in the world, encompassing 6.5 million square feet. It is so enormous that the US Postal Service has assigned it six separate zip codes. It has five floors above ground and two below. Its significance is not merely symbolic, like the Washington Monument or the Jefferson Memorial. It is the actual headquarters of the US Department of Defense—the nerve center of the US military.

Given the Pentagon's significance to US national defense, it has been targeted by America's enemies on several occasions. Most notably, the 9/11 terrorists flew American Airlines flight 77 into the side of the building, killing 189 people. Few are aware that the 9/11 attacks occurred on the sixtieth anniversary of the Pentagon's groundbreaking ceremony in 1941.

On May 19, 1972, left-wing terrorists planted a bomb in a women's fourth-floor bathroom. The explosion caused some damage, but nobody was injured. The terrorist communiqué that followed stated that the bomb was placed in protest of the Vietnam War. The subsequent investigation never revealed that Tim Wallace had driven the woman who planted the explosive device to and from the Pentagon that day. That woman, Susan, would later become his wife.

After his service in Iraq, Colonel Armstrong had been reassigned to the Pentagon, serving as the senior aide to the chairman of the Joint Chiefs of Staff (JCS). JCS Chairman John Conboy had known Armstrong for twenty years and had always respected his counsel. As chairman of the JCS, he was the senior-ranking member of the armed forces. His job was essentially that of principal military advisor to the secretary of defense and the president. All the branches of the military have a representative in the JCS, which is headquartered at the Pentagon. When the opportunity presented itself, Conboy brought Armstrong into his circle. Colonel Armstrong, in turn, recruited Michael into a position at the JCS. Michael's job was to manage a small cadre of analysts who were assigned to research new trends in military technology. After ten years in the military, Michael was in a position to receive another promotion soon. He had the proper pedigree and a powerful mentor. He had full access to the Pentagon and was allowed to sit in on JCS meetings.

All of the family's chess pieces were moving into place.

# TWELVE

## Chess

fter two months on the job, Samantha was growing anxious. Her assignment to a Secret Service group investigating credit card fraud was not what the family needed. Her instructions were quite specific. She had to find a way to an assignment at the White House, either on the presidential, vice presidential, or first lady security detail. Yet she knew it was unheard of in the Secret Service for a new agent to receive such a posting. She analyzed the organization, as she always did, to ascertain its weaknesses. Her experience with Agent Livingstone had reasserted her conviction that, given the right circumstances, any person could be compromised or manipulated.

One day, she saw a flyer on the squad bulletin board announcing a retirement party for Special Agent Rick Gonzalez after twenty-five years of service. She also heard that Gonzalez had been well respected in the Washington office, and several high level management officials would be in attendance. She resolved to attend the retirement party and began the process of selecting the nicest dress for the occasion.

Sullivan had decided to take his own advice, as Lena had so humorously suggested. He invited Kyle to another meeting with his source. Peter had accepted immediately, in the hope that he could ameliorate any doubts Sullivan had about him. He had started to suspect that Sullivan was scrutinizing him beyond what was normal. As they started north to the city of Lawrence again, Sullivan started asking open-ended questions.

"So Kyle, what made you decide to become an FBI agent?"

Peter did not hesitate. "My dad was a cop. He died when I was ten years old."

Sullivan looked over as he drove. "I'm sorry to hear that."

"It's OK."

"Where was he a cop?"

"Little Rock Police Department," he answered flatly.

"What did you study?"

"I studied business, but I don't talk about it, it was pretty boring—as was the school." Peter did not like where this line of questioning was going.

"What about you?" Peter quickly turned the tables on Sullivan. "How did you get interested in the Bureau?"

Not wishing to arouse suspicion on Kyle's part, Sullivan allowed the topic to turn to his own background. They met Isabel in the same location as before, and the meeting was routine. Among the topics discussed were a couple of drug fugitives wanted by the New York FBI office. Sullivan gave Isabel a copy of two photos of the fugitives and asked her to keep a lookout for them, as they were rumored to be in the area.

As they drove back to the office, Sullivan noticed that Kyle had grown silent, almost brooding. Sullivan had received a copy of Kyle's background report that morning from Conrad, and he had yet to review it. He was now more than ever determined to make it a priority. As Sullivan considered his next move, Peter was also scheming. If he felt that Sullivan was becoming a threat, he would pull the trigger on a plan he devised to place him in checkmate.

———

In the absence of any other leads, John O'Neil decided to review Samantha Wallace's application for employment. The SF-86 is the basic application form that every applicant for federal employment must submit. It covers all aspects of a person's life, from prior residences to employments, education, travel, and personal references. It even requires a list of all close relatives. O'Neil scrutinized the form five times, from cover to cover, until his eyes were tiring. As he reviewed the section documenting her close relatives, he noticed that she had two brothers living in the Washington area. Perhaps, he thought, a protective brother stepped in to stop Livingstone's advances? He decided to pursue his only slender lead.

The eldest brother, Michael Wallace, lived in a modest house in Arlington, Virginia. Aside from his date of birth and address, the application requires no further information. There is a small box to check if the person is deceased, and he was not. O'Neil conducted a quick criminal check on the name, and he learned that Michael Wallace had no criminal record. He did not know what to expect as he rang the doorbell at the Wallace residence.

Wearing casual blue jeans and a white George Mason University jersey, Kathy Wallace answered the door. "May I help you?"

"Yes, ma'am, I'm Special Agent John O'Neil of the US Secret Service. Is Michael Wallace here?" He held his credentials open for her to review.

"Yes, but what is this about?"

"If I could speak to him, ma'am." He smiled pleasantly back at her.

"Come inside." She ushered him into their living room.

Kathy went to find Michael, who was upstairs. As he waited, O'Neil was unsettled. He was aware that he was going outside the investigative chain of command. He had not even consulted the FBI agents who had been tasked with the case. He knew Special Agent Roberts would not be happy with him at that moment. He decided to tread carefully.

Michael entered the room, and O'Neil introduced himself. Michael also wore jeans and sneakers. As they sat down on the couch, Michael asked Kathy to wait upstairs. Although she appeared to walk up the carpeted stairs, she stopped halfway and crouched down to listen.

"What is this about?" began Michael.

"I'm investigating a homicide of one of our agents—Special Agent John Livingstone."

Michael cut him off. "What does that have to do with me?"

"I'm sure it doesn't, but your sister Samantha was one of the last people to speak to him. I just need to rule her out as a suspect." O'Neil attempted to sound as reassuring as possible.

"Well, she's one of your own people. Don't you trust your own people?" Michael asked cuttingly.

"Have you talked to her about this incident?" O'Neil plowed ahead.

"I know nothing about it. This is the first I've heard of it...quite frankly, she and I don't speak very often." Michael was getting aggravated, and he was concerned that Kathy might be listening. He tried to keep his cool.

"May I ask, Mr. Wallace, where you were two months ago, on the evening of June 26? It was a Monday night." O'Neil waited for an answer.

"I'm afraid I don't remember that far back. I couldn't tell you. But I don't like your implication. I don't know any Agent Livingstone, and I have nothing more to say." Michael gave O'Neil a harsh look.

It was evident the interview was over. Michael rose and escorted O'Neil to the door. The interview went so poorly, O'Neil didn't even bother to leave his business card.

Later that evening, Michael lay in bed, reading a military journal. Kathy prepared to change for bed, and she looked at how detached he appeared from what had happened only a few hours ago. She had always wondered why his sister Samantha and brother Ryan hadn't bothered to attend their wedding. Further, she recalled that he went out the evening of June 26, with his sister Alexa, who had picked him up. She knew the date, because it was only two days before their anniversary. She couldn't resist asking about what had transpired.

"Michael," she started, "why didn't you tell me your sister Samantha was a Secret Service agent?"

He lifted his head abruptly and gave her an icy stare. "That doesn't concern you; it's my family's business." He turned back to his journal.

His answer left a cold chill in her spine.

The next morning, O'Neil was not entirely surprised when he was summoned into his SAC's office. He had practically expected a call, but he was not completely prepared for what awaited him. O'Neil had no way to know that the Pentagon had called his SAC's office to express their grave concern over O'Neil's unannounced visit to Captain Wallace. They were prepared to fully vouch for their battle-tested officer.

As he entered, he could see that Samantha was seated at one side of the large office. On the other side, seated on a couch, were FBI Agents Roberts and Hernandez. Roberts, in particular, appeared to be seething. Samantha did not seem amused either. He sat in a single seat laid out for him in the middle, facing the SAC, who sat behind his large desk.

They all stared at him for what appeared to be minutes. Finally, O'Neil attempted to defuse the situation.

"I know why I'm here, and I'm sorry. I know I should have cut the Bureau in on my interview," he started, glancing over at Roberts. His attempt at defusing their anger was not effective.

"Sorry?" Roberts said in a loud voice. "That's the best you can do… sorry? After we have cut you in on every aspect of our case? This is an interview that didn't even need to happen."

SAC White raised his hand, as if to stop the rancor. "I'm sure Agent O'Neil realizes his mistake, which will not be repeated." He glared at O'Neil like a scolding father.

"I have something to say." Samantha found her opening. She didn't wait for their consent to continue. "I am tired of this abuse, first from Agent Livingstone, who harassed me nonstop, and now this witchhunt of me and my family. Perhaps, Agent O'Neil"—she paused for effect—"you were not aware that my brother is decorated. He is a captain in the US Army, and his background is above reproach." She stopped, staring directly at O'Neil's eyes.

O'Neil was beaten. "I didn't know. I'm sorry." He bowed his head. He wanted the moment to end, but it did not.

"Furthermore," she stated, directing her comment to SAC White, "I certainly hope that this incident does not affect my prospects for advancement or placement in a position of my choosing in the future…" Her words hung in the air.

After a few more comments of assurance from the SAC to the FBI Agents, O'Neil was dismissed from the room.

———

Conrad had an on-again, off-again relationship with Trish O'Keefe. Her hair was curly and very red. Her skin was pale, her face covered in freckles. Conrad found her intriguing. She was one of the intelligence analysts assigned to his drug squad—in his mind, the best. She had previous experience as an analyst working at a special Pentagon unit, but she never discussed her work there.

O'Keefe was far more taken with Conrad than he was with her, causing her to occasionally break it off with him in spite. Eventually, he would call again, asking for them to get together, and she always relented. She held out hope that their relationship could blossom into a long-term affair, which in her mind meant marriage. It was his fear of that concept that led him to distance himself from her from time to time.

Conrad relied on her routinely in building his cases. Her reports were always on point and furnished him with new avenues of investigation. In particular, her analysis of telephone records was legendary. From reviewing a subject's telephone toll records, she could tell Conrad who was the subject's supplier, client, parent, girlfriend, and wife, in that order, simply by looking at the call pattern. The call pattern evaluated the frequency, time, and duration of the calls, as well as whether they were mostly incoming or outgoing. To obtain such an analysis, Conrad merely needed to write a brief request with the subject's telephone number. She then served the respective service provider with an administrative subpoena, forcing them to furnish the relevant data. Trish usually received the raw toll data first, followed a few days later by the subscriber information, if it was available. Many drug dealers used prepaid cell phones with no subscriber data.

Three days after receiving a request from Conrad for a check of four separate telephone numbers, she received a fax with the requested subscriber data. As she scanned the names and addresses, she was stunned. Conrad had submitted a request for a check on Kyle Grant's telephone.

She immediately dialed his extension.

As Conrad sat at his desk, he looked at his phone's caller ID and noticed it was from Trish's desk. It was ringing loudly, almost ominously. He sensed that it meant trouble. Rather than fight with her over the phone, he got up and walked straight to her cubicle.

As he approached her, he could see she was upset. "Conrad, are you crazy?" He held her by the arm and put his finger to his lips, signaling her to be silent. He escorted her to a nearby conference room.

After he closed the door, she said, "What the hell is going on?"

"I can explain," he said.

"You had better! Do you want to get me fired? What is this about?"

"I didn't tell you so that you could establish deniability. If you are approached about it, you can honestly say you knew nothing."

She was listening carefully.

"Sully is convinced that Kyle is up to no good. He may not be who he says he is," Conrad continued as she listened ever more intently.

"It's just a discreet check on his records. Please do this for me. If you get discovered, just blame me."

Trish had never seen him ask her for anything so desperately. She thought about it for a moment, mulling over the consequences in her head.

"OK," she said finally, "with two conditions."

"Yes, anything."

"First, don't ever keep me in the dark again. I want to go in with both eyes open." She looked up at him, her eyes wide and intense.

"And? What's second?"

"Keep me posted if you learn anything good. I want in on this."

Conrad smiled and kissed her gently on the lips. He was turning to leave when she remembered something. "Hey, one more thing," she said.

"Yes?"

"Be careful of Becky Gennaro on CT-2, Kyle's squad. After seven months in the nursery, Kyle has recently transferred to one of the counterterrorism squads, with ASAC Gibbons's blessing.

"Why?"

"She is his analyst, and I heard through the grapevine that she has the hots for Grant. She might be doing some checks for him, if you know what I mean."

He thought about that prospect for a moment and smiled. If Sully was right, this could become a true battle of wits.

———

Whenever Sullivan initiated a new project, he always sat down with paper and pen. He started with three columns. In one column, he listed the things he needed to do in the short term. In the second, he listed longer-term goals. In the third column, he had a shorter list of pitfalls to avoid. He was meticulous in his analysis.

After reading Grant's personnel file and assessing what information he had gathered from Kyle directly, he decided there were some things that could be checked rather easily. Among those items in the first column were double-checking Grant's educational records and talking to the Little Rock Police Department about Grant's father.

Sullivan called the University of Arkansas and managed to track down one of Kyle's former professors. He left a voice mail for him, indicating he was simply conducting a reference check on his former student. Sullivan felt the chance of this inquiry being revealed was nil. He had also already left a message for Agent Hanford, the polygraph examiner in the Little Rock FBI office. Sullivan was awaiting a return call from him as well.

In his third column, the most pressing item he listed was keeping ASAC Gibbons from learning about his inquiry.

Sullivan circled several items of interest on Kyle's SF-86 and placed it in his top drawer with his notes. He was tired, and he felt it could wait until tomorrow.

———

At least one hundred Secret Service agents were in attendance for Rick Gonzalez's retirement party. The venue was a country club in McLean, Virginia, just outside Washington. There were approximately fifteen large tables scattered about the dining room, with ten people assigned per table. The selected meal was either stuffed chicken or salmon. Samantha chose the latter. She looked about the room, attempting to determine where to focus her attention.

Samantha wore a silky black dress, cut just above the knee, with matching black pumps. She was lean and tan, and her long straight hair fell alluringly by her exposed shoulders. She could see that several higher-ups were in attendance. They could be seen congregating near the bar after the meal. By the time they ordered a second round, she noticed them sneaking occasional glances at her and decided she need not take a direct approach. Instead, she stood against a wall near the bar, glancing at her phone, and waited.

Within five minutes, one of the supervisors approached her and started a conversation.

"Hi there," he began. Samantha knew he was only a supervisor—too low on the food chain. She was not interested and quickly excused herself to the bathroom. When she returned, he was gone. She resumed her position against the wall.

After a couple of minutes, another older man approached her. He seemed to have a commanding presence. She had noticed that most of the others in his group appeared deferential to him.

"I'm Deputy Assistant Director Jonathan Hughes. How are you?" He was direct with her. He was fishing, and she was biting.

"I'm doing well," she replied. "My name is—"

Hughes cut her off. "I know who you are."

"That's a neat trick," she answered him.

"You don't get to my position without knowing who's who," he said confidently. He was almost six three, and Samantha could feel him looking her up and down.

"Well then, I guess I'm in good hands," she said flirtatiously.

"I heard about your situation, and it's not right. You have an impeccable record, and your brother does too, from what I hear." He sipped his drink, looking at her eyes, seeking her attention.

"Aren't you worried I might be a stone-cold killer?" she asked playfully.

"Not in the least."

"I'm glad to hear that. I'm not sure I will ever shake off the stigma among my peers."

"You will do just fine, I'm sure."

Samantha became more suggestive. "Perhaps if I had someone to take care of me, to make sure I get treated fairly."

Hughes gave her a big smile. "Well, I can certainly take care of you." He gulped what was left of his drink.

Now their roles were reversed. Samantha was the one fishing, and he had swallowed the entire hook. She knew not to try to reel the entire fish into the boat immediately. She decided to string him along; otherwise, he might use and then discard her. She would commit to him, but only once he agreed to do something for her.

"Call me," she said after they talked some more. "I want to see you again."

She gave him her number and walked out of the room. She knew Father would be pleased.

Unbeknownst to her, Agent O'Neil had been spying on her from his nearby table. He was surrounded by other agents and support personnel, and she never noticed him watching her every move. Her father would not have been so pleased at her lapse in vigilance.

———

In one hand, Peter held the latest letter from Father, which was addressed to him and all his siblings. He knew immediately what the missive meant—their mission was moving into an operational phase. It was short and direct, as was Father's custom.

It read as follows: *"Children, we now move from phase green to phase orange. To coordinate our plans, we will meet at Michael's residence on September 19. Love and courage, Father."*

It was impactful to him, as he had not yet reached the goal set for him within the FBI. He had less than two weeks before the meeting and didn't want to be the only missing piece in the family's chessboard.

In his other hand, Peter held a cell phone, the one that used to belong to Kyle Grant. The voice mail he just heard was chilling in its implication for his now precarious situation. He listened to the voice mail again.

"Kyle, this is Professor Albertson. I'm glad to see that you appear to be doing well. I got a call from an FBI Agent Sullivan in Boston. He was seeking to confirm a reference for you, I believe. I left him a voice mail but haven't heard back. I just wanted to congratulate you; I know your father would be proud. Call me when you can."

Peter knew he now had no choice. As he had begun to surmise, Sullivan had started to suspect him. He had to implement a plan he had designed for just this contingency. If the plan worked, as he confidently knew it would, the threat from Sullivan would be neutralized, and he would attain the position he was seeking in the Bureau. He sat back, marveling at his tactical brilliance.

# PART II

# ONE

## Terror

On October 23, 2002, led by separatist Chechen leader Mousar Barayev, approximately forty Chechen terrorists seized a theatre in the heart of Moscow, Russia. The 850 innocent and terrified hostages were trapped in the theatre by machine-gun-toting fanatics. During the first two days of the siege, there appeared to be no end in sight. Russian Special Forces soldiers, known as the *Spetznaz*, had surrounded the theatre and were in a stalemate with the terrorists.

The terrorists had suicide vests visibly strapped to their bodies, to thwart any idea of an assault on their position and to further terrorize their victims. The Chechen terrorist group was comprised of both males and females. Their demands were not acceptable to the Russian government, and the terrorists themselves were unyielding.

On the third day, the Spetznaz came upon an innovative plan. In order to incapacitate the terrorists, they pumped a mysterious gas into the theatre's ventilation system. The gas appeared to be odorless, but the terrorists quickly noticed they were being affected and could see their cohorts passing out around them. Those not immediately knocked out by the gas starting firing at the Special Forces soldiers, who began storming the theatre in a coordinated attack. Some of the terrorists also had gas masks. In short order, the Spetznaz killed all of the terrorists.

The operation, however, could not be called a success. The gas used by the assaulting team had also killed 129 of the hostages. Many other hostages, perhaps dozens, were hospitalized from a few days to a few weeks. The Russian government refused to detail all the casualties. The Russians had clearly failed to properly use the right mixture or potency of their secret gas. The dead appeared to have suffered greatly, their faces contorted in agony. In the controversy that ensued, the Russians classified the operation and declared that the gas used during the assault was an official state secret. This further infuriated the medical establishment in Russia, many of whom were forced to watch their patients die senselessly, since they did not know how to treat them.

As the news reported on this terrorist incident, Tim Wallace became electrified. He was obsessed with obtaining as much information regarding the assault as possible. He called a special meeting of the family to discuss and dissect the Russian operation.

As the children sat before him, he showed them video footage of the operation and later instructed them to read news articles about what had happened. He wanted their input, to evaluate their insight. As he waited to see who would respond first, he was certain it would be Michael. After all, he was almost eighteen years old and therefore the most experienced.

Tim was surprised when his youngest raised her hand.

"Yes, Alexa."

She looked pretty sure of herself for a girl of only thirteen years. "If the repressive government forces can use this gas against a progressive movement like the Chechens, then imagine what the gas can do in the right hands. We can use it against the imperialists."

Her siblings all looked at her in amazement. They knew she was right; they had simply failed to articulate it themselves.

"Yes, very good, Alexa." He beamed. He then went on to lecture them for an hour on how this weapon's potential might be maximized. After his lecture, he realized that no assessment could be made of this latent weapon without knowing the details concerning the gas. He searched through all available public source documents and media reporting without success. In frustration, he traveled to Moscow, with sufficient cash, he hoped, to cajole the truth from someone in a position to know. His cover was that of a freelance reporter.

After two weeks of bribing local officials, he was almost arrested by the FSB, which got wind of a suspicious American asking too many questions. A hotel bellman, for the right tip, alerted Tim to the unwanted FSB attention. He evaded them long enough to find a credible source, a Moscow policeman who had a relationship with one of the Spetznaz troops. The information cost him $1,000.

The drug used was Fentanyl, a narcotic one hundred times more powerful than morphine. Applied intravenously, it is used as an anesthetic. Some drug cartels have been known to mix the drug with heroin. When done so improperly, it results in overdose deaths.

Upon returning to the Fortress, Tim began to experiment with the drug on animals of different sizes. With further research, he learned that another version of the drug, Carfentanil, is ten thousand times more powerful than morphine. It is used in controlled doses to immobilize large animals, such as horses or elephants. His biggest obstacle was finding a reliable source for the drug, which was a controlled substance.

Tim became convinced that with the proper use of Carfentanil, the lethality of such a weapon could be practically limitless. If the proper dosage had been used in the Moscow theatre, he was certain everyone inside would have perished. He was ecstatic at the prospect of deploying this weapon at unsuspecting targets.

# TWO

## Cat and Mouse

The next morning Peter made a beeline into ASAC Gibbons's office. He had called ahead, and the ASAC was expecting him. According to his cryptic call, he could not discuss what he had discovered over an open telephone line. After the door closed behind him, the secretary, Millie Spencer, noticed that over the next several hours, other senior managers were coming into and out of the office. SAC Wainwright himself entered the office and was there for at least one hour. When he came out of Gibbons's office, he looked as if he had seen a ghost. Spencer knew this was highly unusual. In most circumstances, the ASACs would meet in the SAC's office, not the other way around. She deduced that they were keeping Kyle Grant isolated for some reason, perhaps debriefing him.

In addition, Gibbons had asked her to place numerous calls to FBIHQ. As the day progressed, incoming calls from FBIHQ increased in frequency. Spencer knew that something momentous was occurring when the FBI director himself, Robert Stuart, called while the SAC was conferring inside with Gibbons and his growing entourage.

At one point, ASAC Billing, who oversaw the counterintelligence program in Boston, emerged from the office to take a cell phone call in ASAC Gibbons's waiting area. He apparently did not want to disturb the discussion taking place inside. Spencer overheard him ordering an emergency command post (CP) initiated on the seventh floor. As she looked at her phone, she could see that all lights on Gibbons's phone were lit up, most of them blinking, as they were waiting to be picked up.

ASAC Rand was responsible for counterterrorism matters in the Boston office. He emerged from Gibbons' office with a mandate—prepare for the arrival of forty agents and ten analysts from FBIHQ and the Washington field office (WFO). Only Boston supervisors were to know about what was happening, and even then, only when authorized by the SAC. No Boston field agents were to be involved in the preparations. ASAC Rand asked every squad supervisor to turn over two of their Bureau vehicles, no questions asked. He needed twenty FBI cars for the arriving agents.

As these events unfolded that day, Sullivan was in his office, finishing a polygraph report from an exam he had conducted that morning. As he ate the sandwich he brought for lunch, he noticed the message light on his phone was lit. He played the message.

"Yes, Agent Sullivan, this is Professor Albertson, the time is seven thirty p.m., and I'm returning your call." Sullivan had missed the call. He listened further.

"I was one of Kyle's professors, and I also knew his father. I hope you call me back, as I would be willing to serve as a reference if needed. Thank you."

Sullivan pondered whether to call the professor back now or wait until he finished lunch. He opted to finish eating.

Fuller was conducting a lengthy polygraph examination on a prospective FBI contractor. She was unaware of the events in the office that day.

Conrad was at his cubicle, preparing a final affidavit in support of a wiretap application. It was 150 pages long, and he was making last-minute corrections. He knew the slightest error would have the assistant US attorney (AUSA) sending it back with embarrassing red ink on the borders. He wanted to make sure it was perfect. He too was oblivious to the maelstrom occurring in his office that day.

As he worked on his project, Trish O'Keefe appeared suddenly before Conrad. She was out of breath and frightened. "I gotta talk to you!"

"What?" he said, not understanding her urgency.

She directed him to the same conference room where they had previously met. He had never seen her so animated.

"I just got off the telephone with a friend at HQ. They...the Bureau"—she was stammering—"they sent a chartered plane with dozens of agents and analysts."

"Are they coming here? Why?" Conrad was confused.

She grabbed him by the shoulders and shook him. "They're coming for Sully!"

"Are they in Boston yet?" His mind was racing.

"Yes! My friend is dating one of the agents. He called her when they landed. They're cabbing it over here right now!"

Conrad processed the information as quickly as possible, given the circumstances and lack of details. He knew that through the Sumner Tunnel, Logan International Airport was only a seven-minute drive to the office.

He ran toward Sullivan's office.

———

In Washington, FBI Director Robert Stuart was more than concerned; he was very close to being in a state of panic. During his tenure, he had never had an FBI agent accused of espionage, and now he faced the prospect of having to brief the attorney general and the president on this new frightening prospect—that the FBI had a mole in its midst again. In August 2001, the FBI arrested Supervisory Special Agent (SSA) Robert Hanssen on charges of espionage. It was the most damaging incident in the Bureau's history. SSA Hanssen had been spying on the FBI for the Russian government for over twenty years. The damage he caused was incalculable. The investigation that led to Hanssen's arrest was a multiyear, painstaking investigation. Now, in this case, the Boston office had decided to round up Agent Sullivan and his conspirators within twenty-four hours. Stuart needed this explained to him, and he expected answers. He waited for another call from Boston SAC Wainwright, flanked by his deputy director and their aides.

The phone on his desk rang, and he picked it up. "Tell me, Wainwright, what is your evidence?" Stuart had a matter-of-fact tone.

"An agent has come forward with a serious allegation that Agent Sullivan may be working with a Cuban agent and furnishing classified information. By way of background, Mr. Director, Agent Sullivan is of Cuban descent; his mother is Cuban and resides outside the city of Boston. Agent Sullivan has operated a female informant for several years, code name Isabel. Sullivan's conversations with Isabel appear to all be conducted in Spanish. She may not be Puerto Rican, as Sullivan has claimed, but in fact Cuban. The agent observed that Sullivan was clearly in a romantic relationship with the informant. She dressed provocatively during her meetings with Sullivan, and this agent observed them touching inappropriately. He also observed that he passed her classified information. At first, the reporting agent didn't recognize the material as classified, because the markings had been removed. He later recognized the secret documents from reporting he had seen in his squad area and realized that Sullivan must have removed the classification markings."

Wainwright paused, anticipated the director's next question. He headed it off. "Normally, of course, we would initiate a logical, methodical investigation in a discreet manner. However, unknown to Agent Sullivan, this reporting agent has a working knowledge of Spanish. He clearly heard them making plans to meet in Cuba at the earliest opportunity. Mr. Director, we can't allow him to defect. It would be a crippling blow to national security and an embarrassment to the Bureau." He waited for the director's answer.

"I sent the resources you requested, based on what I heard initially, but this doesn't sound like an iron-clad case. I hear some 'maybes' in what you are saying." Director Stuart was cautious, even hopeful, that this was all a misunderstanding.

"Agreed," Wainwright stated. "However, all we are seeking to do now is hold Sullivan, in the event he was planning to flee. We can detain him on a material witness warrant until we gather more information. To that end, we are going to execute a search warrant at his home, as well as Isabel's home, later this afternoon."

"Let's be wary of jumping to conclusions. Get to the bottom of this and keep me posted." Stuart's order seemed final as he hung up the phone.

As Stuart looked at his deputy director and the aides, he frowned dejectedly.

"Let's keep this in-house for now, until we can corroborate some of these allegations. We can revisit this in twenty-four hours."

They all nodded in agreement. The crime of espionage was the most serious accusation that could be leveled at an FBI Agent.

"And one more thing," he ordered. "I want to see Sullivan's file."

———

Inside his office, ASAC Gibbons was ecstatic. He was practically salivating at the prospect of giving Sullivan his due—so much so that he was accepting, without question, the allegations of a new, untested, and probationary agent. He continued to ask Peter leading questions, almost cajoling the answers he wanted to hear. As they waited for the arrival of reinforcements from Washington, Gibbons continued to probe Peter.

"Grant, what else can you tell me about him, perhaps about his personal life?"

"Well," Peter offered. "It's rumored that either he has another apartment in the city, or a girlfriend whom he's living with around here, nearby."

"Where does that come from?" Gibbons pressed.

"Well, most of the agents drive into the garage between six thirty and eight in the morning, and Sullivan's car is already parked downstairs. Yet he doesn't stroll into the office until around eight thirty. So how is he getting here? He isn't taking the bus from Medford." His comment dripped with unconcealed sarcasm.

As Gibbons digested the last piece of information, Peter saw an opening.

"Sir, may I make a comment?"

"Of course, Grant, you've earned it." As he answered, Gibbons looked at his watch. He couldn't wait to put Sullivan into an interrogation room.

"Well, sir, the agents here really like Sullivan. I guess he has them all fooled, or most of them. I don't think I can keep working here once this becomes public. I respectfully request a transfer." He looked at Gibbons seriously.

When Gibbons didn't answer, Peter continued. "I'm sure you would agree that my staying here would be untenable, given the circumstances..." He furrowed his brow in a way that indicated that his request was a no-brainer.

"Yes, I agree." Gibbons could see the logic in Peter's request. "What did you have in mind?" He looked at his watch again.

"I was thinking an assignment on the director's security detail, or perhaps the attorney general's detail."

Historically, FBI directors have used security details to varying degrees. Some directors, like former FBI Director Louis Freeh, never utilized a security detail. He was a former agent and drove himself to FBIHQ on his own, with his sidearm serving as his security. Other directors, including Director Stuart, were accustomed to a robust security detail. Several agents traveled routinely with the director wherever he went, including to and from home. The attorney general (AG), as the chief law enforcement officer in the United States, always had an FBI security detail assigned to him. The AG and the FBI director met routinely, and any agent assigned to either security detail would be in a position to put both of them in peril. Their security details were usually staffed with young FBI agents, although rarely with probationary agents.

After some thought, Gibbons answered Peter, "I think that given the circumstances, I can arrange your transfer." He seemed to be pronouncing his declaration as a fact.

Just at that moment, Gibbons answered his cell phone. After listening for a few seconds, he hung up the phone and looked straight at Peter. "They're here."

———

As Conrad ran down the long corridor toward Sullivan's office, he saw Agents Rogers and Wheeler coming out of the bathroom. They were Conrad's squad mates and had also worked with Sullivan in the past.

They were startled when they saw Conrad approaching so quickly. "Guys, come with me. Headquarters is after Sully!" They joined him as they ran the twenty remaining yards to his office.

Sullivan was busy typing the final page of his report when he heard the sound of footsteps. He had his back to the door and turned as they entered.

"What's up guys?" His smile vanished when he saw Conrad's face.

"Sully, I just got word a plane full of agents just flew in from HQ. They're coming to get you. I don't know what it's about yet, do you?"

Sullivan thought for a moment. "No idea, but you know how I feel about coincidences."

"Agreed," Conrad said quickly.

Sullivan assessed his situation. "Guys, if they are coming in stealth mode like this, it can't be good." He looked at the three of them. "Do you trust me?"

They all nodded their heads.

"Then, help me get out of here. I know how it will look if I run, but it can't be helped. This is Kyle's doing. I can't fight him if they have me locked up somewhere." As he spoke, he pulled his gun from the drawer where he kept it and holstered the weapon. He grabbed his jacket with his wallet and a checkbook he kept in another top drawer.

Conrad watched him impatiently "Sully, you don't understand, we have only seconds."

Sullivan answered, "OK, let's roll. I just need to get to the street." Conrad knew what that meant.

Sullivan stood up to leave. Conrad walked in front of him, and Rogers and Wheeler flanked him as they walked to the elevator bank. There were four elevators, and they pressed the down button. Sullivan telegraphed Conrad a knowing glance and gave what appeared to be advice.

"Sometimes, it takes a brotherhood." He smiled, and Conrad looked at him, shaking his head slightly.

As they pressed the button, the agents from HQ had entered the lobby to the building, led by a section chief in the counterintelligence unit, Lee Barrister. He had decided to wait in the lobby until his entire team had arrived, and one of the taxis had been stopped at the light. It would take another minute.

As Conrad and his entourage waited by the elevators, Gibbons spotted him as he went to greet the arriving agents by the reception area. Peter was with him but said nothing.

"Hey," Gibbons shouted, "Sullivan, stop right there!"

Sullivan and his crew ignored them as they approached. As Gibbons and Peter came closer, Conrad, Wheeler, and Rogers formed a human shield around Sullivan, just as the elevator door opened. Gibbons tried to grab Sullivan, but he couldn't penetrate the barrier they had created as he entered the elevator.

Gibbons yelled, "You're going down, Sullivan!"

As the door closed, Sullivan answered him calmly, "Not today."

The elevator headed down toward the lobby. As it did, Gibbons dialed Section Chief Barrister, who picked up on the first ring.

"Barrister, he's trying to escape! He's headed down to you in the elevator."

Barrister and his team were in the lobby, guns drawn and ready, when the elevator door opened. It was empty. They could not have known, nor did it occur to Gibbons in the confusion, that the building has a rear exit on the second floor. The Center Plaza building is on a hill, and the second-floor entrance leads toward the State House and Beacon Hill. Sullivan was gone.

———

By the time Gibbons got a call back from Barrister, it was too late. He realized that Sullivan was now somewhere on Beacon Hill, perhaps headed to the mysterious apartment that Kyle had alluded to.

Gibbons and Barrister conferred, and they decided to deploy their men into the Beacon Hill neighborhood. Gibbons was determined not to let Sullivan escape. He had placed a call to his contacts at the Boston Police Department, and they had sent two dozen officers to help secure the neighborhood. Gibbons, without consulting SAC

Wainwright, had assured the deputy commissioner that the FBI would pay for their overtime expenses.

ASAC Rand was tasked with escorting the arriving agents to the twenty Bureau vehicles, which were waiting for them in the garage. Section Chief Barrister had designated Agent Jeff Warren as the group's team leader. When they got to the parked cars, they could not believe what they saw. All of the vehicles had at least one tire deflated or punctured.

The visiting agents had just received their official welcome to the city of Boston.

———

SAC Wainwright was not happy. He now had to explain to Director Stuart not only how he had allowed a Cuban spy to operate in his office for who knows how long, but he also had to tell him that he had been allowed to flee. Of course, the fact that Sullivan did flee was evidence of his guilt, or so he believed.

In addition, he had to explain to the director how his own employees had conspired to facilitate Sullivan's escape. He had immediately initiated an administrative inquiry against Agents Conrad, Wheeler, and Rogers. Such an inquiry, he realized, would take months to be resolved and adjudicated. He knew that given these circumstances, he needed to address all the employees in the office. He sent out a message to all employees that they were to meet the next morning at nine o'clock. Attendance was mandatory.

———

Within thirty minutes of the incident, the seventh-floor command post (CP) was operational and running on all cylinders. At Peter's recommendation, Gibbons had allowed Intelligence Analyst Becky Gennaro to coordinate with the visiting analysts. Gennaro had already begun the process of pulling Sullivan's telephone toll records. She had placed an emergency request from the service provider and expected a response within three hours. The CP was desperate to link Sullivan to a residence as quickly as possible.

The agents from Washington, joined by the Boston Police reinforcements, had spread out around Beacon Hill, checking all people and cars entering or exiting the neighborhood. The police were given a photo of Sullivan, but they were told only that he was wanted for questioning in a national security matter. The FBI didn't want the press to get wind of the fact that the Bureau was chasing one of its own for espionage, at least not yet. They wanted to manage the media at their convenience, so they could spin the story and minimize any embarrassment.

No longer trusting his own agents, Gibbons, with Wainwright's concurrence, requested an FBI SWAT team from the New York office. They were en route.

In the meantime, Beacon Hill was essentially in lockdown.

# THREE

## Cat and Mouse, Part 2

Fuller had never been pulled out of a polygraph examination, ever. Now, two agents she did not know had asked her to follow them into one of the interrogation rooms. Her interview subject was summarily excused and told to reschedule his appointment. As she sat on an uncomfortable metal chair, she pondered how she was usually on the other end of the equation in these circumstances. Fuller did not know what was happening, only that someone would be with her shortly. She was ordered to wait.

In an adjacent interrogation room, Conrad was likewise seated. He knew why he was there, although he did not know the nature of the allegations against his friend. He had heard that Rogers and Wheeler had been asked to go home for the day. They would be dealt with later. He was considered the ringleader in Sullivan's escape. As he considered the situation, the door opened, and ASAC Gibbons entered the room.

"You are in a lot of trouble, Agent Conrad," Gibbons started. Gibbons knew Section Chief Barrister was watching from an observation room.

"Whatever do you mean, Mr. Gibbons?" Conrad asked slyly.

"You allowed Sullivan to escape. You are now complicit in his crimes."

"I'm afraid I don't understand. What crimes? Escape from what, exactly?" Conrad asked.

Gibbons stared at him, saying nothing.

Conrad continued. "All I know is that you have had a long-standing beef with Sullivan. He wanted to go out for lunch. You tried to mess with him, and I stopped you from harassing him. Is this a crime?" Conrad emphasized the last word.

"You know what's going on, Mr. Conrad." Gibbons was getting angry.

"How could I, Mr. Gibbons? Did you inform me about these crimes in advance? Have you notified the other agents about any alleged crimes? Do you have an arrest warrant? I'm afraid, Mr. Gibbons, that I'm not a mind reader. I have no way of knowing what you're talking about. You have not briefed me into this alleged case you have."

Conrad waited for an answer. He knew there could be no reasonable response. Emotionally, Gibbons was beyond irritation. Intellectually, he knew that Conrad's position was unassailable. He could never prove intent. So he shifted the topic.

"OK, I see how you are going to play this. All I need from you right now is for you to tell me where he is. You know he is nearby, either the North End or Beacon Hill. Where is he?" Gibbons waited.

"I have no idea," Conrad answered with a smile.

Gibbons quickly calculated that Conrad would never give him information of value. He decided they should focus their attention on Fuller. She was always more reasonable.

After Gibbons left the room, Conrad looked at his watch. He knew he had two very important calls to make.

—

Section Chief Barrister and ASAC Gibbons sat before Fuller. They had just given her a full assessment of the information and allegations leveled against Sullivan. She also realized that Sullivan must have sought temporary refuge in Lena's apartment, only two blocks away. She deduced that it would only be a matter of two or three hours before they discovered where that was. In her mind, she could picture the CP in operation, scouring every bit of data on Sullivan and his associates. She turned her attention to her interrogators.

"Who is the source of these allegations?"

"I'm afraid we can't tell you that just yet, Ms. Fuller," Gibbons answered.

"I can tell you quite undiplomatically that it's a crock of shit. Sullivan would never betray us." Fuller sat back with her arms folded.

They were somewhat taken aback with her bluntness. Barrister winced slightly.

"I'm sure you feel a sense of loyalty to Sullivan," Gibbons offered. "However, at this point, let's just focus on finding him. If you are right, then he can explain himself, and this can all be worked out. Isn't that right?"

Fuller was amused at Gibbon's crude attempts to manipulate her. She considered him a novice and decided to throw him off guard.

"Mr. Barrister, are you aware of the Migliore incident?" she asked. Barrister gave her a blank look.

Gibbons headed her off. "Don't pay attention to that," he said, waving his hand in Barrister's direction. "That's immaterial here."

Fuller shot back, "If you did know about it, Mr. Barrister, you would know that Sullivan would never turn his back on us." She kept her arms crossed defiantly.

Gibbons shifted in his seat uncomfortably. Barrister gave them both a puzzled look. Fuller could see that Gibbons would not be placated. She considered her options and shifted gears. "Yes, all right, I'll help. He has a girlfriend, and on occasion he stays with her at her apartment."

Gibbons felt a sense of relief at her sudden change of heart. He passed her a note pad and a pen. "Write down the address please."

"Oh, I don't know the address," she said. "I went there once, but I don't remember the address. But I can show you where it is. I can find it once I get on the street." She looked at them helpfully.

They had no choice but to let her guide them to his hideout. The telephone analysis was taking too long. The phone company had also indicated that the cell phone was not activated. Sullivan had turned it off. They could not track him unless he turned it on.

—

When they emerged from the interrogation room, Gibbons and Barrister were met by the designated team leader, Agent Warren. He had just led a search team at Sullivan's house in Medford and at Isabel's apartment in Lawrence. The latter search yielded nothing. The former, however, gave them the evidence they needed.

Warren explained that in Sullivan's room, underneath a pile of dirty clothes, they found the secret documents recounted by Agent Grant. Just as described, they had the secret markings removed from them. They now had enough evidence to prepare an arrest warrant.

Warren's team had escorted Isabel to another interrogation room. He had done the same with Sullivan's mother, Katarina.

It did not occur to any of them, as they discussed the case, why Sullivan would still have the documents if he had allegedly passed them to Isabel. They could not be bothered with such details with their manhunt underway.

—

"Are you kidding me? Is this fucking for real?" Director Stuart was incensed, his face red. Nobody had ever seen him this angry. He looked around the room for an answer. The conference room was filled with his deputy director, his executive assistant director, and ten other senior managers and their aides. The group was silent; his remark went unanswered. He held a copy of Sullivan's file in his hand, and he displayed it to them for emphasis.

"The FBI's Medal of Valor? My predecessor gave this man the Bureau's Medal of Valor." He repeated his statement, hoping to prod them into an answer.

His deputy spoke first. "It was called the Migliore incident."

"Tell me about it." The director leaned back slightly.

The deputy had memorized the report and did not have to look down at his notes. "In 1998, upon transferring to the Boston division, Agent Sullivan went to a bank in downtown Boston to open an account. Accompanying him was sixty-five-year-old Anita Migliore, a secretary in the Boston office. She wanted him to meet the manager, who was also her daughter. She was making a referral. It was early and the bank had no customers. About two minutes into their visit, two armed men stormed into the bank. Unfortunately, a passing police officer took note of what happened and a ten-hour standoff ensued."

The director was visibly interested. "Go on. What happened?"

"During the incident, Agent Sullivan kept watch over Mrs. Migliore, holding her hand, consoling her, and so forth. Apparently, Agent Sullivan took no action for many hours, hoping that the gunmen would surrender to the negotiators." He paused and looked around the room.

"And?" the director asked.

"Well, at some point he felt the standoff was not going well, so he shot both men point blank with his service pistol. Two shots each. Interestingly, none of the bank employees cooperated with the subsequent investigation. They remained silent. We had only Sullivan's version of events to go on."

The director was stunned. "Great. How are we going to sell this? An FBI Medal of Valor recipient is now a spy?"

One of the assistant directors in the back of the room raised his hand. The director nodded at him, signaling for him to speak.

"We can look at it another way, sir."

"Really, how so?"

The assistant director looked about the room, "We can say he's now a psycho killer, who went off the deep end *precisely* because of the Migliore incident."

The room went silent as they considered this intriguing idea.

# FOUR

## Escape

When Sullivan slipped into the Belvedere, the doorman noticed that Sullivan was not his normal jovial self. He seemed intense and in a hurry. Sullivan had already estimated that he had approximately fifteen minutes before the pursuing agents blanketed the area, making an escape from the apartment nearly impossible. He also calculated that he had perhaps three hours before they discovered Lena's apartment and raided it. Sullivan knew he had to move quickly.

When he entered the apartment, he immediately retrieved his ready bag from her closet. The ready bag was something he used whenever the Bureau asked him to deploy in a moment's notice. It was a holdover from his days working undercover. It was a small backpack containing cash, a three-day supply of clothes, toiletries, a cell phone in his undercover name, and his false identification. He knew that the Bureau had that cell phone number in its inventory of his property, so he could not use it yet.

Sullivan went to Lena's desk and noticed there were three index cards, each with a set of apartment keys placed over them. He looked at the addresses and noticed one was only two blocks away on Joy Street, a fourth-story walkup. He put those keys in his pocket and threw the index card in his bag. Sullivan then took the keys from one of the remaining properties and threw them in his bag. The index card he left.

He wrote a short message on a pad of paper for Lena. He leashed Toby, who had been hovering around him nervously as he walked about the apartment, as if he could sense there was trouble. Sullivan then took the elevator to the ninth floor, where he hoped Lena's friend Melissa, who worked from home, would be.

Melissa answered the door in a T-shirt and khaki shorts. She was surprised to see Sullivan when she opened the door.

"Sully? What's up?" She was even more surprised when she saw he was holding Toby on his leash.

"Melissa, Lena and I need your help. She can't come back tonight and needs you to watch Toby." She listened intently, as he seemed uncharacteristically serious.

"And I need you to give her this." He handed her a note which he had placed in a small plastic bag.

"When will she be back?" she asked.

"Tomorrow morning, I promise." She grabbed the leash, and he walked down the corridor, out of sight. Toby whined gently as he left.

—

When he entered the fourth-story apartment on Joy Street, he was glad to see it had a good view of the street below. He wanted to have an idea when his pursuers were lurking about. He was thrilled to discover that the apartment was fully furnished and had a working landline. There was no way the Bureau had that number. He knew it was clean for at least twenty-four hours.

Lena was in her office when her phone rang. "This is Lena," she answered cheerfully.

"Lena, it's Carlos."

She knew right away from his voice that something was wrong. "What happened?"

"I'm in a little trouble—not of my own doing this time, mind you," he said, attempting to be humorous.

"I see. How bad?"

"Very bad, I'm afraid." Sullivan paused, and then continued. "Unfortunately, you can't go to your apartment tonight—"

Lena cut him off. "What? That's crazy."

"Listen to me carefully. I left Toby with Melissa, and she will take care of him tonight. The FBI will be raiding your place in about three hours, by my estimate. I'm hiding in one of your apartments, but I will be gone by tomorrow night."

"Carlos…" She started to sob quietly as he spoke.

"Lena, it's going to be all right. You need to see Melissa tomorrow morning at nine. She will be expecting you. She has a note for you as well."

He paused as she continued crying.

"Will you help me?" he asked in a hushed tone.

"You know I will," she said, trying to compose herself. "You know how I've taught you about the Russian concept of a debt repaid."

"Yes, I remember."

"Then you know I owe you much," she said.

"OK then, Lena, you must sleep in your office tonight. Tomorrow, see Melissa." His words seemed final.

"Yeah, I heard. Nine o'clock."

"Lena," he said, "I love you."

"I love you more," she answered in the way she always did. It gave him comfort in that moment of uncertainty.

He could think of nothing else to say, and they hung up. As he looked down at the street below, he knew his timing was perfect. Just as he had predicted, he could see agents walking down the street as a Boston Police cruiser sat parked on the corner, its blue lights on. He knew he was trapped for now.

———

After Conrad was excused from his quasi-interrogation, he went directly to his squad's conference room. It had a telephone that he used from time to time for sensitive calls, such as the one he was about to make.

Wheeler and Rogers never noticed the message Sullivan had cryptically relayed just before he escaped. But to him it was unmistakable.

The person he called picked up on the third ring.

"Jorge?"

"Si, Conrad." The man recognized his voice instantly.

"I have a mission for you and your brother."

———

Trish O'Keefe had news for Conrad. They both knew that in any crisis, the best antidote was reliable intelligence about the events as they unfolded. Conrad listened pensively as O'Keefe gave him an animated update on the situation.

"I've learned that Kyle and that bitch, Gennaro, are basically running the show at the seventh-floor CP. They are running point for the team leader from HQ, Jeff Warren. She has set up everything they need to trace his phone. The problem they have is Sully turned it off as soon as he left the building. She's also trapping his undercover phone, as if he's stupid enough to use that. I also know she put in an emergency request for his toll records. That should be here shortly."

O'Keefe put her index finger to her chin, trying to recap everything without error.

"Oh, right, and Fuller is on the street right now, taking Warren and some of his agents on a tour of Beacon Hill."

Conrad chuckled as she continued. "We think it's hilarious—they actually think she is going to take them to Sully's!" She couldn't help but laugh. "There's also a SWAT team headed here from New York. Not sure when they will be here."

O'Keefe sat in front of Conrad, clearly pleased with herself. She had left the best for last.

"What's that look about?" Conrad asked her.

"It's in place." She answered coyly.

"What's in place?"

"Grant's phone…I have it trapped. I can tell you all of his calls, and I can track him. Only he *is* using his phone, unlike Sully. I thought you might like to keep track of him," she said with a wry smile.

"Oh, yes, very good, little Trish. Very good."

—

The attorneys entered the FBI reception area in a brash and unceremonious manner. Three of the best criminal attorneys in the city of Boston were intent on upending a small part of what was occurring within the walls of the office. Representing the firm of Adams & Noble, they belonged to a firm that had more than a hundred-year presence in the city, and which made people tremble in their wake. They announced themselves as attorneys for Katarina Robles.

The Boston FBI's chief division counsel, Samuel Kritz, and his assistant division counsel made hasty arrangements to meet with their unwelcome visitors. Over the next two hours, the attorneys laid out their case.

The classified documents in question were found in the living area of agent Sullivan, over which Ms. Robles had no access. There was no evidence linking their client to the documents. She was a naturalized US citizen, not an alien. She had no criminal history. As the Bureau's legal minds listened, the attorneys kept at them with more and more exculpatory information.

The Bureau did not know that as he grew up with Sullivan, Conrad had come to consider Katarina Robles to be a mother figure for him. She cared for him when his own mother died after he turned fourteen years old. Over the years, Conrad had made a lot of connections, and many people owed him favors. The thought of her being held in an interrogation was unacceptable to him. By the time the meeting was over, the Bureau decided that as long as she turned over her passport, they would release Ms. Robles pending further investigation. In truth, they knew they had no case against her.

Conrad had decided to cash in all of his favors. He also wanted to have some good news for Sully when he called, as he knew he would soon hear from his best friend.

———

The four black Chevy Suburban SUVs with New York license plates were parked ominously in front of the State House. Passersby noticed the vehicles were running, but their tinted windows concealed whatever was happening inside them. Inside the lead vehicle, Special Agent Justin Stryker was conflicted in his role as the SWAT team leader. While he did not know Sullivan personally, he had friends back in New York who had spoken highly of him. In the Bureau, it's not six degrees of separation, but usually only two degrees. Despite his reservations, he knew he had an assignment to complete, and he intended to do it as professionally as possible.

Agent Warren had received a welcome call from Peter in the CP. He had been walking fruitlessly with Fuller through Beacon Hill on what he quickly determined was a stalling tactic. Finally, his team received actionable intelligence.

Becky Gennaro had reviewed Sullivan's telephone toll data, and she had located a residence she believed belonged to Sullivan's girlfriend, based on her analysis. She had identified Lena Hall as a resident of apartment 8L at the Belvedere building on Beacon Street. As she relayed the information to Peter, other analysts in the CP began developing a profile of Ms. Hall and all of her contacts.

Agent Warren conferred with Stryker, who had stepped out onto the sidewalk, in the shadow of the State House. Stryker's team was going into and out of their vehicles, grabbing their equipment, prepping for their raid. Fuller stood a few steps away, attempting to listen to the conversation. She knew that the Belvedere was less than a hundred yards from where they were standing. When she saw Warren pointing at the building, she knew they had located Lena's apartment.

Warren's men evacuated the surrounding units on the eighth floor in preparation for Stryker's assault on the targeted apartment. The doorman, Joe, had confirmed that Sullivan had entered the apartment but could not recall seeing him leave. They would not be cutting Sullivan any breaks, as he was technically considered armed and dangerous.

As the door was breached, a flash bang was thrown into the small apartment. The floor seemed to buckle from the blast's concussive effect. It took Stryker's team less than ten seconds to clear the unit. As Stryker had suspected, the apartment was empty. His team went back to their vehicles, as Warren and his men entered the unit to search for new clues.

Within short order, Warren found the address for another apartment on Grove Street, on the other side of Beacon Hill. After his team hit that apartment and again came up empty, Warren approached Stryker, who seem relieved. The last thing he wanted to be known for was harming another agent, no matter the circumstances.

"I told you that was just bait he left for us," Stryker said plainly.

"It did seem a little too easy," Warren agreed, "but we have to leave no stone unturned."

Stryker was not in a patient mood. "Really, is that what they teach at HQ, 'leave no stone unturned'?"

When Warren said nothing, Stryker added, "you are going to have to be a little cleverer if you are going to find this guy. He's been two steps ahead of you the whole time."

Stryker unstrapped his bulletproof vest as he walked away.

———

The next morning, Sullivan awoke to the sound of a siren. He jumped off the couch where he had slept. A quick glance down to the street revealed it was an ambulance. On the corner, he noticed the same cruiser watching the intersection. Also on the corner he could see several agents talking, sipping their coffee. He looked at his watch. It was seven o'clock. If he ever hoped to get out of the city, Sullivan knew he would have to make a bold move soon.

———

On most occasions, FBI employees had to be dragged kicking and screaming to their all-employee meetings, if they even went at all. That was not the case this morning. Everyone had heard about or seen first-hand the events that had occurred over the last twenty-four hours. By eight forty-five, the eighth-floor meeting area was already overflowing with agents, analysts, and other support employees for the nine o'clock meeting. The air in the room was electric. It did not escape notice that sitting in the front row was Rebecca Scola, the granddaughter of the now deceased Anita Migliore. She sat with her legs crossed, her hands placed gently on her knees. At the age of twenty-five, she was now a secretary in the FBI herself, having followed in her grandmother's footsteps.

Standing to one side were Fuller, Conrad, and O'Keefe. They had agreed to say nothing. They would let others do the talking at this meeting.

At nine o'clock, SAC Wainwright finally arrived at the meeting, accompanied by ASACs Rand and Billing. He could instantly sense the energy in the room, and it did not seem particularly welcoming. His intent was to calm the office, which was nearly in a state of revolt. The plan did not begin as he had scripted it in his mind.

Rebecca Scola stood up before he could get his first words out. "Mr. Wainwright, you cannot possibly believe these allegations that are being thrown about. Sullivan is one of the good guys." Her voice was rising as she continued. "That man is one of the good guys—he saved my mom and grandmother!" She was nearly in tears.

As she sat down, Agent Thomas, with thirty years of experience, rose to speak. "Mr. Wainwright, it seems like there has been a rush to judgment here."

Wainwright kept raising his hands up in an attempt to stop the onslaught, but others kept rising to talk. After five minutes of listening to his employees harping, he caught sight of ASAC Gibbons approaching him. He had been in the CP, and he seemed animated.

"Call the meeting off," Gibbons whispered in his ear. "We got him."

The excitement in the CP was palpable. At exactly 9:07 a.m., Becky Gennaro detected a signal from Sullivan's phone. She quickly determined that it had emerged from the underground parking garage at the Boston Common. It was within a stone's throw of the State House, near Beacon Street. Gennaro quickly surmised that the signal had been blocked because he had been underground.

After confirming her findings, she yelled, "I got him!"

Everyone made their way over to her workstation.

"I got him!" she yelled again. "He was underground; he's on the move now!"

Peter quickly arranged for a radio message to all the units in the area, as Wainwright entered the room.

"All units, repeat all units, the subject is on the move. He has emerged from the Boston Common parking garage."

When the message was received, all the surveillance teams on the street were relieved. Their work might soon be over. They moved quickly. Stryker and his men were already at their Suburbans when they got the call. More messages were coming from the CP.

"All units, he is headed west on Beacon Street, into the Back Bay. Corner of Beacon and Arlington Streets!"

Stryker's vehicles were only a minute away. They gunned their engines, followed by the police cruisers that had been providing assistance. Each cruiser had an FBI agent in it for coordination purposes.

By the time the pursuing units reached Beacon and Arlington, Sullivan's signal was detected on Storrow Drive, headed east now.

"All units, the subject is now headed east on Storrow Drive, he's trying to get on the highway, possibly Route 93." The radio operator was trying to portray a calm demeanor over the air.

Stryker and his team were closing in on their target, even as Sullivan was now traced to Route 93 northbound. Gennaro continued to relay real-time intelligence to the surveillance teams. Peter, Warren, and Barrister stood over her, observing.

"All units, subject is now on Route 93 northbound, traveling approximately eighty-five miles per hour!" Despite his attempt at calm, his voice rose as the excitement mounted.

As he continued to get intelligence on the location of the signal, Stryker and his men identified their target. It was a late-model Ford Taurus, gray in color, and they were closing in. Following their training, they moved in methodically. One SUV passed the car and moved in front. Stryker's vehicle moved next to the target on the left, while his other units fell in behind their subject. They were boxing him in.

Stryker was in the passenger seat of the flanking vehicle and had a perfect view of their target. His gun was out, ready.

"Do you have a visual yet?" The CP radio operator asked. Everyone in the room held their breath in anticipation.

"Oh, yes I do," replied Stryker.

"Do you have him?" Gibbons had taken over the radio. He could not contain himself.

Stryker's vehicle was now matching the speed of the Taurus. He had not yet made the call to take the car down. He was too amused at what he was witnessing.

"No, I don't have him," Stryker answered.

"Why not?" yelled Gibbons.

"Because he is a she. And she's flipping me the bird."

As he looked out his window, Lena was steering with her right hand. Her left hand was extended out her open window.

———

Within two minutes of ASAC Gibbons's dramatic entrance at the all-employee meeting, Conrad received a call on his cell phone—the one he had been expecting. Sullivan was calling from the apartment's hard line, as he knew it wouldn't matter now.

"Has all hell broken loose yet?" Sullivan asked.

"Just about," Conrad answered.

"Are we on track?"

"Yes, just say when and where."

Sullivan didn't know how to thank his most loyal friend. "You know, Conrad—"

"Stop," Conrad interrupted. "We are a team. We always have been. We always will be."

"OK," Sullivan said, almost in a whisper.

Conrad was focused on their plan; he felt there was time for reminiscing later.

"Listen," he said, "once you are settled, we will focus on taking Kyle down. I can track him now. We will get to the bottom of this." He was trying to give Sullivan some encouragement. "One other thing, Sully."

"Yes?"

"Your mother is safe. She's been released. She'll be OK. I will get a message to her when the moment is right."

"That must have cost you some favors. I guess the beer is on me next time."

They exchanged thoughts about the situation for another moment. Before ending his call with Conrad, he gave him the address to his location.

Exactly seven minutes later, he walked out of the building and stood on the sidewalk, his ready bag slung over his shoulder. The streets were now devoid of any pursuing officers. A dark-blue van pulled up to the curb, and the sliding door opened. Sullivan quickly slipped into the well of the van.

"*Hola,* Jorge," Sullivan said as he took a seat.

Jorge's brother, Miguel, was in the passenger seat. They exchanged handshakes and smiles.

Sullivan was on his way out of the city.

# FIVE

## Lena

Lena sat pensively in her interrogation chair. She knew what to expect, or so she thought. Sullivan had always told her that in the FBI, a suspect was never told they were going to be interrogated. They were always told it was merely an "interview," which of course sounds less confrontational. After hearing Sullivan, Fuller, and Conrad swap stories, she knew the mind games employed to get a person to confess. The interview would begin with the agents building rapport and then convincing the suspect that they were there to help him. During the interview, the interrogator would spin stories and themes that might appeal to the suspect, a process meant to allow the guilty to save face or rationalize his behavior.

She always thought it was a quaint process. In her native Russia, no such subtleties were employed. The police were always guaranteed a confession, whether they beat it out of their suspect, or they simply made one up. In her case, she knew there was nothing to confess to; she was merely helping her boyfriend, a decorated FBI agent.

Lena was pulling back her long black hair, trying to knot it into a bun. She was using the long mirror in the room, which she assumed had agents behind it observing her. Her emerald-green eyes shone back at her from the glass. Without any warning, two agents unceremoniously entered the room and sat across from her. One appeared to be in his fifties, with gray hair and dark-rimmed spectacles. The other was perhaps ten years younger. Both wore dark suits with crisply pressed white shirts. The younger agent spoke first.

"Ms. Hall, I'm Assistant Special Agent in Charge Gibbons, this is Section Chief Barrister from Washington, DC." He placed his hands on a white notepad that lay before him.

"I've heard of you," Lena said with a knowing grin.

"Yes, well, Ms. Hall, you are in a lot of trouble," Gibbons said coldly.

"No, no, that's not a good way to start," Lena shot back.

"Excuse me?" Gibbons seemed confused.

"You're supposed to tell me how I'm not in so much trouble, that it's nothing that can't be resolved, and so on. It's called minimizing the crime." Lena looked from one to the other.

"This is not a game, Ms. Hall. You need to tell us where Agent Sullivan is right now!" Gibbons raised his voice.

"Wrong again," Lena responded calmly. "You are supposed to build rapport with me, convince me you're my friend."

Gibbons was growing frustrated. He looked at Barrister, who crossed his arms and watched impassively. Barrister seemed to be enjoying the show. Behind the mirror, several senior managers, including the SAC, were watching. Peter was the only nonmanager in the observation room. It was a packed house.

Lena continued. "You should try saying that it's all Sully's fault, that he manipulated me, and I'm just a victim. That's called projection, when you project the blame onto some other person."

Gibbons realized he was being watched, and he knew he was being bested. "OK, Ms. Hall, you're right," he said. "I think Sullivan did trick or coerce you into helping him. Would you agree?"

"Your transition seems unnatural." Lena's lip curled into a slight smile. "You see, you didn't lay a foundation built on good rapport, so now you seem insincere."

Gibbons was regretting not having someone else conduct the interview. And he was not getting any help from Barrister, who seemed like a statue in the room.

"You aren't an interrogator, are you?" Lena looked directly at Gibbons.

Gibbons put his hands on the table, as if to leave, cuing Barrister to do the same, when Lena saw an opportunity.

"Mr. Barrister, these allegations against Sully, they are coming from an Agent Kyle Grant, are they not?"

Gibbons raised his hand as if to dismiss her, but Barrister placed his hand on his forearm, signaling Lena to continue. Inside the observation room, all eyes moved to Peter.

"You are wondering how I could know that, right?" Lena could see she had his attention. By Barrister's reaction, she could see that she was indeed correct.

"A few days ago, Sully told me that he believes Agent Grant is a fraud, an imposter."

Gibbons jumped in. "That's absurd. You are simply trying to protect your boyfriend!"

Barrister looked at Lena but said nothing. He did not attain his position by acting rashly. He would weigh this new information in due course. Meanwhile, in the observation room, Peter could feel the weight of all the eyes in the room on his back. He tried to stand nonchalantly, uninterested, but inside he was fuming.

"Ms. Hall"—Gibbons went on the offensive—"you will be charged with harboring a fugitive."

"Really?" she retorted. "On what basis? I did not know he was a fugitive, actually, until you just told me now."

"You had his cell phone in your possession," he replied.

"Sure, so you say. He has used my car many times; he must have dropped it there accidentally," Lena knew she was on solid ground.

"This interview is over." Gibbons declared as he stood to leave. He paused for a moment and looked down at her.

"Ms. Hall, is that a Russian accent I detect?" he asked accusingly.

"I am an American citizen, Mr. Gibbons," she answered, without elaboration.

"I see." Gibbons said derisively.

Lena couldn't help but give him a parting shot. "Perhaps you could charge me with speeding. I might have been going too fast."

They walked out of the room as quickly as they had entered.

Assistant United States Attorney (AUSA) Ben Weinstein had been observing the interview with interest. He had been assigned the prosecution of Agent Sullivan and any coconspirators who might be uncovered. He had already determined that there was insufficient evidence to charge Lena. As a courtesy, he conferred privately with Samuel Kritz, the FBI's chief division counsel in Boston, so they could be on the same page. Both of them agreed that Lena should be released until such time as their investigation developed new evidence of collaboration with Sullivan. They were also concerned about the doubts cast on Kyle's credibility as expressed by Lena. The animus of Sullivan against Kyle could muddy the waters of their case.

Upon hearing the news of Lena's release, Gibbons met with Peter to decide on a strategy.

"We should tail her." Gibbons said to Peter.

"Mr. Gibbons, I don't think there's any way Sullivan is going to meet with her now. There's too much heat." Peter leaned in conspiratorially as he spoke.

"Let me give Becky her numbers, and we can keep track of her that way, more discreetly."

"Gibbons put his hand on Peter's shoulder. "Good thinking, Kyle. Make it happen."

Whenever Lena needed to clear her head, she always took Toby for a late-night walk along the Esplanade, bordering the Charles River. She stopped briefly for Toby's sake, looking across the river to the Cambridge side. The moonlight shimmered off the dark waters as small waves lapped against the shoreline. So much had occurred over the last twenty-four hours, her head was spinning. As she recalled the circumstances of her interview hours earlier, she realized that Carlos was right after all. She was certain that Kyle must have set up her man.

Mostly, she wondered when she would hear from him again. She missed him deeply.

As she walked, she noticed a man following her at a distance of about thirty feet. He had a phone to his ear and appeared to be talking to someone. For a moment, she considered that the FBI might be following her. When she saw another woman walking by with a dog, she thought she was just being paranoid and kept walking slowly down the Esplanade.

A short distance behind her, Peter was lurking, watching her intently. He did have a phone to his ear, but it was turned off. He had seen a passerby and was waiting for the right moment.

As Lena pulled on her leash, she noticed Toby turn his head back quickly. She also sensed that someone was approaching.

Peter came out from the shadow of a tree, a knife in his hand.

"You must be Kyle." Lena said in fear.

Peter was incensed at Lena, and the doubts he now had to endure from those who had been watching her interview.

"You bitch," he said, his face red. "You are going to tell me where your boyfriend is."

He lunged at her, kicking Toby, who crashed into a tree, dropping unconscious to the ground.

Lena ran as fast as she could in the direction of the boathouse. It was only fifty yards away, and she could hear his footsteps behind her getting closer. She knew if the side door was locked, she would not have time to unlock it, though she had the key. She reached the door, which was miraculously ajar. But he was right on her, placing his hand on the door, so she could not swing it open. Instinctively, she swung her elbow back, hitting him on the side of the head. As Peter fell back, she slipped into the boathouse and locked the door.

Peter, enraged, started kicking the door down. As the door buckled with each blow, Lena realized that in her haste, she had dropped her purse. She had no phone, no way to call for help.

Suddenly, she noticed that he had stopped pounding on the door. Peter had noticed somebody approaching, and stopped, waiting for the person to pass. After a minute or two, he talked at her through the door.

"Hey, Russki, you realize it's only a matter of time before I get in there," Peter hissed at her.

"I'm a girl, so it's Russkaya. But go fuck yourself," she answered back.

"If you open the door, I won't hurt you. I just want to talk."

"Is that why you brought a knife, asshole?" Lena looked about, searching for a weapon.

"I will put it away. Let's talk," Peter insisted.

Lena recalled how Carlos always told her that in any engagement, action is always quicker than reaction. She had to act decisively, or he would eventually break down the door.

As Peter considered his options, he stood with his shoulder about a foot from the door. Suddenly, the door crashed against him, knocking him back. In her hands, she held one half of a broken oar that was left in the boathouse. She swung at his chest, but he moved back, and she missed. He pulled out his knife and started circling her, closing in slowly. He tried striking a knife blow, but she quickly swung the oar, hitting him in the hand, causing him to drop the knife. Peter winced as he tried to massage his bruised hand. It was already starting to swell.

Sensing she had caught him off guard, Lena swung the oar as strongly as she could, at his chest. Peter saw it coming and saw an opening. He absorbed the blow to the chest, but at the same time he grabbed hold of the oar. He was momentarily winded, but now she was defenseless. As Lena tried pulling the oar back, he punched her straight in the nose. Warm blood started oozing out of her broken nose as she fell onto her back.

Peter knelt over her as she looked up to the night sky, dazed. Despite her pain, she slowly lifted her left hand, giving Peter the finger.

"Good night, Lena," Peter said softly, placing his weight directly on her as he gripped her neck firmly with his good hand, slowly squeezing the life out of her.

In the seconds before her death, as she lay motionless in the dark, she thought about her love. Where, she wondered, was her Carlos?

# SIX

## The Brothers

The moon shone brightly in the Rhode Island night sky at a campground outside of Newport, where Sullivan had once gone camping with Lena. He knew it to be an isolated and safe spot from which to plan his next move. As he sat on a rock, his concern was for Lena and what she must have endured after helping him. Sullivan considered how he and Lena had pitched a tent only a few feet away from where he was sitting.

He heard the brothers talking and turned to listen and watch them.

When Jorge and Miguel Restrepo's father Luis was killed in their own living room, as they watched helplessly, they vowed to get their revenge. They were only nine and eleven years old respectively, living in the small Colombian village of Santa Rubina, in an area controlled by the rebels. In the seventies, those rebels were the communist-inspired Fuerzas Armadas de Revolucion Colombiana, known simply as the FARC. At that time, the FARC had control over vast areas of the country, and they effectively ran a government with its own army. The FARC, fueled with money from Castro's Cuban government and trade in narcotics, terrorized much of Colombia. They routinely planted bombs in markets and clubs, even in the capital, Bogota. They took hostages for ransom, often government officials or policemen. Usually, however, ordinary Colombians were taken prisoner until their families paid ransom.

In the eighties, the US government, under the anticommunist policy of President Reagan, started a campaign to fight the narco-traffickers and the FARC. Covert funds were sent to the Colombian government, and antiterrorist units were trained by the US military. Among the first to fight in these anti-FARC units were the brothers. They were all too eager to fight against the rebels and eventually formed their own units under the auspices of the US government. Their potential was so valued that they were even trained to pilot helicopters, a skill they used repeatedly in their raids on FARC encampments. This skill led many in the war to dub them the "flying brothers." Over time, the Colombian government, with the assistance of these units, had the FARC on the run, defeated.

This was the case at the time Sullivan met them in the late nineties. Sullivan was serving a tour of duty at the FBI's legal attaché office at the US embassy in Bogota, Colombia. At this time, with the FARC on the defensive, the US government wanted to shift the focus of the antiterror units toward the drug cartels, which were still very powerful. Sullivan developed a professional relationship with the brothers that led eventually to a social one. He respected the honest, direct approach they had always displayed with him. If they felt a particular operation was not viable, they pulled no punches in saying so.

Sullivan realized the potential they represented as cooperating witnesses to the FBI in the United States. To an investigator, a good source is worth his weight in gold. In the case of the brothers, they were even more valuable, because they could accomplish more as a team. One day, the brothers reported to the embassy with urgent information. They had word that one of the drug cartels they were targeting was actively seeking personal retribution against them. They were looking for their mother, to assassinate her and send a message.

Sullivan worked tirelessly to relocate the brothers, and their immediate family members, to the United States. Since that time, they worked as FBI cooperating witnesses, resulting in the arrests of dozens of drug traffickers. When Sullivan left the drug arena, they continued working under Conrad's direction.

The brothers were aware of the debt they owed Sullivan. Until this most recent incident, Sullivan had never asked them for a personal favor. They were not going to hesitate now.

Miguel was the older and more intense of the brothers. With a large build, deeply set eyes, and a large nose, he was an intimidating presence. Jorge was smaller and more sociable. He appeared to always be smiling, although he had a temper and could turn in anger instantly. Both had spent their years in the United States learning English as best they could.

After watching them argue for a time, Sullivan walked over to them.

"OK, boys, what have you got for me?" He stood over them, as they sat on a blanket they had placed on the ground.

Jorge went to the van and retrieved two black duffel bags. He opened the first, which contained several pistols, cartridges, and boxes of ammunition. He placed them on the ground, displaying them for Sullivan.

From the second bag, he pulled out a MAC-10 machine gun, and two Remington 12-gauge shotguns. Sullivan arched an eyebrow, surprised.

"Were you two planning on invading Canada?" he asked them sarcastically.

Miguel looked back at him and smiled. "We no know how bloody this mission going to be, Sully," Jorge replied, in his thick Spanish accent.

"I don't want to know where you got these," Sullivan answered dryly.

"No ask, no tell," replied Miguel.

"OK, what about phones?" Sullivan inquired.

Jorge slipped his hand into one of the duffel bags and retrieved three cell phones.

"These are clean," Jorge said as he tossed one of them to Sullivan.

"Excellent." He knew he had calls to make.

# SEVEN

## Fallout

**B**y the time Peter returned to the office, his right hand had turned purple. He stopped at a pharmacy on his way back, purchased a bandage, and wrapped his hand. He calculated that it would be best if he was back at the office when they received word of Lena's murder. The CP was now a twenty-four-hour operation, with the evening shift having taken over at six o'clock. He also knew that Becky was working overtime and would be there waiting for him.

As he entered the CP, he noticed several agents around the conference table, reading various reports, presumably background information on Sullivan. Agent Warren was at the far side of the table, typing into his laptop. Another agent was on the phone with headquarters. He had little information to relay, as they had no clue where Sullivan was, or where he might be heading, other than the elusive rumor about his travel to Cuba. All of the airports had been placed on alert.

Becky spotted him as he entered the room. "Hey, there, you're back early. I thought you were going to get some shut-eye."

"Bad luck. I fell down my stairs and hurt my hand." He showed his bandaged hand, thinking it best to not appear defensive about his wound.

"Let me see it," she asked him, reaching for his hand.

"Nah, it's nothing." He pulled his hand back. "We have work to do. What's the latest?"

Becky went to her computer. "Well, I told you her phone was headed to the Esplanade…you know, by the river. It's still pinging in that same place."

Of course, he knew all too well, as this was how he was able to track Lena. With his adrenaline level dropping, Peter suddenly realized he was hungry.

"We should eat. Is anyone here hungry?" Peter called out to the group.

"We ordered pizzas. They should be here any minute," answered one of the agents.

"OK, great." Peter leaned back and grabbed one of the reports lying on the table.

———

Conrad and O'Keefe were working late, unsettled by all that had happened. Fuller had also stopped by for a moment, checking in with them. She left them upset, uncertain how they should proceed. Now Conrad's phone was ringing, and he recognized the number as Boston Police Detective Bob Harrington, whom he knew well. He contemplated not answering. He assumed the detective was looking for an update on the events of the day. After giving it more thought, he thought it best to answer.

"Conrad, I have some bad news." Conrad sat straight up in his chair. O'Keefe noticed his change of demeanor.

O'Keefe had never seen Conrad so enraged. He screamed something incomprehensible and flung his phone across the room, shattering it against the wall.

"What is it?" she asked as she followed him down the corridor.

"He killed Lena," he whispered under his breath as he walked toward the CP.

"What! That's crazy," she said, desperately following him, trying to grab his arm as he walked more quickly. "Don't do anything crazy."

He flung open the door to the CP and saw Grant sitting with his feet casually propped up on the table. Peter had no time to react before Conrad was upon him, pummeling him with all his strength. It took five agents to pull them apart as O'Keefe watched, horrified. In the confusion, nobody even noticed that Peter's hand was bandaged.

Conrad pointed at Peter furiously. "You killed Lena!" he screamed as ASAC Gibbons arrived in the room.

"Take him out of here," Gibbons ordered the agents holding Conrad. Gibbons followed them out into the corridor. "You are losing it, Conrad."

"I'm telling you he killed Lena," Conrad said flatly, composing himself.

"That's outrageous," Gibbons answered. "Your judgment is clouded."

Conrad turned and started walking back to his cubicle.

"You need to go home!" Gibbons yelled at him as he walked away.

O'Keefe silently followed Conrad back to their squad area. When they got back to their stations, Conrad looked at her.

"Now what?" she asked.

"You said you had his phone tracked, so let's track it."

———

The stunned agents looked around the room. Papers had gone flying everywhere during the melee. Becky was tending to a cut under Peter's eye when Gibbons returned to the room.

"Pack your bags, Kyle," Gibbons said dryly. "You're headed to Washington—the director's detail. You clearly can't work here any-more. You were right."

"All right, thanks."

Becky was not happy with this development. "What about me?" she asked, almost pleading.

"Would you move to DC with me?" Peter asked. He wanted to keep her as an ally.

"Yeah, I can ask for a transfer," she said, smiling.

As they spoke, Agent Warren announced that their pizzas had arrived, and he placed them on the conference table. Happy to feed her new boyfriend, Becky opened the top box and let out a horrified shriek. The agents all turned to see the problem. A black snake slithered out of the box and across the table.

"Ah shit," Gibbons muttered. "This is getting out of hand."

"Son of a bitch," added Warren. "I even tipped the delivery guy."

—

Trish O'Keefe alternately stared at her computer and at Conrad, who sat next to her.

"I think you are right after all," she said.

"You can place his phone at the crime scene?" Conrad asked excitedly.

"No, but interestingly, he turned his phone off two hours ago. And it's still off." O'Keefe grinned knowingly. They both knew agents never turned their phones off.

"Let's get out of here. We need time to think," Conrad said. He was exhausted, his eyes puffy. As they walked toward the elevators, Conrad looked at her sadly. "Trish, I don't know how I'm going to tell Sully."

"I know." As they rounded the corner, they ran into Becky, who had just called for an elevator.

"You bitch!" Becky screamed at Trish. "I know your uncle owns that pizza shop!" The elevator arrived, and she got on.

Trish gave Becky a sly smile. "I'll take the next car." Becky shook her head angrily.

Conrad had forgotten that O'Keefe's uncle owned the Cambridge Street Pizzeria. He laughed the entire way home after she told him the story. It was a brief respite from the day's events.

—

The next morning, SAC Wainwright convened his senior staff and legal counsel for a meeting. Section Chief Barrister was also there, representing FBIHQ. It was now clear to them that Sullivan had killed his girlfriend, either to cover his tracks, or because he simply lost it.

He was no longer simply wanted for espionage. He was now a murder suspect as well. In a new twist to their case, they also learned that Lena Hall was Russian. She could have been part of the conspiracy.

With Grant transferred to HQ, any possible conflict of interest was put to rest. It was decided that Agent Warren would remain in Boston and direct the team hunting Sullivan. To further shield the investigators from any further harassment, all Boston agents were given strict orders to stay away from the CP and the investigation. The SAC made it clear that the director was expecting results, quickly.

As the meeting was concluding, Agent Warren entered the room with news. It was not the kind of news they wanted to hear. He had just heard from one of his agents on the night shift. They had arrived at their hotel, and their room keys were disabled. When they checked at the desk, the manager informed them they had received a call that evening from an FBI official, canceling all of the FBI reservations. The SAC was upset and embarrassed. He seemed to be losing control of his office.

"Did they get a name, anything?" he asked, exasperated.

Warren shook his head in disgust. "Yeah, they said he gave them your name."

—

The next morning, Sullivan began making his phone calls. His first, to Professor Albertson, was revealing.

"Yes, Professor Albertson, this is Special Agent Sullivan. I'm sorry it took so long to get back to you. I got tied up."

"No problem," he answered. "How can I assist you?"

"Yes, I'm doing some follow-up as part of Kyle's background investigation. You indicated you knew Kyle Grant's father. Please tell me more," Sullivan asked politely.

"Well, his father died in the line of duty, as you must know. He and I went to high school together, so his death was pretty shocking to me."

"I see," Sullivan answered. "Did Kyle do well at school?"

"Absolutely, and he was actively involved in campus life. He had the time of his life."

Sullivan frowned, thinking about his previous conversation with Kyle. Any minor doubts he might have had immediately vanished.

"Is there anyone on the police force who might have more information about Kyle?"

"Well, interesting that you mention that, because his father's partner, Detective Johnson, was recently killed. He had become a sort of surrogate father to Kyle."

Sullivan was momentarily stunned. "Killed?" he asked, "How? Why?"

"He was murdered. It's a big deal in these parts. From what I know, he was strangled. It's an unsolved homicide." There was silence on both ends of the phone as Sullivan pondered what he had just heard.

"Are you there, Agent Sullivan?"

"Yes," he said quietly. "Thank you for your time, Professor." With that, he hung up.

The next call was also informative. It was only seven in the morning in Little Rock when Agent Pat Hanford's phone rang at this desk. He was an early riser and was sitting at his desk. Usually, his caller ID revealed the incoming number. On this occasion, his screen only displayed a series of ten zeros. It was a private call.

"Good morning, This is Pat," he answered cheerfully.

"Good morning, Pat, this is Carlos Sullivan." The two knew each other. There are fewer than one hundred polygraph examiners in the FBI, and they meet during regional training initiatives, as well as during their annual polygraph conference. They were not friends, but they were part of the polygraph fraternity. The news of Sullivan's situation had traveled like wildfire throughout the Bureau. He paused for a moment before saying anything. Hanford knew he was talking with a fugitive.

"Well, Sully, perhaps not such a good morning for you," he said, arching his eyebrows slightly.

"Yes, it could be better," Sullivan conceded.

"I'm not sure I should be talking to you, Sully," he said seriously.

"You know you will. You're too curious."

"Indeed, indeed," Hanford answered. "How can I help you?"

"This kid, Kyle Grant, my accuser. You tested him, no?"

"Yes, I think so..." Hanford reached into his drawer and pulled out his journal. Most polygraph examiners kept a logbook with a record of each test they conducted. Hanford was no exception.

He leafed through the journal until he found the entry for his test of Kyle Grant.

"Sure, I found it. What about it?"

"Do you remember anything about the test? I know you run a lot of exams, but do you recall anything out of the ordinary?" Sullivan asked hopefully.

"I vaguely remember him," Hanford answered. "He was really kind of plain vanilla."

"OK, thanks anyway," Sullivan said dejectedly.

"Wait, there was one thing," Hanford said. Sullivan listened intently.

"I see in my notes that I wrote he had serious PVCs. I've never seen anything like that. It was like he had a heart condition." Hanford seemed sympathetic.

"All right, that's good. It might help. Thanks."

"Oh, Sully."

"Yes."

"You know I have to report this phone call, right?"

"Yeah, I know. Thanks for your time." Sullivan disconnected the call.

Sullivan knew his next call was fraught with more danger. His pursuers would surely be tracking any of his friends and associates. While unlikely, he was concerned that Conrad's phone might be monitored.

O'Keefe sat at her desk when her phone rang, her caller ID indicating it was coming from a blocked number. She was busy with Conrad's latest tasking, which involved conducting an analysis of Grant's telephone toll records.

"This is Trish."

"Hey, Trish, how are you?" Sullivan said nonchalantly.

She recognized his voice instantly.

"Oh Sully, my god." She gasped. "Let me get Conrad. Hold on."

Sullivan immediately sensed something was amiss. The fifteen seconds it took for Conrad to pick up the line seemed like an eternity.

"Sully—" Conrad began.

"What happened?" Sullivan cut him off.

"I'm sorry to tell you this, Sully, but the bastard killed Lena," Conrad said plainly.

Sullivan said nothing for several seconds. He was numb. His head slumped sharply.

"Sully…are you there?"

The brothers were watching Sullivan. They could tell there was a problem.

Finally, after a moment, he tried to govern his emotions. "How?"

"He beat her and then strangled her." Conrad was direct. He knew Sully would not want it sugarcoated. Trish watched as Conrad rested on her desk, the phone to his ear.

"This changes everything now," Sullivan said, his tone flat.

"I know. We have to finish it now."

"I'm going back to get him." Sullivan was more determined than ever.

"Don't come back here. He's headed to Washington. Word is he got himself on the director's detail. He reports there in two days, September 13."

"Then that's where I'm headed."

For the next several minutes, Sullivan shared the information he had gathered in his earlier calls. When he finished, he turned to the brothers, who were watching him closely.

"Boys, it is going to get bloody after all."

# EIGHT

## Fuller

gents Rogers and Wheeler could see the Boston skyline as they
approached the city from the north. The sky was cloudless and
bright blue. In the rear passenger seat, Isabel shifted uncomfortably.
Conrad, at Fuller's suggestion, directed them to find Isabel and bring
her into the office. While Isabel preferred to speak Spanish, she understood English well. They convinced Isabel that they were there on
Sullivan's behalf. They wanted to clear both of them. After careful
thought, she decided to cooperate.

During their meeting, Fuller suggested that they start developing
actual evidence which could exonerate Sullivan. She would submit
Isabel to a polygraph examination, to directly challenge the underly-
ing premise of the espionage allegations.

For the plan to work, Isabel would have to be brought in secretly.
Fuller's polygraph suite was down the hall from the CP. Agent Warren,
in charge of the operation, had already met her during the search of
her apartment. If he saw Isabel, he would object to their meddling.
ASAC Gibbons would no doubt also feel they were being obstructionist.

As it was, they were all under suspicion for the ongoing harassment
of the agents from HQ.

When the agents pulled into the garage, they explained to Isabel
their plan and reasoning. When they escorted her into the FBI office
on the sixth floor, she was handcuffed and masked. They walked

past Warren, who gave them a puzzled look. Isabel was ushered into Fuller's polygraph suite. Rogers and Wheeler stood guard outside the door.

Almost half an hour later, ASAC Gibbons appeared before them. He had heard the reports of a masked prisoner being escorted through the office. "Who's in there?"

"Fuller is, sir, with a polygraph subject," replied Rogers.

"Who is she testing?" Gibbons asked with suspicion.

"Not sure," Wheeler answered.

Gibbons walked away unsatisfied. He decided he would confront Fuller later.

Meanwhile, Conrad and O'Keefe were watching the test from the observation room. The relevant questions developed by Fuller seemed to be right on point. She reviewed them with Isabel, who sat calmly and listened intently.

1. *Have you committed espionage against the United States?*
2. *Have you conspired with Agent Sullivan to commit espionage?*

Isabel assured Fuller she could truthfully answer no to each question.

After the exam, Fuller took the components off her test subject. She called for Rogers and Wheeler to escort her back home, which they did, in the same manner as they had arrived. This time, nobody noticed them.

Fuller was smiling when she entered the observation room. Conrad and O'Keefe were giddy with anticipation, their arms up, nonverbally screaming "What?"

"Well, Kathy? Cut it out! What's the word?" Conrad could wait no longer.

"She passed with flying colors." She stood, her arms crossed, grinning proudly.

O'Keefe jumped in. "Let's go to management right now! The SAC has to know the truth."

"Not so fast," Fuller answered. "Let's get more evidence, so we can lock this down."

"I think you're right," Conrad responded.

"Didn't you say that the professor knew Grant? If Sully's right, we can send him a picture of our Kyle and see what he says. If it's not Grant, then we have an airtight case," O'Keefe strategized.

"Yes, that occurred to me," Conrad added. "Can you get a picture off our internal directory?"

"I can try," O'Keefe offered.

Conrad volunteered another idea. "Fuller, what about that stuff from Little Rock, that he had these 'PVCs'?"

"If I could get him in my polygraph chair, it might help," Fuller answered.

"How likely is that?" O'Keefe asked, rhetorically.

———

Peter was packing the last of his personal items into a box when he noticed Fuller at his cubicle.

"Can I have a word, Kyle?" Fuller asked nicely.

He considered her request warily. "Sure."

Fuller accompanied him into her polygraph suite, but it now contained no equipment. The table was bare, and the polygraph chair was gone. There were two simple chairs in the room, and they each took one.

"I just wanted to say I'm sorry how this all turned out for you," Fuller said sympathetically.

When he didn't answer, she continued. "I mean, you having to leave here, so suddenly. And the circumstances. I thought you were going to flourish here. I was looking forward to it." Fuller was practically gushing.

Peter shifted in his seat. He was wondering what the purpose of this talk was. Especially since he knew she was Sullivan's partner. He was having second thoughts about agreeing to this conversation. "I know you are a friend of Sullivan's," Peter said to her, looking her right in the eye.

"Kyle, that was before he killed his girlfriend. You don't think I could stand behind him now?" Fuller tried sounding as sincere as possible.

"You don't?" Peter asked.

"Of course not," Fuller said. "Now that he's wanted for murder, it just vindicates everything you alleged."

"I see." Peter seemed to lower his guard. He was starting to hope that any suspicion of him was now a thing of the past.

Just at that moment, there was a knock on the door.

"Come in," Fuller said.

At the door was Gloria Beckwith. She was a twenty-two-year-old support employee, assigned to the mailroom. She was holding a box in her arms.

"This came for you. It's from HQ," she said helpfully, placing it on the table.

"Thank you, Gloria," Fuller said, smiling.

As she left, Fuller stood up and started peeling open the box. Peter scrolled through his Blackberry. Fuller looked into the box and started pulling polygraph components out of it.

"It's my new polygraph equipment."

Peter stood to leave. "I'll let you get back to work."

"Actually, Kyle," Fuller asked, "would you help me out? I'd like to check and make sure the components are all working."

Peter did not flinch. "I don't think so."

"It won't take long, just a few minutes."

"No." Peter was unwavering as he moved toward the door.

"It's harmless," she pleaded.

Without another word, Peter walked out door and back to his cubicle. He knew the entire scenario was a trap. He grabbed his belongings and briefly stopped by Becky's desk to kiss her good-bye. Peter then walked out the door, slamming it behind him. He looked back at the office as he crossed the street. He knew he would never be back in Boston again.

In the polygraph observation room, Conrad and O'Keefe had watched the show with amusement. They had both told Fuller her plan had zero chance of working. She insisted on trying. They were now proved right.

Fuller walked into the room. "At least I tried," she said, frustrated.

"I was about to puke," Conrad said.

O'Keefe stood up abruptly. "Now it's my turn at bat," she said.

# NINE

## The Gaslight Rendezvous

The impending demise of summer meant that Boston got darker with each passing day. It was only seven, but already the streets seemed eerily still and gray. Conrad watched the street from his corner table at the Gaslight Grill, only a few blocks from his apartment in the South End. The Gaslight bar was filled with young professionals enjoying a nightcap after work. The restaurant section was also bustling with patrons, mostly young couples. It was at the Gaslight that Conrad first took O'Keefe on a date. He liked the Gaslight's discreet location far from the FBI office. Conrad looked up from his menu occasionally, watching the door for O'Keefe. He had told her in coded language to meet him there. Since the incident with Sullivan, they had become increasingly paranoid that they were under observation.

Conrad was relieved when she finally arrived and took a seat across from him, her face flushed.

"You know I like this place, Jimmy," she said, "but parking isn't so easy."

"I was getting worried." He looked at his watch.

She ignored his implication that she was late. "I could use a drink."

"I've already ordered your favorite."

"I thought you would." As she looked at him, Conrad could tell that she was nervous. He reached across and held her hand.

"Jimmy, I'm worried how this is all going to play out. You know I love Sully, but I have to worry about my job, you know—"

"I know." He cut her off in midsentence. "It's all going to work out, I'm certain of it." He tried his best to reassure her. She nodded, appearing to relax a bit.

A young waitress appeared, seemingly out of nowhere. She had her black hair tied up in a ponytail. She wore a white polo shirt with the Gaslight logo.

"Hey there, Conrad, good to have you back," she said as she placed O'Keefe's drink in front of her.

"Hello, Nancy."

O'Keefe wasn't surprised. She knew he was a regular at the Gaslight. They ordered their food, and Nancy was gone as quickly as she had arrived. Apparently she could tell they wanted privacy.

"So Trish, what have you learned?"

"Well, Kyle is registered at the Standard. It's a new boutique hotel about three blocks from headquarters in Washington. I googled the place, and it's a refurbished historic property. Small, only three floors. He checked in yesterday. Today was his first day on the director's detail."

"What room is he staying in?"

"You are joking, right?" She looked exasperated.

"Yeah, yeah…just kidding."

"OK then." She sipped her drink. "I can also tell you his phone is active. He hasn't seemed to stray far from the hotel since checking in. Or"—She paused—"I should say his phone hasn't left the hotel. He has kept it on continuously."

"Yeah, that asshole only turned it off when he went to kill Lena." Conrad looked more angry than disgusted.

As they talked, Conrad caught sight of a vehicle parked across the street. It was a late-model Ford, and its windows were tinted. Although he could not see inside, at one point through the darkness he glimpsed a light briefly shining from inside the car. He instantly realized it must have been a phone or other electronic device emitting light. Someone was inside the car.

During a break in their conversation, Conrad excused himself to use the restroom. As he walked away, O'Keefe noticed him reaching for his cell phone.

Conrad returned in short order.

O'Keefe seemed more serious than ever. "Jimmy, you're going to think I'm crazy, but I have a feeling we're being watched at work." Her eyes widened slightly.

"It's not crazy at all." He paused briefly as he looked out the window. "They no doubt think we can lead them to Sully. So they will be watching us."

"I heard Becky had a meeting in the office with some representatives from the phone company. I think they are trying to tap into our extensions."

"Can they do that?"

"It's not that easy. Our extensions are part of one trunk line. To eavesdrop on a call made directly to our extension, say from an outside caller, can only be done from the switch in our office." O'Keefe always got animated when talking about any telephone issue.

"Have they done it?" Conrad continued looking at the suspicious car outside.

"I'm not sure; I'm scared they will see me at the switch box. It's the only way to know for sure." Trish bit her lip slightly, which she always did when nervous.

Conrad gave her a look of reassurance. "It doesn't matter, Trish. Just assume the lines are tapped. We will never use them to contact Sully again. I've already worked that out."

Nancy arrived, a plate in each hand. She smiled. "Here you go, guys. Let me know if you need anything else!"

After she left, O'Keefe leaned closer to Conrad. They were getting more intimate. Conrad sensed an opportunity.

"So Trish, what exactly did you do for the Pentagon?" He looked up at her hopefully.

"Nice try." She half smiled. O'Keefe then tried switching the subject.

"Jimmy," she asked, "what really happened to Sully in that bank?"

Conrad's face turned red. He lost some of his composure. He was not so much mad as he was embarrassed.

"I'm not sure, Trish; he's never discussed it with me."

She had always wondered why the bank employees had refused to give a statement. Yet she detected that it was a sore subject for him, so she dropped the issue.

As the couple ate their meals, Agent Warren was watching them with a small pair of binoculars. The agents in the rear seat were aiming a parabolic antenna toward the diners, hoping to pick up their conversation.

Warren was flustered. "I can't pick up what they are saying, there's too much ambient noise in there!"

His partner seemed to sympathize. "I wish I could read lips."

When they finished their meals, Conrad uncharacteristically pulled out his cell phone and sent a text message. O'Keefe knew that Conrad had a rule about not texting during their dates. She watched him with curiosity.

As Conrad paid the check, a Boston police cruiser pulled in behind the suspicious Ford and turned on its blue light. Two officers emerged from the cruiser, tapping loudly on the driver's side window.

"Boston Police, license and registration please," one of the officers bellowed.

Warren lowered the window and flashed his credentials. "FBI."

"FBI?" the officer answered sarcastically. "So what? License and registration!"

"I'm not even driving, I'm parked."

"First of all, FBI, your keys are in the ignition. So, technically you are considered to be driving. Have you been drinking?" The officer was quizzing Warren, clearly enjoying the scenario. "Second, if you were actually parked, you are 'parked' more than twelve inches from the curb."

As the officers hassled the frazzled agents, Conrad and O'Keefe, arm in arm, walked out of the Gaslight and crossed the street, in plain sight of the harried surveillance team. They shook their heads as

Conrad smiled right at them. As they walked away, they could still hear the officers berating Warren.

"This is the city of Boston. We have laws here, Mr. FBI..." His voice trailed off as they got farther away.

"You are something else, Jimmy." O'Keefe beamed.

They disappeared in the dark streets of the city.

# TEN

## Alexandra

The international corporate headquarters of Xion Corporation was located on the outskirts of the city of Wilmington, Delaware. The large glass-and-steel structure was built on the banks of the Delaware River. Xion, one of the largest pharmaceutical companies in the United States, was important to the Delaware economy, given its status as one of the largest employers in the state.

From her riverfront office on the fifth floor, Alexandra Wallace leaned back in her chair and stared at her phone, expecting it to ring at any moment. In only two short years, Alexandra had become one of Xion's best saleswomen. She was a superstar. A week earlier, Benjamin Steel, the deputy sales director for the western region had approached her in the hallway. She was going over the incident in her head.

"Ms. Wallace, please come with me," He had instructed her.

As she sat in his office, she puzzled over what seemed to be the problem.

"We have recently been audited by the DEA," Steel began. "It seems that one of your clients out west has drawn their scrutiny. As you know, the DEA is responsible for policing controlled substances."

"Which client drew their interest?" she asked, already knowing full well the answer.

"Benton County Veterinary & Relief Corporation of Benton County, Arkansas. It is one of your biggest clients."

"What is their concern?" Alexandra asked quietly.

"Your sales of Phoenixium. They claimed it seems like a lot for only one client." Steel looked at her, attempting to discern any concern on her part, and saw none.

"It's perfectly legitimate," she answered confidently.

"That's what I told them. But one of their investigators wants to talk to you anyway. I told them you would be available next Friday at one o'clock." He lifted his hand and pointed to the door. It was her cue to leave.

As Alexandra recalled the meeting, she went over everything in her mind one more time, as Father had instructed her since child-hood. He insisted that there was no substitute for preparation. At one o'clock exactly, her phone rang.

"I will be right down to get her, Sally, thank you," Alexandra told the receptionist.

Agent Beatrice Simmons was a veteran and dogged investigator. She was top of her graduating class at Howard University, and was the most senior woman in her department at the DEA. She was dressed in a conservative gray suit, with black heels. Simmons glanced around the office as she took her seat in front of Alexandra. She noticed that there were no personal photos or items on display.

"Ms. Wallace," she started, "as you know, I'm here about your large sales volume of Carfentanil to one company—the Benton County Veterinary & Relief Corporation."

"We sell it under the name 'Phoenixium,' Ms. Simmons. What exactly is your concern?" Alexandra asked innocently.

"Yes, I know what you call it here at Xion. Other companies use other names, obviously. The concern is that we track these sales, and this particular drug is very powerful. No other veterinary firm in the country, that we can detect, has purchased so much in the last two years." Simmons gave her a grave look.

Alexandra placed her folder on the table before them. It was labeled "BCV & RC."

"Ms. Simmons, as you can see from my paperwork, this is a legiti-mate client. Their operating license has been reviewed and confirmed.

I have personally visited the ranch in Arkansas where they operate. I have a professional and direct relationship with their director of operations, John Wellington." Alexandra was calm and deliberate, just as she had practiced.

"Why do they need so much Carfentanil?"

"Phoenixium," Alexandra corrected her. Simmons said nothing and waited for an answer.

"You may not be aware, but the western part of this country has a problem with wild horses."

Simmons arched an eyebrow, more in interest than skepticism.

"There are too many wild horses. They have no natural enemies. Fewer ranches mean fewer horses are needed, so they are not domesticated. More wild horses results in more competition for scarce food resources, which means many of these animals are dying of starvation. It's a disaster. Many environmental groups, in conjunction with state and local governments, have herded the animals."

"Please continue."

"Well, the BCV & RC is one of the few facilities with the resources capable of putting these horses down. They are paid only a nominal fee by these groups for the work they do. In fact, it is considered a charity. We sell the Phoenixium at a discount. Our legal department is actually trying to see if we can claim a write-off as a charitable expense."

"I see," Simmons said.

"So you see, they need Phoenixium so the horses can be putdown humanely." Alexandra wanted to end strongly. She opened the folder and pulled out a series of photos. She displayed them for Simmons. One was a picture of the BCV & RC ranch and its beaming Director Wellington. Another showed a picture of Alexandra on a horse at the ranch. Still another showed a veterinary doctor in a lab coat, injecting a resting horse. Simmons could never have imagined that all the photos were staged. There was no BCV & RC.

Simmons stood to leave. "Very well, Ms. Wallace. I will file a conclusive report very soon. Thank you for your time."

After she was gone, Alexandra went back to her office and closed the door. She was expecting her phone to ring again.

At exactly two o'clock, Alexandra picked up the phone on the first ring. Now that the operation was in its final stages, Tim Wallace knew the use of telephones was necessary.

"Father," Alexandra said, smiling.

"Alexa, it is good to hear your voice."

"Yours as well, Father."

"I've just received your last shipment. I believe this will be all that is needed."

"Understood."

"Any problems on your end?" Tim had carefully read Alexandra's message about the audit and the scheduled meeting.

"None," she replied proudly. "How are you and Mother?"

"We are both well and excited to see you soon, Alexa."

"Me too, Father"

After she hung up the phone, she retrieved the BCV & RC folder and destroyed every document and photo in the shredder. She packed a few personal items in anticipation of her permanent departure from Xion.

———

Twenty-five hundred miles away, Kyle Grant lay on the ground of his cell, exhausted, breathing in the shallow way to which he had become accustomed. Over the previous months, he had overheard his captors enough to know that one was named Bill, and his leader was Tim. He recognized their voices as they spoke from outside his cell. Recently, he felt he had been having hallucinations. In some of them, he was visited by a ghostly apparition of Tina.

Through a slit in one of the walls, Kyle had watched his jailers kill a horse in the same hideous way he had seen them kill numerous other animals. He had become deadened to the scene. After they tied the horse to their truck and dragged it away, they returned, walking near his cell. Throughout it all, Kyle was unsure if it was a hallucination, a horrible dream, or some evil reality.

Kyle's pale skin sagged from his drastic loss of weight. His back was grievously scabbed from the large and numerous insect bites. He listened intently as they pondered his fate.

"We leave tomorrow," Tim stated.

"Do you want me to be done with him?" Bill asked in a matter-of-fact manner.

"He's starving. I think it's interesting. I've never seen anyone starve to death," Tim responded.

"So what do you want me to do?" Bill asked again.

"Give him half rations for the time we're gone. Let's see how it plays out."

Even in his weakened condition, the remarks left Kyle stunned. It confirmed that his fate was sealed. He lay back and stared at the ceiling. He was too dehydrated to cry.

# ELEVEN

## The Standard

The Standard hotel was listed in Washington's historic registry, having been built shortly after the Civil War. Sandwiched between the National Museum of Crime & Punishment and the International Spy Museum, Peter found it quite an ironic retreat for him. The hotel was best known for its central courtyard, where many Washingtonians and their visitors would while away the evening. The service was exceptional, the drinks expensive. This did not concern Peter, who did not drink. He was taught as a young boy at the Fortress that drinking clouded judgment. He needed to keep a clear mind, now that his mission was nearing its conclusion. As he walked toward the hotel, Peter could not help but consider the fact that in a few days, he would certainly either be dead or in prison. He knew it was necessary. The mission was more important than any one person, including himself.

Peter, dressed in a crisp blue suit with a red tie, crossed the street toward the hotel entrance. Across the street, Sullivan watched him from the brothers' van. Jorge noticed that as Sullivan watched Peter, he clenched his fist tightly. He looked at his brother, anticipating that they might have to restrain Sullivan if he became unable to govern his anger.

"That's him." Sullivan pointed at Peter on the sidewalk.

"OK," replied Jorge.

"Go!" Sullivan ordered.

Miguel opened the sliding door, allowing Jorge to get out of the van and cross the street. Moments after Peter entered the lobby, Jorge followed. As he entered the hotel, Jorge scanned the area quickly, observing that Peter had stopped to talk to one of the employees working the desk. Jorge moved toward a small table with a house phone and pretended to make a call, all the while watching Peter.

Once Peter finished at the desk, he stopped at the elevators and pushed the button. Jorge followed suit. The door opened and Peter entered first, followed by Jorge. There were only three floors, and Peter pressed 3. Jorge leaned back, his hands clasped behind his back. Peter looked at Jorge sharply, observing him closely. He started by scanning Jorge's running shoes and moved up to his thick black hair. Peter made no attempt to conceal his scrutiny of his elevator mate. Jorge seemed completely still, not appearing to even blink.

When the elevator stopped on the third floor, Peter used his hand to signal Jorge to get out first. Jorge hesitated but had no choice.

"OK, thank you," Jorge said faintly.

As he got out of the elevator, he had the choice to go left or right down the hallway—a fifty-fifty gamble. He chose right. He could hear Peter in his dress shoes walking behind him. The floors were tiled, not carpeted.

Jorge walked down the hallway slowly, listening intently. Finally, he heard Peter stop and slip the key card into the door. He turned back in time to see a door close. He turned back down the hallway to see the room number: 313. He took note of the number from an angle such that Peter could not see him through the peephole. Rather than cross in front of the door, Jorge decided to walk to the end of the hallway and take the stairs. He did not notice that Peter had quietly opened his door, looked down the hallway, and noticed him approaching the stairwell.

Jorge returned to the van and with Miguel at the wheel, they drove off. Sullivan did not have to ask, Jorge was ready.

"Numero 313. It's on the right side of floor three. The room is side with view out…toward street."

"Maids?" asked Sullivan.

"No maids."

"I guessed not. They're usually working in the morning." Sullivan thought about his options.

———

Early the next morning, Sullivan and his team were back on the street, across from the Standard, waiting for Peter to emerge from the hotel. Miguel was at the wheel once again, Jorge in the passenger seat. Sullivan sat in the back, wearing dress pants, a white shirt, and a tie, which he'd bought the night before.

As they waited, Miguel spoke. "What the plan?" he asked in his heavy accent. The team had rehearsed their operation, including worst-case scenarios. Still, Sullivan never mentioned what his ultimate goal was. Miguel was curious.

"I need to learn what this is all about." Sullivan watched the entrance intently as he continued. "Maybe if I can get in—"

Jorge cut him off, pointing to the hotel. "Look, he there." Sullivan had made the same observation.

They watched Peter cross the street and turn the corner out of sight. Sullivan got out. Before closing the door, he displayed his cell phone to them. They knew what that meant. Sullivan walked across the street and entered the hotel. After he entered, Miguel moved the van a block away, on the opposite corner but still within view of the hotel. Out of habit, and as rehearsed, Miguel positioned the vehicle for the quickest exit in an emergency.

By then, Sullivan was already on the third floor. He spied room 313 and noticed a maid working in room 316, across the hall and down one room. He gently tapped on that door, calling to the maid. He smiled as the young woman approached the door, and he noticed her name tag: Iris.

"Senorita," he said nicely. "I left my key in the room. Could you please help me?"

She scrutinized him for a moment. As she decided what to do, Sullivan turned on his charm.

"De donde eres?" he asked her politely.

"El Salvador."

"San Salvador?" he asked. "I was there recently." He then spoke to her for a minute or so in Spanish. As he talked to her, he moved toward the hallway, as if willing her toward room 313.

She followed him out, and he pointed to room 313. After she let him in, he looked back at her and smiled again. "Gracias, Iris."

He quickly closed the door and started looking about the room.

Outside the hotel, the brothers heard the screeching sound of tires. Several large SUVs swung around the corner and stopped exactly where they had been parked previously. They boxed in a nonexistent vehicle. A large force of FBI SWAT members started pouring out of the SUVs. Before they could scan the surrounding area for the missing van, Miguel had swung down a side street, gunning the engine. One of the agents managed to fire a volley of rounds at the van, striking several bullets into the side of the vehicle before it disappeared around a corner. The SWAT team focused on the hotel, where they hoped to snare their main target.

Simultaneously, Jorge dialed Sullivan, who picked up on the first ring.

"Get out!" Jorge yelled into the phone.

Sullivan looked around the room one last time and noticed an envelope with the name SULLIVAN written across it. He picked it up and put it in his pocket. He knew he had only precious seconds.

The SWAT team stormed the hotel yelling for anyone in their path to get out of the way. One team took the elevators, two others split off in opposite directions, each taking a stairwell up to the third floor.

Sullivan ran into the hallway. The large service cart was outside of room 316. That door was still open. He took the cart and pushed it into the room, as Iris looked at him, astonished and scared. He closed the door behind him.

"No te preocupes," he reassured her, holding a finger to his lips. "Nothing will happen to you."

He looked at her sternly. "Sit!" She sat on the bed, a tear welling up in her eye.

Sullivan opened the curtains and looked out the window to the courtyard below. On more than one occasion, he had enjoyed warm summer nights with friends on that patio while visiting headquarters. He had actually stayed at the Standard on two occasions. He observed that the windows were sealed and could not be opened.

He looked about the room for a tool. The bedside lamp was about five feet tall and made of metal. He removed the lampshade and felt the large metal base of the lamp. Without hesitation, he swung the base at the window and cracked it on first impact. The second swing broke the rest, the glass raining down to the ground below. Seconds later, the SWAT team was entering room 313. Sullivan deduced that they used Peter's room key, given the lack of noise upon entry. All he could hear was the sound of the agents calling out commands.

"FBI! Come out, Sullivan!" One of them yelled, assuming he was under the bed or in the bathroom.

As they quickly cleared room 313, Sullivan was tying the bed's sheets and blanket together. He pushed the cart against the window and tied one end of his makeshift rope to it. The other, he threw out the window. Iris looked at him as if he was a crazy man.

"I'm sorry," Sullivan said to her as he climbed out the window.

He was able to scramble down about half the distance to the ground and jumped to the patio floor. He knew from previous visits that the courtyard was required to have emergency exits, given the number of people that it could hold. As he looked for one, he looked up to room 316. Iris must have bolted immediately, because two SWAT team members were peering out the window, pointing at him.

"Sullivan, stop right there!"

In an instant, Sullivan turned and ran to one corner of the courtyard, where he saw an Exit sign. He pushed open the emergency door and was on the street. He ran toward the Gallery Place Metro station, only about a block away.

The radio call had gone out. All units were on the street, and several agents had seen Sullivan running. They were close on his heels. However, the agents were weighed down by their bulletproof vests, weapons, and equipment. Sullivan was unencumbered and could easily outpace them. When he reached the Metro escalator, he pushed several people out of the way as he descended as quickly as possible. Morning commuters were surfacing in the opposite direction, creating another obstacle to the pursuing agents.

The agents descended the Metro like a herd of bulls with commuters, some screaming, scrambling to get out of the way. The agents assumed he was getting on a train, as one was approaching when they got to the station. However, Sullivan knew that the Gallery Place Metro Station had another entrance in Chinatown, two blocks from where he had entered. Rather than go to the platform, he ran straight to the other exit, running up the escalator as fast as possible. The pursuing agents never saw him go up. They ran to the platform, yelling for everyone to get on the ground. They forced the conductor to shut down the train as they searched, car by car. As the agents started their painstaking train search, Sullivan emerged on the surface, free.

Two blocks away, back at the Standard, Agent Warren was scolding the SWAT team leader. Peter was at Warren's side but said nothing.

"How could you let him get away?" Warren yelled. He continued a stream of profanities until the SWAT leader simply turned his back on him and started walking away.

"What do you have to say to me?",Warren screamed, walking behind the agent.

"Fuck you," the agent muttered in disgust.

—

The strong current on the Potomac River had churned up mud from its banks, giving it a gray color. The afternoon sun was blocked by large dark clouds, and the scent in the air hinted of an approaching rainstorm. Sullivan, pensive, stood on the Virginia side of the riverbank, his arms crossed. A plane flew low over his head, its landing gear down, preparing for a landing at Reagan National Airport. He looked up at the plane, then back to the van, then again across the river to Washington. He pulled out the envelope he had retrieved from the room, opening it slowly. Inside was a piece of paper, with a single word scribbled on it: "Gotcha." He crumpled it up and held it tight in his fist.

Inside the van, Jorge and Miguel watched him silently. After they picked up Sullivan at their predesignated emergency rendezvous point, he had said nothing to them. Not a word. They felt that somehow they had let him down. Jorge got out of the van as Sullivan approached them.

"Sully, I'm sorry, he must have made me—"

"Don't worry, my friend, it doesn't matter." Sullivan cut him off and put a hand on his shoulder.

"It was a risky plan anyway. We got lucky they were poorly prepared," Sullivan said to them.

"It was no luck that I moved the van," Miguel said proudly.

"Yes, Miguel, but they caught us by surprise. That can't happen again."

The brothers noticed that Sullivan appeared serene and resolute as he scanned the horizon. They knew Sullivan would not stop until his mission was complete.

# PART III

# ONE

## The Meeting and Mission

**K**athy Wallace sat at the kitchen table, processing what she was hearing. "What do you mean your whole family is coming over here in the morning?"

"Yes, and I will need you to clear out by eight." Michael stood over her with a serious look.

"Clear out? What does that mean? I haven't seen your folks since our wedding." Kathy was flustered.

"I'm sorry, but it's family business. You can't be here." His tone gave her no hint of flexibility. He walked into the living room and turned on the TV.

After he was out of her sight, Kathy sobbed quietly, her hands covering her reddened face. Michael never bothered to check in on her again.

⌣

The morning of September 19 seemed like any other Saturday morning in Northern Virginia. It was cloudless, bright, and quiet. Most Northern Virginians were sleeping in, or enjoying their breakfasts over coffee as they read their morning copy of the *Washington Post*. Some young families were preparing to take their children to their soccer or lacrosse games. One family, two doors down from Michael's residence, was loading their kid's equipment into the rear of their SUV. They never noticed the silver rental van that passed by their home and pulled up to the Wallace residence, carefully backing into the driveway so that the license plate could not be seen from the street.

Tim Wallace opened the door to the SUV, stepped out of the vehicle, and walked to the sidewalk, scanning the area. Bill and Susan stayed in the vehicle until he signaled them that it was safe to exit. They walked up the steps and knocked on the door.

Michael was watching from his front window, having spent the last hour watching the street, looking for any suspicious vehicles. The family was of the consensus that they were not under surveillance of any kind, but they knew to take all security measures nonetheless. He was waiting at the door, opening it before Father could rap on it a second time. Michael ushered them in quickly, closing the door as soon as they entered. Once the door was closed, they all embraced.

"Kathy?" Tim asked his son.

"She's not here, of course, Father."

"You know what has to happen, son…when the moment comes."

Michael was almost offended that his Father felt the need to lecture him, but he knew that he was only being overly cautious. He knew nothing could be left to chance.

"Yes, of course, Father, I will take care of her when the time is right."

His mother was watching her beloved son, beaming. "Let's sit and wait for the others."

As they sat in the living room, Bill started unpacking the duffel bag he held in his hand. As previously requested, Michael pulled out two large corkboards from a closet. Bill and Tim started pinning photos they had brought onto the boards in preparation for their presentation.

One by one, the children arrived at the residence, after first conducting their SDR, known as a surveillance detection run. It consisted of watching their rearview mirror as they drove down side streets, occasionally pulling over, watching to see if any vehicles were following. If they were on a highway, they pulled over in the emergency lane for a minute or two. They knew from their studies and training that it was almost impossible for a surveillance team to react to these techniques without revealing themselves. They also looked to the sky, attempting to detect if there was any aerial surveillance deployed against them. They saw nothing.

Alexandra arrived first. As her father had done, she also positioned her car so that the license plate could not be seen by passersby. She was wearing light-colored blue jeans and a dark-blue sweatshirt. She practically jogged up the stairs, eager to see her family after so much time away.

Ryan was next. In his hand he carried a black garment bag. He also was happy to see his family. He was also excited to see how their long-anticipated operation was to unfold.

Samantha circled around the residence twice before she eventually parked her car, a black two-door Nissan, in a similar manner. She was never as sentimental as her siblings. Her anticipation centered upon seeing their mission to completion. She knew that was now imminent.

They awaited Peter's arrival with concern. Tim and Susan had briefed the others on the events surrounding Peter's transfer to Washington and the position that he had been targeting all along. Despite Peter's apparent success, Michael expressed grave concern when he heard all the details.

"With this Sullivan character in the wind, we are at risk," Michael said sternly.

Because he was a man of few words, the others were impacted by his statement.

Michael continued. "Once Peter's deception is discovered, our entire house of cards will come tumbling down."

Father interjected, "Yes, I share your concern, Michael. That is why we are accelerating our plans. Our mission is at hand. It will be too late by the time they learn what happened."

Susan stood up, as if to stop the conversation. She did not like them talking about Peter in a negative light.

"We will all give our briefings *after* Peter arrives." She sat back down.

They took their cue and stopped their discussion. They turned to personal matters. Ryan and Michael took this as an opportunity to reconnect. Similarly, sisters Alexandra and Samantha shared stories of their lives since leaving the Fortress.

Miles away, Peter was exercising extreme caution. Since his near capture of Sullivan, he had obsessively checked his movements, which under other circumstances might be considered paranoia. In this case, it was prudent.

Five hundred miles away in Boston, as O'Keefe hunched over her monitor, Conrad sat a few feet away. She was tracing Kyle's phone on a real-time basis. His cell phone's location was vectored to within approximately twenty yards at any given moment. She would read out a location, and Conrad would relay the directions to Sullivan, who was following Peter with the brothers. He was careful to stay far enough back that Kyle could not see him. Occasionally, the signal stopped abruptly, often for as long as five minutes. Sullivan surmised that Kyle was engaging in an SDR.

Peter felt something was wrong. He should have already arrived at Michael's home, but he was reluctant to finally get there for fear of compromising the mission. In the back of his mind, he wondered if Sullivan had found some way to trace his movements. He certainly knew that Sullivan had allies, especially in the Boston office. He also knew enough about Conrad to not take anything for granted. He sat in the drivers' seat of his gray Chevrolet Impala. Peter looked in the rearview mirror pensively, deciding what to do. He was new to the director's detail, and he could still hear his supervisor's direct order ringing in his ears. Supervisory Special Agent (SSA) Thomas Diamond, in charge of the director's security detail, was a serious man with a SWAT background and twenty-five years of experience. Peter correctly assessed him to be an intimidating man. He played the order out in his mind once more.

"Never... *never* be out of contact. I have to be able to reach you at any moment. Whenever the director needs to go somewhere, we need to be available." Diamond's order was unequivocal.

As he looked about one last time, he grabbed his phone and turned it off.

O'Keefe's jaw dropped when she noticed she lost the signal. "He shut if off!" she yelled.

Conrad slumped visibly. "Sully, he turned it off."

Conrad did not expect Sullivan's response on the other end.

"No problem. He's only two blocks away. I will find him."

———

Peter's arrival was greeted with unbridled relief. They had been waiting nervously, and as was his custom, Father had assumed the worst. In fact, Peter had not called to relay his delay for the simple reason that he was too focused on his SDR. He wanted to take every precaution to protect the mission. His last act—disobeying a direct order from his new supervisor—could possibly jeopardize his new position, but it was a risk he knew was necessary. He could sense Sullivan's reach.

Peter's worries evaporated instantly once he saw his family. All the stress of living a double life for a year was now lifted from his shoulders. He could finally be and act like himself. Just hearing his family call him Peter had a soothing effect on him. He hugged all of them affectionately.

Once they exchanged pleasantries, their work began in earnest. Through his body language, Tim indicated their meeting was to begin. Bill reached into his bag and passed them each their operational cell phones.

"These are safe and untraceable. They are to be used only to coordinate our mission among ourselves. They are not to be used for any other purpose." As Bill spoke, he turned to see Tim watching from behind, approvingly.

Tim stood before the group. "First, each of you will brief us on your status, and then I will lay out how the mission will proceed. This is your final briefing."

———

Once Sullivan heard that Kyle's phone was turned off, he surmised that he must be close to his final destination. He was prepared. Utilizing a map book, he began a grid search of the area, ordering Jorge to drive in ever expanding concentric circles from where the signal was lost. As they drove, Sullivan scrutinized each home as they passed by. After about twenty minutes, Sullivan spotted his best prospect.

"That's it," Sullivan said. As he said it, he could feel the van slowing down.

"Don't stop. Keep going."

"OK." Jorge sped up.

"Circle around the block."

Without any further instruction, Jorge drove around the block and positioned the van a block from their targeted residence: 18 Webster Street. By the time he parked, Sullivan was looking down at the residence through his binoculars.

Miguel made a simple observation. "I see, Sully, from the cars…the way they are parked."

"Yes, Miguel." Sullivan was frustrated. He quickly realized none of the vehicles' license plates was visible from the street. He made notations of the makes and models, occasionally glancing at the front window, but saw no movements. He reached for his phone. He knew Conrad would be anxious for an update. The phone rang only once.

"Did you find him?"

"Yes, I need your girl to give me a full workup on 18 Webster Street, Arlington, Virginia."

"No problem." Conrad hung up and turned to Trish.

Sullivan scanned the residence again with his binoculars. He then placed them on the floor and looked at the brothers.

Jorge sensed an opening to ask a question. "Sully, how is possible that they want you in prison? Those are your people?" He was genuinely perplexed.

Sullivan leaned back and thought of Lena. She always had a smart Russian saying for every occasion. He could picture her smiling, quoting one of her favorites. "Jorge, there is an Old Russian proverb. 'Never say never to jail or poverty.'"

The brothers looked at each other. Jorge shrugged. Miguel smiled. Sullivan reminisced.

"Settle in boys, we will be here for a while."

———

"Samantha," Tim called out. "Let's start with you."

Samantha leaned back slightly in her chair and crossed her legs. Her hair lay across her shoulder, and she tossed it back. They all knew that Samantha loved drama and being the center of attention.

"Well, the Secret Service has a rule that special agents need at least five years of field experience before being assigned to a protective detail, especially numbers one and two." They understood she was referring to the president and vice president.

Her smile also told everyone that she had found a way around the rule. She always seemed to get her way.

Ryan jumped in. "But…" He gestured, questioningly.

"But Deputy Assistant Director Jonathan Hughes seems to think that I have potential beyond my experience level. He arranged for me to get a waiver. I'm working on the vice president's protective detail. His Secret Service code name is 'Cowboy.'"

Father beamed proudly. "Go on."

"The president and the vice president only have one scheduled meeting per month. When that happens, I *may* be in a position to take them both out. Otherwise, I can definitely eliminate Cowboy at any time during my shift. If he is the only target, Father, then I can even probably escape. If both are the target, then I will be killed or captured." Her statement was flat and emotionless.

Tim ignored her implied question and turned to Ryan. Father pointed at him.

"I am now a sergeant with the Capitol Police. I am trusted and have full access to the Capitol building, where Congress meets, as well as the Hart building, which houses some of the senators' offices. At your request, Father, I have familiarized myself with the ventilation system within the building." He reached into a notepad and retrieved a series of diagrams and schematics. He passed them to Bill, who pinned them on one of the corkboards against the wall. "With my access, I can sneak anybody in that you want. No problem."

"The canisters?" Father asked.

"I can allow your van to pass through. The people under my watch trust me completely. I can even have one of my subordinates let you in."

"Excellent," Tim exclaimed. He then pointed to Alexa.

She leaned forward, excited that their plan seemed to be on track. "I've arranged for you to have the gas you needed. I have destroyed any evidence related to the sale and delivery of the poison. I'm ready and excited, Father, for my next role."

"Very well," Tim answered. He then pointed to Michael.

"I'm a captain in the US Army. Much like my dear sister Samantha, I've earned the trust of a powerful mentor, Col. Gustave Armstrong. Through this connection, I've been assigned as an aide within the Joints Chief of Staff. I have full access in the Pentagon. I also have diagrams," he stated as he handed those over to Bill. As before, Bill placed the diagrams on the corkboard for all to study. Susan continued taking notes.

"Continue," Tim commanded.

"The JCS usually convenes an official meeting only once a month, unless a threat surfaces. Then they convene an emergency meeting. I can place one of your canisters in the JCS command center discreetly. Or I can take them all out with my weapons. The latter would put me at greater risk, meaning I would be killed or captured, the same as Sam. I leave the decision to you, Father, of course."

"What about their ventilation system?"

"The building is so massive; there is no central ventilation system. There are several dispersed throughout the Pentagon." Michael replied calmly. He had done his homework.

"Very well," Tim said with a hint of disappointment.

All eyes now turned to Peter. While Peter was proud of his accomplishments, Father was not so pleased.

"Peter, please explain the drama you are involved in," he said sarcastically.

"I have achieved my objective, Father," he said defensively, looking about the room for any sign of support.

"And this woman you killed?" Tim arched an eyebrow disapprovingly.

"It was necessary to further my scheme and guarantee my reassignment to Washington." He was unwavering.

"It made the situation personal, no?" Tim countered.

"It was unavoidable." As he looked about the room, he noticed his brothers were looking down at the floor.

"Perhaps, if you hadn't attracted unwanted attention from this Agent Sullivan—"

Peter cut him off. "It's a done deal; I can't change the past, Father."

Samantha rose to defend her brother. "Father, how was this any different from Agent Livingstone? People are not always predictable. Things happen."

"Perhaps. He is correct that it is now history," he conceded. "Now, Peter, continue."

"I have been assigned to the FBI director's security detail. He meets with the president once a week. However, once he is in the White House, security falls back to the Secret Service." He looked at Sam, smiled, and continued. "However, he does meet weekly with the attorney general as well. The AG works across the street from FBIHQ and has his own FBI security detail. During these meetings, I will be in a position to kill them both. If the director is the only target, I can kill him at any time inside the Hoover building. I can also probably kill his top deputies at the same time. As with Sam and Michael, the more targets selected, the greater the likelihood of my being killed or captured."

Peter then handed Bill a diagram of the director's office and conference room area. Bill placed the diagrams on another corkboard.

The children were anxious to hear the exact details of how their combined pieces were to be placed for the mission. Michael spoke for the other children.

"Father, how will the mission play out?"

———

One hour had elapsed, and Conrad's phone was vibrating. He answered without any exchange of pleasantries. "What have you got?"

"I'm gonna put Trish on the line. She found something interesting."

Trish had worked feverishly since obtaining the address Sullivan was watching.

"Sully, the house belongs to a Michael and Kathy Wallace. No prior record. In fact, he is listed as a veteran, US Army. Some clever Internet searching, and I learned he attended George Mason University."

"So what's so interesting?" he asked, frustrated.

"I did an off-line NCIC search."

Sullivan knew that only an experienced analyst would know to conduct such a search. In essence, it a reverse search. It is a way to determine if anyone has conducted a search in the database of a particular name or license plate, among other items.

"Yes, Trish, tell me something good," he said hopefully.

"It turns out that two weeks ago, Special Agent John O'Neil, US Secret Service, ran a criminal history check on Mr. Wallace." Trish was grinning from ear to ear. Conrad was listening by her side.

"That *is* interesting."

"I know how you don't believe in coincidences, Sully."

"No, I don't, Trish. Something is up. What do you have on this O'Neil?"

"I looked him up. He's an SSA assigned to their Washington office." She looked to Conrad and passed him the phone.

"Sully, it's me. I know what you're thinking. I'm on the next flight to Washington."

———

Tim looked over at Susan, then at Bill, before finally laying his gaze on his children. He had envisioned this very moment for years. All of their training and preparation were about to bear fruit. He was ecstatic. He paused for dramatic effect, and then he started. "The operation is officially code named Coyote One. All references to this mission between us can be shortened to simply 'Coyote.'"

A hush came over the room. All of them recognized the significance. After a moment, Michael raised his hand.

Tim seemed mildly annoyed at the interruption. "Yes, Michael."

"The code name seems to imply there is a subsequent mission, yes?" Michael sat rigidly still, as if he was at attention.

"You may infer that, but for security reasons, I can say no more about it."

Michael looked at the group and realized it had been several years since they had all gathered like this. He had fond memories of the Fortress and Father's lectures.

Tim continued. "Coyote One is a two-stage mission. Stage one is the trigger, which will lead to a glorious chain of events. The trigger is Peter. As we are all aware, he is the only one who cannot be traced back to the rest of us." All eyes turned to Peter.

"Peter, when is the next scheduled meeting between the director and the attorney general?"

"Three days—on Tuesday morning." Peter had been briefed on his first day. It was at that same briefing that he was warned never to turn off his phone. He looked at his watch nervously.

"Very well, then. Coyote will be initiated in seventy-two hours. At that meeting, Peter will eliminate the attorney general and the director, as well as any other senior deputies you can get to before you are neutralized."

Peter smiled, unconcerned with his own demise.

"Once this occurs, as in previous crises, the president will want to speak to the nation. To ensure they don't attempt to cover up the attack, Peter will, if possible, call or text me when the mission is complete. I will then notify a preselected member of the media. Once the news is out, the president will hold a press conference. Most likely, the vice president will be in attendance, as well as senior aides. Regardless of the press conference, I have no doubt that the two men will meet in the White House after stage one. Ideally, we can cut off the snake's head on national television. Samantha?"

Samantha was listening intently. She knew how Father thought. The plan was intended to sow fear among the people.

"Father, I have seen the press room. It is relatively small. I know the entry point from which the president emerges. I would have access to that corridor, so long as the vice president is in attendance. If that occurs, I will find a way to get into the press room. I will kill them both before the entire world. It will be glorious."

Tim was stern. "It is critical that, once Peter initiates stage one, we utilize our phones to coordinate an exact strike time for stage two. Samantha will keep us informed when the conference is scheduled, and this will be the second trigger."

The excitement in the room was thick. Occasionally, Michael would walk to the window and check for passing cars and then return to his seat. Each time, Tim would pause from his presentation.

"One hour before the president's speech, Ryan will allow Mother and me to enter the Capitol grounds. The timing is good, because the Congress has just returned from their August recess. We will be there to repair the ventilation system. In reality, we will be preparing the gas dispersal. The goal is to kill as many of the 435 members of Congress as possible." He paused another moment, gathering his thoughts. "The Senate is another matter. Almost half the senators have offices at the Hart building. He stepped toward a corkboard, pointing to photos Ryan had provided that illustrated the targets. "This will be Bill and Alexa's mission. Ryan?" He motioned to his son.

Ryan walked over to a duffel bag he had brought with him. From within it, he pulled out two Capitol Police uniforms. He handed one each to Alexandra and Bill. "I went by the measurements you provided."

"Ryan, you will escort Mother and me into the critical ventilation area to launch the gas. You will remain with us during the operation. It is critical that we be allowed access." He stressed his last sentence.

Ryan nodded in acknowledgement.

"Bill and Alexa will arrive with us, and take your Capitol Police vehicle. Once there, they will take it and initiate an emergency evacuation of the Hart building. They have been studying the photos of all one hundred senators, who are their primary targets as they start leaving the building. They will clearly also have to kill other Capitol Police officers. Your use of their uniforms will only enhance their confusion. You will have the advantage. Ryan will walk them through the area tomorrow. It will be quiet on a Sunday. I want them to know the area like the backs of their hands."

Tim again paused for emphasis. He stared at Samantha. "It is critical that you text me five minutes before you initiate your mission. This will allow us to know exactly when to launch our attacks on Capitol Hill."

"Yes, Father, without fail," she said obediently.

Tim turned to Michael. "Once these attacks unfold, the Pentagon will be cranked into high gear. The crisis will initiate an emergency meeting of the Joint Chiefs of Staff. All military assets will be put on high alert. Americans are easy to predict. Michael, you know what to do, correct?"

"I will kill as many military leaders as possible, concentrating on generals, admirals, and other high-level officers." His siblings nodded their heads in agreement.

"What is your prospect for escape?" Tim asked him.

"It's possible, although unlikely. In the confusion, and with my uniform, I could manage to escape."

Tim stepped closer to his children. He placed his hand on Alexandra's head, as she was the closest to him. Susan rose to address them and stood next to her husband.

"You all have your homework assignments. Make sure you study your mission plan. As you were trained—practice and rehearse." They knew the meeting was coming to a conclusion.

"One final matter," Tim said as they started to gather their belongings. He caught their attention. "Do you all remember our fourth mission, to New York?"

They all nodded their heads.

"Then you recall where we had our final meeting the night before we left?"

"Yes, Father." Michael was answering for all of them.

"Good. If by some miracle some of us survive our assignments, we will meet there forty-eight hours after our mission."

"Understood, Father." Michael again responded for the group. None of them believed that there was a chance of survival. They understood that Father was merely covering all the bases.

Tim then issued his final instructions, bringing the meeting to a close.

"Before we all leave, make sure you have each programmed everyone else's phone numbers into those cell phones. After this moment, only I or Mother can issue the abort order. Coyote One is now in effect."

As he gathered his possessions, Tim called Peter for a private conversation.

"Yes, Father?" Peter asked.

"Son, is there any loose end that might jeopardize Coyote One before it commences in seventy-two hours?"

Peter didn't hesitate. "There is one thing I've been worried about." He and his father walked toward the kitchen together for a private discussion.

Unbeknownst to the conspirators, a small gray, digital recorder had silently documented their entire meeting.

—

One by one, Sullivan watched from a distance as the vehicles pulled out of the residence. He noted the time but made no effort to follow them.

Miguel spoke first. "Sully, we follow?"

"No. We have a good lead for now. I don't want to get burned and ruin it."

Sullivan waited ten minutes after the Wallace family meeting was over. The van then quietly slipped down a side street and left the area.

# TWO

## Connecting the Dots

The sunrise that Sunday morning was spectacular. The sky was clear and bright blue. From his favorite spot on the Potomac River, Sullivan watched as Conrad spoke with SSA John O'Neil at his car. After a few moments, he observed them approaching his van. Conrad slid the door open.

O'Neil's eyes widened. He gasped under his breath. "Carlos Sullivan?"

"You recognize me?"

"Yes, I saw the law enforcement bulletin." O'Neil took a step back. He was unsure how to proceed.

Sullivan could sense his trepidation. "Let me explain why I'm here." He put up his hand, trying to reassure his potential new ally.

"I think you should, quickly." O'Neil reflexively placed his right hand on his holster.

Sullivan and Conrad noticed it but chose to ignore the threatening gesture. Conrad spent the next minutes outlining what had happened to him. With each passing minute, O'Neil's body language softened. He listened intently, waiting to ask questions.

"So what do you need from me?"

"Yesterday, Kyle Grant visited the home of Michael Wallace, 18 Webster Street, Arlington. I can see you recognize the name and address, correct? We know you ran a criminal history on him just two weeks ago."

"Really." O'Neil's response was not asked as a question. He was connecting the dots in his head.

"We are curious why you were looking at him."

Conrad and Sullivan looked at each other as they listened to O'Neil's story.

———

Kathy Wallace went outside to pick the Sunday edition of the *Washington Post* from their driveway. She placed it on the kitchen table, where her husband would look for it, reading the paper over the breakfast she was preparing. She went to the stairs, listening for Michael to jump into the shower. As soon as she heard the water running, she quickly retrieved her digital recorder and put it in her pants pocket. She had used that same device to record her class lectures. Her mind was racing. "What if he finds it? When can I listen to it?" She kept asking herself these questions, uncertain how to proceed.

During the course of the day, it seemed that Michael would not leave Kathy out of his sight.

At one point, she attempted to leave the house. "Honey, I'm going to the supermarket. I will be back in a few."

"No, I want you here today." His response was abrupt and jarring.

Later, when she went to the bathroom, he rapped on the door.

"Are you all right in there?"

"Yes, honey. Out in a minute." Kathy was terrified, her heart racing.

She could not have imagined that her husband was already plotting her death.

———

"We are agreed then, that we should coordinate together?" Sullivan asked.

"Yes, but through Conrad. I can't be talking to you. You are a wanted man, Sullivan," O'Neil answered.

Conrad interrupted, "That's understood."

"What will you do now?" Sullivan asked.

"I'm not sure what it means yet. This Samantha Wallace is protected by an assistant director..." O'Neil said, thinking. "I have to proceed carefully."

"It sounds like you believe this agent of yours is involved in Livingstone's murder."

"I do. Yes. I also learned that there is another sibling in law enforcement. Ryan Wallace is a cop with the Capitol Police," O'Neil stated.

Conrad spoke up. "But what is their connection to Kyle Grant?"

"I think that by working together, we can solve all these mysteries," Sullivan declared.

O'Neil shook his head and glanced at his watch. It was their cue that the meeting was over. They all shook hands before departing. O'Neil thought to himself that he was letting a fugitive escape. He consoled himself with the thought that there was not much he could do against two armed agents. In addition, he was certain in his heart that Samantha was involved in Livingstone's murder. He would not pass up this opportunity.

———

Ryan Wallace spent Sunday morning touring the grounds of Capitol Hill with Uncle Bill and his sister Alexa. He showed them all the entry points and emergency exits. The tour included the Hart Senate Office Building, their primary target. They drove in the same vehicle that Ryan would be handing them for their assignment. He taught them how to utilize the radio, emergency lights, and siren. When the tour ended, Bill leaned over to Ryan.

"Take me to the airport."

Alexa and Ryan gave him a surprised look.

"It's OK," he said quietly. "I have one final matter to take care of."

Back in Little Rock, Agent Hanford's Blackberry light was blinking. He sat in his living room, watching TV and digesting his lunch, a dry pastrami sandwich. Instinctively, he reached for his phone, wondering who was sending him a message on a Sunday afternoon.

He opened the e-mail, which contained an attachment—a photo of Agent Kyle Grant. The message, from Agent Kathy Fuller, contained only one line. "Please expect a call in five minutes."

Hanford dutifully answered as requested. "Yes, Ms. Fuller. How can I help you on this Sunday afternoon?" Fuller could hear the irritation in his demeanor, even through his deep southern drawl.

"Yes, Pat. I do need your assistance. From one polygraph examiner to another."

"What?"

"First of all, do you recognize Grant in the photo as the same person you polygraphed a year ago?"

"Are you kidding? I can't remember that far back. It's been too long. There is a resemblance, I guess." Hanford shook his head in frustration. He had heard about Sullivan's conspiracy theory.

"Can you check his file photo then, see if they match?" Fuller asked.

"It's Sunday. I have no files here."

"On Monday morning then, please." Hanford could sense Fuller would not take no for an answer.

"OK, is that it?" He wanted to hang up the phone.

"No, I will be there on Monday. We are going to put this issue to rest once and for all."

Hanford was stunned. "How, exactly?"

"We are going to show Grant's photo to Professor Albertson, University of Arkansas. I don't know my way around there. You will help me." Her request was simple and direct. Before Hanford could object, Fuller hung up the phone.

Kathy Wallace spent the night in bed staring at the ceiling. Her husband snored gently, but he was a light sleeper. She knew he would awaken if she tried getting up. She also knew he would go to work in the morning, and she would have her chance. Her curiosity about what might have been recorded was consuming her. Her attempts to fall asleep were in vain.

# THREE

## Twenty-Four Hours

After the latest incident with Sullivan, Peter had moved into another hotel under an assumed name. On Monday morning, he had work to do before his mission the next day. He wanted to get in early and walk through the area where the attorney general (AG) and the director would be meeting. During his briefing, he had learned that the director usually walked across the street to the Department of Justice building to meet with the AG for their monthly meeting. Every third month, however, the AG made the walk to the Hoover building. That would be the case for their meeting tomorrow. Peter was especially cautious going to work, continually looking behind him. Sullivan had made him paranoid.

Once at work, Peter called Becky. He wanted any intelligence available. Nothing could be left to chance. "Becky?"

"Hey there, how are you?" She was excited to hear from him.

"I'm good, Becky. Getting used to the new job."

"I heard what happened down there. That Sullivan is crazy."

"Yeah, what are you hearing? Any leads on him?"

"No leads," she answered flatly. "We don't know what phones he's using. I've had no luck on this end tracking those internal calls."

"OK, then," he said, disappointed.

"I did hear this morning that Conrad did not come in today. Rumor has it that he went to DC."

"Thanks, babe. I will keep an eye out for him." He looked out the window, half expecting to see Conrad or Sullivan staring at him with binoculars. He glanced at his watch, calculating. He only needed another twenty-four hours.

"Be safe," she cautioned. It would be their last conversation.

———

The Monday morning sun shone into Kathy's Wallace's window and reflected off a mirror, illuminating her bed. While it bothered her on occasion, she knew it was the best alarm system in the world. She never overslept. On this occasion it was superfluous since she had not slept at all. She lay in bed, aware that Michael had gotten up and was in the shower. Kathy was both excited and frightened at the prospect of finally hearing the recording. It had been the longest night of her life.

She watched him eating breakfast and kept peeking at the digital clock on the microwave oven. Every second felt like a minute, every minute, an eternity. It seemed to her that Michael was moving in slow motion.

"Can I get you anything else?" Kathy asked helpfully.

Michael looked up from the newspaper and stared at her. She felt his eyes going right through her.

"No," he answered quietly. He then continued reading, much to her consternation.

After ten more minutes, he finally rose from the table. He grabbed a windbreaker and walked to the front door. Before leaving, he turned to her as she held the door.

"Is there something wrong?" he asked her suspiciously.

"No, honey. Of course not," she answered nervously.

Michael scrutinized her silently for a full thirty seconds. She seemed to squirm under his observation. Finally, he stopped staring at her.

"I will see you later," he said, walking down the driveway. She watched from the window until he drove off and was out of view. She then pulled out the recorder, flipping it on. She kept watching from the window, fearful that he would return.

———

Pat Hanford's Bureau car was idling at the airport terminal when Fuller emerged, tired from her long flight from Boston, which had required a connection in Dallas. She spotted Hanford, having met him at their annual polygraph convention, and walked over, putting her bag in the backseat and sitting in the front.

"Thanks for picking me up," she said with a faint smile.

Hanford was not in a generous mood. "Explain to me, please, why we couldn't just e-mail the professor a photo?"

"I want to document this interview. I want to see his reactions. I need to know for sure."

"I see." Hanford's answer dripped with sarcasm.

"Did you check his file photo?" Fuller asked him.

"Yes, and I can see a resemblance. It could be someone else. I can't be sure."

"Well, no matter, the professor knows we are coming. I called him, and he agreed to meet us." She scanned the area, looking for any sign pointing to the university.

"I hope he is a patient man," Hanford replied.

"Patient? Why do you say that?" Fuller seemed puzzled.

"Where do you think the University of Arkansas is, Fuller?" he asked.

"Little Rock, right?"

"No Agent Fuller. It's in Fayetteville."

"Where's that?" she asked, surprised.

"It's a three-hour drive, if I go seventy-five miles an hour." He smiled at her.

She didn't blink. "OK," she replied, "then drive eighty-five."

———

Peter again glanced at his watch. He knew he now only had eighteen hours to maintain his cover. He thought of the family meeting only two days ago. He was disappointed that his siblings, especially Michael, didn't seem to appreciate how much more difficult his mission had been than theirs. They were not lying about their identities as he was, only their goals.

Anxious, he called his Arkansas connection, Jeff Wilson.

"Kyle?" Wilson answered on the first ring. "How are you? Did you not get my rent payment?"

"Of course I did," Peter said reassuringly. "Just checking in, seeing if you are all right."

"I am well."

"How are things with you?" Peter asked.

"Good, I heard your message last week about your new assignment. I haven't had a chance to get back to you."

"Not to worry. I've had a lot on my plate."

"Yeah, I heard about the Boston situation. Man, that sounds crazy!"

"You could say that," Peter answered.

"It's funny, but I heard a Boston agent landed in Little Rock today. Pat Hanford is meeting that agent. Is it connected to that situation?" Wilson asked, curious.

"Who's the agent, do you know?" Peter asked, analyzing the situation.

"No, just that it's a female agent."

The line was silent for a moment. "All right, thanks, Jeff." Peter hung up his phone. Wilson stared at his telephone for a moment, wondering about the purpose behind Kyle's call.

After thinking about the call, Peter knew he needed to relay his newfound intelligence.

He sent a one line text to Father: *Boston FBI Agent Kathy Fuller is in Arkansas.*

By the time Kathy Wallace had finished listening to the recording, she was quivering. Her heart was palpitating, her face red, her skin sweating as if she had just run a two-mile sprint. She couldn't believe what she had heard. She knew she needed to report it but wasn't certain where to turn until she remembered about the Secret Service agent. It was now obvious to her that Michael was involved in that murder. Kathy had the habit of talking to herself when she was nervous.

"Was it John O'Brien?" she muttered. Then, after a second, she whispered, "No, John O'Neil." She seemed certain and ran to the closet in the foyer. She needed the phone book.

Her hand was shaking as she dialed the phone.

"US Secret Service," the switchboard operator answered on the second ring. "How may I direct your call?"

"Special Agent John O'Neil," she blurted out. "Please, quickly!"

"One moment please," The operator forwarded the call to O'Neil's extension.

As the desk phone rang, O'Neil was engaged in a conversation on his cell phone. He contemplated not answering, but decided to end his call early. He picked up just as the call was about to go to voice mail. Kathy was desperate, concerned that he would not answer. Finally, she heard his voice.

"This is O'Neil."

"Oh my god, Mr. O'Neil, this is Kathy Wallace. I'm married to Michael Wallace. You came to my home—"

"Yes, Ms. Wallace, I remember. Slow down. What's wrong?"

"My husband—he is a terrorist! Something horrible is going to happen. I don't know what to do!" Her voice was rising. She was hysterical.

"Take it easy, when is this horrible thing going to happen?"

"Tuesday, but it's complicated…" As she spoke, she had the sudden realization that she heard a car door in the driveway.

"Let's meet in person. Let's say one hour, at the Washington Monument?" O'Neil quickly suggested.

"OK," she answered. "I gotta go!" She hung up her phone as Michael placed his key in the door lock.

During their long drive to Fayetteville, Fuller looked out her window, amazed at the Arkansas landscape. It was so far removed from the view she grew up with in Maryland's Chesapeake Bay. The ubiquitous Arkansas billboards provided her endless entertainment. She glimpsed one sign in particular, flashing the neon message *WARNING: YOU ARE ABOUT TO MEET GOD*. Hanford could see her chuckle under her breath. He looked over at her.

"Don't say it." He raised his right arm up.

"I'm just a visitor passing through," she said, smiling. "I think the message must be for you."

Hanford smirked and gunned the accelerator. He wanted their mission to be over.

As Hanford finally pulled his car into the campus grounds, Fuller looked at the digital clock on the dashboard. She was quite certain they would have arrived thirty minutes earlier, had she been driving. She looked about to get her bearings, surprised at the size of the campus.

"This place is huge," she said.

"There are twenty thousand students and almost a thousand professors. So, yeah, it's big," Hanford said, looking for a parking spot.

"Well, Professor Albertson teaches at the Sam Walton College of Business, so we need to find where their faculty building is."

"Just follow me," Hanford said dryly. "I'm an alum."

As they approached the building, Bill was walking up a rear stairwell, making his way toward the professor's second floor office. He wore dark-brown hiking boots with rubber soles. They made no noise as he reached the second floor landing. He had received a warning text from Tim, so he was warily looking for any female faces that might be FBI. As he saw no danger and proceeded toward the professor's office, he noticed the door was ajar. The name "Professor John Albertson" was etched on the door, so he had no doubt he was in the right place. He could hear the professor talking to a student, so he waited outside. He wanted minimal casualties.

After waiting about two minutes, the student, a female with a backpack slung over her shoulder, walked out the door and past Bill. She didn't even look up to see his face. Bill slipped into the office and closed the door as Fuller and Hanford walked up the stairwell.

"Do I know you?" the professor asked, startled at having his door closed.

Bill looked about the room quickly, searching for any weapons the professor might reach for. He saw none. His immediate impression of the professor was how small he was. Bill assessed his prey to weigh no more than 150 pounds. He wore a white collared shirt, with neat blue jeans. He sat at his desk, not yet comprehending the danger he was in.

"I asked you a question," Albertson stated sternly.

Bill walked behind his desk as the professor started to stand. He went around him and grabbed him in a choke hold. "Shut up," Bill ordered as he squeezed his neck tighter and tighter. Albertson didn't have the strength to break the hold. He tried to yell, but could not. His arms and legs were flailing wildly. He was in a desperate panic. Bill had lifted him up, and Albertson was dangling as if he were hanging from a noose. As he kicked forward, he knocked over some of his belongings, including a glass, which broke when it crashed into the floor.

Outside the door, Hanford and Fuller heard the commotion. Instinctively, Hanford called out as he reached for the door. "Professor? Are you OK?" As he opened the door, Fuller followed close behind.

As his victim slumped to the floor, Bill hustled to the door to intercept them. When the door fully opened, Bill punched Hanford in his face, knocking him back and into the hallway. He grabbed Fuller by the neck as she reached for her weapon. With his large right hand, Bill was choking her to the point where she felt she might pass out. As she started to feel herself panic, she heard his voice, slow and eerie.

"Hello, Agent Fuller."

The words gave her an immediate jolt of adrenaline. She reached up and scratched him across the face, but he would not yield. Fuller then kicked him squarely in the balls with all her remaining strength. The sudden pain forced him to release her.

Finally free, Fuller knelt to the ground to catch her breath. She gasped for air. As she did so, Hanford started to get up from the floor, but Bill kicked him directly in the chest. The blow from Bill's boot winded Hanford, who lay on the ground.

Sensing an opportunity, Bill ran through the hall and then down the stairs, determined to escape.

Fuller composed herself and stood as he reached the stairwell.

"See to the professor," she yelled. "I will get him."

Hanford was still on the floor when Fuller was already outside, chasing Bill across the campus grounds. Most students were too distracted with their friends, or iPods, to immediately notice a woman with a gun chasing a large man across the yard. What finally caught their attention was when Bill reached for his pistol and started firing backward, all while running forward. He was not aiming, only hoping to get a lucky shot. Everyone who heard the "pop, pop, pop" of the gunshots fell to the ground or ran to safety. Running past frightened students, Fuller continued her chase, which led into the Mullins library.

Once at the entrance, she proceeded cautiously, worried that he was setting a trap. Some of the students inside were running out of the building past her. Fuller reached for a fire alarm and pulled it. More students streamed out of the building. She grabbed one student by the jersey, stopping him cold.

"Did you see which way he went?"

"He went into the stacks!" he yelled. "Straight ahead." The startled student ran off.

Bill had turned off the lights. The only illumination was light streaming in from the windows, causing large dark and shadowy areas in the library. Fuller walked in slowly, crouching. She knew that the longer they were in the building, the more time was on her side. Reinforcements would be arriving shortly. Yet she also knew he was making the same calculation. He would be desperate to leave. Rather than go any farther, exposing herself, she decided to assume a fixed position near the closest emergency door. She would wait for him to come to her.

After two minutes, she began to doubt her theory. Perhaps he had left before she arrived. The sound of the emergency alarm was piercing. She would not be able to hear his approach. It would have to be visual. As she waited, suddenly, she saw a shadow cross the floor, by the emergency door. She sat motionless on the floor, her gun pointing at the door. As her target came into view, she saw his back as he reached for the emergency door. As he glanced back before exiting, he saw her but it was too late. She fired two rounds. He fell to his knees, stunned, clutching his bloody chest.

Fuller ran over to him as he lay on his side, drawing his final breath. As she looked down at him, she noticed something unusual. He died smiling.

———

John O'Neil waited patiently at the base of the Washington Monument on the National Mall. As the one-hour mark approached, he kept replaying in his mind the bits and pieces Kathy Wallace had blurted out. Only two things seemed certain from what she said. Her husband was a terrorist, and something was to occur on Tuesday. If he could corroborate her information, his hunch about Samantha will have been proved correct. He had no doubt about her involvement in Livingstone's murder. Proof, however, was another matter. After ninety minutes had passed, O'Neil gave up. He reached for his phone and dialed a number.

"Conrad?" O'Neil said.

"Yes," Conrad replied as he put the call on speaker phone.

"She didn't show."

Conrad could hear his disappointment.

"We should meet again and strategize. It's a whole new ball game now."

Conrad glanced over at Sullivan. "Agreed."

———

Michael was not exactly certain what Kathy had said or done that prompted him to suspect her loyalty. Perhaps it was her tight smiles, or when she was overly solicitous. It mattered little now. They were too close to their grand day to take any chances.

He lifted Kathy's lifeless body and placed her in the trunk of his car, which he had backed into their garage. Her face was blue, her tongue sticking out grotesquely. He placed a blanket over her, although not out of pity or care. He had actually enjoyed choking her slowly to death. In his zeal to kill her, he never noticed that there was a small recording device on the kitchen counter. She had not had time to hide it.

Michael drove off with the immediate goal of disposing of her body. He was expected back at the Pentagon.

# FOUR

## Twelve Hours

The sun had set on the locked-down campus in Arkansas. Dozens of police and federal agents had descended on the campus to facilitate the investigation of the attempt on the professor's life and the shooting. Emergency blue lights were still seen intermittently around different parts of the campus, as well as at the crime scene. Whenever an FBI agent discharges a weapon, the Bureau's protocols require that a shoot team respond immediately to conduct a review of the incident. This situation was no different, although it took several hours for the team to arrive. Fuller was isolated in an office provided by the university. They had taken her phone, leaving her incommunicado. This was more for her benefit, since it was always preferable for an agent to give only one statement after a shooting. As she was being escorted by two state troopers to the room, Agent Hanford had managed to walk by her side.

"When I get out of that interview, I want a full briefing on the investigation," she said sternly. Hanford nodded in agreement. The incident had turned him into a full convert to her cause.

Fuller sat uncomfortably, anxiously waiting to get back in the game. She felt as though she was in a penalty box. In the meantime, Conrad and Sully needed to know what was happening. She wondered if word had reached them. As she pondered that, she kept remembering the assassin's smile, and his words. "Hello, Agent Fuller" kept echoing in her ears.

———

Across the country, the media had begun broadcasting the story, shooting images of the bucolic campus. Interspersed with the reporting was a summary of other shootings at college campuses, most prominently the shooting at Virginia Tech years earlier. Tim and Susan watched the broadcaster intently, turning up the volume.

"*For now, the university is only reporting that there is one victim, shot dead by an FBI agent. They are reassuring the community that no students were injured. I can report at this time that there is an unconfirmed report that a professor was injured in the incident. He is reportedly in stable condition at a local hospital. We will have more to report as this story unfolds.*" As the broadcaster spoke, the camera panned behind him, showcasing the university library and one of its doors, which was closed with yellow evidence tape.

"*Over to you, Jim,*" The broadcaster said seriously.

Tim turned off the TV and sat apprehensively. Susan sat next to him, her hand over her mouth, upset. Unwilling to cancel the operation, he knew their plan would need some tweaking. He felt certain that Bill would not have anything on his person that could trace the authorities back to the family.

He reached for his phone and composed a text for the family. Each member read it with relief. "*Operation Coyote is still in effect.*"

———

The digital clock on the desk read 8:15 p.m. The mood in the room was grim. O'Neil, Conrad, and Sullivan sat silently around the small coffee table in Conrad's hotel room. Sully's hair was still wet. It had been several days since he had taken a warm shower, and he wasn't going to miss the opportunity. The news from Arkansas was making its way through the Bureau like a California wildfire. They were awaiting a briefing from Fuller, but she was still incommunicado. Conrad's phone was placed at the center of the table; its speaker phone was on. Hanford was on the line with them.

"Mr. Sullivan, it appears that you are on to something after all," Hanford said, his Southern drawl accentuating every word. Whenever possible, Hanford used the title Mr., as opposed to Agent, when addressing colleagues. It was unusual in the Bureau.

"Am I to conclude from your remark, *Mr.* Hanford, that you are now on my team?" Sullivan said with a slight smile.

"You may."

"I'm glad to hear that." Sullivan leaned back in his chair.

"And if I may say so, I'm very impressed with your associate, Ms. Fuller," he stated in a serious manner.

"Yes, I've always been impressed with her. So, Hanford, I'm here with Conrad and Secret Service SSA John O'Neil. What can you tell us?"

"Well, first of all, I just came from the hospital. Professor Albertson is alive but sedated. He won't be available until the morning. As for our dead suspect, a fingerprint check turned up negative. He's not in the system."

O'Neil was on the edge of his seat. He pounced when he saw an opening. He briefed Hanford on the Kathy Wallace call. "She had information that something will be happening tomorrow, Tuesday."

"Well, is there something scheduled for tomorrow?" Hanford asked.

"Not from a Secret Service protective detail, as far as I'm aware," O'Neil answered. "What about at the Bureau?"

"I checked with my contacts at HQ. There's nothing out of the ordinary," Conrad answered.

"So what would be normal tomorrow?" Sullivan interjected, looking at Conrad.

"Well, only a meeting between the director and the AG. It's scheduled for tomorrow morning," Conrad answered, somewhat puzzled.

"Don't you get it?" Sullivan answered. "Kyle is on the director's detail. That was his mission." He seemed sure of himself.

"So what's his connection to Michael Wallace?" O'Neil asked.

"I'm not sure," Sullivan answered, "but they were meeting together. I know that for certain."

At that moment, Fuller burst furiously through the door. Hanford seemed to relax, in relief. She picked up his phone, seemingly aware of the conference call.

"Sully," she said, almost breathlessly into the phone.

"Kathy! Are you OK?"

"Listen to me Sully, the guy I killed...he knew I was coming!" she practically screamed.

Sullivan, Conrad, and O'Neil looked at each other, confused. Hanford arched an eyebrow. They waited for her to explain.

"He called me by my name. He said, 'Hello, Agent Fuller,'" She said it in a manly voice, theatrically.

They all sat silently for a moment, pondering the implication of what they were hearing.

Sullivan reacted first. "It has to be Kyle. The information that you were going to Little Rock was only known within the Bureau. Therefore, it was inside information. Michael Wallace does not have that information." Sullivan leaned back in his chair, as his colleagues watched him elaborate. "Under my theory, Kyle has the most to gain from Professor Albertson's demise. Plus, he is the only one who could have known Fuller was going to be there. It's obvious." He thought for another moment. "Hanford, does Kyle have any contacts in the Little Rock office?"

"Actually, yes," he replied. "He is renting his house to a fellow classmate, Agent Jeff Wilson."

Fuller jumped in. "I'm on it."

Hanford raised his hand in a blocking gesture. "No, he's in my territory, let me deal with it. And I will check on the professor tomorrow. Perhaps he will be lucid."

Sullivan agreed. "Hanford, I appreciate that. Fuller, I need you on a flight back tonight. Whatever is going to happen next, I have a feeling it's back here, not in Arkansas. I need you here."

O'Neil gave words to their unspoken thought. "I have a feeling we don't have a lot of time here."

Sullivan closed the meeting as he usually did. "Let's reconvene tomorrow morning."

After the call was disconnected, Sullivan turned to Conrad. "You have to get me into the Hoover building tomorrow. Kyle is going to do something, and we have to stop him."

———

Judge Kenneth Waterman looked at the papers before him; his thin eyeglasses perched precariously on his nose. Waterman was in his fifties, his hair salt-and-pepper gray. As he flipped through each page, his face betrayed increasing skepticism. The walls of his study were filled with books from floor to ceiling. His desk was a large mahogany antique. The chair was dark leather and comfortable. O'Neil sat across from the judge, watching intensely. He looked at the clock on the judge's desk. It was 12:30 a.m. He knew Waterman was the judge on duty. He knew little of Waterman's reputation. O'Neil was hopeful that the judge was pro-law enforcement. He knew he was engaged in the equivalent of a legal coin toss. He continued observing the judge intently, awaiting his decision.

The judge seemed to read the last page of O'Neil's affidavit twice. He dropped it on his desk and looked at his desperate visitor. "It's missing something," Waterman said flatly.

"What's that, Your Honor?"

"Probable cause," he replied sarcastically.

"You see no merit in my argument?"

"Mr. O'Neil, you have a reasonable suspicion. It's not the same as probable cause. I sympathize with your zeal. But I can't sign off on this search warrant of the Wallace residence."

"But Your Honor—"

"It's late, Mr. O'Neil, and you are on a fishing expedition."

The judge stood, waving O'Neil toward the foyer. He escorted him to the door.

"I'm sorry," he said.

O'Neil took back his affidavit and nodded to the judge. He knew in his heart he was right. He also knew he could not meet the proper legal threshold. The judge was legally correct. In his mind, O'Neil knew what he had to do, and he was prepared to take the next step.

"Thank you for your time, Your Honor." O'Neil said calmly. He stepped off the porch and walked quickly down the dark driveway toward his car.

# FIVE

## Showdown Prologue

The alarm on O'Neil's cell phone rang loudly, startling him into consciousness. He had leaned his car seat back at a comfortable angle, allowing him to sleep as best he could, given the circumstances. It was still dark at 5:30 a.m., and there was no movement on the street. O'Neil noticed that two or three of the homes within sight had lights on. People were stirring, preparing for their tedious commute to work. Most significantly, through his binoculars, O'Neil observed that a light in the second-floor window at 18 Webster Street had been turned on. He waited patiently.

Inside the residence, Michael was shaving. He had slept peacefully, knowing that his day of glory was at hand, and he wanted to look good. Michael also felt the freedom of not having to deal with Kathy. He was unencumbered. He played out the events that were to unfold in his head, over and over again. He was mentally dress rehearsing.

———

Sullivan awoke instantly when Conrad tapped him gently on the shoulder. Fully dressed, he jumped up instinctively, evidence that he had been dreaming.

"What time is it?"

"Five thirty," Conrad answered.

"Did Trish come through for us?" he asked, hope filling his eyes.

"Yes," Conrad said, smiling.

Sullivan rubbed his eyes, thinking. "Good, let's review all of our assets again. We have a lot to do."

———

The crew of Delta flight 2108 from Dallas was tired. Despite routinely handling the red-eye flight to Washington, something about this last run had them exhausted. The pilots themselves were fresh, mostly because the flight was on autopilot for most of the trip.

The flight attendants were not as rested. There was no cruise control for their jobs. As the plane started its descent into Washington, one of them could be heard over the public address system, intoning wearily, "We have started our descent into Washington. We hope you have enjoyed your flight. Please put your seatbelts on and your tray tables up, and place your seat in the upright position."

Fuller awoke from the announcement. She was groggy from the long trip and looked out her window. The city lights of Washington were still not visible. She glanced at her watch. It was 5:30 a.m.

———

Peter sat in silence, meditating. He had slept little that night, knowing that the success of the family's mission rested squarely on his shoulders. It was pitch black in his room at the Washington Lodge. His curtain was drawn, obscuring any outside light. The only illumination was from the hallway, beaming underneath his door. He knew he would not be returning to his hotel room once he left it. His only goal meant certain death. He thought about his ideals and why he was engaged in this mighty struggle. The values he was raised with were on his mind. He considered how large a tip he would leave the hotel maid. After all, he was fighting this battle for her and other such oppressed workers.

He glanced at the digital clock on his night stand. It blinked 5:30 a.m.

Peter got up and started dressing one final time.

—

As Michael drove from his residence for the last time in his life, he looked cautiously about for any surveillance. This was second nature for him. As he glanced down the street, he saw nothing alarming about the dark sedan parked a block away on the street. In the early dawn light, he could not see inside the vehicle, which was deliberately parked away from the street light. O'Neil, on the other hand, noted the 6:15 departure. A shot of adrenaline surged through his body. He waited ten minutes, then he walked to the residence and climbed the steps to the front door. O'Neil observed that although some of the neighbor's lights were on, nobody was on the street. The house next to the Wallace residence was still completely dark.

O'Neil quickly determined that the front door had a sturdy dead bolt, and the front windows were sealed tight and had double panes. He quickly bounded back down the steps and went to the rear of the house. His eyes lit up when he detected a weak point. One of the rear windows was kept shut with only a flimsy lock. He gave it two strong jolts and pushed it open. He took off his coat then shimmied himself through the window and into the Wallace home. O'Neil shook his head as he did so, wondering about the chain of events that had forced him—a decorated federal agent—into a criminal act: breaking and entering. Once inside, his first act was to go to each window in the residence and pull down the curtains. O'Neil was glad to see that they were opaque. He could now turn on the lights so he could work in freedom, meticulously. In truth, O'Neil considered that other than Kathy Wallace herself, he had no real idea what he was looking for. Nevertheless, he was determined to conduct a thorough, although quite illegal, search.

—

The lobby of the Washington Lodge, located on the edge of Chinatown, was unusually quiet for a Tuesday morning at 6:30. The décor was dated, circa 1972. The walls were old wood paneling. The floor was covered in a cheap faux carpet with an oriental design. Two dusty chairs covered one corner, a dark frumpy love seat another.

The sole desk clerk, Amy Ying, was a short woman. Her turn on the night shift was almost over. "Were you satisfied with your stay at the Lodge, Mr. Peters?"

"It was acceptable," Peter answered dryly, quite pleased at the pseudonym he had given himself.

Ying reached out to hand Peter a copy of his receipt, but he stopped her with a wave of his hand.

"No need," he said quickly. "Keep it."

She seemed surprised and watched Peter walk briskly out of the hotel. Peter started walking the five blocks to the Hoover building. In his excitement about what lay ahead, he failed to take notice of his surroundings. Across the street from the hotel, Sullivan had perched himself at the window of a Starbucks coffee shop. Several other patrons were inside. One read a newspaper. The rest perused their electronic tablets as they sipped their coffee. Sullivan watched them. He sympathized with the newspaper reader—the new dinosaur in a digital era. He then turned his attention back to the hotel.

Sullivan stood upright when he saw Peter emerge from the hotel. His eyes locked on his prey. He was resolved to take action and began his pursuit.

After two blocks, Peter started to get the feeling that he was being watched. It was a strange sensation, one he could not pinpoint. He looked around and saw nobody he recognized. But the feeling persisted. He slowed his pace, Sullivan did not. Finally, as he prepared to cross the street at the next intersection, he turned completely. Sullivan was less than thirty feet away and closing. Instinctively, Peter ran.

Several cars navigating the intersection had to swerve or stop to avoid hitting Peter. The screeching tires drew the attention of dozens of morning commuters on the street. Sullivan was in immediate pursuit, closing in on his target. He used the hood of one of the stopped cars as a springboard, as he bounded toward the fleeing Peter.

Peter ran one more block but could hear Sullivan closing in on him. He knew he could not outrun Sullivan to headquarters. As he ran, he measured his limited options. Just as Sullivan was about to grab him from behind, Peter reached for a passing woman. She wore a conservative gray business suit, with sneakers for her commute, as is the custom in Washington. She cried out in a panic as Peter spun her around by her hair. He placed his gun at her temple. Sullivan stopped, silently weighing a response. Sullivan had drawn his pistol, but he pointed it downward, out of concern for Peter's hostage.

"Give it up, Sullivan!" Peter yelled at him.

"Please let me go!" she screamed, crying.

Peter began dragging her backward, toward a small deli a few feet behind them. Startled commuters ran in every direction, away from the incident. Sullivan kept moving toward Peter and his hostage, keeping up step for step with his target.

"I will kill her! Not one more step!" Peter was furious, spit coming out of his mouth.

Sullivan stopped. As Peter reached the deli door, he smashed his gun against the woman's face, throwing her toward Sullivan. He quickly ran into the deli.

Sullivan kneeled down to comfort the woman. "Are you all right?" All the while, he kept his eyes on the door Peter had entered.

The woman groaned slightly. She had a cut above her eye, but he could see her injuries were not life threatening.

"You will be OK," Sullivan said, standing up. He cautiously went to the deli and swung the door open.

Inside, a waitress cowered near the counter. Another patron was also on the floor beside her. He looked at them both, hoping they would give him a sign. After a moment, the waitress pointed and mouthed the words, "Out the back." Sullivan ran toward the back of the deli. The rear door was wide open. He stepped out carefully and looked in every direction. Peter was gone.

———

Attorney General Jonathan Mitchell was expected at the Hoover building for his scheduled meeting with the director in one hour. SSA

Diamond was in his office, going over his personnel roster when his secretary informed him he had an unexpected visitor. Agent Conrad had insisted on a meeting. Sitting next to Diamond was his deputy, Agent Will French. Both of them had worked on the same detail for over a year, and they thought alike. Out of respect for Conrad's reputation in the Bureau, Diamond agreed to a meeting. He and French listened to him, with one eye on the clock on the wall. They were getting impatient.

"Conrad, I understand your buddy is in a trick box over these allegations, but I can't help you," Diamond said in a lecturing tone.

"We are convinced that Grant is up to something. It could very well involve the director's security. Aren't you listening?" Conrad was exasperated.

"You Boston agents are a pain in the ass. What would you have me do, with no evidence?" Diamond asked.

"All I'm asking is that you keep an eye on him," Conrad pleaded. He could tell from French's demeanor that he was in agreement with his boss.

Diamond looked at Conrad and considered what he had just heard. He thought for a moment. He shifted in his seat slightly. Conrad waited. After a few seconds, Diamond looked at Conrad directly with his decision.

"My responsibility is the director's security. If there is even a slight chance you are right, I can't ignore it. So I will, as you describe it, 'keep an eye on him.'" Diamond rose, signaling an end to the meeting. French also got up.

Conrad also rose. "Thank you," he said and walked out of the office.

As he entered the hallway, his cell phone rang. He could hear Sullivan's distinctive voice clearly as he told Conrad what had happened.

"What do you mean, you're coming here?" Conrad asked.

"I mean exactly that, I'm coming to headquarters."

Conrad stared at his phone for a second before responding, "Are you crazy?"

⌐⌐

After searching the Wallace residence for an hour, O'Neil was ready to give up. His methodical search of every room had proved fruitless. Dejected, he finally sat on a stool in the kitchen, next to a long counter, pondering his next move. He flipped through some of the mail that was stacked there. He found nothing of interest. O'Neil looked at his watch. It was 7:30 a.m. As he glanced across the counter, O'Neil spied something unusual. He reached for the curious item, holding it in his hand, inspecting it.

⌐⌐

The white van pulled into the Capitol Hill complex at exactly 7:30 a.m. The sign on the side of the van read Capitol Area Air & Heating Services. Sergeant Ryan Wallace was there to greet the van, dutifully checking the driver's identification, as well as the corresponding work order. At his side was a new Capitol Police officer, Alexa Wallace. Her uniform fit her perfectly. He waved Tim and Susan, both wearing their khaki Capitol Area Air & Heating Services work uniforms, into a visitor parking spot. As they pulled out their equipment from the back of the van, Ryan handed them each a visitor pass. Ryan never smiled during their interaction. He escorted his parents into the bowels of the Capitol, where the ventilation center was located. He knew that his parents would disapprove of any hint of emotion during the operation. Alexa mimicked her brother's demeanor. Everything was going according to their plan.

# SIX

## Coyote One

O n a large flat tract of land, on the banks of the Anacostia River, lay the Capital Area Helo Tours Corporation. Owned and operated by retired Marine Captain Jim McDougal, it catered to both tourists and businessmen seeking quick trips to small airports in the metropolitan Washington area. McDougal was an affable man, always with a warm smile for his clients. Behind the smile, nevertheless, was the unmistakable visage of a man who had seen the horrors of war. There was a deep, serene quality to his dark brown eyes.

His business was small, operating only ten functioning helicopters. An eleventh, a Bell 460, had been under repair for almost a year. Business had been slow, and McDougal saw little need of repairing it quickly.

As McDougal looked out his office window, he noticed a van enter his property. The van parked in a visitor's spot. McDougal noticed that the persons inside seemed to hesitate before coming out. He saw this often, usually from tourists who were having second thoughts about flying in a helicopter. In anticipation of receiving new clients, he looked at his tarmac and quickly made a mental note of which helicopters were available. He only had two pilots ready to go. He waited behind his desk, patiently expecting his new visitors.

Sullivan entered first, flanked by the brothers, both wearing heavy jackets that concealed their machine guns. Sullivan walked to the counter and flashed his FBI credentials. "I'm FBI Agent Carlos Sullivan."

McDougal stood up, his interest piqued. "Yes, how may I help you?"

"I will need one of your helicopters."

"Sure, let me get our pricing—" McDougal was cut off abruptly.

"No, you don't understand. I need to commandeer one of your choppers. My associates are pilots. They noticed the black Bell Jet Ranger 260. Is it operational?" Sullivan said flatly to a stunned McDougal.

"I'm afraid that—" McDougal shook his head, but was cut off midsentence.

"No, this is nonnegotiable. There is a national security emergency. We are taking one of your birds." Sullivan handed McDougal his business card. "This is my card. I give you my word; you will get the chopper back. We are wasting time. Get the key and walk with me."

McDougal hesitated for a moment, assessing Agent Sullivan. His gut told him that his surprise visitor was genuine. "OK, let's go," he answered.

—

FBI Director Robert Stuart sat at his large mahogany desk reviewing the latest intelligence reports compiled by the Bureau. Among the reports in his in-box was the latest information in the Sullivan matter. In sum, there was nothing new. Sullivan had disappeared, the evidence against him thin. Stuart would never get to read that report.

As he breezed through some of the files, he knew he was only killing time in anticipation of his impending meeting with the attorney general. In truth, he didn't care for AG Jonathan Mitchell, whom he considered condescending. Yet he knew he had to make nice with the person who was nominally his boss. Despite the immense power he wielded as FBI director, he knew that Mitchell had the president's ear. He had to keep up appearances.

Two offices down the corridor, SSA Diamond sat behind his desk. Given his responsibility in protecting the director, his office was quite close by. In reality, as long as the director was inside the Hoover building, security was never a major consideration. The Hoover building was considered a secure location. There was no need for armed agents to follow the director around his own building. As such, whenever the AG visited, the AG's security detail would wait outside the conference room. SSA Diamond had summoned Kyle Grant into his office. Without alarming Grant, he was prepared to tell him that until the Sullivan matter was resolved, he wanted Grant to stay by his side at all times. He considered how Grant would take his edict, just as he heard a loud knock on his partially opened door.

———

Professor Albertson looked up at the ceiling, his body bruised and his chest and neck discolored. His hospital bed was comfortable, but his sleep had been disrupted by the loud snoring of a man who shared his room. They were separated by only a thin blue curtain. He winced in pain as he looked at Agent Hanford, who was holding a photo in his hand.

"Mr. Albertson, you had previously agreed to help us in a certain matter."

"Sure, yes," he answered slowly.

"Please take a look at this picture. Do you recognize this man?" Hanford asked.

"No," he replied dryly.

"Are you certain?" replied a surprised Hanford.

"I've never seen that person before in my life," he said resolutely.

"So to be clear, then, this is not the person you know as Kyle Grant?" Hanford's chest was beginning to tighten at the realization that there truly was a conspiracy.

"Absolutely. That is not Kyle Grant," Albertson said with finality, his weary head falling back into his pillow.

If Hanford had been sitting down, he would have fallen out of his chair. He steadied himself by holding onto the edge of the professor's bed as he decided whom to call first.

Peter sat across from his supervisor, processing the words he was hearing. For an instant, he was unsure if or how this would affect Coyote One. In his mental rehearsals, he had anticipated killing Diamond anyway, inasmuch as he was usually within arm's length of the director. So this new policy would most likely not alter his plans, he calculated. As he prepared his first question, Diamond's phone began buzzing.

"Will this have an impact on today's visit by the AG?" Peter asked, concerned.

Diamond pulled out his phone and looked at it. He could tell from the number that the call was coming from within the Hoover building itself. He held up one finger, signaling for Peter to wait.

He paused for a moment before answering the phone. "Diamond here."

Peter watched Diamond closely as Conrad revealed what had unfolded. He noticed Diamond's eyes widening slightly as he listened to the caller. He could not hear everything the caller was saying, but caught enough words, such as "professor" and "Hanford," that he knew his cover was blown. Diamond started shifting his weight. He moved the phone from his right ear to his left, leaving his right hand free to draw his weapon.

Without warning, Peter jumped up and leaped over the desk, kicking Diamond in the forehead with the heel of his shoe. His phone flew from his hand, smashing against the wall. The attack was so swift and accurate, Diamond had no time to react. He was on the floor and disoriented as Peter put him in a choke hold from behind. In seconds, Diamond was passed out. Peter took an extra fifteen seconds, tightening his grip, ensuring that his supervisor was dead and not simply incapacitated.

Peter knew his time was limited. He correctly assessed that Conrad was making his way to the director's office at that very moment. He walked to the director's office in seconds and greeted his secretary, Miss Easton. She looked up at Peter with the usual disdainful look she reserved for rookie agents.

"Yes?" was the only word she managed, as Peter fired a single bullet into her brain without breaking his stride. She jerked back violently, her left foot landing on the corner of her desk as she fell to the floor. It was a grotesque image that Peter took a short second to enjoy. He proceeded into the director's office, who by now was standing rigidly behind his desk, startled.

"Mr. Director," Peter said quietly

"What are you doing?" Stuart asked, confused.

"I am killing you, sir." In an instant, Peter fired two rounds directly at the director's chest. He fell to his knees, clutching his chest, and then fell face forward.

Peter walked briskly out of the office and into an adjacent hallway. He found an emergency evacuation switch he had scoped out earlier and pulled it. As he started down a stairwell, he took out his phone. He was alive. He now had a message to relay.

———

The five-seat Bell Jet Ranger 260 is the most popular civilian helicopter, with a maximum speed of approximately 125 miles per hour. Jorge was at the controls, pushing the limits of his newly acquired aircraft. On Sullivan's orders, Jorge stayed clear of the White House, for fear they would be shot out of the sky. They flew low, about two hundred feet over the top of the DC skyline. Within a few short minutes, the chopper was approaching the Hoover building. As it did, Sullivan could feel his phone buzzing.

"Yes!" Sullivan yelled over the roar of the chopper's engine.

"You were right! The professor confirmed Grant is not who he said he is!" Conrad screamed back into the phone.

Sullivan smirked. Conrad continued loudly. "I'm on my way to get the bastard!"

"I will be on the roof. Find a way down for me!" Sullivan yelled back.

"Somehow I will. I already warned the AG's detail. He is safe."

Conrad then hung up and ran toward the director's office.

———

From deep within the Capitol building, Tim felt the buzzing of his phone and excitedly opened the text message. His shoulders slumped as he read the message and then showed it to his wife. It read simply, "*Director is dead.*" Although pleased that phase one was complete, he was disappointed that the attorney general was not also eliminated. Susan could sense his discontentment and put her hand on his shoulder.

"No matter," he said. He scrolled through his phone contacts, pulling up the media contacts he had researched.

"Let phase two begin." He dialed the first number and put the phone to his ear.

# SEVEN

## Phase Two

Tim had estimated that once news of the assassination began to circulate, it would take the government only about one hour to begin mobilizing itself in defense. The Washington News Network had already issued one bulletin, and the other cable services began airing images of the Hoover building. Beneath the image, the scroll read *"FBI director feared dead. Panic and mayhem reported in the Hoover Building."* From within the Capitol building, Tim and Susan had no access to a television. However, from their phones they started to read the news reports. They were delighted. Phase two would soon be initiated.

⁓

Once Conrad saw that the director lay dead, he quickly moved to check the surrounding offices for any signs of Kyle. He found Diamond's and Easton's bodies, but no sign of Kyle. As he prepared to find the stairs in the hope of reaching the roof, he heard the building's emergency evacuation alarm. It was loud and piercing. As he noticed people starting to file down the stairs, he realized that Kyle was going to try to use an evacuation in an attempt to sneak out of the Hoover building.

Agent French arrived seconds after Conrad.

"We need to get to the roof," Conrad barked at him.

"Follow me," French answered. "We found a way up there during one of our exercises."

They ran through the corridors, Conrad close behind French.

———

In the basement of the vice president's mansion at the US Naval Observatory, in northwestern Washington, the Secret Service agents on shift were watching the news of the crisis at the FBI building on the television monitors in the operations center. Among the agents on the vice president's detail watching the breaking news unfold, only Samantha was unsurprised at the speed with which the reporters had arrived on the scene. They could see images of FBI employees streaming out of the Hoover building as ambulances began to arrive. It was a jarring image to Samantha's colleagues. They were so engrossed in the story, none of them noticed Samantha smiling.

One of the senior agents took a phone call at the far end of the operations center. He said nothing, but listened intently. When he hung up the phone, he turned to his colleagues. "That was the White House detail. They want Cowboy at the White House now. Everybody suit up!"

Samantha quickly typed a message to the family and hit the send button. It read "*Cowboy summoned to the WH.*"

Samantha then reached for her bulletproof vest.

———

Across the Potomac River, deep within the Pentagon complex, Michael was watching the same news reports on TV monitors at the Joint Chiefs operations command room. The room was beginning to stir with excitement. Phones started to ring with more frequency, and Michael could see more personnel arriving. His cell phone rang, and he could see from the caller ID that it was his mentor, Col. Armstrong.

"Yes, Colonel," he answered sharply.

"It seems there was some sort of incident at the FBI. We're gonna activate our emergency protocols out of an abundance of caution. So I need you to head to the command center."

"I'm way ahead of you, Colonel. I'm already here."

"Excellent, Mike. You never know, this could be a prelude to some other attacks," Armstrong cautioned.

"Yes, of course, Colonel," Michael answered.

"I also heard word that Chairman Conboy is headed your way, too."

"Very well, Colonel. I will start calling some of our analysts." Michael ended the call as he continued watching the news reports. He smiled at the irony. It was the very security protocols the government was initiating that would be their undoing.

In the days preceding Coyote One, Michael had arranged for a new water bubbler to be installed in the command room. In the lower half of the bubbler, Michael had hidden his gas canister. He had tied a rubber hose from the canister's nozzle to one of the water activation handles. By turning the handle counterclockwise, he could unscrew the handle, slowly releasing the gas into the room. He had spent three weeks testing the system, and it was foolproof. His only decision now was when to release the gas. He was waiting for a packed command center, with the biggest fish he could catch.

He typed a simple message into his phone for the family.

"*JCS chairman and staff en route.*"

———

Tim and Susan had just read the latest message when Ryan appeared. He had left them alone momentarily and returned to check on them. The ventilation room was cold. Both Susan and Tim had zipped their jackets tight.

"What's happening outside?" Susan asked

"Just as anticipated, more and more congressmen are arriving. They are getting into their patriotic mode, getting ready to rally around the flag."

"Excellent. Once I release the gas, I will send you a text. You and Alexa need to be in position. You should start heading out," Tim said.

"Technically, you are supposed to be escorted at all times. I'm worried one of the men will challenge you if I'm not around." Ryan sounded concerned.

"Don't worry about that, we are very close to executing phase two. Where is your sister?" Tim asked.

"She's in my cruiser, waiting for me," Ryan answered.

"Go to her now. We're almost all set. I just need Sam to get to the White House."

Back at the cruiser, Alexa double-checked both her pistol and machine gun, making sure she was fully loaded. She checked her watch. Almost an hour had now elapsed since the director's assassination. As part of her training, Alexa was visualizing the attack she was about to participate in. She was completely unconcerned that the trunk of her car contained a large payload of explosives. Ryan had rigged the device to explode via cell phone signal. She scrolled through her phone's memory, making sure that the number was there when she needed it.

———

O'Neil sat on the Wallace family couch with his left hand on his forehead. He could not believe the recording he had just listened to. His first instinct was to replay the recording, but he knew he had no time. As a Secret Service agent, his first and most important priority was protecting the president and his VP. He got up and raced for the door.

# EIGHT

## Feds Counterstrike

Sullivan waited impatiently by the only door he could find on the barren roof of the Hoover Building. The brothers waited inside the now silent helicopter. After what seemed like an eternity to them, Conrad sprung the metal door open and emerged onto the roof, accompanied by French.

"It's too late. He killed the director," Conrad blurted out. Sullivan shook his head in disgust.

Sullivan peered over the edge of the building. He could see the multitudes trying to exit the massive structure. Sullivan knew that security at headquarters, as in most buildings, is designed to screen people coming in, not leaving. He imagined that Kyle was attempting that very moment to blend in with the crowd leaving the building. There were at least twelve thousand employees, none of whom had ever had to evacuate FBI headquarters. It would take a lot of time to get that many people out of the building. Also, the director's office was on the seventh floor, so Kyle could not have been among the first to get onto the street.

Sullivan pointed at French. "Get to the FBI Police with a picture of Grant. Have them start circulating with the crowd outside, looking for him. Make sure they do it openly!"

They both nodded. Sullivan then directed his attention to Conrad. "You need to hook up with Fuller."

Sullivan then turned to face the brothers, who watched from the chopper. He twirled one finger in the air, and they turned on their ignition, which in a moment had their engine whirring to attention.

"I have a plan!" Sullivan yelled over the noise. Conrad and French watched in amazement as Sullivan boarded the helicopter.

—

The specially equipped Cadillac limousine that would carry the vice president was idling on the oval driveway outside the VP's mansion. The limousine's capacity was seven passengers, which meant that on the short trip from the mansion to the White House, six Secret Service agents would accompany Vice President Rand Tolland. Special Agent Tucker Smith was the VP security team leader, and he traditionally rode shotgun. As Tolland walked toward the limo with his security team at his side, Smith held open the rear door for them. When the last man was aboard, Smith closed the heavy door. The door was so heavy that Smith had to use both hands to shut them in. He then went around and jumped into the passenger seat as he usually did. Once sealed inside the limousine, they were protected by five-inch-thick armor plating.

Samantha was seated in the follow-on Secret Service vehicle, a specially equipped, heavily armored Suburban van that followed closely behind the limousine at all times. The glass on the limousine's windows was so thick that very little light entered the vehicle. For this reason, Samantha could not see the people inside the limo once the doors were closed. The six other agents in the Suburban with her were quiet. She resisted the urge to send the family another text. It would look odd to her colleagues, and she wanted nothing to derail their plan, which was so close to realization.

Behind the Suburban were several police cars. In front of the limo were several motorcycle police units. Those units would close upcoming intersections during the trip, allowing the caravan to proceed without interruption.

Once all the units were in place, they heard Smith's voice crackle over their radio speaker. "Limo two has a green light." Limo two was the code name for the vehicle carrying the vice president.

With that command, the caravan proceeded out of the vice-presidential compound.

———

Across town, Robert White, special agent in charge of the Washington field office of the US Secret Service, sat behind his large mahogany desk watching the news reports, as were most other people around the nation. He understood that if the FBI director was truly dead, as the reports were indicating, the United States was potentially the victim of another terrorist attack. As he saw the reports, he was hoping it was the act of a deranged employee, rather than some part of a larger plot.

He anticipated that the Secret Service director would soon summon him for a conference. The Secret Service would have to ramp up security in light of these events. He had called his own senior staff for a security meeting. He wanted to have a plan of action to present to his director. As he rose to go to the meeting, his phone intercom came alive. It was his secretary, Olivia Summers. She had worked in that capacity for the last five years, and they had developed a good relationship. White could sense fear in her voice.

"Bob, you need to pick up on line one. It's important." Her voice cracked slightly.

The senior staff studied their Blackberries as they waited for the meeting to begin. Among those waiting at a conference room table for White's arrival was Deputy Assistant Director Jonathan Hughes. As Hughes waited, he was daydreaming of the rendezvous he had scheduled with Samantha for later that evening. He pictured her in one of the sexy black dresses that she liked to wear for him. The next thing that happened jarred him to attention.

White bounded into the conference room, his reddened face scowling, and bellowed to the startled group, "Where the hell is Special Agent Samantha Wallace?!"

Jorge had lifted off the roof with ease. On Sullivan's orders, he had swooped around the building, leaving them hovering over Pennsylvania Avenue, where most of the employees had begun to congregate. The Washington police had quickly shut down the intersections on Pennsylvania Avenue that led to the Hoover building. Thousands of FBI employees were milling about. After a few minutes, they seemed to forget that there was a helicopter over them—all of them except for Peter. Having managed to leave the building with a small cluster of employees, he decided to stay close to them so he would not stand out. He was hesitant to leave the area, for fear that the police checkpoints had been alerted to his identity. Peter looked up at the helicopter warily, attempting to discern which law enforcement agency was operating it. He found it odd that it had no markings. He started to assess his options. In truth, he had never imagined that he would still be alive. The idea that he could actually escape and arrive at the family's rendezvous point never really crossed his mind. For the first time in his life, he had no direct plan of action.

Having been alerted by Agent French, the FBI Police took no notice of Sullivan and his helicopter crew. They were told of the search for Kyle Grant, and a photo of Kyle was distributed to all FBI Police officers on duty. On French's orders, they began to fan out among the crowd, looking for their assassin. In their bright white uniforms, the FBI Police officers stood out from the hundreds of employees, most of whom were wearing business suits. As such, Sullivan could see the scene clearly unfold from above. He scanned the crowds, hoping his plan would work.

From the ground, Peter suddenly came to the realization that the FBI Police was not simply present for crowd control. He could see them holding something, which he quickly assumed was his photo, as they waded through the throngs of employees. He knew he had to bolt.

Peter started walking away from the crowds, heading south on Pennsylvania Avenue toward the US Archives building. As he got farther from the outer ring of the crowd, he started walking faster.

From above, Sullivan pointed down at him. "I got him!" he yelled.

———

Less than two miles away, the Limo Two caravan was heading into the heart of Washington. The Suburban stayed close on the limo's tail. The follow-on vehicle had an important role in the security of the convoy. In addition to providing additional armed agents in the event of an assault, the Suburban had equipment to detect approaching heat-seeking missiles or chemical attacks. From within the Suburban's front passenger seat, the vehicle's team leader, Agent Lance Benetti, could launch countermeasures to protect the limousine.

Seated next to Samantha was Agent Russell Roberts, a senior agent with fifteen years of experience. He, like the other members of the team, was not pleased at how Samantha had obtained her posting. They had all heard the rumors of her affair with Assistant Director Hughes. As they barreled through the closed intersections, he watched her as she looked out the Suburban's tinted window. He noticed her calm demeanor, which he found interesting, given her inexperience.

The silence within the van was disrupted by Agent Benetti. "Two minutes!"

They were closing in on the White House.

———

When Peter saw the helicopter move in his direction, he began a full sprint toward the National Mall. As he cornered the National Archives building, Sullivan's view of Peter was temporarily blocked. Jorge deftly lifted the chopper higher, over the Archives, and again they could see Peter, who was now running across Constitution Avenue, as cars swerved to avoid hitting him. The chopper followed him across the wide expanse of Constitution in seconds, while Sullivan looked at Jorge and pointed down. Jorge knew what this meant. Sullivan was itching to get his hands on his prey.

Peter sprinted onto the wide open area of the National Mall, and he decided to run toward the Smithsonian Institution, which was overrun with tourists. His strategy was to blend in with the throngs of people milling about.

Conrad and French had observed the chopper's movements, and they followed it on foot as quickly as they could.

The helicopter touched down on the grass of the National Mall within view of their fleeing fugitive. Sullivan aggressively leaped out of the chopper.

"Wait here," he ordered. He instinctively lowered his head as he ran underneath the chopper's whirring blades. His pursuit began in full.

Peter was fatigued, and Sullivan was fresh, enabling him to gain on him quickly. Sullivan ran past families with their children, as well as tourists, many of them having watched the helicopter landing with interest. Most of them moved out of his way as he ran past. Some were taking pictures of the surreal scene. Sullivan was focused exclusively on Peter, who was now only one hundred feet in front of him as they approached the Smithsonian.

Once again, Peter's senses were on high alert. He was almost out of gas and was now working on pure adrenaline. He was in full survival mode. He could feel Sullivan closing in on him. He turned and saw Sullivan racing toward him, less than fifty feet away. He knew he only had seconds. Peter ran toward a young family of four—an overweight man wearing a green T-shirt, his short wife wearing a red blouse with gray shorts, and their two children, a boy about five, a girl perhaps three years old. The man had a large camera hanging around his sweaty neck. The woman was attending to her daughter. Without warning, Peter approached the group and shot the man in the face. The sharp sound of the pistol stunned everyone around to attention. The man's blood spattered onto his wife and across the grass. Peter grabbed the boy off the ground and held him to his chest. The woman screamed hysterically, blood dripping down the side of her face. She grabbed her daughter, covering her eyes, as she knelt down to the ground.

With one hand holding the boy, Peter used his other to point his gun at Sullivan, who now stood before him. Because of his fatigue, and the weight of the child, his gun hand was unsteady. Sullivan could see that weakness and started circling them, making it harder for Peter to shoot him. Peter fired one round and then another, missing.

"Please understand it was never personal with you," Peter yelled as he clutched the boy closely. He was stalling for time.

Sullivan continued circling, faster. "It's time to pay!" he shouted back.

Peter raised his hand a little higher, again pointing at Sullivan, steadying for another shot. The child squirmed and kicked, making him harder to handle. With one swift movement, Sullivan pulled out his pistol and fired one round, hitting Peter squarely on the jaw, missing the boy by mere inches. The child instantly dropped to the ground, as Peter fell back, arms outstretched helplessly to his side.

Sullivan quickly picked up the child and took him to his stunned mother. She ran away as fast as she could muster, with both children. Sullivan walked back to Peter and kicked the gun out of his clenched hand. Blood was pouring from his caved in jaw into his open throat. Peter could not breathe or even gasp for air. He was drowning in his own blood. He looked up at Sullivan in his final seconds of life.

As Conrad and French approached the scene, passing frightened onlookers who were fleeing the area, they saw Sullivan kneel next to Peter and whisper something into his ear. Peter's eyes then closed for good.

Sullivan conducted a quick search of the body and found a small cell phone, which he pocketed. He stood as they arrived.

He greeted them somberly, holstering his weapon. "I think we are done here."

Conrad was breathing heavily from his run.

"No—no," he stammered. "It's not over."

---

Limo Two was speeding across Constitution Avenue, two blocks from the White House, as the helicopter touched down on the Mall. Samantha and her colleagues watched the scene unfold as they continued toward their destination. She did not know that her brother was at that moment fighting for his life. She glanced at her watch and then focused herself, rehearsing in her mind again how she envisioned the events would play out once she was inside the White House.

After the attacks of 9/11, the section of Pennsylvania Avenue in front of the White House was closed for added security. On both ends of the closed street, a Secret Service security booth was installed. Steel security columns were built into the street to prevent vehicles from entering that section. However, with the push of a button, the Secret Service uniformed officer within the booth could lower the barriers, allowing Secret Service personnel, or a presidential convoy, to pass.

Limo Two was only two blocks away from the checkpoint, which was now visible to the convoy, when Samantha noticed Team Leader Benetti receive a call on his cell phone. Seated in the front passenger seat, she noticed him warily glance back at her.

"What?" Benetti said into the phone, confused.

In the background, she could hear the raised voice of VP security detail chief, Tucker Smith, who was in the limo seated next to VP Tolland. Samantha's antenna went up as she saw Benetti whisper something to their driver, Agent Kenneth Swindon. She felt the Suburban start to slow down as the limo surged forward.

Seated next to Samantha, Agent Roberts turned to question the driver. Without hesitation, Samantha pulled out her pistol and pumped two rounds into him. Because he was wearing his vest, she put one in his throat, the other in his forehead. She turned to the two other agents in the back with her. They froze. Before they could react, she fired two more rounds into each of them in the same manner. They slumped lifelessly in their seats. Pointing her weapon at Benetti, she clambered up to where she was within two feet of him.

"Gun the engine!" she ordered as the limo raced toward the checkpoint. She could see the barriers being lowered.

"What are you doing, Wallace?" Benetti screamed in fear.

"Get on that limo's tail or you die!" she shouted, desperate to make the checkpoint.

Benetti looked at Swindon, who gunned the engine, trying to gain on the limo. The limo passed through the checkpoint, and the guard started to raise the barriers just as the Suburban was passing through. One of the steel columns rose up and clipped the rear of the Suburban, lifting it two feet off the ground. The Suburban bounced off the ground but passed through. The impact swerved the van off track, and the vehicle stopped in the middle of the plaza, stalled. Samantha could see the White House gates opening to allow the limo to pass through. She pointed her gun at Benetti, then Swindon.

"Get out!" she shouted.

Without a word, Benetti and Swindon both opened their doors and got out of the Suburban, running back toward the security booth. Wandering tourists on the White House Plaza now started to scatter. Samantha quickly slipped into the driver's seat just as the limo passed through the heavy metal White House gate. She needed to use both hands to close the heavy doors, which cost her precious seconds. Samantha put on her seat belt and turned the key, starting the ignition. She floored the accelerator as hard as she could and steered directly at the now closed gate. The impact was jarring. The gate buckled but held. She pulled the van into reverse and again rammed the gate with all the Suburban's might.

As Samantha rammed the gate a third time, she could see Smith escorting VP Tolland into the White House, surrounded by his security detail. She started receiving incoming fire from other agents who were streaming out of the White House. The bullets bounced harmlessly off the armored Suburban. Samantha kept rocking the gate back and forth with the Suburban. As she did so, the gunfire she received became more intense and of higher caliber, causing more damage to her vehicle. Samantha gritted her teeth in determination, certain she was the coyote in her epic battle. The wolf was hers, if she could only get inside. As the gate finally crashed to the ground, she saw another agent leaning against a tree, holding a rocket propelled grenade (RPG). She saw the projectile shoot toward her, but she drove the

Suburban forward just in time. The grenade exploded against another section of the gate she had just broken through.

As the Suburban gained traction again, she headed straight for the front steps of the White House, determined to crash through. She was operating now on an emotional level. Samantha knew her chance to actually kill the wolf was beyond her reach. Yet her determination was indomitable.

As the Suburban closed in on the White House itself, another RPG round hit the rear of the vehicle, spinning it 180 degrees. Inside the smoky Suburban, Samantha was shaken, but alive. In the hazy smoke, she felt for a machine gun that was stored under the passenger seat. She could still hear bullet rounds pinging against the impaired vehicle.

With the machine gun in her hand, she inserted a magazine and racked the action. She unlatched the door with her free hand and pushed the door open with her legs. Samantha quickly poked her head outside and identified three approaching targets. Without further exposing her face, she reached out her hands and fired a volley of rounds in their direction. Two of the agents were struck, falling to the ground. The other took cover behind the rear of the Suburban. Samantha jumped out of the still smoking vehicle and ran toward the cover of a large tree in front of the White House. A sniper, positioned on the rooftop, fired two rounds at her but they hit the ground, missing her. She moved too quickly.

Leaning against the tree and from her partial cover, Samantha started firing additional rounds at the agents who were rapidly encroaching on her position. For good measure, she fired at the White House itself, which at that moment was sheltering her despised wolf. Sensing encirclement, Samantha decided to move again, closer to her target. As she moved forward, she continued firing when suddenly she felt a sharp pain in her shoulder. A bullet had passed through her left clavicle. She knelt in pain, dropping her machine gun. As another agent came forward, she reached for her pistol, taking it out of its holster. In the instant before she fired at the agent, who was only a few feet in front of her, she felt a shock to her system. From behind, she heard the fateful round fired at her, and she knew. She only had a minute or so to live as she lay motionless, facing the blue sky.

From two feet away, O'Neil had placed a bullet at the base of her neck, just above the protection offered by her vest. She could not move, but she could feel the shadow he cast over her as she rested on the ground. Her breath grew increasingly shallow. O'Neil cautiously pulled her pistol, which she still clutched, out of her hand, tucking it into his waistband as other agents appeared at his side. He looked down at her without pity.

"Why?" he asked simply.

She mouthed a few words, and O'Neil leaned down to hear her answer.

Her voice was soft in its last few breaths. Yet he could hear her clearly.

"Because…I'm a coyote."

# NINE

## Coyote Pushback

The Washington press corps was now in full frenzy. Dozens of media outlets seemed to instantly appear outside the White House, where a full war had taken place only minutes before. From his phone's browser, Tim Wallace started to read the incoming reports. "*Vice presidential convoy assaulted. White House grounds breached by terrorists. Firefight reported outside the presidential compound.*"

Although unsure whether Samantha had succeeded in assassinating her targets, he knew there was not a moment to waste. He activated the gas release into the Capitol. He then texted a one word order to his remaining children: *Proceed.*

---

Conrad related the full conspiracy to Sullivan as quickly as possible and as faithfully as he'd heard it from O'Neil.

"O'Neil said he would take care of the Secret Service end of the conspiracy. He told me the rest was up to us. He has his hands full protecting the vice president."

He finished the briefing just as he rushed Sullivan to a waiting FBI car parked on Constitution Avenue, only blocks from the Capitol Hill complex. In the driver's seat of the idling car was Fuller. She was exhausted from her late-night trip but otherwise ready for action. Sullivan could always tell when she put on her game face.

Sullivan opened the passenger door and leaned inside.

"Hey there, Fuller, ready to play?" Sullivan asked with a serious expression. He too was determined to bring his A game to the unfolding scenario.

"Ready," she answered.

Sullivan looked at Conrad and French. "You guys go with Fuller to the Capitol building. I will get to the Pentagon."

French looked at Conrad, then back to Sullivan. "How will you get there?"

"You forget that I have a helicopter." Sullivan smiled.

Conrad nodded as Sullivan turned toward the Mall again. "Good luck!" He yelled at his friend. Sullivan ran toward the helicopter and the waiting brothers.

——

The cavernous JCS command center was buzzing with a mixture of excitement and nervousness. Everyone moved with a machine-like efficiency, knowing that much rested on their shoulders. Rows of analysts were on the phone, sharing incoming intelligence about the attacks with their counterparts at the CIA, NSA, FBI, and the Secret Service. The command center was designed like a wide well, the lowest point being in the center. Every twenty feet from there, the room gained another foot, a higher platform. The outer ring, manned by the lowest-level analysts, was almost ten feet higher than the center, which contained a large table for the chairman, his deputy, and the chiefs of all the services. JCS Chairman Conboy had taken his place at the largest, most comfortable seat in the center, his ear to a landline phone. No cell phones were allowed into the command center, as it was considered a SCIF, a room designed for secret communications, which strictly prohibits any electronic devices. Next to him, on a landline with the White House, was the secretary of defense, Jason Whitworth.

His presence made Michael's target far richer than the family could have imagined. They had not anticipated that Whitworth would be a viable target.

The command center had two entrances at opposite ends of each other, known as the eastern and western entrances. The doors were solid metal and when closed, sounded like cell doors. They were opened by punching a security code into a secure pad. Every employee with access had his own individual seven-digit code. At the eastern entrance, the door had been secured shut with a neatly printed sign, which read Eastern entrance closed for maintenance. Michael had bolted the door, ensuring that employees could only enter from one side.

Several large television monitors were hanging on the northern wall of the command center. Michael watched the news as images were displayed of the still smoking, bullet-marked Suburban on the White House lawn. Other screens showed actual scenes from the firefight taken from the recorders of visiting tourists. Some of the reports showed people being taken out on stretchers, some of them covered in blood-soaked sheets. He knew something was amiss. Samantha clearly was compromised before she could reach her target. The news reported that the president and vice president were both safe. Her mission had failed. Michael wondered if the remaining mission would also be derailed. He knew it was inevitable—he would soon be identified as Samantha's brother, and logically a person of interest. Just as he pondered how long that would take, he felt his cell phone vibrate. He knew having a cell phone in the command center was a security violation, but this infraction seemed insignificant next to the mass murder he was about to commit.

The phone contained his father's one word message. He found comfort in it. Michael walked calmly to the watercooler, which was strategically placed in a corner twenty feet from the center of the room, and reached for its nozzle. Just as he touched the nozzle, he felt a hand on his shoulder.

"Mike," Col. Armstrong said firmly, "I'm glad you're here." Michael pulled away and stood up straight.

"Thank you, sir," Michael responded, feeling the tug of the water-cooler. He had to turn on the switch before it was too late. He wanted to succeed where Samantha had failed.

"We have a lot of work to do," the colonel said, pulling Michael away from the cooler.

"Yes, sir, I'm getting reports from a contact at the FBI. Let me consult with him, and I can brief you." Michael lied, determined to get back to his device.

"Very well, then," Armstrong said. He turned and walked back toward Chairman Conboy.

Michael finally reached the watercooler, releasing the gas slowly. He then briskly walked toward the only exit in the room. He had every intention of both succeeding in his mission and surviving it.

—

As Sullivan's chopper crossed the Potomac, Miguel sat in the front passenger seat and glanced back. He could see Sullivan feverishly texting on his cell phone. After a few seconds, Miguel saw him smiling. Sullivan looked up at the brothers and displayed his telephone screen, which showed a man's picture with the name MICHAEL WALLACE in bold letters underneath.

"That's our target," he shouted.

Miguel and Jorge both gave him a thumbs-up sign. They understood.

From her cubicle in Boston, Trish O'Keefe had been reviewing all the data she had gathered on the Wallace family, which she had begun to do after Sullivan's earlier surveillance. Sullivan knew that with Trish on the case, their chances of success had increased considerably. As he considered this fact, he felt a vibration from the phone he had confiscated on the Mall. It had a one word text: *Proceed.* Sullivan shook his head silently at the sobering message.

As the chopper closed in on the Pentagon, Miguel pointed at the approaching building and yelled back to Sullivan. "How you get inside?"

"Drop me on the roof," he said confidently. "I have a plan."

Miguel and Jorge arched their eyebrows simultaneously.

———

Before Michael had even crossed the Potomac, Fuller had reached the security perimeter of the Capitol building, using her police lights and siren. Capitol Police Captain Ross Reardon, the highest-ranking officer on duty that day, ran down to greet the arriving agents when he heard the commotion. When he got to them, he could hear one of his sergeants arguing with the female agent. Sergeant Joss Black, a ten-year veteran of the force, stood with his arms crossed in a skeptical pose.

"We don't have time to waste," Fuller yelled at the flustered officer. "You need to evacuate the Capitol building!"

"I'm in charge here," Reardon said firmly. "What's the situation?"

"It's more than a situation," Conrad said seriously. "Where is your officer Ryan Wallace?"

———

As instructed by Sullivan, Jorge descended and let the chopper hover a foot or so above the Pentagon's roof, allowing him to jump down without actually landing the aircraft. To absorb the impact of the jump, Sullivan rolled over. He then sat on the ground, his legs crossed. He watched the helicopter bank away from the building, back toward the Potomac River. Sullivan had quickly surmised that he would be unable to get into the building. He knew, however, that the Pentagon Police, already on high alert after the events of the day, had clearly watched his approach and landing. His plan was to let security come to him in the hope that his information, as well as his power of persuasion, would win the day. Sullivan suspected that people were dying that very moment in the heart of the Pentagon. Sullivan sat and waited with his badge and credentials in his hand, at the ready.

Within a minute, a large metal door flung open from the ground, approximately fifty feet from where Sullivan was seated. A SWAT team of ten heavily armed Pentagon Police officers swarmed toward him yelling, "Hands on your head!" Sullivan did not even have time to display his badge, they were so quickly on top of him. In seconds, he was in handcuffs, face down on the concrete, gasping for air as two of the officers kept him pinned down by kneeling on his back.

They patted him down, and one of them shouted, "Gun!" as he confiscated his weapon.

From the ground, Sullivan heard one of them use his radio. "Subject in custody!"

Sullivan, his face on its side, tried to talk to his captors.

"I'm an FBI agent. It is important you listen to me." He tried talking as calmly as he could, given the circumstances. He knew they probably thought him a madman.

From behind the SWAT team emerged another officer. This one clearly walked with the swagger of authority. Sullivan could deduce the man was an officer of some high rank, from the insignia on his uniform. The man, in his fifties, barrel-chested with an oversized head, walked to the scene and stood over Sullivan.

One of the officers handed the man Sullivan's badge and credentials, which the man scrutinized skeptically. As he reviewed the document, his cell phone started ringing. He was prepared to ignore the call, until he noticed the caller ID, which read a series of ten zeroes across his screen. He had never seen that before. Intrigued, he answered the phone.

"Is this Miles Nickerson, deputy police chief, Pentagon Police?" a female voice asked him.

"Yes, it is."

"Please stand by. I have a call from Attorney General Jonathan Mitchell." Nickerson looked at his phone for a moment, then pulled it tightly to his ear, straining to hear over the ambient noise.

"This is Attorney General Jonathan Mitchell," the AG said flatly. "Do you have a Special Agent Carlos Sullivan with you?"

"Yes, well, not exactly with me…but yes, he is here." Nickerson was getting quite agitated.

"Well, you should extend him any cooperation he needs. I have spoken to the president, and we are of one mind. Do we understand each other?" Mitchell's tone allowed for no discussion or argument.

Nickerson was stunned. He barely had a response. He hung up the phone and turned to his officers. "Release him."

As he was being freed from the cuffs and lifted to the ground, he said a silent thanks to Trish. She'd come through for him again. Although he looked forward to hearing how she had pulled that off, he knew he had precious seconds to act.

———

After listening to Conrad for a minute or so, Captain Reardon was incredulous. He had come to rely on Ryan Wallace as one of his most reliable officers. He felt that there must have been a misunderstanding. Without even realizing he was doing it, Reardon had been shaking his head as he stood listening in disbelief. As Conrad continued to speak, Reardon reached for his radio.

"Officer Wallace, over." The radio crackled with Reardon's voice.

While the others waited for a response, Fuller walked over to a parked van with the words "Capitol Area Air & Heating Services" written across the side. Fuller had noticed the suspicious vehicle as soon as they had arrived. She looked inside the locked vehicle but saw nothing alarming. She walked back to the group, which waited in nervous silence.

Reardon again called out, "Officer Wallace, please respond." His disbelief morphed into concern.

"Has anyone seen Officer Wallace?" Reardon pleaded over the radio. A response was immediate.

"Officer Breen here, Captain. He was headed over to the Hart building in a cruiser. He had a new officer with him—a female, over." Reardon looked down at the ground.

Reardon knew there was no new officer. Conrad, Fuller, and French read his face like an open book, and Reardon could tell. He looked up at them. "What do we do?" Conrad spoke first. "If you have a tactical team, deploy them now."

He then pointed at Reardon. "Take French and me into the Capitol building, the ventilation area."

Then Conrad pointed at Sgt. Black. "You take Fuller to the Senate building."

Fuller managed a slight smile. "Finally, let's roll," she said to the group quietly as she opened the trunk of her car. She knew they needed more than their pistols from that point forward. Inside her trunk were several vests, as well as two M4 carbines.

A few blocks away, outside the Hart Senate Office Building, the largest of three buildings used by the Senate, Ryan and Alexa heard the radio call-out with alarm. They realized there could be no further delay.

—

Several dozen congressmen were in the Capitol building gallery, listening to and preparing speeches designed for consumption in their local districts. Many had aides or interns at their side. Most of the speeches were meant to reassure their constituents that they were tough on terrorists and would give no quarter to the enemy. Because of the enormous size of the gallery, none of them could yet feel the effects of the gas that had been released into the chamber.

Tim and Susan Wallace, having released their deadly toxin, discussed their next course of action. After a quiet talk, they decided to head out of the building. Their gas was released and filtering into the gallery. There was no further need for them to remain in the ventilation room. They would head out of the building, wreaking as much havoc as they could as they attempted an improbable escape.

—

The Hart Senate Office Building was connected to another building, the Russell Senate building. The complex took up an entire city block, with entrances on First Street NE and Second Street NE. Across from the Hart building on First Street was the third Senate office building. The Senate complex was a short walk from the main, iconic Capitol building.

Alexa positioned their cruiser as close to the Second Street side of the Hart building as possible. At the Capitol Police guard shack, Ryan waved at the guard behind the glass. In seconds, the metal barrier blocking their passage was lowered, allowing them to pass. After parking the vehicle, Alexa and Ryan walked around to the front of the building on First Street, and as an extra precaution, walked another two hundred feet back from the structure. Alexa retrieved her cell phone and dialed the number that would trigger the blast. As she dialed the number, she and Ryan both noticed three other Capitol Police officers emerge from the building. They had received a phone call tasking them with finding and detaining Officer Ryan Wallace. They were too late. An earth rattling explosion knocked them off their feet, rendering them partially unconscious. Had they been at the rear of the Hart building, they would have been eviscerated.

On the other side, the enormous blast left a large crater, which destroyed all four above-ground floors of the structure on the rear side, caving it in. The concussive effect also shattered the windows of two buildings across the street. A gray haze seemed to descend on the city block, much like the closing of a dark curtain. Glass and concrete were sent in every direction. Dozens were killed instantly. Hundreds were injured or dazed, yet the carnage was only commencing. As part of their plan, Alexa and Ryan, with machine guns slung over their shoulders, were prepared to fire at the survivors evacuating the building from the front doors. The front of the building, while damaged, was still structurally sound.

From two blocks away, Fuller and Sgt. Black, in their car, felt the explosion.

"Fuck!" yelled Sgt. Black. "Did you hear that?"

"Yes," Fuller responded. "We are too late. Fuck." She gunned the engine, roaring toward the smoky scene of terror.

After a quick briefing from Sullivan, Nickerson sensed that he had a major security problem at the Pentagon. He knew Michael Wallace by reputation, which was impeccable, but he had been around long enough to hear a compelling story. From the roof of the Pentagon, he had attempted to call Col. Armstrong, a personal friend, on his cell phone, but it went directly to voice mail. He was not immediately alarmed, because he knew that mobile phones are not allowed in the command center. However, Nickerson's concern was magnified when he was unable to reach anyone inside the command center's hard lines. They all agreed that reaching the command center was their first priority.

Nickerson felt he needed to share a critical piece of information. "Someone else very important is down there."

"Who?" Sullivan asked, annoyed at Nickerson wasting time.

"The secretary of defense. He arrived fifteen minutes ago."

"Then let's go!" he urged.

As Sullivan, Nickerson, and his SWAT team made final preparations to descend into the Pentagon, they heard an explosion unlike any of them had ever heard. It was a powerful, deep sound that seemed to create a disturbance in the atmosphere. Sullivan looked across the Potomac and saw a large plume of smoke, coming from behind the Capitol. From his knowledge of the city, he knew that one of the Senate office buildings had just been attacked. And from the sound of the blast, he knew that damage was significant.

The moment jarred him into a new level of awareness—the explosion crystallized in his mind the nature and extent of the evil conspiracy they were facing.

It started with a cough. JCS Chairman Conboy was sitting in his regal-looking chair when he looked over at Col. Armstrong, who was briefing his aides, and noticed that he coughed. He had known Col. Armstrong for twenty-five years and had never heard him cough or sneeze. The man was never sick. As he pondered that fact, he realized he was not feeling well himself. He started feeling nauseated. Then he started coughing, gasping for clean air. He tried standing up, but didn't have enough oxygen in his system. He felt immobilized. As Conboy looked around the room, he saw people falling to the ground. Next to him, he witnessed Secretary of Defense Whitworth lying prostrate, his eyes pleading. It was the last thing he saw as he blacked out, slumping to the floor.

———

Nickerson and Sullivan, followed by the SWAT team, arrived at the western entrance of the JSC Situation room with lightning speed. As they traversed the long corridors of the Pentagon on their journey, the employees they encountered all moved to the side, letting them pass unimpeded. Because the SWAT team members were in vests and helmets, they were winded when they arrived. Immediately, they could see the sign placed at the entrance in bold letters: JSC Situation Room closed for briefing. They observed that the access pad had been destroyed, possibly with a heavy object. Michael was already on his way out of the Pentagon.

Sullivan could also see their obstacle. "No way to open it, right?"

"Fuck!" Nickerson shouted, banging on the door with his fist. It seemed immovable.

"Blow it!" Sullivan said. He knew the Pentagon SWAT team must have explosives.

"Now!" Nickerson ordered. His SWAT team leader, Officer Welsh, started the process with two of his men. Using small amounts of RDX explosives, they quickly rigged the door's large steel hinges.

They cleared the hallway and took cover around a corner.

"Fire in the hole!" bellowed Walsh.

The explosion reverberated down the hallway and beyond. Even after covering their ears, it was bone jarring. The door was blown off its hinges.

Once inside the Situation Room, Sullivan could see that those closest to the doors were dazed, some sitting, most kneeling. Some of them were vomiting. Those in the center of the room were in worse condition, immobilized, possibly dead. He knew what they were facing. Having been briefed by Sullivan, Nickerson had ordered his SWAT team to don their gas masks.

"As I said, Mr. Nickerson, it's a gas!" he said, covering his face with his left hand.

The SWAT team began escorting those on the outer fringes out of the room, one by one, as quickly as they could. Sullivan looked from the door's threshold for Secretary of Defense Whitworth, but could not see him. As Nickerson looked on in disbelief, Sullivan held his breath and bounded into the Situation Room, descending each level quickly, headed toward the lowest point. He imagined that the leaders were most likely in the center of the room. He had seen Whitworth on TV dozens of times; he scanned the victims, searching for that familiar face. Finally, he saw Whitworth lying on his side, eyes closed.

Sullivan reached down, braced himself, and pulled him over his shoulder, still holding his breath. He started the climb to safety. Level by level he ascended, each second testing his endurance. His first thought was how fortunate he was that Whitworth was not a large man. Yet the 160 pounds he was carrying seemed like the weight of the world. As he finally crossed the threshold, he laid the secretary down as gently as he could. He then dragged him another twenty feet from the door, concerned that gas might still be a threat. Sullivan could not have known that all the gas had been released. It had started to dissipate.

EMS teams had started arriving at the scene. Sullivan called two medics over, and they placed an oxygen mask over Whitworth's face.

As other medics started to tend to the victims, and still more went in to retrieve others from the room, Whitworth started to breathe fresh oxygen. His eyes opened. The first thing he saw was Sullivan, kneeling next to him, still slightly winded. Sullivan patted him on the shoulder and rose to confer with Nickerson.

Nickerson spoke first. "You were right. Thank you," he said, wiping his brow.

"There's no time for that," Sullivan said impatiently.

"You want Michael Wallace," Nickerson said rhetorically.

"I will find that man," Sullivan said.

Nickerson detected no doubt in Sullivan's eyes.

At that moment, Michael Wallace, driving a rented green Nissan Maxima, drove out of the Pentagon parking lot, satisfied that he had accomplished his mission. The car had a small decal on the left side rear window: Dominion Car Rentals. In the trunk was a suitcase with his clothes and a stack of money. In his wallet, he had false identification in the name of Michael Christian, which he would use to start a new life. As he drove off the lot, he threw the cell phone his family had given him out the window. He knew that was the only thing that could be used to track him. He was a free man.

# TEN

## Escape

The moment they arrived at the intersection of First Street NE and C Street, Fuller and Sgt. Black witnessed the unthinkable. Two Capitol Police officers—one of whom Black had considered a trusted colleague—were shooting at survivors as they came out of the building's entrance. Several bodies lay at their feet. One of the victims appeared to be an officer, his white service uniform stained red with blood. Black could not fathom what he was watching. He was stunned. Fuller, however, had been briefed on the macabre plot. She displayed no fear or hesitation. She positioned the car so that the engine block offered them tactical cover. They were fifty yards from the terrorists.

"Get over here, behind me," she ordered, the sound of gunfire ahead of them piercing the air. He clambered over her seat to get out of the car. His side of the vehicle was exposed to the gunmen. Once behind her, he pulled out his gun.

Fuller waved for him not to shoot. "They haven't seen us yet. I want to get off a surprise shot." She leaned over the hood, positioning herself as best she could. From fifty yards, Fuller was a decent marksman at the range. She usually hit at least 80 percent of her targets from that range with her pistol. With the M4 carbine she was holding, she was much better. Yet she knew this was not a range, and her target was moving. Sweat was beading down her neck and brow as she aligned for a shot. She identified the male suspect as the better target, because he was closer to her. Fuller clicked a small button on the M4's sight, turning on the red dot function. On a small sight screen, a red dot lit up, which indicates to the shooter where the bullet will strike if it is properly sighted. The red dot does not project outward and is only visible to the marksman. With Ryan Wallace in her sights, she waited for him to stop moving, even for an instant.

Ryan fired another round at a senate employee escaping the building. The victim, a small female with pink-colored glasses, fell to the ground, wounded. As Ryan aimed his gun down at her to finish her off, he stopped for a moment. Fuller fired.

The M4 carbine shoots a .223 round. It is small, about the size of a .22-caliber bullet. However, the speed at which it travels enhances its lethality. The round penetrated Ryan's left temple and went out on the opposite side of his cranium. Death was instantaneous.

"You got him!" Black shouted, incredulous.

In that instant, Alexa turned her attention toward them. She fired a furious barrage of rounds at them, demolishing their windows and front tires. They were safe behind the engine block, which absorbed several rounds. The firing then stopped for two or three seconds. They peeked over the car, hoping they were clear. Instead, they saw the female changing magazines, reloading. They ducked as another volley of rounds hit their cruiser.

Alexa then turned and walked south, away from their destroyed cruiser. As she walked quickly down the street, a Metro Police cruiser sped toward her with lights and sirens blaring. She waved for them to stop. Two officers climbed out of their cruiser. Before they could say anything, Alexa coldly took them down at close range.

Fuller and Sgt. Black watched in horror as the officers fell, lifeless, to the ground. They ran toward her, guns drawn, but were too far away from her. She got in the cruiser and peeled around the corner. They ran to the corner in an effort to see which direction she took and noticed she turned left after two blocks. Just as this occurred, a Capitol Police cruiser arrived at their corner. Sgt. Black recognized his colleague, Officer Blake, who rolled down his window.

"What the fuck is going on, Black?"

"Just let us in, we need you," Sgt. Black responded. Fuller and her new partners were now in pursuit of a police cruiser. As they drove off, they saw numerous other police and ambulance units arriving.

"Take that left, there!" Fuller ordered from the backseat. She knew where she would go if she wanted to hide.

———

In a remote hallway, unable to see into the gallery of the Capitol building, Tim and Susan Wallace were eager to peer into their targeted chamber and see the results of their handiwork. Susan waited in a hallway while Tim found a passageway from which he could see the damage they had caused. When Tim finally saw that the gallery was almost fully evacuated with no casualties, his face turned pale. He felt like had been punched in the stomach. All the work he had done in preparation for this moment now seemed wasted.

He took a moment to pinpoint his failure. Without a large enclosed room with which to conduct more extensive tests, he had miscalculated his gaseous formula for death. At the dosage he had prepared, the room would have required at least an hour to cause serious injury or death. As a result, after forty-five minutes, the gas had caused only slight nausea to those in the upper level of the chamber, closest to the vents. The evacuation ordered by Captain Reardon had been successful.

When he finally composed himself, Tim did not have the heart to tell Susan about their failure, but she could see the concern on his face. They walked together down a hallway, determined to inflict as many casualties as possible. For Tim, this now seemed more important than ever.

Captain Reardon now accompanied Conrad and French to the upper levels, to the ventilation room. Reardon's SWAT team was two floors below, gearing up as they heard the sound of gunfire.

"Did you hear that?" French asked.

"Yes, that was gunfire," Conrad said, cradling the M4 carbine that Fuller had given him.

"We should wait for the SWAT team," Reardon said hesitantly.

"No way," Conrad said. "People are dying."

Less than twenty-five yards from their position, not yet visible to them in the circular passageway, Tim and Susan Wallace had just shot a congressman and his young intern. Each received one bullet to the head. After finishing off their two defenseless victims, they continued walking down the hallway, looking for more people to assassinate. They were walking toward the south.

Walking north, Reardon, with his pistol drawn, led his two new companions forward.

As they rounded the curved hallway, the groups locked on their opponents, the encounter seeming like a Wild West shootout. Tim and Susan fired at them, and they returned fire instantly, Reardon and French each with their pistols, Conrad firing three-round bursts with his M4. After several seconds of gunfire, a sudden silence shrouded the hallway. The acrid smell of gunpowder overwhelmed the scene. Conrad still had ammunition but stopped firing because he saw French fall back. He was lying on his side, bleeding from the head.

Conrad could see that the woman had been hit in the shoulder. She was kneeling as the male terrorist started pulling her back, retreating away from them. Conrad looked to his left and saw Reardon had fallen back, struck several times. Two rounds were absorbed by his vest. Another round, however, hit him in the hip. He was immobilized. Miraculously, Conrad was unscathed.

His breath shallow, Reardon placed a hand on Conrad's shoulder.

"My SWAT team is on the way," he said. "Just wait."

"I can't let them regroup. They are wounded," Conrad replied.

"Just rest until your team comes for you," he said, turning his attention back toward the retreating team of terrorists.

Several yards away, Tim tried reassuring his wife. "Susan," he said calmly, "you will be fine, let's just compress the wound." He reached in his small backpack for a towel, all while walking backward, slowly. Susan had dropped her weapon, unable to hold it in her hand.

Despite his stated reassurances, Tim knew she would not be all right. The wound was serious, and they had no hope of escape. Susan was aware of their plight, but their mission had always been the priority. She did not complain or cry out.

"Did we kill them all?" she asked weakly.

"Yes," he answered. "Of course."

She could tell from his look that they had failed but said nothing more.

As Tim tended to her, Susan was looking down the hallway. He saw her eyes widen. He looked up, lifting his weapon toward their threat. The sound of gunfire pierced the air.

Dozens of rounds were fired in their direction. Firing three-round bursts, Conrad walked toward them, his M4 carbine his only shield. Susan was struck in the forehead, with pieces of her cranium spraying Tim, who returned fire.

Conrad emptied his thirty-round magazine and then reloaded. His enemy lay twenty feet ahead, and both appeared to be down. As he approached them cautiously, he fired three more rounds into their bodies, to be certain. They were dead.

With the adrenaline coursing through his body, Conrad had not immediately noticed that he had been struck. Two bullets had pierced his left arm. He stood for a moment, looking at the blood on his shirt. As the reality of his situation dawned on him, he dropped the M4 and sat against the wall. He started feeling light-headed. His breathing was shallower. Knowing that panic was the biggest enemy when wounded, he started repeating over and over, out loud, "I'm alive, I'm alive, I'm alive…"

―――

Union Station, in the nation's capital, is a large three-level retail mall. It is also a regional rail center and has a Metro station. It is only a few blocks from Capitol Hill. A taxi stand is always busy with activity at the mall's entrance on Massachusetts Avenue.

With all the commotion underway in the city, the waiting taxi drivers did not think it odd when a Metro Police cruiser pulled up to the mall and parked in front. A female officer got out of the car and calmly walked into the mall. Nobody, even the security guards standing outside the station, noticed that the officer was wearing the wrong uniform for that cruiser. Indeed, they waved hello to Alexa as she walked inside. She waved back, pulling her police cap tightly onto her head, careful to conceal as much of her face as possible from the surveillance cameras.

One minute later, at Fuller's instruction, Officer Blake pulled up to the mall and parked behind the police cruiser. She could see from their expressions that she had impressed them.

"Gentlemen," she said, "this is a great place to blend—and escape."

They got out of the car and walked to the security guards, who watched them approach.

"The female officer," Fuller said, pointing to the cruiser. "Did you see her?"

"Yeah," one of them replied. "She went inside."

They walked inside and could see how daunting their task was. There were hundreds of people, walking, shopping, and eating. None seemed the least concerned that the city of Washington was under attack. At that moment, Alexa was in the restroom of the lower level, near the food court. Inside a stall, she quickly removed her uniform. Underneath it, she was wearing street clothes—a pair of gray slacks and a green T-shirt. Her hair, which had been held in a bun, she let loose down past her shoulders. The uniform, as well as the family cell phone, she put into the trash bin. The person who walked out of the bathroom looked nothing like the person who had entered.

As Fuller and her team searched for her one level above, Alexa walked to the Metro station and retrieved from her pocket a Metro card, which she had purchased earlier, in anticipation of this moment. Using the card, she walked to the platform and waited for the first train.

For ten minutes, she waited patiently on the platform, watching for danger. None appeared. When the train arrived, she boarded with several others. She found a seat, and the doors closed. As the train departed, Alexa loosened her shoulders and relaxed for the first time. She was free.

Fifteen minutes later, with the aid of the surveillance cameras, Fuller tracked her terrorist using the escalator, headed toward the lower level. It showed her turn a corner toward the restroom. After a quick search of the bathroom, Fuller retrieved the disposed uniform and cell phone. Unfortunately, she knew the camera did not actually capture the bathroom door. So many people walked by that area, no description would be possible.

Fuller went upstairs to make a phone call. Dozens of police cruisers were now parked outside Union Station. Hundreds of Metro Police officers had joined them in their search for the cop killer who had left their brothers dead and wounded on the streets outside.

———

Michael Wallace, having left all traces of his former life behind, drove silently through the Pennsylvania countryside, his headlights piercing the dark night like a saber. He had planned his escape meticulously. As he drove north, toward the family rendezvous point, he wondered if his wife's body had been found yet. He doubted it.

———

Sullivan looked at his phone. "Fuller, are you all right?"

"Yes," she said.

"Have you heard from Conrad?" he asked, worried about his friend.

"No"

"What happened?"

"Sully, the damage they caused...I can't even believe it." As she spoke, her hand went to her face. Now that she was alone, with the adrenaline out of her system, she was starting to feel a wave of emotions—a mix of fear, anxiety, and compassion for the victims.

Sullivan could tell she was upset. "We need to all meet up," he said, attempting to reassure her.

"One more thing," she said.

"What?"

"One of them got away—a woman." Fuller could feel herself start to cry, and she bit her lip to contain herself.

"The Pentagon suspect got away, too." He looked down at the ground in disgust.

"What do we do now?"

Sullivan thought silently for a moment. "I know someone who can help." He smiled tightly, hopefully.

# ELEVEN

## Regrouping

**A**s evening fell upon their wounded capital city, the team re-grouped at the foot of Conrad's hospital bed. Within minutes of being found by Reardon's SWAT team, both men were on their way to the George Washington University Hospital. Both were awake and conscious, in rooms across from each other. In Conrad's room, the TV was tuned to the National News Network, which was broadcasting pictures of the death and destruction caused by unknown terrorists. The images were horrifying. The scroll beneath the images described much of what had occurred: "*Seven dead at the Pentagon, including JCS Chairman Conboy. Dozens killed at the Senate office building, at least one ter-rorist reportedly escaped. Assault on the White House thwarted, several Secret Service agents killed.*"

The volume was turned down as Conrad, Fuller, and Sullivan watched the monitor in silence. As they watched, an anchorman was speaking in what appeared to be his most somber manner. Two photos were suddenly flashed on the screen, and Sullivan spoke first.

"Turn it up," he ordered. Fuller had the remote and complied.

"*These are photos obtained by the National News Network of two of the terrorists involved in today's siege of the capital,*" the anchorman explained dramatically.

The team was glued to the TV.

"*They are Ryan Wallace, a sergeant with the US Capitol Police and Samantha Wallace, a member of the Secret Service. Both were reportedly killed during the attacks.*"

Then another picture was posted.

"*A third suspect, seen here, is Michael Wallace, a captain in the US Army, reportedly attached to the Pentagon. He escaped and is wanted by the FBI.*"

"Good," Fuller blurted out. "Let's get his picture out there."

"It won't matter," Sullivan replied. "I'm sure he's changed his appearance by now."

The announcer shifted in his seat, to address a terrorism expert on the NNN staff. "*Jim, the nation is reeling from another major attack, this one apparently from homegrown terrorists. And it appears we have a family of terrorists here, all of whom had infiltrated sensitive government agencies. We were attacked from within. What are your thoughts?*"

"Turn it off," Sullivan said quickly. "We need to focus."

"Agreed," Conrad said weakly from his bed.

"OK," Sullivan looked at Fuller, "where do we stand with the female?"

"I reviewed Metro surveillance footage of the Union Station platform, and I've identified a woman who matches the age and body type of my suspect. She boarded an in-bound train, but it will take days to review footage at all the other possible terminals, to see where she might have gotten off." Fuller was not optimistic.

"Days?" Conrad asked in disbelief.

"It's not like the movies, Conrad. You know that," Fuller scolded, pulling her hair back in frustration.

"It won't matter," Sullivan chimed in. "By the time we know where she got off…she could be anywhere."

"What about the people I tangled with?" Conrad asked quietly. "What is their connection to all this?"

"Well, they had no identification on them. Their fingerprints came back with nothing. But I would guess, based on their ages, that they are the parents of the other terrorists. I could be wrong—" Sullivan was cut off.

"No, I like it," Fuller interrupted. "And if so"—she hesitated—"then my female, and Kyle Grant, or whoever he really was, are also siblings of our three known suspects."

"Exactly, Fuller," Sullivan could see all the pieces now emerging.

"This explains why they needed to kill the professor in Arkansas." Sullivan was on a roll. "They needed to keep Grant's true identity a secret, because he was the only mole operating under a false cover."

Conrad listened raptly from his bed.

"Yes!" Fuller exclaimed. "Once you were onto Grant, they needed to cover their tracks."

"And it also explains Livingstone's murder. He must have been in a position to know something about Samantha Wallace's infiltration," Sullivan mused.

Conrad lifted his one good arm up to stop them.

"That's great, guys, but how does all this help us catch our remaining fugitives?"

"I'm not sure yet," Sullivan answered, "but your girlfriend is going to help us. She's been worried about you…said you weren't in a talking mood."

Conrad reacted with a frown, as Sullivan pulled out his cell phone and dialed Trish. She picked up on the first ring.

"Hey, Sully!" Trish said excitedly.

"I have you on speakerphone. I'm with Fuller and your boy."

"I love you, Conrad," she gushed, her voice amplified by the speaker. Sullivan and Fuller smiled when they saw their friend's embarrassment.

"OK, Trish, what have you got for us?" Sullivan rubbed his hands in anticipation.

"Well, I analyzed the phones you were able to get off those terrorists. They only called each other, it seems. There were a total of eight lines. With five terrorists killed and two fugitives, that leaves one other unexplained."

Fuller jumped in. "No, Trish, we believe the eighth would be the guy I took out in Arkansas. So they are all accounted for."

MICHAEL C DE LA PEÑA

"OK then, I have been monitoring the lines to see if any of them come to life, but they have all been silent since that last text earlier today." Trish was animated.

"Don't bother," Sullivan responded. "They won't be using those lines anymore. The woman left her phone at the restroom, and Michael Wallace's was found near one of the Pentagon exits."

Sullivan was growing concerned that Trish was finally going to let him down. But he knew that she had a habit of leaving the best for last. Fuller and Conrad shared the same concern as they waited for her to continue.

"Well guys, there is something. As you know, I've been doing a full work-up on Michael Wallace ever since Sully's surveillance at his house. A complete analysis of his e-mail, home phone, cell phone, work phone…" Trish was trying to build suspense.

"Out with it, baby!" Conrad shouted in the air.

Trish seemed to hold her breath for a moment. "I believe I have a solid lead for you."

———

After a complex combination of bus and train routes, Alexa had managed to arrive at the heart of Times Square. Although she was ahead of the timeline for the rendezvous point, she was anxious to meet Michael. From the news reports, she knew he had also escaped, and she was elated. Michael had always been her favorite. Alexa watched the news footage with keen interest. She was impressed with their handiwork. Yes, the mission did not follow the plan in its entirety, but she knew from her training at the Fortress that a mission rarely goes exactly as scripted. Nevertheless, the coyotes had managed to do some impressive damage. Despite the fact that she was certain she could not be traced to her siblings, at least not for a very long time, she followed her training, taking every precaution to avoid detection.

———

The team's meeting was interrupted by a commotion outside the hospital room. Several loud voices were heard, which got their attention. After a moment or so, a knock was heard at the door.

Annoyed, Sullivan rose to answer.

"Mr. Attorney General," Sullivan said, surprised. "What brings you here?"

AG Mitchell was flanked by two men in expensive suits. Mitchell was a bear of a man, with a larger-than-life swagger. He always made an impression when he entered a room. Sullivan recognized one of the men with him as the FBI deputy director. The other "suit" he did not know. Behind them were several members of his FBI security detail, whom he recognized by their demeanor and attire. They waited outside the open door.

"This must be the Boston team I've heard so much about," Mitchell said loudly, almost beaming. He was a politician at heart.

"Where is my niece?" He looked about the room, "She is very impressive, isn't she?" The team exchanged confused looks, which Mitchell quickly picked up on. "Oh, it's like Trish not to talk about me…" Mitchell said to the silent group.

"That explains a lot," Sullivan interjected.

"Well, is she here?" he asked.

"She's the only Boston team member actually *in* Boston, Mr. Mitchell," Sullivan answered quickly.

"Well, please extend my gratitude to her for her efforts." He then shook their hands and patted Conrad on the shoulder.

"From the briefing I've received," Mitchell continued, "I have you guys to thank for being alive." Hearing the slight Boston accent, Sullivan recalled that Mitchell had grown up in the Boston area. Trish had never revealed the connection.

"I only wish we could have saved the director, sir," Conrad replied for the group.

"Well, yes. On that note…" As he spoke, one of his suited guests stepped forward, and Mitchell put his hand on his shoulder.

"This *was* FBI Deputy Director Anthony Franklin. With my recommendation, the president minutes ago announced he is the acting director, until confirmed by the Senate, of course."

Franklin spoke to the group. He had waited patiently for his turn to speak, in deference to Mitchell. "Sullivan, you have been cleared of any suspicion, of course. I am making you lead investigator in the attacks of today and charging you with capturing the remaining fugitives." Franklin pointed at Sullivan.

Sullivan raised an eyebrow. One half of him wondered when he was getting his apology. The other half knew that it would never happen. He knew to let it go. He waited for Franklin to continue.

"Normally, having been involved in a shooting incident, you would all be put on administrative leave, and I would have to take your weapons." He looked at all of them sternly. "However, given the national security crisis that has occurred, and the possibility of further attacks on the nation, I am waiving that action as acting director."

Franklin waited for them to acknowledge his gesture, but the team was silent.

After an awkward moment, Sullivan responded. "Mr. Director, thank you for the gesture. It is appreciated. However, that wasn't on our minds right now. We have a lead to pursue."

Franklin had heard that Sullivan was a difficult personality. He wanted to assert his new authority. "Very well, but you will keep me posted of any and all developments immediately. You will keep me in the loop." He gesticulated with a pointed finger.

"Yes, of course, Mr. Director." Sullivan answered with a half smile.

"OK then," Franklin said, turning to leave. "Let me know what resources you need. Nothing is off the table, given this situation."

Sullivan pounced on the offer. "Actually, I do need something." He swooped in. Franklin gave him an inquisitive look.

"I need two assets I have been using deputized for this case." Sullivan beamed.

"Those two pilots of yours, correct?" Franklin sounded annoyed.

"Yes, actually." Sullivan was certain this was the best opportunity to get what he wanted. He was concerned for the brothers and their legal status in everything that had transpired.

Mitchell had been listening intently. "That was some stunt, boy," he interjected.

The team knew that Franklin was boxed in. There was a momentary silence.

"Very well," he finally agreed.

With that, the visiting entourage left the room. Sullivan was close behind them.

# TWELVE

## Capture

The offices of Dominion Car Rentals were located in a small lot only two miles from Reagan National Airport, in Arlington, Virginia. Smaller than the better-known national car-rental companies, they specialized in long-term rentals. Their typical client rented month to month. The company was small, employing only eight people, most of them related in some way to the owner and manager, Tyler Van Kleef.

The morning after the attacks, the city was eerily quiet. There was stillness in the muggy morning air. Many people had simply refused to go to work, concerned that the city might still be in danger. The sun shone intermittently through scattered clouds hovering over the nation's capital. Americans awoke to the feeling of having been sucker punched again, and they wanted justice.

Sitting behind the wheel of an FBI car, Sullivan watched Dominion Car Rentals from across the street, searching for any sign of life. He knew it was not scheduled to open for another thirty minutes, but he also knew that many managers arrive to work early. Next to Sullivan sat Jorge, holding his new, shiny badge authorizing him special duties as a special federal officer, known in law enforcement simply as an SFO. Miguel was alert in the rear seat, quietly scanning the area for any danger. Sullivan had made it clear that the business could be a source of information, or it could have some more sinister connection to their fugitive. They would watch for a while before approaching.

MICHAEL C DE LA PEÑA

As he waited, Sullivan imagined all the activity occurring across the city in Tyson's Corner, Virginia, at the Terrorist Screening Center. He had left Fuller in charge of coordinating all their leads from the TSC, which is a major joint command center, comprised of FBI, CIA, and most other federal law enforcement entities. By now, he knew that teams were raiding and searching the homes of all the identified terrorists. Those searches would, they hoped, yield evidence identifying all the perpetrators and their motives. Perhaps some leads might help capture their fugitives. In addition to that, Fuller also had a team of electronic surveillance specialists listening to the recording O'Neil had discovered, amplifying the recording, and analyzing every aspect for any detail which might be useful. Linguists would be asked to evaluate the accents of the people on the tape. The task ahead of Fuller was formidable. Sullivan preferred his current role in the field. As he pondered the value of his current lead, his cell phone buzzed at his hip. His caller ID let him know it was Trish.

"I was just thinking of you," he said.

"I'm checking to see if anything panned out." Trish always wanted feedback on her analysis. It was her way of sharpening her skills.

"I hate to sound skeptical, Trish, but tell me again why you think this is significant."

"I ran all their numbers and e-mails—"

Sullivan cut her off. "Yeah, yeah, you said that."

"Yes, and I found nothing," she said flatly.

"Nothing? But you—"

"Yes," she interrupted. "Nothing of what I would typically expect from someone who was planning an escape. For instance, no calls to airlines, railroads, hotels, motels—"

"Or car rental companies." He completed her sentence.

"Exactly!"

"So what am I doing here again?" he asked.

"I went back to his work cell phone and analyzed all his calls for the week preceding the attacks."

"Go on."

"I found one call to the main Pentagon switchboard."

"That's it?" Sullivan asked. "He worked there, Trish!" He was exasperated.

"Yes, but when he called the Pentagon on every other occasion, he dialed a direct extension. This was the only time he called the main switchboard." She grew more confident with every retelling of her methodology.

"Maybe he forgot someone's extension."

"Perhaps, but I don't think so." Trish sounded confident.

"Continue," he urged her.

"I analyzed the date and time of that call—which by the way was placed two days before the attacks—and noticed that it lasted four minutes. Four minutes, Sully. Remember, he's calling the main switchboard!" She grew more animated.

"And?"

"That's a long time. Sully, most calls are far shorter. Four minutes or more on a call, and it's either a lover, or you are giving information to make some sort of reservation."

"You know this?" he asked, again incredulous.

"Yes."

"OK, go on," Sullivan retorted.

"So I went down to our switchboard and talked to our operators and made some inquiries. And I found out something very interesting."

"Yes," Sullivan now sounded interested.

"There are occasions when some agents will call the switchboard and ask the operator for a 'patch' to another number. The operator then dials the number and patches it into the agent's cell phone. By doing this, the agent avoids having the number appear in his call history. There is no trace. Usually, they tell me, the reason is innocuous, such as the agent wants a patch to a police department or some number he doesn't know offhand. Or the agent has someone on the line and is trying to set up a conference call. There are many reasons why a person might do this."

"Like a terrorist not wanting to leave a trace of a phone call…"

"Yes, exactly. So based on this tip, I analyzed all outgoing phone calls from the Pentagon switchboard that corresponded with the exact time of his call," She said proudly.

"All the Pentagon outgoing calls? How did you manage that?" Sullivan said in genuine surprise.

"That's another story," she said, guarding her secrets.

"OK, so I guess the call in question was made to this location."

"Exactly."

"You really need to find another word," Sullivan teased.

At that moment, two vehicles came around the corner, toward Dominion Car Rentals. From the backseat, Miguel tapped them both on the shoulder.

—

A hundred and fifty miles to the north, in the small town of Milford, Pennsylvania, near the New York and New Jersey border, Michael looked warily out of his motel window. He had no reason to believe he could be traced, but he wanted to make sure. He scanned the parking lot from his second floor unit and saw nothing unusual. A light drizzle sprinkled the pavement, causing miniature ripples in the pools of water that had formed from an overnight storm. His rented Nissan was parked exactly as he had left it—with a clear path to the exit.

From watching the incessant news reporting in the aftermath of Coyote One, Michael learned that Alexa had also escaped. He felt a pride beyond measure. Perhaps because she was the youngest, and he felt more protective of her, he and Alexa had developed a special relationship. He lamented that he had no way of communicating with her prior to their rendezvous, yet he knew it was probably for the best.

As he listened to the continuing coverage of the attacks, he perked up when they again announced his name, with a photo of him obtained by the Department of Defense. In the photo, he wore glasses. He had already altered that by using contact lenses. He had also started using a false moustache. He headed into the bathroom for one final touch.

He would dye his hair from its natural black, to a light brown. Michael considered going blond but felt that it would not match his overall features and would attract more attention rather than less.

He turned on the hot water. In a little more than twenty-four hours, he would be hugging his sister.

———

After seeing the two employees enter the small offices of Dominion Car Rentals, Sullivan watched them carefully from behind a pair of binoculars. One employee, who had opened the door with a key, was a tall male with graying hair and a handlebar moustache. The other was a female, perhaps twenty-five years old. The large glass window and door in front allowed for an easy view into the business. Both employees alternated between answering phones and typing into computers. The male was at a desk. He appeared to be the manager. The female sat behind a small counter. After thirty minutes, Sullivan decided it was safe to enter.

"Miguel"—Sullivan looked back—"wait here. Keep an eye out." He pointed two fingers to his eyes, emphasizing he was their lookout.

"Si."

Sullivan walked in first, followed closely by Jorge.

The manager stood to welcome the two visitors. "Good morning!"

"Good morning to you," Sullivan started. "Are you the manager?"

"Owner, manager, and everything else. I'm Tyler Van Kleef, and this is my daughter, Amanda," he said, extending his hand.

Sullivan shook his hand and then pulled out his FBI credentials.

"I'm Special Agent Carlos Sullivan, and this is my associate." Sullivan looked back at Jorge. Even though he attempted an uncomfortable smile, Jorge looked like a coiled snake, ready to spring into action.

"How can I help you?" Van Kleef asked.

"I need to know if you recently rented a vehicle to a Mr. Michael Wallace."

"No," Amanda answered quickly.

"No? That quickly? Could you check your computer, please?" Sullivan's tone told them he wasn't really asking.

"You don't understand, Agent Sullivan." Van Kleef stepped in to help his daughter.

"We are a small operation. We would remember a name."

"Yes, of course," Sullivan answered, retrieving his cell phone. In an instant, he pulled up a picture of Michael Wallace on his screen.

"OK," Sullivan countered. "Please tell me if you have done business with this man."

He held the phone for them. Van Kleef slowly shook his head, but Amanda hesitated. She cocked her head to one side slightly, quietly analyzing the photo, her mouth smirking as if she was unsure.

"You seem to recognize him," Sullivan looked directly at her. She was still scrutinizing the picture.

"Well," she answered, "he kind of looks like another guy who rented from us two days ago. But he didn't have glasses." She kept looking at the photo.

"Who was that?" Sullivan could barely conceal his excitement. It appeared Trish was right after all.

"His name was Michael Christian," Amanda offered. "Let me get you his paperwork."

"Does this have something to do with yesterday's attacks?" the father asked, suddenly concerned that he might have inadvertently given aid to terrorists.

"I can't address that," Sullivan answered.

While they waited, Amanda started pulling up the file on her computer. After a moment, she looked up helpfully. "Yes, two days ago, he took a two-week rental on a 2011 green Nissan Maxima."

Sullivan smiled as Amanda continued looking at her screen.

"I can give you his entire file." She then caught herself and looked at her father for approval.

"Yes, of course, anything you need," Van Kleef offered.

Jorge listened quietly from the door, his stance relaxing as he could see they were getting cooperation.

"I will need the plate number," Sullivan thought for a moment and then added, "Do you recall anything in particular about him?"

"He was very businesslike. I tried engaging him in conversation, and he just wasn't interested." Amanda scratched her head as she talked. She tried to remember every detail.

"I see," Sullivan said pensively.

"Oh, he wanted a car without a GPS system," she blurted out.

"GPS!" Sullivan interrupted. He couldn't believe he hadn't considered that. It dawned on him that he had been off the street and behind a desk for too long.

Van Kleef moved closer, putting his hand up to calm Sullivan. "You have to understand. Almost half of all rental cars in the US now use GPS to track their vehicles. All of the national rental companies now have their fleets rigged with GPS. Some people object to that. We have cultivated a reputation as a company that doesn't use the devices. We don't actually advertise this, but through word of mouth we have a niche clientele. More and more people are worried that their wives, employers, or the government will track them down. We cater to those who want privacy," Van Kleef explained. As he did so, he could see Sullivan's excitement sour.

"So you have no way to track the car," Sullivan said. "Great." He looked down at the floor.

"Oh, not at all, Agent Sullivan," Van Kleef said seriously. "The GPS allows us to stop or retrieve any stolen cars. This gives me a discount on our insurance policy. Plus, it allows me to see if a car will be returned when the client promised, or if it's too far away, indicating that it won't make it back in time. It helps me keep inventory."

"But you just said..." Sullivan was momentarily confused.

"We lie to them," Van Kleef said flatly. His daughter looked at Sullivan sheepishly.

To her surprise, Sullivan's face beamed a great smile. He grabbed a startled Van Kleef by the shoulders in pure joy. "Today Mr. Van Kleef, I'm glad you lie."

Having rented a bicycle at the Chelsea Piers, Alexa rode the bike path on the West Side Highway along the banks of the Hudson River. She was the youngest child, so her recollection of the exact spot along the river designated as the rendezvous point was not exact. She had a general idea where the family had gathered, but she wanted to lock in the location before her anticipated meeting with her brother. After two hours of riding, she finally spied the spot from the side of the highway. It was a small park along the water, with a picnic table in a clearing. Alexa looked about, searching for any tactical weak spots. She thought it a good location, from which any approaching persons could be seen clearly. She got back on her bike, excited that she would see her brother in twenty-four hours.

———

"That's fantastic!" Fuller said, a cell phone to her ear. All the agents in the TSC command center turned their attention to her. They knew she was waiting for news on a solid lead. The room grew quiet as everyone strained to hear the news.

She turned to the group, still on the phone. "Virginia license plate RDX-450! Get that BOLO out right away!" She ordered a standard "be on the lookout" alert for law enforcement units on the street.

"I'm on it," responded an analyst from behind his computer screen.

Sullivan was outside the business, looking through the glass at Jorge guarding his two new witnesses. His partner listened intently on the other end of the line.

"Fuller, another thing—you need to get an emergency warrant. They can track the car with its GPS system. I want this fucker alive, and I don't want to tank the case on a technicality." Sullivan paced back and forth in front of the business. He could see Van Kleef pointing at something on his computer screen. Across the street, he saw Miguel still in the backseat, watching the street, scanning the horizon.

"Agreed," she replied. All eyes were on her as they continued talking.

"And send some agents down here to watch these witnesses."

Fuller pointed to an agent standing next to her. "Dominion Car Rentals, now, take two agents," she barked.

"Fuller, by the time I get to my chopper, I want that warrant!"

After finishing his conversation with Fuller, Sullivan walked into the business.

Van Kleef looked up from the screen prepared to help. He was by now wholeheartedly on team Sullivan. "I can tell you that the Nissan is in—"

"No!" Sullivan raised his hand up, stopping the manager. "No, don't say a word. Anything you do now is at the behest of a government agent. I need a warrant. I appreciate you are trying to help, but let's wait."

"OK," Van Kleef said meekly, chastened.

"We are leaving now. Please listen carefully." Sullivan looked at them both. Amanda had a shocked look on her face. Van Kleef stroked his long moustache silently.

"I will call you once I have a warrant. You will then relay the car's location. I want updates every ten minutes, which you will text to my phone. Keep your phone line open. Other agents will be here shortly. Don't let anyone but them in this business. This is now a crime scene." Sullivan enunciated every word crisply, to emphasize his seriousness.

They listened with a mixture of amazement and disbelief. Nothing had prepared them for what they were experiencing.

"Do you understand?" Sullivan asked finally, pointing his finger at each separately, for emphasis. He stared at them, waiting for them to vocalize an answer.

"Yes," they answered simultaneously.

Sullivan turned and walked out of the business, Jorge close behind him.

———

On the evening of the terrorist attacks, retired Captain Jim McDougal was still at work when Sullivan and the brothers returned with his helicopter. After the events that day, he was proud of his involvement. Several news outlets had aired footage of his helicopter in different parts of the city. There was one image of the chopper on the National Mall, another of the helicopter's daring landing on the Pentagon. He was quite sure that he would use the incident in a future marketing campaign. More importantly, he was glad to have had a hand in defending the nation.

McDougal stretched his hand out to Sullivan as they disembarked.

"Thank you, Agent Sullivan," he said simply.

"It's not over," Sullivan had answered wearily. "We will be back for it again."

"Anytime," McDougal offered.

Sullivan thought of that exchange as he and the brothers headed back to Washington Helo-Tours to retrieve their helicopter. He wondered if McDougal had gassed it up for them.

—

Judge Kenneth Waterman sat on a leather couch in his chambers, watching news footage of the terrorist attacks and their aftermath. One of the reports was live footage of a search at the home of terrorist fugitive Michael Wallace. He immediately made the connection. This was the same home for which Secret Service Agent John O'Neil had requested a search warrant the night before the attacks. Now, as he sat in solitude, he was having second thoughts. In that moment he was grateful that he had a lifetime appointment to the bench. As he replayed the meeting with O'Neil in his mind, the telephone on his desk rang loudly, jarring him out of his reverie.

"Judge Waterman?"

"Yes," Waterman answered.

"This is FBI Director Anthony Franklin."

—

Sullivan stood next to the Bell 260 as Jorge and Miguel jumped aboard, initiating preflight preparations. McDougal was next to Sullivan, prepared to offer any assistance requested.

Sullivan had the phone to his ear. "Tell me you have that warrant!" He shouted over the whirring blades.

"Yes! We have emergency authority granted by Judge Waterman," Fuller answered.

"Excellent," he said. "I will send you a message en route." He hung up and then dialed Dominion Car Rentals. Van Kleef nervously answered on the first ring.

A minute later, Sullivan boarded the chopper. He tapped his pilots on the shoulder.

"North, gentlemen." He pointed up and to the north.

"Si, jefe." Jorge smiled. "Norte."

As they ascended, Sullivan placed a duffel bag next to his feet, containing several pistols, a machine gun, and a sniper rifle. Before he had time to compose a full message for Fuller, the helicopter had already left the city limits.

———

The George Washington Bridge (GWB) is the most heavily trafficked suspension bridge in the world, with two levels and a total of fourteen lanes. Opened in 1931, it has two massive steel towers on each end that soar more than six hundred feet above the Hudson River, which it spans. The two towers are connected by enormous cables, which hang down like tentacles. The GWB connects Ft. Lee, New Jersey, to midtown Manhattan, a distance of about three-quarters of a mile. A toll is collected, but only when cars are crossing from the New Jersey side.

New Jersey State Trooper Malcolm Stanton, a fifteen-year veteran of the force, was ticketing a speeding vehicle on the New Jersey Turnpike, only three miles from the George Washington Bridge (GWB). His cruiser was equipped with the latest computer technology, including a scanner that automatically runs the license plate of any vehicle within its range. Thousands of license plates can be scanned for warrants or other violations within minutes. Whenever the device gets a hit, the patrolman is alerted. After 9/11, the federal government had offered grants to some law enforcement departments so they could equip their vehicles. Stanton's cruiser was a fortunate recipient of this largesse.

After crossing through Newark, Michael started north on the New Jersey Turnpike, headed into New York City. He was unaware that Sullivan was approaching his position from above, only minutes away. He passed cautiously by Stanton's cruiser with its flashing lights on the side of the road. He was unconcerned, not only because he was following the posted speed limit, but also because he knew nobody could be looking for his car.

Stanton was in his cruiser, writing the ticket, when his onboard computer screen repeatedly flashed an alert. He looked up and punched in his security code.

The computer flashed again. *"Virginia License plate RDX-450, FBI BOLO, Nissan Maxima, 2011, green in color, wanted in connection to the terrorist attacks in Washington, DC, consider armed and extremely dangerous."*

Stanton could not believe his eyes. He reread the screen again for confirmation. As he did so, he peeled out of the emergency lane, northbound, in pursuit of the fugitive vehicle. By the time Stanton had gunned his engine and pulled into the left lane, Michael was almost a half a mile ahead of him, closing in on the GWB.

From above, with the coordinates relayed by Van Kleef, Sullivan's Bell 260 had caught up with the Nissan. Sullivan was looking down at the highway through his binoculars.

"There!" He pointed. "That's it."

Miguel, in the passenger seat, had a larger view because he was not using binoculars. He pointed south of the Nissan, at the approaching cruiser with its emergency lights flashing.

"Sully," he yelled. "Look behind it!"

Sullivan pulled the binoculars to one side and looked down again. "Shit! We just lost the element of surprise!" He cursed to his team.

Michael looked in his rearview mirror and saw the lights headed toward him. At first, he was not apprehensive. The cruiser certainly must be after someone else, he thought. However, as the trooper got closer, his blood pressure began to rise exponentially. Now only one hundred feet behind the Nissan, Stanton continued to relay information to other troopers, two of whom were ahead of him on the turnpike, just shy of the GWB entrance.

Traffic was heavy, and Michael was forced to slow down in the left lane. When the cruiser reached him, Stanton rammed his vehicle. The loudspeaker crackled to life.

"Stop the vehicle immediately. That is an order!" Stanton bellowed.

Michael ignored the bump and continued forward, himself bumping the car in front of him, forcing it out of the way. As others in front of him saw and heard the approaching cruiser, they started moving out of the way. They were plowing the road for Michael, who continued driving, even as he was rammed twice more by Stanton.

As Michael approached the tollbooths, he saw that two other troopers ahead were ready to throw down the spike strips as the Nissan passed by. Michael realized his car was surely doomed. He would need another vehicle. Not having any maneuvering options because of the traffic, he continued driving, directly over the strips, which shredded his tires. He pulled over and reached down to the backpack on the passenger seat. Michael retrieved a machine gun that was already locked and loaded.

The two troopers started walking toward him, crouching behind other gridlocked cars for cover. In their zeal to capture their fugitive, they failed to consider that all around them were innocent drivers and passengers in other cars, stuck in traffic, exposed. Michael instantly realized the tactical advantage this gave him.

From the driver's seat, through the closed rear passenger window, he turned and discharged a volley of rounds in their direction. One round clipped a trooper on the shoulder. The others peppered several vehicles. People started screaming, exiting their cars, and running in every direction. The troopers retreated, with the sudden realization that they were outgunned, and civilians were at risk. Stanton reached his two colleagues as the mayhem and gunfire erupted. They had sent a radio call for backup but were told there would be a delay because of the highway congestion.

The chaos had disrupted traffic on the GWB completely. Michael saw an opportunity. He decided to simply walk across the span and commandeer a vehicle on the New York side. He had neutralized the New Jersey troopers, and he knew the NYPD had nobody stationed on the other side of the bridge. His plan was to get there before the police. He started spraying other vehicles on the bridge with gunfire as he walked across the span, fomenting more chaos to help in his escape.

Watching the unfolding scenario from two hundred feet above, Sullivan hatched his own plan of action. "I have to get on that bridge!"

"No es posible!" Jorge answered in Spanish, pointing to the suspension cables. "No place to land!"

Sullivan looked at the massive GWB in awe; it was so large.

"There!" Sullivan yelled back. "On the steel tower!"

"I can't land there, jefe!" The helicopter was too large for such a landing, plus the winds would make any such attempt deadly.

"I know. Just me. I will jump onto the tower!" he said, locking his eyes on both pilots.

Jorge knew it was a crazy plan, but he also knew there was no point arguing with Sullivan. He moved the helicopter over the tower on the New York side. Sullivan slid the chopper's side door open as they ascended to the top of the steel tower. As he looked down, he saw how daunting the task was. There was no solid landing spot. Each corner of the tower's roof had a large X shaped crossbeams.

As they moved closer into position, Sullivan gave a final order. "No matter what happens, we must take him alive—at any cost!"

They both nodded in agreement.

Jorge held the chopper as steady as possible against the wind, as Sullivan, one hand grabbing the door handle, dangled above the tower. When Jorge lowered the chopper as much as he could, Sullivan finally leaped down.

He landed awkwardly, one knee banging against one of the steel plates. Prior to jumping, he had deliberately not looked down to the water below, for fear of backing out of his crazy scheme. Now he had no choice. He knew that for maintenance purposes there had to be a ladder. And once he found the ladder, there could be no escaping looking downward.

Almost three hundred feet below, Michael was making his way toward the New York side of the expanse, all the while continuing to fire at the stalled vehicles. His aim was not to kill anyone but to create panic, which would cause confusion as dozens of people would be streaming across the bridge on foot. Sullivan could hear the gunfire from above as he found the steel maintenance ladder. The rungs were small, only about eighteen inches wide, which hindered his descent. Yet with each round of gunfire he heard, he quickened his pace, ignoring the pain in his knee.

When Sullivan finally made his way close to the street level, he stopped about ten feet above the surface to get a tactical advantage. From his perch, he could see people running toward him, fleeing the gunfire. In their midst, he saw Wallace, a machine gun cradled in his arms, perhaps only ten cars away from his position. Sullivan then finally climbed down to the street, making his way toward Michael. As he did so, he tapped on several car hoods, waving his gun, ordering the passengers to lie down on their seats for safety.

From two cars away, Michael sensed danger. He stopped, scanning ahead. He was almost to the other side of the bridge. He could see freedom again. Then he spotted Sullivan crouching behind the hood of a car in front of him. He had heard a helicopter throughout the ordeal but lost sight of it when it rose toward the tower. Even now, he could hear the chopper but ignored it. When he first spotted it, he saw no police markings. Plus, his goal was freedom on the other side of the bridge.

Michael raised his weapon and fired at Sullivan. Several rounds glanced off the hood of the car protecting Sullivan, bouncing into a car behind him. He fired again, but this time his rifle jammed. Sullivan was close enough to hear it. He surged forward, running as fast as he could, gritting his teeth at the sharp pain in his knee as Michael tried to clear the weapon. Michael could see with his peripheral vision that he would not have time to unjam the machine gun in time, so he flung it to one side, reaching for his pistol.

As he swung the gun forward from his hip, Sullivan was already there. Following his training, he reached for the gun with one hand and then reinforced his grip with his other hand.

A life-and-death struggle commenced. Sullivan started twisting the gun sideways, away from him and toward Michael. This technique forced Michael to either release the gun, use two hands to attempt to gain control of the weapon again, or break his wrist. Michael chose a fourth option—as Sullivan slowly twisted the gun with all his strength, Michael started punching him in the face with his free hand.

Closing his eyes to protect himself, he absorbed several brutal punches to the face, but he ignored the injuries, willing himself to pry the weapon from his adversary. He continued twisting Michael's hands until he released the gun. As he did so, Michael kicked Sullivan in his weak knee. The gun fell to the ground, as did Sullivan, wincing in pain, barely able to open one eye.

Michael walked calmly to the pistol and picked it up. He walked back to the injured Sullivan, who was kneeling on his one good knee, and pointed the weapon at his temple execution style. Sullivan could feel the metal barrel against his head.

As Michael squeezed the trigger, a round was fired that pierced Michael's shooting hand. A large bullet hole was torn through his right hand, forcing him to release the weapon. Michael, in shock, clutched his bloody hand and fell to his knees.

From his wounded position, Sullivan could hear the helicopter had moved closer to them. Without the necessity of clear sight, which he currently did not have, he knew what had occurred. As the chopper hovered over the upper deck of the bridge, Miguel had trained the sniper rifle on his adversary, making a shot few could have made.

Sullivan, peeking through his one useful eye, found the gun, and pointed it at a defeated Michael Wallace.

"You are under arrest, you son of a bitch," Sullivan declared.

# THIRTEEN

## Aftermath

That evening, Alexa saw the news footage documenting the capture of her beloved brother Michael. In one clip, several FBI agents could be seen escorting her shackled sibling, his right hand bandaged, into a federal building in New York. For the first time that she could remember, she wept. She was now alone in the world.

---

After he received treatment for his facial injuries, some of the swelling on Sullivan's face subsided. Having returned to Washington following the dramatic capture of their fugitive, he sat with Jorge, Miguel, and Conrad, the latter with his arm in a sling. They sat in a circle. The TV monitor flashed images of what had transpired, but the volume was off. Conrad thought his friend looked like a mess. Sullivan detected the look he was receiving, and he waved at Conrad in frustration.

"Don't say it," Sullivan said.

"I know, I know," Conrad teased, "I should see the other guy, right?"

Sullivan turned his attention to Miguel, who always listened with interest.

"Miguel, that was an unbelievable shot."

"Horrible shot, jefe."

"How was it horrible?" Sullivan seemed perplexed.

"I aim for his gun," Miguel said with a smile.

They all chuckled loudly. After the laughter subsided, Conrad spoke.

"Sully," he said, "what was it you whispered to the guy you killed on the Mall?" He raised an eyebrow as he asked his question.

"A Russian expression," He answered, "Dolg platejom krasen. It refers to the repayment of a debt." He thought of Lena in that moment.

"I get it," Conrad responded. "Payback."

They all nodded silently.

After another minute of silence, Conrad again spoke. "Sully, when are you going to tell me what really happened in that bank fifteen years ago?"

Sullivan smirked slyly. "One day my friend. One day."

The next morning the entire team reunited at the Terrorism Screening Center in Virginia. Fuller had news from Arkansas. She took center stage at the center of the massive meeting room. Dozens of agents and analysts were in attendance. Sullivan sat next to Fuller on the stage. Conrad, Jorge, and Miguel were in the front row.

Fuller stood to address the group with a microphone in one hand.

"First of all, Acting FBI Director Franklin personally called the TSC to thank the group for the capture of Michael Wallace." She looked over to Sullivan, as did the entire audience. As this occurred, Franklin unexpectedly walked into the room. He saw them turn to him, but he waved dismissively, indicating that he was there only to observe. He did not want to detract from what they were doing. Fuller understood the gesture and continued.

"We cannot forget, of course, that we still have one female fugitive out there. Sadly, as we know, we have little to go on. No prints. No real good picture. The images we have are too grainy or distant to be of any use. We have no phone. We are going to need the public to come forward." She paused for a moment to catch her breath. "To that end, we have established a hotline for the public to call with any information about our elusive female. Hopefully someone will call and give us the tip we need. We will be staffing that 24-7."

The group knew that this meant more agents would be needed. Some of them would be asked to work overnight shifts, a sacrifice they were all willing to commit to.

"From Arkansas," Fuller continued with a dramatic flair, "I give you Agent Pat Hanford on a live video feed."

The TV monitors all lit up green for an instant, then white, before turning into an image of Hanford in camouflage clothing, wearing a helmet.

"Hanford," Fuller said over the activated speakerphone. "Can you see and hear us?"

"Yes, Fuller. I can see you."

"What do you have for us?"

"Well, we have located the Wallace family compound," He said with his heavy Southern drawl.

"It wasn't easy, but we located it. I am with a SWAT team just outside the road leading to the compound. It is deep in the Ozark Mountains. We have had a sniper watching the compound all night, and he has given the all clear. He indicates that most of the structures have been burned to the ground. He reports no movement. Nevertheless, we will make entry with the SWAT team now. I will be with the team, and you will have a live feed as we go in."

"Excellent," Fuller declared. The audience was now quite engaged in the unfolding investigation. They were all on the edge of their seats. Fuller had managed to keep this aspect of the case a surprise for them.

"We will engage now," Hanford stated. "I'm activating my helmet cam."

He turned, and as he did so, the camera attached to his helmet swung around to capture the SWAT team, lined up next to their vans. As the action unfolded, they jumped into their vehicles and drove down the dirt road leading to the Fortress. The sound of radio communication between the men in the vans punctuated the silence every several seconds.

"Approaching phase line green," the SWAT team leader announced as they reached the clearing where the Fortress lay in ruins.

"*Go, go, go!*" he barked as they drove up to the fallen structures and slid their doors open. The team could be seen exiting their vans and swooping around the ruined structures, looking for any threats.

After the all clear was given, Hanford was escorted to a small shed which was the only structure remaining. The audience in Virginia watched raptly. Upon further inspection, the shed was clearly a jail cell. Taped to the door was a folded note. Everyone watched as Hanford pulled it off the door with his gloved hand, slowly.

"It appears they have left a note," he said, knowing he had a large audience. "It reads as follows: 'Inside this cell lies Kyle Grant. We want you to know that he died a long and agonizing death. We want you to know you could not save him, as you will not be able to save yourselves. The Coyotes." He folded the envelope and placed it into an evidence bag.

He leaned into the window of the cell and saw the ravaged, starved body of Kyle Grant. Insects had started to feed on his rotting flesh. The grotesque image flashed across the screen at the TSC, revolting many in attendance. Several in the audience left quickly for the bathroom. Sullivan shook his head in disgust. Silence descended upon the chamber.

"There's not much I can say right now. Over to you, Fuller." Hanford signed off in anger.

After turning his microphone off, Hanford reached for his radio. A large team of agents waited for orders to enter the Fortress and commence a meticulous search of the grounds for evidence.

"Hanford to evidence team one, over."

"Evidence team one leader here," an agent responded.

"Please proceed into the compound. Make sure you have Agent Wilson report to me immediately."

"Copy that, sir."

Several minutes later, Wilson appeared before Hanford. Without saying anything, he walked toward Grant's death chamber. Wilson followed quietly.

"Poke your head in there, Wilson," Hanford ordered.

After looking in the cell, Wilson's chest started heaving, convulsing with nausea. As he walked to a corner of the woods to throw up, Hanford leaned over him.

"Wilson, I wanted you to meet your friend, Kyle Grant," he said angrily.

# FOURTEEN

## Conclusion

The memorial service for Lena was held in the Fair Oaks cemetery in Medford, Massachusetts, not far from Sullivan's house. Never envisioning her untimely death, Sullivan decided on a familiar setting. His own father was buried in the same cemetery. In attendance were several dozen colleagues from the Boston office who wanted to pay their respects, despite the fact that they were unaware of Lena's existence until her demise. Also attending were Jorge, Miguel, Conrad, Fuller, and O'Keefe who, as a surprise, had brought Toby. After Lena's death, O'Keefe had tended to the dog, arranging for his treatment by the best veterinarian she could find. Despite being in a cast with a broken rib, Toby was quite animated at the sight of Sullivan, his tail wagging furiously.

During the ceremony, Toby sat quietly next to Sullivan, who wiped a small tear from his sad eyes. A sense of heavy loss hung over them.

Standing silently in the rear was Rebecca Scola. She waited for a moment alone with Sullivan and walked toward him when she saw the opportunity.

"Sully, I just wanted to—" She was cut off by Sullivan, who put his index finger to his lips, shushing her.

She hugged him tightly, both of them sobbing.

—

A week after the terrorist attacks, no new leads had been developed regarding the phantom female fugitive. On the eighth day, a nervous caller dialed the FBI hotline.

"This is Agent Stilson, thank you for calling the hotline." The agent waited as he heard nothing on the other end.

"Is there anyone there?" Stilson asked.

"Yes...I may have information, but I'm not sure," the voice said, hesitating.

"OK, what's your name, sir? I'm sure you want to help your country, right?"

After almost a minute of silence, the man finally spoke. "I'm Benjamin Steel, deputy sales director, western region, for Xion Corporation."

"Yes, please go on."

"We had an employee who disappeared right after the attacks. She worked in this office for some time now, and it's not like her to just disappear. She is very dependable." "All right, I'm listening," Stilson said carefully.

"Well, she kind of matches the description I heard about that fugitive," he continued tentatively.

"Yes, is there something else?"

"Well, she sells Phoenixium, a gas that sounds like what was used in those attacks. Oh, and she had the same last name as the other terrorists..."

Stilson almost fell out of his chair.

———

Within an hour, Xion Corp in Delaware was swarming with FBI agents. The building was secured as the team arrived to conduct their investigation. An evidence team from the Philadelphia office, the closest available, was on the scene, dusting for fingerprints and other DNA evidence. They found none.

After several hours interviewing employees at Xion, the team was frustrated at how little they were able to squeeze from the one solid lead they had. Dozens of coworkers were interviewed, and nobody seemed to really know who Alexa Wallace was.

Sullivan, Conrad, and Fuller stood in Alexa's office, looking out her expansive window to the Delaware River below. They had studied the office and immediately noticed that there were no personal photos in the room at all.

Fuller spoke first. "It seems like she socialized with nobody."

"Well, at least we know her name," Conrad offered.

"But she has no driver's license," Fuller said, "so we still have no picture."

"What about a corporate photo?" Sullivan asked.

"Mr. Steel informs me that somehow her photo was deleted from their system. They are looking into it." She bowed her head in frustration.

"What about the search of her apartment?" Conrad asked.

"It will take time to process the scene, but the evidence team leader phoned me an hour ago—no photos at all."

"They won't find anything," Sullivan said flatly.

"It's not like you to give up like that," Conrad admonished him, adjusting his sling. In truth, he knew his partner would never give up. He was probing to see Sully's reaction.

Looking out the window, Sullivan's forehead and right hand were pressed hard against the glass. Behind him, the team watched Sullivan carefully.

"We will get her. Don't worry, my friends. We will get her…" His voice trailed off quietly.

———

One hundred and eighty miles away, Alexa lay in bed at a hostel room in New York City's West Side, close to her family's rendezvous site. After her brother was captured, she saw no need to visit the place. However, for days after her escape, she did not sleep well. Every night she tossed and turned fitfully in bed. From her small room, she considered her options. For days, she was tormented about what to do or where to go. She was spiritually lost.

One morning, she awoke abruptly, to a dreamy vision. Alexa sat up in her bed, drenched in sweat. Her father's voice resonated in her dream, repeating over and over again, "Meet us, meet us, my daughter."

Not knowing what this meant, she finally visited the family's meeting point. She took a taxi to the park and quietly walked to the site. A few feet from the picnic table, she spotted a rock where her father had once sat to tell them the story of the wolf and the coyotes. She sat on the rock, envisioning the scene in her mind. Alexa's heart was crushed by the loss of her family.

As she replayed the dream in her mind, she kept seeing the rock that Father had sat on. It seemed somehow central to the message. After two hours at the site, she had a thought.

She rose and tugged at the rock. It barely moved. Again, she tried. Using all her strength, she finally pulled the rock onto its side. Feeling beneath it, she touched a ziplock bag, which she pulled out of the ground. Inside it was a small piece of paper. Scrawled on the paper was a series of numbers.

41–1 44 10/35–18–21–142

Beneath the riddle was another handwritten message, which she read, smiling broadly. She recognized the writing instantly.

*"My gift to the five of you. With love, your father."*

She clutched her new lifeline tightly and walked out of the park. Alexa had a new lease on life.

———

At an Irish pub two blocks from her hostel, Alexa sat at the bar drinking a draft beer. On the bar was a pad of paper and a pencil, with which she tried to decipher her father's puzzle. The bartender, an Irishman in his forties, watched her with curiosity. She seemed different than other patrons, more focused. As he watched her work, suddenly a news report flashed on the TV monitor that seemed to catch her attention.

The newscast showed Michael Wallace being taken out of a US marshal's van and escorted into a federal courthouse in Washington. The scroll beneath the screen indicated he was being taken in for his initial arraignment. The image of her brother, shackled like an animal, embarrassed in front of the world, enraged her. Her face turned crimson.

As the barkeep watched his customer, for a moment he thought he heard her growling.

Alexa locked her eyes on the screen, her teeth bared like a coyote on the hunt.

*The End*

Michael C. Delapena has been a Special Agent of the Federal Bureau of Investigation (FBI) for 24 years. He is an FBI-certified undercover agent and polygraph examiner. The author resides in Boston, Massachusetts. Discussions, questions, and comments can be forwarded to thecoyotewars@gmail.com.

Made in the USA
Middletown, DE
27 May 2015